LITTLE DEAD MAN

JAKE BIBLE

LITTLE DEAD MAN

JAKE BIBLE

PERMUTED PLATINUM

LITTLE DEAD MAN

ISBN (paperback): 978-1-61868-505-6
ISBN (eBook): 978-1-61868-265-9

Published by Permuted Press
109 International Drive, Suite 300
Franklin, TN 37067

Cover art by Dean Samed, Conzpiracy Digital Arts.

Follow us online:

Web: http://www.PermutedPress.com

Facebook: http://www.facebook.com/PermutedPress

Twitter: @PermutedPress

ACKNOWLEDGMENTS

There are a lot of people to thank for making this novel happen.

Readers and fans that have given me great feedback over the years; my former agent, Adrienne Rosado, for championing the novel in the beginning, and the authors James Melzer, Jenny Melzer, and Jonathan Maberry for putting the bug in my ear to write a YA zombie novel.

I, of course, have to thank my wife for all of her support, too.

But, most of all, I thank my kids, Sam and Annah. They were in the forefront of my mind the entire time I was writing this. They are my inspiration and my drive for keeping the keys a clickety-clacking each and every day. Love you guys!

FOREWORD

*L*ittle Dead Man has had a wild journey as a novel.

The idea came to me when I was driving home from a convention in Pittsburgh in September of 2010. I had spoken with quite a few horror writers that weekend, but the one conversation that stood out was with James and Jenny Melzer. We talked about how Young Adult zombie fiction was gonna be hot and that getting on that bandwagon would be a great career move. Then I had a very brief chat with Jonathan Maberry after a panel we did together and he said YA zombies was the way to go. Agents were looking for zombies!

I took that to heart and during the long drive home from Pittsburgh to Asheville, I happened to look over at a car I was passing and saw two brothers in the back seat (I assume they were brothers). The idea slammed into my brain of writing a novel about brothers: one alive, one dead. But the idea that a zombie brother would be kept alive didn't fit. Unless the brothers were conjoined twins and severing the connection put the living brother's life at risk. Bingo! I had my idea.

I had to finish up the novel I was working on before I could start *Little Dead Man*. But the second I started I rocked right through that thing! I started writing at the end of November 2010 and had a finished manuscript out to agents in February of 2011. In March I signed with an agent and we worked hard to get the novel polished for submission to publishers.

Within just a few months we had quite a few positive rejections. Things along the lines of: "Great writing, great novel, but not sure how to market it." That sort of stuff. So long story long, *Little Dead Man* never found a home and just sat there, doing nothing.

Until now. With a quick stint as a self-published novel, *Little Dead Man* has finally found a home with the perfect publisher, a publisher that gets dark fiction and especially post-apocalyptic zombie horror—Permuted Press!

I'm looking forward to seeing the new life *Little Dead Man* will lead. Can't keep a good zombie (novel) down, right?

Cheers,
Jake

CHAPTER ONE

CHAPTER ONE

I

Today my brother and I turn seventeen and Mom baked us a cake. Well, she baked me a cake. Garth is dead, so he doesn't eat real food.

I should probably explain better. Mom actually *burned* us a cake. It was a small fire and I put it out quickly, so no real harm done. It's okay since Mom's not the greatest cook and I would have had to choke down a few polite bites anyway. It's the thought that counts, right?

"Sorry, sweetheart," she says as I open the doors and windows to air out the RV.

"No worries, Mom," I smile. "It'll clear out soon."

"Don't tell your father, okay?" she pleads, knowing it will upset him and he'll start in on the psych questions. That usually ends in tears. Hers and his. Of course, Dad has been out on his studies since before we woke up, so he won't have a clue anything happened.

Dad's always said Mom used to be an amazing cook before the world died and before Garth and I were born, but she hasn't been the same since. At least that's what Dad *says* and, well, he isn't always paying attention, so I take it with a grain of salt.

"I know it's your birthday and all, but can you go pick the rest of the blackberries?" Mom asks me. "They're gonna dry on the vine in this heat and I'd hate for them to go to waste."

I give her an awkward hug (I'm seventeen now, after all)

and set off to get prepped before leaving camp. Small compound really. We have a converted RV that has been backed into a rock outcropping that juts from the ground, which serves as our storage area and safe zone if any necs come wandering by. Usually they don't make it up here, but lately we've seen more than our share and Dad puts them down right away ("Headshot, son. Headshot") even though he says killing anything is a crime these days and should only be done as a last resort or for survival.

The total compound is about an acre surrounded by a ten foot chain link fence with razor wire on top and strung through out. There is a second row of chain link and razor wire spaced two feet out from that and then an eight foot deep by six foot wide trench. Mom and Dad were prepared when the world ended.

The compound, and especially my loft bed above the RV's driver's seat, is all I've ever known for a home. I read about houses and condos and apartments and mansions, but I've never seen any. Dad says he'll take me down the mountain sometime to see what the world used to be like and what it has become. But, as with so many things, he hasn't told me when. I've never been more than ten miles from the compound ever.

So, for now, my impressions of the world, or at least the way the world used to be, are from the books I read. And I've read a lot of books. Dad has to make trips to scavenge every once in a while and he always brings me back books.

Mysteries, fantasy, non-fiction history, fictional history, medical books, technical books, horror, romance, teen, pulp. You name it, I've read it. What else is a kid going to do in a dead world?

Sure, I can hunt and fish and all that other outdoorsy stuff, but that gets old. Reading doesn't. Not for me.

2

Seventeen... Wow...

In all the books I've read, turning sixteen was the big deal in the old world, back before the necros came to be. Kids used to get their own cars and have huge parties, at least the girls did. Something called "sweet sixteen". Dad says the parties were for the pretentious elite and were a huge waste of money and resources. I don't really understand the whole "money" thing, but Dad says it was what made the world go round. Since my parents couldn't give me a car, Dad spent a couple weeks last year showing me how to operate the RV. I didn't get to drive it, since it's our house, but I know what all the buttons and pedals do.

Even without cars, money, and cake, I guess seventeen is pretty important since my parents never thought I'd live past one or two. Having an undead conjoined twin stuck to your back can really worry the parents. Dad tried to separate us more than once, but my blood pressure dropped too low every time and it wasn't worth the risk. Mom doesn't ever speak of Garth. She acts like he isn't there, but I do catch her staring when she thinks I'm not looking. I'm not sure what the problem is really, I'm used to Little Man and he's used to me. Just like brothers in the books we get on each other's nerves, but that's life, right?

Well, "life" might be stretching it a bit when talking about Little Man (that's mine and Dad's nickname for Garth). Mom got pregnant just as the world ended, when the necros came to be, and my parents were able to escape up here to the camp. Dad's a scientist, behavioral virology, and Mom was a surgeon, so they had everything prepared: all the supplies, equipment, resources, just in case there were any complications.

There *were* complications. Best laid plans and all that... (That's Steinbeck, not my favorite author, but beggars can't be choosers).

I think about all this as I go through my equipment and weapons checklist: machete in sheath and strapped to my leg; spiked baseball bat on my back, next to Garth; 9mm Beretta on my hip with three extra magazines; ten inch serrated hunting knife on my belt with heavy gloves tucked next to them; folding shovel in my satchel along with matches, a canteen, a large plastic bag and two smaller plastic bags, an extra t-shirt and a towel. Over the years, in order to keep from tearing my skin, Little Man was supported in a deer hide sling that would strap under my arm, across my chest and around back. Now my skin and his has hardened, becoming rough, but pliable. Sorta like a big callus that surrounds where his body connects to mine. The only problem now is it gives him more mobility and as I drape the alert whistle over my neck, Little Man grabs at its cord, as always, and I have to swat his hand away. He grunts at me, but I ignore him.

Mom and Dad knew they were having twins and everything was going fine until a week before the due date. Mom was checking vitals and could only find one heartbeat. That alone would be terrifying, but even though there was only one heartbeat, she could feel us both moving. Dad had to cut us out. Like I said, Mom hasn't been the same since.

Garth had his umbilical cord wrapped around his neck. He was dead for only a day since Mom checked our vitals like clockwork. But dead for a day is all it takes with the necros. Twenty-four hours from death to undeath. Such is the way of the necros.

Necros... *Homo Sapiens Necrosii*. That is what Dad has classified them. A new species all together. It's his obsession and keeps him away most of the day, and sometimes all night.

He calls them HSNs. I call them necros, or necs, but Dad doesn't like this. He says it's derogatory and I should know better because of Garth.

Mom never speaks about them and prefers we don't either. Dad calls it denial. I call it crazy, but I keep that to myself. Crazy moms are in a lot of my books, so I guess she isn't breaking any new ground.

I systematically unlock the inside gate, relock it, double check that it is secure, walk the thirty yards to the outside gate, unlock it, relock it, check that it is secure and finally make my way down the trail to the creek and the blackberries waiting to be picked.

Little Man died in utero (in the womb), but since my parents only had a portable ultrasound machine, they couldn't tell that he and I were connected. Conjoined. When I was young I'd read all these books about kids with normal lives, without their brother hanging from the top of their spine, and I'd be so jealous. But, over the years, I've gotten used to it. He's Little Man.

"He ain't heavy, he's your brother," Dad jokes. Says it's lyrics to some song by a guy named Neil. I haven't heard it. They brought equipment, food, weapons and other supplies, but Dad forgot the music (still makes Mom pretty angry), so all I know is what Mom sings while she works or what I've read about. Dad doesn't sing, or at least we tell him not to.

Apparently, Little Man and I share spinal fluid and major blood vessels. This is why Dad can't separate us, although he hasn't tried in quite a few years. He isn't the surgeon like Mom, but she's taught him a lot and if he has one thing going for him, he learns fast.

"When you're older, maybe," he says. He wants my body to stop growing first so he knows what he's dealing with. Garth's body hasn't grown since we were born. He's a nec and necs are dead and the dead don't grow. They just erode.

"They *petrify*, not *putrefy*," Dad has told me.

The virus that turns a human into an HSN (to use Dad's term) kills everything, not just the host body. It kills all bacteria, other viruses, microbes, yeast, anything and everything a human body could have in it or be exposed to. This means that once a person turns into a nec they don't rot away. Instead, they end up changing with the weather. They become kinda spongy when it rains or hard and dry during a drought. Their body only breaks down by natural exposure to the elements, or friction as they move. This leads to some interesting looking necros out there.

But, since Little Man is connected to me, and my blood and spinal fluid, he doesn't erode like the rest. He just stays Little Man. I get bigger, he stays the same size.

He does stink though.

Nec farts are awful.

"**H**ush," I warn Little Man. "Stop wiggling and moaning." He quiets down quickly. He's usually pretty good about minding me which fascinates Dad.

Dad...

He spends most of his time out "in the field", as he likes to say.

"We have to study the HSNs, Garret," he'll tell me when he knows Mom isn't listening or when we are out on our hikes. "They are the dominant species now and we must learn from their behavior so we can survive."

Not sure what we can learn from them. Only thing they do is look creepy and eat. Eat people. Not animals, but people. What's to learn?

We get about a half mile down the three mile trail when Little Man shifts again and gives a high squeak. This time I don't tell him to hush. Instead I get off the trail quickly and duck behind one of the many large pines that are everywhere here in southern Oregon. That squeak means necs are getting close.

Little Man squeaks again, just to make sure I'm listening and I reach behind and pat his head. As usual, he tries to bite me, but he wasn't born with teeth, and being dead, they never came in. I swat at him absentmindedly and he growls a little, but hushes up. I'm usually pretty good at knowing when necs are close, but I'm lost in thought today. Birthday musings. Dad thinks my sensitivity to necs has something to do with Garth. That I'm naturally more aware of the necros. Whatever the reason, I don't care, since it's the only way Dad was able to talk Mom into letting me out of the compound on my own.

Now, here's the thing about necs: there's more than just one kind.

Dad calls it "genetic variability". His theory (God, does he have some theories) is that since each person has many genetic variables and predispositions when alive, it stands to reason they will have the same variables when they are dead. Or undead. Whatever.

Some necs are just slow, shambling creatures. They walk from place to place, their noses and ears leading them to what they hope will be food. They never run, they never make any noise, they just shamble. They're the easy ones to deal with. We've had a surprising amount make it all the way up to our camp and we just wait until they shamble off. Dad usually goes out and puts them down once they are far enough away.

Other necs are a little more animated. Like the lurkers. Those guys wait. They'll be in a ditch, a hole, a cave, behind a tree, under a bush, behind some rocks. Doesn't matter, they just wait for prey. There is always one around somewhere. They are pretty quick, but not too bright. They think since they can't see you, you can't see them. Usually parts of them are sticking out from their hiding place, so they really aren't too hard to spot. All you have to do is circle around, come up from behind quietly and SPLAT! Off goes the head.

Now, the ones you have to watch out for are the runners. These guys you don't mess with. It's easier to hide and let them move on than to face them. Mostly because they run in packs.

"The runners are the evolution of the Hunter gene," Dad says. "Some people were born to farm, some were born to hunt. Runners are the latter."

Runners are fast. And I mean *fast*! Trust me, runners can, and will, chase you down. Dad and I have come close before, but luckily we've gotten away every time.

"Know your surroundings, G," is another of Dad's sayings.

"Always know where you are in relation to what's around you. That knowledge can mean the difference between life and death."

Oh, and runners can climb too. That's why we have the razor wire on the compound fence.

But what Little Man has warned me about is none of these. What's close to us is one of the broken.

4

The broken...

The poor, pitiful thing grasps at the dry dirt of the trail, desperate to pull itself along. I can see that its legs were gnawed off by other necs when the thing used to be alive. Used to be a person.

From the look of its torn chest and the matted pony tail hanging down its back, my guess is it used to be a woman. Its clothes have long since rotted away and its grey-blue skin is shiny from what Dad calls "dead sweat". That's just ambient moisture that seeps from its undead pores.

Its head is barely attached to its body and dangles down from the neck. With each movement the head bobs slightly, reminding me of one of my childhood toys. It's kinda comical, but not really when you think that this used to be a person.

I unsheathe my machete and stand over the nec. It struggles to raise its eyes to me, but its head won't cooperate and the thing starts to hiss in frustration.

"Kill it, Garret," my Dad's voice whispers from directly behind me, causing me to yelp and nearly drop my blade.

"Dad!" I fume in a hushed yell, since where there is one nec there are usually others. "Don't do that!"

"Sorry, G," he apologizes, squeezing my shoulder. "You shouldn't let them suffer. Just do what's needed."

"Yeah, I know. It's just I wasn't looking forward to digging."

Part of killing a nec is disposing of the body. Even though

necs don't eat other necs, they are attracted to the dead ones. Dad has a theory on this, of course. The main problem with necs is they don't decompose. So the body has to be covered in at least three feet of dirt or they attract others. If they decomposed, it wouldn't be such a problem since they'd just rot away to nothing eventually. But, as I said, one of the many wonders of necs is that not only are *they* dead, so are the trillions of bacteria and yeasts that inhabit a living human body. Microorganisms that would normally breakdown the dead flesh don't. Nothing lives on or in a nec. Nothing.

We spend a lot of time burying necs.

"Kill it, G," Dad says again.

I step close and bring the machete down through the thing's skull. It collapses instantly and is still forever. I look at Dad and roll my eyes, take off my satchel and pull out my shovel. "Over there looks good," I say, pointing to a spot well off the trail that doesn't look choked with tree roots. I hate tree roots.

"I agree," Dad says and we both pull on our heavy gloves to keep from getting infected.

Viruses are contagious. This is something Dad has drilled into me since I was old enough to understand. What changes the living into living dead is a specific virus that can be transmitted by bodily fluids, including blood, saliva and dead sweat. This isn't one of Dad's theories. He states this as fact. I've asked how he knows for sure, but he never answers and Mom usually changes the subject or stares off into space like she hasn't heard anything.

We each grab an undead arm and pull the nec from the path. Dad and I are big folk, as Mom likes to tease. We're not fat, that's not really possible these days, but we are tall and muscular, so we have the thing off the path and to its final destination in no time.

"Start digging. I want to take a sample," Dad says.

"Why? You've taken thousands of samples. You never find anything," I complain, more from having to dig alone than because he's wasting time taking a sample. "Give it a rest, Dad! They're all the same: dead!" As soon as the words are out of my mouth I regret them. Garth. That's why Dad takes samples. Even though I'm connected to Little Man night and day, I forget sometimes he's a nec. He's just, you know, my brother. "Sorry."

Dad gives me a weak smile, but I can see that it'll be a while before he lets my comments go.

"Just dig, Garret," he mutters as he pulls out several vials and a scalpel from his own satchel and proceeds to slice bits of skin and hair from the corpse.

I push the shovel blade into the ground and start furiously tossing dirt to the side. Usually I don't let things get to me, having an undead twin teaches you patience, but this time... well, it's my BIRTHDAY!

After a few shovelfuls of dirt *accidentally* stray towards Dad he sets the vials aside and stands, giving me his sternest look.

"So, what's eating you?" he asks, his hands on his hips, ready to argue.

"Nothing," I mutter and continue digging.

"Out with it, Garret. I don't need any whining today."

"You don't...?" I toss the shovel on the ground and laugh. "Oh, well, wouldn't want to get in the way of Dr. Weir's important day!" He starts to speak, but I cut him off. "Do you even know what day it is?"

"Of course. It's Thursday, August 29th." He just stands there, all grumpy faced, and I wait for it to hit him. Three... two...one... "Oh, crap! It's your birthday! I'm so sorry, G."

"You're about a foot and a half too late for sorry, Dad," I grumble, picking up my shovel and starting at the hole again.

"Stop, Garret. I'll finish for you. I really am sorry I forgot."

"I'm sure you are, but I'm already a sweaty mess so I might as well finish up here. Why don't you go pick blackberries. I'll be down to the creek to wash off in a minute." He starts to speak again, but once more I cut him off. "Just go. I'll be there soon."

He gives me an apologetic nod, grabs up his things, and heads back to the trail.

I keep digging.

5

Living in southern Oregon is no picnic.

By the time I'm done digging the hole, tossing in the corpse and then covering it over, I'm drenched in sweat from the hot, dry air.

It doesn't help that Little Man is grunting and hissing the whole time, complaining over the exertion and the sweat that's covering him. His small fists swat at my back with every angry grunt and it's all I can do from reaching back there and slapping him silly.

"Stop!" I yell, way louder than I should. I'm answered by another string of hisses and then his feet start in. "Garth, I swear I will hold you under for at least five minutes once we get to the creek!"

After a few more grunts he shuts up, knowing I'll make good on my threat. You see, necros don't need to breath. Their lungs work since their muscles still work and the diaphragm is nothing but a big muscle that pumps the lungs like a bellows. Well, the side effect of having working lungs is that they can fill with water. Little Man hates it. His little body gets all bloated and heavy and he can't vocalize or move right. This isn't a problem for other necs since they're dead. But, Little Man is connected to me and different. I'm pretty darn sure he thinks and feels (despite what Mom wants to believe or not). And, being the brother that I am, I take advantage of this when I can.

"Yeah, you're quiet now," I mutter as I grab up my things and start back down to the creek.

We walk for a few minutes and the trail is extra dusty (we haven't seen rain in weeks) and I wish I hadn't emptied my canteen back there digging, but the creek is close, I can hear it, and cool, clean water is in my future. I can almost feel it on my skin when Little Man squeaks.

I guess before I get to cool down, I have to get past the shambler. Dammit, don't the necs know it's my birthday?

"It's because you made me yell," I blame Garth. He growls a bit and slaps me, but keeps still after that, sensing the other nec.

I know better, I really do, but I'm just so tired and dirty and all I want to do is get clean and have a swim and eat a few blackberries (if Dad doesn't get distracted and forget to pick some). Even though I know better, I pull my 9, take aim and put a bullet right between the nec's eyes. Skull, brain, blood and hair splatters against the trees behind the nec and its now truly dead body crumples to the ground.

I know the second I pull the trigger I'm in deep trouble.

6

"What did you do!" Dad shouts as he runs up the trail from the creek. "That shot can be heard for miles! We'll have even more making their way here!"

"Then maybe you shouldn't be shouting!" I shout back.

"I wouldn't be shouting if you hadn't been so stupid! What were you thinking?"

"I don't know! I wasn't! I'm tired and hot and dirty and I just want some damn blackberries!"

"Well, I left the blackberries back at the creek! I was lucky to grab my satchel!" He stands there glaring at me, blaming me. I don't care. "Get your gloves on and help me get rid of this thing." He sighs and puts his own gloves on for the second time today. "Did you get any back spray on you?"

"No, I was far enough away." I just get my gloves on when the sound of twigs snapping makes us both stand straight and grab for our weapons. Garth starts to squeak over and over, his legs and fists slamming against my back and shoulders.

"Hush!" I whisper, knowing necros are on the way. Little Man isn't ever wrong and my gut is telling me there's more than one.

Dad drops the nec's arm he is holding and pushes me back up the trail. The sound of branches breaking and underbrush being shoved aside grows louder. "It's gotta be runners! They must have been following the shambler! Go!"

"What about...?"

"Forget the corpse! We don't have time! We have to zig-zag back to the camp. We can't lead them there!"

I nod and sprint to the right, off the trail and away from the oncoming noise. I'm yards away before I realize Dad isn't with me.

"Dad!" I cry, trying to keep my voice down. "Dad!"

Nothing.

Little Man starts up again and won't stop, no matter how many times I swat at him or tell him to be quiet. "Okay, okay! We're going."

I run. Legs and arms pumping, the dry air burning my lungs, but I don't dare stop. Little Man has quieted down except for when I have to leap or duck suddenly and jar him. It's times like this when I know he can feel, when I know he has pain in his life...well, in his death.

Dad and I have practiced the zig-zag escape many times, so my feet know where they are going automatically and I'm back at the compound in no time. And so are the necs. Lots of them.

7

I can see them before I break from the tree line, so I'm able to stop myself without being seen.

Of course, Little Man can't see them, just knows they are near, and starts squawking. I reach back to shush him, but it's too late. They see us.

Six runner heads whip about, their undead eyes locking onto us.

Time stands still.

Six of them. I've never seen that many at once before. Dad's said he's seen dozens packed together down the mountain, but I always had a bit of doubt about that. Until now.

Garth can sense my fear and his squawks turn to yelps, high and loud. I don't try to quiet him, knowing it doesn't matter now. Stumbling backwards, I reach out to steady myself against a tree, but my hand hits semi-soft flesh. Dead flesh.

I spin and the thing is already on me, growling and clawing. I shove hard, knocking the nec back, but it's enraged and hungry and my shove is like the wind. It reaches for me and my eyes fall on the thing's hands, just sinew holding bone together, the skin and muscle long worn away by years of erosion. Without muscles and tendons, it can't close its hands, can't grab onto me and it just swipes at me over and over, trying to get close enough to sink its teeth in.

I kick out, connect with its right knee, and send it to the ground with an audible snap of bone. I reach back for my spiked bat and as I do I feel teeth clamp down on my fingers. I cry out and spin around, grabbing at my hand. My heart leaps into my chest and for a split second I think I'm dead, that it's all over, that I'm infected, but I realize I never took my gloves off and the nec couldn't get through the tough leather.

"Garret! Down!" I hear Mom scream and I fall to the ground just before I hear the rifle shot. I cover my head with my arms as brain and bone spray everywhere and the nec crumples. I hear eight more shots and then silence.

The nec I took down claws at my jeans and tries to pull my leg over to its mouth, but I get my 9 loose and put two in it's left eye.

"GARRET!" Mom screams. "GARRRET TELL ME YOU'RE OKAY!"

I roll onto my side, careful as always not to crush Little Man, and take a deep breath. "I'm fine, Mom!" I shout back, taking a couple more breaths before I push myself to my feet. "Are you okay?"

I can see her inside the fences, tears are streaming down her face and she lets the rifle fall from her hands as she falls to her knees sobbing.

"Hold on, Mom! I'm coming in! Everything will be fine!" I yell as I get to the ditch and toss the planks in place. My feet barely touch the wood I'm moving so fast and I'm inside with both gates secure in a matter of seconds. I scoop Mom into my arms and let her bury her face in my chest, her body shaking violently as she cries and cries.

"Shhhh," I soothe, stroking her hair. "Shhhhhh. I'm fine. They didn't get me. I'm fine and Little Man is fine too." She cries harder at the mention of Garth and I regret the words instantly.

"They...were...so...close," she stutters. "They...were... going...to eat...you."

I laugh a little. "That's what they do, Mom. But I'm alright." I push her away a bit. "See? No marks. No bites. Nothing."

She gives me a weak smile. "There've never...been that... many so close...before."

She's right. We've had the occasional shambler, lurker and broken make their way up the mountain, even a runner or two, but never a pack.

"They know we're here, Garret!" she gasps. "They know we're here!" Her sobs double and Little Man starts in with the moaning too and it takes me twenty minutes to quiet them both down. All the while there's no sign of Dad.

Happy Birthday to me....

CHAPTER TWO

I fix myself a dinner of cold roots, leftover squirrel and raccoon and sit eating it as far away from the RV as possible. I'd have cooked something nice, but Dad insists we hold off on fires for the next day or two until we know the area is clear of necs.

Dad makes it back to the compound about an hour after I do and Mom hasn't stopped laying into him since. It's obvious he doubled back for his samples and supplies before heading to the camp and Mom won't let it go. They've been yelling at each other in the RV non-stop.

As their voices rise, so does Little Man's irritation and I finally have to set my food aside since it's near impossible to eat while he's grunting and thrashing. I pull up my right jeans leg and expose a long scab. I pick at it for a minute until I get a good size chunk. Reaching back I stuff it in Garth's mouth and he hungrily munches on the treat. It's a trick I've learned over the years to get Little Man to calm down. I've never told Mom or Dad and never will. They wouldn't understand.

The RV door slams open, banging against the side, and I see clothes fly from the vehicle and into the dirt.

"Get out!" Mom screams. "You selfish son of a bitch! GET OUT!"

Dad stumbles down the two metal steps and backs away, dodging shirts and pants, socks and underwear. "Dammit, Helen! Just calm down!"

"You left him out there!" Mom screams, following him out of the RV, an axe handle in her hand. "You left our son to fend for himself while you went back for your precious samples! I had to save him, Thomas! They had him surrounded and I had to shoot them! I could have missed and the stray bullets could have killed Garret! What if I had missed?!"

"You didn't, though. You didn't miss!" he pleads. "He's fine!"

"No thanks to you! UNFORGIVABLE!"

She takes a wild swipe at him with the axe handle and he steps out of the way easily. I get up wearily and walk towards them, knowing I'll have to be the one to break it up.

"Stop! You're going to do something you'll regret later!" Dad warns. "Just stop!"

"My whole life has been something I regret, Thomas! I regret leaving everyone without warning them! I regret you talking me into coming out here! I regret getting pregnant! And I regret you talking me into it all and carrying a monster! I REGRET EVERYTHING!"

I stop, stunned. A monster? Doing what needed to be done?

"What do you mean 'talking you into it'?" I ask and they both turn and notice me. "What does that mean? I thought it was all an emergency? You both said you didn't know until it was too late."

I can see the pain in Mom's eyes as she struggles with the thoughts bouncing around in her head. She jabs the axe handle into Dad's chest. "Your fault..." she mutters and is gone inside the RV with a bang of the door.

Dad ducks his head and averts his eyes from my burning gaze.

"Dad? What did she mean?" I ask quietly as I struggle to keep my anger in check. "Did you know about Garth?"

"It's complicated, Garret," he answers and walks away, leaving me, and a newly agitated Little Man, to stare after him as he walks around the outcropping and out of sight.

2

"**M**om?" I quietly knock on the RV door and step into the dark space and close the door behind me. "Mom, are you okay?" I can hear her sniffling, but she doesn't answer.

The place is a wreck. Clothes are everywhere: hers, mine, Dad's. There are broken dishes and books tossed about. I try not to look at the books, hoping she hasn't ruined any of my favorites.

"Mom?"

"Go away, Garret," she whimpers. "I don't want to talk right now."

I find her in the back curled up on the bed under the blankets with the pillows piled around her head. "Come on. Please. I just want to talk."

"I know you do, but I can't talk right now. Just go, please." Little Man snorts a few times and Mom flings the pillows away, her face filled with rage. "Go away, Garret! I don't want to talk!"

I back out of the bedroom and slide the partition closed. My heart is beating a thousand miles an hour and feels like it's lodged up in my throat. I'm seventeen now, but sometimes I feel so small.

I will the tears not to flow and begin to pick up the mess in the RV. I neatly fold the clothes and put them back in their drawers. I'll let Dad deal with the ones outside.

I'm keeping it together fairly well until I see the copy of *The Wizard Of Oz* laying next to the couch, its spine ripped and several pages torn and sticking out. Picking up the book I plop onto the couch and feel my heart rise and rise until hot tears drip down my cheeks. Little Man can smell them and tries to reach around to get a taste and I slap his hand hard. He lets out a yelp and slaps me back. Soon we're slapping at each other over and over.

"Knock it off!" I yell. He growls back and pinches the back of my neck. I flick him in the eye and he howls, his hands slapping at his eye over and over. "Stop being such a baby! It didn't hurt that much!"

The panel slides open and I see Mom standing there, her eyes puffy and hair a mess. "Leave your brother alone," she whispers as she walks past me and to the RV door. I'm not quite sure which one of us she's talking to.

Little Man stops freaking out and looks over my shoulder as we both watch her step out into the evening light.

3

Standing at the RV door, I watch Mom begin the process of getting the cook pit ready.

"Dad says not to light a fire tonight," I warn, but she ignores me. I go to her and gently touch her elbow. "Mom?"

"It's your birthday and you deserve a hot meal, not leftovers," she says sadly. "You deserve more than that..."

"Its okay, Mom. Please don't worry about me. Really, I'd rather go without than..."

"Than what, Garret?" she asks, her voice rising. "Than make the good professor angry? Trust me, son, if you knew half the truth you wouldn't give two spits about your father."

I've never heard her say anything like this before and I'm stunned. I don't know how to respond. So I just stand there, watching her get the tinder box lit until she has a nice cook fire.

"Get me some water, please. I need to boil the potatoes," she says after a couple minutes of silence. "You like mashed potatoes."

I look down at the ground and fear what I have to say. "I, um, didn't have a chance to fill the jugs today."

She sighs and sets the cook pot down and grabs a Dutch oven. "Then it's roasted potatoes. You like those, right?"

She finally looks at me and I can tell from the look in her eyes that she's stepped over and isn't quite here anymore.

"Yeah, I love roasted potatoes," I lie. She burns the

potatoes every time which is why I prefer the mashed ones even though those are lumpy and flavorless. "I'll see if we have any garlic."

She nods and mumbles something, but I can't make out what it is. I turn and head into the RV. The sight of my father standing at the edge of the RV stops me instantly.

"Go ahead, G," he says kindly. "Get the garlic."

"Not if you two are going to start fighting again," I say defiantly. Mom starts to hum behind me, oblivious. "You already ruined my Oz book."

His lips turn down and he steps towards me. "It's a kids book anyway, G. You're seventeen now. Time to let go."

"Let go? And move on to what, Dad?" I ask annoyed. "Shall I pop down to the local library and browse their selection of new releases? Should I bring back the Internet thing and order a bestseller to be delivered to Middle of Nowhere Oregon?" I sweep my arms about. "There is no moving on, Dad. This is all I have and all I know! No one is going to make more books! No one is going to make more of anything! The world is dead and I'm just living my life until I join it!" He steps closer and starts to speak, but I shake my head and wave him off. "I don't want to hear it."

"Let me speak, Garret. I know you're pissed, but I'm still your father. Just hear me out." I glare at him for a few seconds, but finally nod. "Thank you," he continues. "You're absolutely right. This is all you know. And it's probably time we changed that. Go get the garlic so we can fix you a birthday dinner. We're going to sit down like a family and eat some food, celebrate your birth, and then we are going to discuss your future. We're going to discuss the future of the whole family."

4

The meal isn't bad. After some heated resistance, Mom lets Dad help with the potatoes while she shreds rabbit jerky and toasts that up with some seeds. Mixed together, it's actually quite good.

After an exaggerated belly pat Dad takes mine and Mom's plates and sets them aside. "I'm sorry for today, but in a way I'm glad it happened." Mom opens her mouth, but Dad presses on. "Let me finish. I'm not glad for the danger you were put in, Garret. Or the pain I caused you, Helen. What I'm glad for is that this was a wake up call. We've lived in this spot for nearly seventeen years and up until today we've been pretty lucky. We've had a few HSNs wander by. A couple run-ins with some of the cougars and black bears, but we were more a danger to them than they were to us. We out lasted a few brutal winters and a couple wildfires. Overall it has been a great home." He pauses and Mom and I wait for the 'but'. "But...things are changing down below. This mountain is isolated which is why we chose it. That isolation only works if the HSNs, for the most part, stay centralized, which they have for a long while now. Something has forced a change out there. They're moving out of the towns and cities and starting to migrate."

"Why?" I ask.

"I'm not sure," Dad answers. "My guess is their hunger is finally forcing them to. With no bacteria to break them down and only time and the weather against them, their animal brains have finally pushed them past the zombie state and are driving them forward. The runners have always hunted. I think now they all are."

"I don't want to leave," Mom says quietly. "We don't know what's out there, Thomas. It's not just the zombies..."

"HSNs," Dad corrects. "And that's the other reason we need to move. We're sitting ducks here. That fence will hold out the undead, but it's not going to hold everything out."

I look back and forth between them, puzzled. "Wait...what do you mean 'everything'? What else is there?"

Dad pauses for a long while and Mom looks away. "People, Garret," he finally answers. "It won't hold out people."

I'm on my feet in an instant. "People...? Did you say 'people'?"

"Yes, son. There are still people out there. Quite a few actually. And not all of them are nice or like to share. It's only a matter of time until they find us. If it's the wrong sort then we won't be able to defend ourselves."

I don't know what to say. People? There are people still alive?

5

"Garret? Are you alright?" Mom asks, getting up and taking my hand. "You've been still for a while."

I blink a few times and realize the camp has gotten a lot darker. "How long have I been standing here?"

"Just a few minutes. Your father started to worry, but I know you're just processing."

"Are we really leaving?" I ask turning and looking into the twilight of the forest beyond camp. "Where are we going to go? If there are people out there, won't they just find us once we start to move? What's to keep us safe then?"

"Great questions all," Dad responds from the RV steps. "Come inside and let me show you."

I look at Mom, but she's no help. "Go inside, Garret. See what your dad wants to show you," she says. "I'll clean up out here and put the fire out. Go on. I'll be in soon."

I nod, give her hand a squeeze, and I follow Dad into the RV.

"What?" I say and plop on the couch.

Dad lets my attitude slide, but I can tell from the look on his face he isn't in the mood for more of it. I decide that if Little Man starts acting up I won't shush him. That always starts to get on Dad's nerves.

"This is what you need to see," Dad says, sliding open a panel in the wall of the RV and pulling out a thick notebook stuffed with papers and bound by a thick rubber band. He opens the notebook and sets all the loose papers aside, keeping them out of my line of sight. He knows I notice this, but neither of us comment on it. He slaps down a map on the table and opens it, waving me over. I reluctantly get off the couch and lean over the table.

"This is a map of the US," he starts.

"Yeah, I can see that," I say snottily.

Pinching the bridge of his nose he squeezes his eyes shut. "It's been a long day for both of us, Garret. Zip the lip and just listen."

I pantomime zipping my lip and he gives me a sharp look. "Sorry," I apologize, though I don't really mean it.

"We are here. See?" He points to a green X just south of Crater Lake and I nod. "The red circles with Xs are dead zones. Places that are completely overrun by HSNs and no one should go near for any reason."

"I thought that was most of the world, really?" He glares. "Zipping it. Sorry."

"You can see that pretty much every urban area in the US is crossed out, as are most of the smaller rural towns. Anywhere there was a concentration of humans is now off limits." He points to some blue circles. "However, these areas have been cleared and are fairly secure. At least as secure as our area."

He lets me puzzle over the circles for a few minutes. "But, you have places all over the country circled. How can you know that?"

He grins and actually looks slightly embarrassed. "Because your mother and I have kept you in the dark on a few things. This being one of them." He crosses back to the panel in the wall and reaches in, pulling out a small box with a handset. "This is a short wave radio. It can pick up radio broadcasts from all over the world if I have enough power. Usually I have to take it to the peak and set up an antenna, but some-times I can get signals here in camp. It's rare though because of the topography of this mountain."

I step back and shake my head. "So you've always known there are others out there?"

"Yes, son."

"Why didn't you tell me?"

"Because you would have wanted to find them. Because children are social and long to be with other children. We didn't want you to have that longing."

"But, that doesn't explain why we aren't with the other people. Why are we stuck up here all alone?"

Dad glances at my back and frowns. "Because of Garth. Your mother can't even handle the reality of him. Do you think others that aren't family will understand? I barely do. You'd both be killed out there. We stay here for your safety as well as for Garth's."

Little Man gives a grunt and a fart. Dad waves his hand in front of his face.

"You've been feeding him scabs again, haven't you?" he complains.

My eyes go wide in surprise. "You know about that?"

"Kid, all I do is observe. There's not a lot that escapes my attention around here."

"Except my birthday."

He averts his eyes. "Yeah...sorry about that."

I turn the subject back to leaving. "So, we've stayed here for mine and Little Man's safety, but now we have to leave? Aren't we in just as much danger out there as we would be here?"

Dad is obviously glad I don't rub in his forgetting my birthday and points once again at the map. "Yes and no. You see this circle here? That's outside what used to be Cottage Grove. I've been in contact with them since almost the beginning. They were lucky enough to already have a type of commune built and self-sustainable when the world ended. All they had to do was fortify it against others and the HSNs. They've been surviving ever since."

"Against others? You mean other people?"

"Yes, other people. The HSNs are dangerous and deadly, but the scariest animal on Earth has always been humans." He points to a few blue circles between us and the Cottage Grove commune. "None of these can be trusted. They are either run by men and women that don't think anyone's survival is more important than their own. Or..."

I wait for him to elaborate, but he doesn't. "Or...?" I ask, trying to draw him out.

He sighs and rubs at his face. "Some weren't prepared or don't have the survival skills needed." I wait some more and he can tell I'm not going to drop it. "Food, Garret. It's about food."

6

"I don't get it," I say and honestly I don't. "How is food a problem? Why don't they hunt? There's plenty of game out there. And gardens. Ours isn't large, but that's because we don't get much rain. I'm sure other places get more and could have great gardens."

"Ideally, yes," Dad answers. "But, something you have to learn about human nature, son, is that ignorance is a powerful thing. It takes a person over and is almost as infectious as a virus. Many times it's even more dangerous."

"You're not answering my question, Dad," I complain. "Just tell me what's going on out there."

He takes a deep breath and I can see he is seriously debating whether to tell me or not. Finally he speaks. "They eat other people, G. They're cannibals."

I feel my body go numb with shock. I hear Dad speaking to me, but none of the words are making sense. It's all just gibberish in my shocked brain.

Cannibals? People that eat other people? I thought that was all in stories and happened on the "Dark Continent" like in the novels by Defoe and Conrad. How can that be happening here and now? I just find out that there are other people out there and now I have to worry about whether they're going to eat me?

"Garret? Garret!" Dad yells.

I snap out of my head and look him square in the eye.

"Cannibals? That's messed up."

"Did you hear anything I just said?" he asks, concern on his face. I shake my head no and he puts a hand on my shoulder, giving me a reassuring squeeze. "I know it's a lot to take in, but I need you to focus." He turns back to the map and pulls out a black pen from his pocket. "See these two areas?" He crosses them off. "As of this morning I have confirmation that they don't exist anymore. At least not in a good way."

"What does that mean? Are they dead?"

"No, they've been wiped out by this group." He taps the map. "We call them the SATs. It's short for sick and twisted. Pretty much sums them up. They are led by two people, Charles and Charlotte Griffin."

I let out a short laugh. "Charles and Charlotte? Really? That's worse than some of the paperbacks I've read."

"Their names may be laughable, but they are pure evil as far as I'm concerned. I'll never take for granted what atrocities they are capable of. Never underestimate them, G. They are a million times worse than the HSNs."

Little Man starts to twitch a bit, but I ignore him. He's just going to have to sit through all this. I don't have time to give him attention right now.

Dad looks at Garth, but then continues. "If we leave here, we are going to have to get past the SATs in order to get to Cottage Grove. It isn't going to be easy and it's going to take a lot of preparation." He fixes me with his 'Serious Dad' look. "Garret, if for some reason we are separated, you need to never go near the Griffins' compound. Do you hear me? This is vital. Promise me."

"Um, sure, I promise." Easy promise since I have no desire to get anywhere near people known as 'Sick and Twisted'. I point to the area south of us and the blue circles there. "Why not head that way?"

"California isn't an option anymore. None of us have heard from any of the survivor groups down there in weeks." Little Man grumbles and lets out a squeak. We both ignore him and Dad taps at San Francisco then Los Angeles. "I'm pretty sure the HSNs are moving north. There's enough of them from both of these cities to overrun any survivors."

"What's to stop them from getting to us?"

"Climate. Geography. There's an entire mountain range between us and these groups. It'll be a long time before any HSNs make it our way. But, we still need to get going. A long time will be here sooner than we think and we need to be with others."

Little Man slaps at my neck and tries to scratch my face. He lets out a long, loud squawk. This gets my attention.

So do Mom's screams from outside

D ad and I have guns drawn and are out the RV before Mom is even at the steps.

"What is it?!" Dad asks, his eyes sweeping the camp.

Little Man is beside himself. He won't stop squawking and his hands beat at me faster and faster. I had been so wrapped up in what Dad had been telling me that I had assumed the sick feeling I had was from finding out I could become some nutjob's next meal. Instead that feeling had been a warning of what was coming. What was now here.

"Runners!" Mom screams, her face filled with terror and panic. She shoves past me and Dad and into the doorway of the RV. "Out there! Look! They're at the fence!"

Mom has already put out the fire so we both stare into the gloom of the night. I can't see a thing, but I can hear them. Dad reaches into the RV and pulls a large flashlight from the wall. He flicks it on and I nearly piss my pants.

I have never seen so many before. I thought today was crazy with six runners at once, but I'm now staring at a dozen at least. They go nuts when the light shines on them. They tear at the fence, ripping their dead flesh apart on the razor wire. Dad flicks the light about and there are more clawing their way out of the trench and even more behind them coming out of the trees. Not just runners, but shamblers and even some lurkers hanging back, their heads hiding behind trunks, but the rest of them sticking out for all to see.

"No... No, no, no, no, no..." Dad mutters. "We need more time. They shouldn't be up here already."

"What are we going to do, Thomas?" Mom screeches. Little Man answers with his own screech and I reach back and pat his head. He just tries to bite me.

"We can't leave now. I haven't had time to tear down the lab," he says. "It's too soon. I can't leave everything..."

Mom slaps him upside the back of his head. Hard. "To hell with your lab! We need a plan! They're going to get in here!"

The lab. Dad's personal sanctuary. It's where he spends most of his time when he's not in camp. The lab is a good four miles away. Dad built it into a cave, so there's only one way out and one way in. We've had to hide there before if we couldn't get back to camp and we had a runner or two on us. It's pretty secure, but there's no way we can get to it in the dark. And not with the necros knocking at the gate.

Dad turns on Mom, his face red with anger. "We have to have my research! We have to!"

"No we don't! What we have to do is get away from here! Get to Cottage Grove like you said!" Mom yells.

I wonder how long they have been talking about leaving and wonder when they were going to tell me if the runners hadn't shown up today.

"You don't understand, Helen! It's the research that they want! Without that research we are just three more mouths to feed! Plus, it's the only way they'll let Garret in..."

He trails off and Mom goes quiet. She doesn't look at Garth, but I know she realizes what Dad is saying.

"Fine," she relents. "How do you propose we save your precious lab?"

Dad switches off the flashlight and looks at us. "You two will have to pack up the camp as fast as possible and get the RV ready to go." He takes a deep breath. "I'll go out the back and around to the lab. I'll meet you back here before dawn."

"Before dawn?!" I shout. "They'll have the fence down before that!"

He turns to the fence, switches the flashlight back on, takes aim and fires into the necs. Six shots and four drop as their heads explode. "You thin their numbers. I don't know any other way."

I stare at him, but I can't figure out any alternative, and nod. "Okay. What if you don't get here by dawn? How long do we wait?"

"You don't," he says gravely. "You ram through the fence and drive. Get down the mountain. If I'm alive, I'll find you." He dashes into the RV and comes back out with the map. "See the green lines leading to I-5? That is the route you take. It isn't exactly safe, but it's better than these." He shows us the black lines. "Stay away from those roads. Those are SAT routes. See the red lines? Those lead into dead zones. Stay away from those, also."

He runs back inside and I follow. He shoves some supplies into his satchel, grabs a rifle and a box of ammo and pushes the map into my hands. "Keep this safe! Do not lose this map! It's all that will keep you from driving into danger!" He looks me in the eyes and gives me a hug. Little Man growls and Dad laughs. "You watch your brother, okay? Keep him hidden. If you come across anyone before I find you, do not let them see Garth, got it?"

I nod, but I'm too choked up to speak. I can see he understands this and he gives my cheek a pat then moves on to Mom. "I love you, Helen. If I don't come back in time just get this thing down the mountain. I'll catch up. It'll be slow going at places and you may need to winch your way out, but we've gone over this and over this. You know what to do."

Tears stream from Mom's eyes. "Don't you die out there. You hear me, Thomas Weir? Don't you die and leave us alone."

He kisses her and I turn away.

"I won't, sweetheart. I'll get the research and be back by dawn," he says, wiping at his own eyes. He turns to me as he's stepping out the door. "Take care of your mom and watch the roads! And, Garret?"

"What?"

"Trust no one. The world is a selfish, self-serving place now."

"Sounds like the same world I've read about, at least according to Ayn Rand," I laugh hollowly.

"Except this free market is run on lives, son. Never forget that. And stay away from the Griffins!"

Then he is gone into the night, leaving me with a crazy mother, an undead brother on my back, and a howling pack of necros at the gate.

I'll say it again, Happy Birthday to me...

CHAPTER THREE

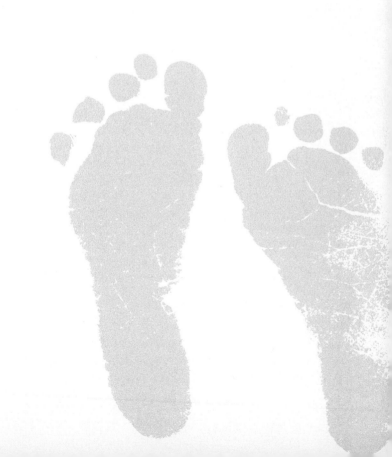

I

The night is brutal. I start killing off the necs with one of the hunting rifles, but Mom makes me stop and use my 9 since we have three times the ammo for that.

Of course, this means I have to get closer to them.

I kill thirty-eight total with Little Man howling on my back the whole time. Mom brought me ear muffs to protect my ears from the gunshots. She was wearing a pair herself, even in the RV, but I think it was more so she couldn't hear Garth.

She had helped with the shooting at the start, but her nerves were so frazzled she was only getting a kill shot every fourth bullet, so I told her to wait inside and not waste the ammo. She pretended to be mad, but I know she was grateful.

Now, I sit in the passenger's seat of the RV, staring at the five or so necs that are still out at the fence, and watch the forest get brighter and brighter as the sun rises.

"Almost dawn," I say sleepily. I roll my head about and my neck pops several times, startling Little Man. He slaps at me a couple of times, but settles back down. "How long do we wait?"

Mom sits in the driver's seat, her hands gripping the steering wheel and white knuckled. "As long as we can."

"Which is how long?"

"Don't pressure me, Garret!" she snaps.

I ignore the outburst and go back to staring at the necs.

Three are runners at the fence, one's a shambler and the last is a broken, both still on the far side of the trench. How the broken made it all the way up the mountain to us with only one arm, no legs and an exposed rib cage (now with half a tree's worth of twigs caught in it), I don't know. Maybe it lost the other arm along the way, but I can't tell because the empty shirt sleeve covers the shoulder socket. Usually you can tell if the limb has been lost, ripped off or if it was chewed off when the person died. I watch the thing inch along to the edge of the trench then tumble over, lost from sight.

The first rays of light pierce the pine and fir needles and cast that orange glow that I've known all my life. It's the only way I have ever seen the sunrise and now I'm about to leave that. About to leave everything that defines me and, honestly, I'm terrified.

I have no idea what the world is about.

We wait another twenty minutes and I can see a couple more shamblers making their way up the trail to our camp.

"I think it's time, Mom," I say and wait for the backlash. But none comes. She starts the engine, releases the brake and slowly pulls away from the outcropping.

Before prepping the RV I had to brace part of the fence with sheet metal and wood planks. Mom says Dad designed only this section of the fence so the segments don't overlap, but line up perfectly. This is our exit. As we hit the fence, the section brakes apart, slams into the next section and they both fall across the trench. Mom guns the engine and we shoot over the trench, crushing two of the runners and the shambler. I look out my side window as we zoom across and see the broken staring up at us from the bottom of the trench. Has to suck for that one to crawl as far as it did and then have breakfast speed away in a Winnebago.

Once across the trench, Mom yanks the wheel and we just miss the tree line.

"You sure you know how to get us down the mountain?" I ask. "Are the trails wide enough for the RV?"

Mom gives me a look, but doesn't answer.

"No, really, are you sure?"

"I'm sure, Garret!" she yells. "Go sit in the back if you aren't going to be helpful! There's an old logging road about a quarter mile ahead. It's overgrown, but we'll be able to get down it."

I know the road she's talking about and it doesn't exactly strike confidence in my heart.

I get up from the passenger seat, since I know my anxiety will just get her more worked up.

In the living world of the past, sixteen year olds knew how to drive, not to mention seventeen year olds. But, I don't live in the living world.

2

I guess I must have fallen asleep because the next thing I know Mom is shaking my shoulder and her face is bone white. I was so tired I didn't even notice Little Man freaking out.

"Wha...?" I start, but she puts her finger to her lips and points out the windshield.

I slowly get off the couch and peer out the glass.

Necros. Lots and lots of necros. All crossing the logging road, heading up through the woods, taking the most direct route to our camp. Most look like runners, with maybe a few shamblers in tow.

"Where did they come from?" I whisper.

"I don't know," Mom whispers back. "I came around the bend and there they were."

I watch the necs, but luckily they seem to ignore us, almost like they're being led or called and won't be distracted.

"Have you ever seen them act like that before?" I ask.

Mom shakes her head.

"So what do we do? Just wait until they pass?"

Mom nods.

We both make sure we are back in the shadows inside the RV. Necros aren't smart enough to know what an RV is, so as long as they don't see us watching them we shouldn't have a problem.

Of course, we also have to be quiet.

Little Man's protests increase in volume and I slap at him. "Garth! Hush!" I say. "They'll see us!" Little man doesn't listen. In fact, he starts to get louder and his tiny arms and legs beat at me. "Stop it!"

Before I know what's happening, Mom is on us. She has a frying pan and is swinging it at my back, at Garth.

"MOM! NO!" I shout.

I shove her away and she slams her head against one of the cupboards and falls to the floor in an unconscious heap. Little Man lets out a long, loud wail. Between my shout, the sound of Mom crashing into the cupboard and Little Man's wail there is no way to stay hidden any longer. I look out the windshield and my blood turns cold.

All of the necs have stopped and are staring at the RV.

I reach back and cover Garth's mouth with my hand. His jaw opens and closes over and over, trying to get a piece of my hand, but this isn't the first time I've had to shush him up to hide from necs.

"In the creek, Little Man," I growl. "Shut your butt up or I'm putting you in the creek."

He stops his thrashing, but doesn't quiet completely. Small grunts of annoyance repeat from behind my head, but I let it go, pretty sure I'm the only one that can hear them.

I catch myself holding my breath as I watch the necs stand in the overgrown road, just waiting there, their lifeless eyes focused on the RV. None move, not even a little twitch and I feel like hours go by before they gradually turn and continue across the road and up the mountain. Within minutes they are all gone and the road is clear.

I sigh and kneel down next to Mom. She has a large bruise on her forehead, but her breathing is steady. I lift her up and set her on the couch, covering her with one of the many knitted afghan blankets we have. I hate the afghans. My toes always get caught in them and it wakes me up at night.

Mom stirs a bit and lets out a small moan, which Little Man parrots back at her.

"You need to shut it," I snarl at him. "This is your fault."

He's silent, but gives me a quick jab.

I sit in the driver's seat and look at the dashboard. Mom and Dad have shown me what everything does many times,

I've even read manuals from some thing called the DMV, but I haven't ever driven before. Dad has made sure to keep the RV running, but it always stayed put in the camp.

I glance back at Mom then out the windshield.

How hard can it be?

3

Okay, so driving isn't as easy as it sounds in books. And all those signs in the DMV manual don't matter at all when you're escaping down a mountain road.

I've nearly run us off the mountain five times so far. I finally learn that you use one foot for the gas and the brake, not two feet at the same time with one foot on each pedal. I also learn that it takes a lot to control an RV. They are big, heavy and not made to go around corners at high speeds.

I am now creeping down the mountain at a steady ten miles an hour. That's just fine with me.

Mom is still fast asleep on the couch. I've stopped a couple times to make sure she's breathing and she seems fine. I figure she's catching up on all the sleep lost from last night.

On the other hand, Little Man is wide awake. I think he likes driving. Not that he's doing anything, but he can watch the trees go by through the driver's side window. He'll be quiet for a few minutes then start hooting and slapping at my back. I don't know what he sees, but it makes him pretty excited.

We haven't seen a single nec since that close call with the group back there. Every once in a while I can feel Little Man tense, but then he relaxes. I think moving at the speed we are helps keep him from freaking out.

The road is starting to level off a bit and I think we're getting close to the base of the mountain when Mom puts her hand on my shoulder and I scream myself silly, yank on the wheel hard and nearly send us into a ditch. I get control of the RV and slam on the brakes, causing Mom to slam into the dashboard.

"Holy hell, Garret!" Mom yells. "Are you trying to kill us?" I grip the steering wheel with all my might and stare out the windshield. "Garret? Are you alright, son?"

"I think I almost peed my pants, Mom," I gasp. "You can't sneak up on the driver like that."

She watches me for a moment and then bursts out laughing. Tears start to leak from the corners of her eyes and she is holding her stomach she's laughing at me so hard. It isn't until Little Man joins in with some small grunts that she slows down and stops.

"What's so funny?" I ask, my feelings hurt a little.

"Sorry," she says, giving me a kiss on the cheek. "I just never thought I'd hear you say something like that. 'You can't sneak up on the driver like that'. Oh, that's just too rich!" She starts up laughing again.

I frown at her and she quickly stops.

"Glad I could amuse you," I say.

"Oh, don't be like that, Garret," she pleads. "It's been so long since I've had a good laugh. Don't ruin it."

I think about this and realize I can't remember the last time she really let loose and laughed. I give her an apologetic grin. "Sorry. I guess it is kinda funny."

She hugs me, careful not to touch Garth. "I love you."

"Love you too, Mom."

She looks out the windshield. "Have you seen any more HSNs?"

"Nope. Not a one."

"Good. Look out. I'm taking over."

I let my shoulders slump and keep my hands on the wheel. "Really? I'm just getting the hang of it. I think I can keep driving for a while. I'm not tired at all."

"I'm sure you could drive to the ends of the earth. It's what teenagers do. But, we aren't doing any more driving."

"What? What do you mean?"

She points at the bend in the road just ahead. "We're going to stop there for tonight. Move. It's gonna be tricky getting us into the trees."

"Trees?"

"Just move, Garret. Listen to your mother."

I grumble a little, but get up and let her take over. She drives us only a quarter mile more or so then pulls off to the side. Without saying anything to me she turns the wheel all the way to the left and pulls forward, making us perpendicular with the road then puts the RV in reverse, starts checking the side mirrors back and forth and before I know it we are backed well off the road and surrounded by a thick cluster of young pine trees.

"What are we doing?" I ask. "We still have a good couple hours of daylight. Why don't we keep driving?"

"Because this is the first rendezvous point," she answers, turning the ignition off. "If your father is going to find us, this will be the first spot he'll look." She gets up and goes to the door. "Come on. We're pretty well hidden, but we need to add a little more camouflage."

I stare after her as she steps out of the RV. "Camouflage?"

4

I'm pretty sure Mom has fully gone insane as I watch her kick and shove old, dry branches out of the way.

"What are you doing?" I ask. "What are you looking for?"

"I'm not looking for anything. I'm just getting this crap out of the way. See that branch over there?" She points to one of the taller pines in the front of the cluster. I do see a branch sticking out at a weird angle.

"Yeah. So what?"

"Grab it and pull it over to me," she responds as if this was a normal request any mother would make.

I shake my head and walk over to the branch, grab hold ready for a struggle and give a good, hard pull. I nearly fall on my butt as the branch comes away easily. But, to my surprise, it isn't just a branch. Connected is a long net stretching from the forest floor to a good three feet above me. "Holy crap!"

"What? You think your father and I had only worked on the camp? There's secluded spots like this for the next forty miles. After that..." She lets the words fall away.

"We're on our own, right?"

She nods and helps secure the end of the net to another tree then starts grabbing up brush and branches, weaving them into the net. "Finish this, Garret. I'll work on the other sides."

I do as she asks and in about an hour and a half we have

the RV completely hidden from the road and from the rest of the forest. Anyone wants to see us they'll basically have to walk right into the side of the RV.

"Hungry?" Mom asks.

I nod yes even though I know whatever she makes won't be the most appetizing thing. I don't care, I'm famished.

She puts together a quick meal of some of the rabbit jerky, some flatbread Dad and I call "gutbusters" and a couple of apples. I wolf it all down in just a few bites.

"You're gonna give yourself gas," Mom laughs.

I let out a loud belch in response and we both laugh. At least until Little Man gives a small squeak.

We quiet up quick and freeze, both listening as hard as we can. I slowly look about us, trying to see what Garth feels. I personally don't feel anything, but he's the one with the real gift. After a couple of minutes a few crows let out some caws and we relax.

"False alarm," I say, knowing it wasn't false at all, we just didn't see what Little Man was sensing.

Mom doesn't say anything and hands me a full canteen.

"Drink up," she orders. "We have to stay hydrated. You never know what can happen when you are on the run."

"Were you and Dad on the run when you came here?" I ask.

"Sorta," she answers, but doesn't offer any details. I can tell she doesn't want me to push, so I let it drop. We'll have plenty of time to talk once we're back on the road. She can't dodge me forever, especially when we're alone in the RV.

I watch the evening light turn to twilight and start gathering up kindling for an evening fire.

"Not tonight, Garret," Mom says. "No more fires from here on out."

"What? What do you mean no more fires?"

"They're too easy to see. They'll bring anything out there right to us. This isn't the camp. We're exposed and unsafe at all times." I watch a shiver go through her. "Come inside. We're gonna lock things up for the night."

"The sun isn't even fully set yet!" I protest. "Come on!"

"Don't argue!" she growls, her voice turning cold. "One thing you aren't going to do while we run is argue! When I tell you to do something you do it! Understand?"

I can see the steel in her eyes and know she isn't going to bend.

"Yeah, sure. Okay." I quickly realize that all this time I figured things would be just as they were. We'd have the RV so life was going to be just as it was, only in a different scene each day. I was an idiot to think this. The RV may be home, but my life as before is over. Forever.

5

The flames of Hell have always haunted my dreams ever since I first read the Bible as a child. I've always wondered if I would be considered unclean. If I was an abomination, a demon, because of Garth. Some nights I would toss and turn, my subconscious torturing me.

Tonight I'm revisited by these horrible visions of pits of fire. I hear voices crying out for mercy and I search for them through the sulfur smoke that gets thicker and thicker. Soon I can't see anything and I'm blindly wandering around, the calls of the damned mocking me, laughing at me, screaming for me to join them.

"GARRET! WAKE UP!" Mom's voice screeches in my ear, ripping me from my nightmare and thrusting me into another one.

"What? What?!" I ask, swatting at her arms as she shakes me over and over. Little Man is crying out since Mom isn't concerned for him and every time she shakes me it slams him against the mattress. "Stop it!"

I push her away and she falls roughly to the floor. I know it's night, but strangely I can see my mother's face clearly, her features illuminated by a red-orange glow. Then I smell it.

Smoke. And where there's smoke there's...

"Fire!" I yell and leap from my loft bed. I grab up my jeans and pull on my shoes. "How close is it?"

"I don't know," Mom says. "But we have to get the fuel into the RV fast!"

I look at her, puzzled. "Fuel?"

"There are fuel cans hidden in a covered storage ditch just behind the RV. Your father put them there years ago and has checked them repeatedly. Without that fuel we aren't going to get very far!"

I'm stunned. Why didn't we put that in the RV last night? I ask her as much.

"I didn't know the forest would be on fire! I thought it would be better to wait so we didn't have to breathe fuel fumes all night long!" she says.

I understand the argument, but still...

"Where are the fuel cans?" I ask, throwing on my shirt and shoving the RV door open.

The second I feel the intense heat, and thick smoke forces its way into the RV, I know it's too late to get to the fuel cans. Mom is at my back and I shove her away from the door, slamming it closed. "We have to leave now!"

I've been in a couple wildfires and I know how fast they can move. It could already be too late.

"We don't have enough gas to make it to the next stop, Garret!" Mom screams, bordering on hysteria. "We have to have that fuel!"

Even from inside I can hear the hiss and pop of the pine trees as their pitch begins to boil and catch flame. Several small explosions, like gunshots, go off a good distance away and I know it's just a matter of time before the trees around us do the same. We are in the middle of a grove of time bombs.

"Mom! Listen! You need to get behind the wheel and drive! If we don't leave now we are going to burn to death! We have to go!"

She stares at me, her eyes wild and uncomprehending. We don't have time for her insanity. I shove her aside, rougher than I should, get in the driver's seat and start the ignition. I put the transmission in drive, hit the gas, and the RV rockets through the camouflage net and out onto the road. We thrash about quite a bit and Little Man protests loudly, as does Mom. "Shut it!" I scream at both as I struggle to control the vehicle. I almost put us in a ditch, but manage to get us going straight.

The image in the side mirror of the forest behind us is one straight out of my nightmares. Flames reach into the night sky, the trees burning and exploding from the heat. I put my foot down to the floor and coax as much speed as I can from the RV. If we don't get moving faster the wildfire will catch up to us and I really, really don't want to end up a crispy critter.

Mom sits down in the passenger seat, her eyes glued to her side mirror. "Faster, Garret!" she cries.

"I'm going as fast as I can!" I scream. Doesn't she know how terrified I am? I haven't ever driven until today and now I'm racing to save our lives! This is insane!

The pine tree explosions are getting louder, which means they are getting closer. I look in the mirror and see that the flames are only about twenty yards behind us! The road and the sky are now engulfed, like a tunnel of burning death coming at us. There's a massive explosion and I watch a fire-ball reach high into the night sky. I guess that was fuel.

"Garret! WATCH OUT!" Mom screams.

I pull my eyes from the mirror and see we are about to hit one of the last major bends in the road. "Oh, CRAP!" I turn the wheel hard and the RV rocks. I actually think it is up on two wheels for a moment as we go around the curve. I get the vehicle under control, but now we are perpendicular with the mountain as we race down the road.

The fire is no longer behind us, but right next to us. I try not to throw up from the adrenaline pumping through my veins.

I can see the flames racing through the trees, coming straight for us and the next thing I know, Mom's foot is on mine, trying to press the accelerator down even further.

"Get off me!" I shout and shove her away. She lands back in the passenger seat and I know she's not in her head any-more. Her eyes bug from her skull and her mouth just keeps opening and closing, opening and closing, like a trout that's just been caught. She's focused on the fire that is coming to consume us and I doubt she even sees me anymore.

Little Man begins to screech and screech. Mom joins him, her eyes now closed and her hands planted firmly on her ears. Garth's fists beat at me, his heels digging into my back.

"I don't have to time to look for necs, Little Man!" I shout. "Stop hitting me!"

His warnings get louder and louder and I finally look out my window. Silhouetted against the flames are the shapes of dozens of different forest animals. Deer, bear, coyote and probably many more too low to the ground to see. They're all trying to stay ahead of the fire, to try to get to safety. But what makes my breath catch is what's behind them.

The silhouettes of necros. Runners.

There must be a hundred of them.

A stag and two does break from the tree line directly in front of the RV and I swerve to miss them. More animals cross the road and I miss a couple, but several squirrels and possibly a raccoon or two end up crushed under the RV's tires. I can see another turn ahead, this one away from the fire, and I pray we can make it.

BAM!

The RV shudders and I look in the mirror to see a deer crumpled on the road having just slammed right into the side of the RV.

BAM! BAM! BAM!

More animals fall and I struggle to keep the RV from going off the road. Little Man's screeches are near deafening and I find myself yelling for him to stop. Mom's screams are mixed with ours and I'm pretty sure we will all be deaf when this is all over. If we live.

BAMBAMBAMBAMBAMBAM!

I don't even bother looking into the mirror anymore. At least, until I hear the sounds on top of the RV. Hands scratch and claw at the roof. I risk a glance and actually do pee myself a bit. Some of the runners have made it out of the trees and have leapt onto the RV! I see three of them gripping onto the grooves and nooks of the RV's siding. They scramble up on top and are replaced by more instantly. There must be at least fifteen right on top of us!

"MOM! Get the guns!" I shout, hoping she'll snap out of it. She doesn't. "Crap..."

I hit the curve and yank the wheel to the side, the tires of the RV skidding, and several shapes fall from the roof and hit the dirt road. Even though I can still hear more up there, I breathe a little easier with the fire behind me. Although it's not very far behind.

I straighten the wheel once again and press the gas as hard as I can, willing my foot through the floor. A couple more runners fall as I accelerate and they are quickly consumed by the flames as we speed away.

Seconds feel like minutes and minutes feel like hours as I finally drive us out of the dense forest and into open scrub brush. Cinders from the fire drift on the thermal winds that the heat has created and they look like demonic snowflakes as they float past the windows.

I can still hear the necs on the roof and the moment I feel we are safely away from the flames I slam on the brakes.

"HOLD ON!" I shout, but Mom has had her hands firmly planted on the dash of the RV for miles and she doesn't even notice the jolt. Eight necs tumble from the top and fall in front of the RV. I don't even hesitate as I gun the engine and smash right into them, crushing their undead bodies.

For the next few miles, all I do is listen for the sound of necs scrambling on the roof, hitting the brakes and crushing those that fall off. But after an hour of driving I finally feel it's safe and slow the RV to the side of the road.

"Mom?" I ask. She doesn't move. "Mom? I'm taking the shotgun and going outside. Okay?" Nothing.

Little Man gives a squeak and I figure there's at least one still on top, so I grab the shotgun, load a few rounds into the chamber, and slowly open the door. I let the door swing wide on its own and wait. Miles away the pops and roar of the raging wildfire can still be heard, but I hear nothing directly outside the RV. I take a deep breath and step outside.

S pinning about, I aim the shotgun at the top of the RV, see nothing, then spin around again to check my surroundings. Nothing. I close the door quickly to keep anything from getting in.

Little Man squeaks, but it's a weak one. "Whatcha feel?" I ask. He doesn't answer.

Slowly, I walk the length of the RV, take a deep breath and turn around the side, expecting to see a runner on the back ladder. Again, nothing.

"What the hell?" I mutter and then I hear it. A faint scratching and moaning. Its coming from underneath the RV. I take a couple of steps back and kneel down, the shotgun ready to blast anything that jumps out at me. What I see isn't jumping anywhere.

Trapped by one of the axles and smashed up against the undercarriage of the RV is a nec, once a runner and now a broken. It bares its teeth at me and hisses, its eyes hungry for flesh. No legs and only one arm, the thing still fights, clawing at the steel axle, trying to free itself. I get back up and walk around the vehicle, crouching every few feet to get a better view of all angles. Once I'm satisfied I won't hit anything vital to the RV, I pick my angle, brace the shotgun and fire, blasting the thing's head right off. The dirt under the RV is sprayed with brain and bone and the headless corpse just hangs there, its broken body still wedged into the axle.

"Great," I mutter and go to get a pick or shovel to try to work the body out. I just get the RV door open when my spiked baseball bat swings through the air. I'm barely able to duck my head out of the way, but one of the spikes catches Little Man across the skull. He howls in pain and starts slapping at his head then at me.

"What the hell, MOM!" I yell as she raises the bat to swing again. I rush her, slamming my shoulder into her gut, and knock her on her butt. The bat falls from her hands and I pick it up before she can grab it again. "You almost killed me!"

I see nothing but fear in her eyes. There isn't even recognition anymore and she scoots away from me.

"Mom? It's me, Garret. Your son, remember?"

She whimpers and tucks her legs up to her chin. I go to her and she swats at me, her nails raking deep gouges in my arms. "Hey!" I shout and grab her by the shoulders, giving her a good couple shakes. "Stop! It's me!"

She closes her eyes and shakes her head back and forth over and over and over. There's no way I can leave her alone in the RV while I try to get rid of the nec corpse, but if I don't pull the thing off then they'll find us when we stop.

I make a hard choice, grab a length of rope and tie my own mother's hands together then strap her to the table.

"Sorry, Mom, but it's for your own safety." More for mine really. I find a shovel and get back outside.

Glancing at the wildfire I can see necs far down the road. They are moving quickly, but I think I have time to get the body free before they are too close.

It takes me a few tries, but I'm finally able to work the corpse loose and I toss my gear onto the floor of the RV, take the driver's seat for the third time in less than twenty-four hours and get us the heck out of there.

I'm becoming quite the driver. Eat that old world teenagers!

We get a few more miles and I look over my shoulder at Mom. Her eyes are wide open, but I know she doesn't see the outside world. She hasn't been this bad in a long time, but in the past it would sometimes be hours, or days, before she would snap back to reality. Great. Just what I need.

I turn back to look at the road and realize that Little Man didn't move or make a peep when I was looking back at Mom. Usually if I turn my head he tries to grab my face or starts squawking about something. This time there's nothing.

"Hey, Little Man? You doing okay back there?"

The RV is quiet. I reach back to pat his head, expecting him to try to chomp on my finger, but instead I feel his wet skull. That's not good.

I slow the RV and stop in the middle of the open road.

"Little Man?" Still no answer.

I get up and go to the tiny bathroom and grab a hand mirror. Turning so I can see in the bathroom's mirror I reach back and lift Little Man's head. There's a long gouge running from his right eye, across his temple and around to the nape of his neck. Garth is pretty tough, but Mom really got him this time.

This isn't the first run in Little Man has had with Crazy Mom. And each and every time there's only one solution to help him heal up quickly.

I pull my knife from my belt, grab a hand towel and slice my forearm and let the towel soak up all the blood. I grab a second hand towel and wrap it around my bleeding forearm then cut the bloody one into strips. I carefully reach around and lift his small head up, pull his lips apart and place the blood soaked strip of towel in his mouth.

"Come on, Little Man. Eat your bloody towel."

I wait for an eternity, but slowly I see his jaw start to move and within a few minutes he's making disgusting sucking noises. He starts to choke on the towel and his eyes snap open. He spits the towel out and growls. I have to laugh.

"You're welcome," I say as I get back in the driver's seat. We keep driving and I feed him a new strip of towel every few miles.

The bloody strips run out right about the same time the gas does. I let the RV coast to the side of the road and pull the hand brake.

Little Man grunts and growls, wanting more blood soaked towel.

"I'm all out. Sorry."

I look back at Mom and her eyes are closed, her chest

rising and falling rhythmically as she sleeps.

I really hope she wakes up semi-sane, because I have no idea what to do about the RV.

On the bright side, Little Man is back to his normal grouchy, undead self.

CHAPTER FOUR

I

"AAAAAAAAAAAAAAAHHHHHHHHH!"

I bolt awake and realize I fell asleep in the driver's seat. Hurrying to my feet I slam my head on the roof and quickly fall to my knees.

"GARRET!" Mom screams. "Why am I tied up?! GARRET!"

"I'm right here, Mom!" I shout, rubbing at my head. Little Man begins to scream too, but I slap him and he quiets down.

"Why am I tied up?" Mom asks again, straining against the rope.

"Because you tried to kill me and Garth!" I shout at her. "If you promise not to attack your children I'll cut you loose!"

She glares at me for a moment then starts to cry. "Did I really try to kill you?"

"Yes," I say, rubbing at my eyes. The sun has risen and the light is near blinding. "You caught Little Man pretty good, but I got him fixed up." Mom turns away and won't look me in the eye, so I wait until she stops blubbering before I pull out my knife. "Promise not to go crazy on us?"

She nods and adjusts her hands so I can cut her loose. The rope falls away and she rubs at her wrists, trying to get the circulation back to normal. I help her to the couch and she looks about the RV in surprise.

"You got us out of the fire?" she asks.

I nod.

"Wow, Garret. That's just...wow..."

"Thanks, Mom," I say, but then frown. "Only problem is we're out of gas."

"Get the map. Let's see where we are," she says, getting to her feet and fetching some water. She takes a long drink as I spread the map out on the table.

"I think we're here," I say pointing to a specific spot at the base of the mountain.

"How do you know?" she asks.

"The mileage would be right and there's supposed to be a town about fifteen miles ahead. We didn't pass anything, so I figure we're still back here."

She lets out a sigh of relief. "We haven't passed the last supply cache. There's an old barn right here." She points at the map. "It looks like it's collapsed, but your father was able to fix it right so we could hide fuel and other essentials under it. It will take some clearing of the debris, but we'll have enough fuel to get us almost all the way to Cottage Grove. There should be some rations, water, and a cow catcher also."

"Uh, a what? Cow catcher? You mean like on trains?"

"Yes, well, sorta. It's more like a wedge made of steel and iron. It bolts to the front of the RV and even has its own wheels for stability." Mom can see I'm not following at all. "Once we start getting to the areas of population the roads are going to get clogged with cars. I'm sure they've been cleared by, well, others. But a vehicle this size is going to have some problems. The wedge will help shove other cars and trucks out of the way."

"Wow, that's good thinking," I say, actually impressed my parents thought of this.

Mom frowns and looks disappointed. "We've had almost two decades to plan, Garret. We knew this time would come and we've been prepared for it."

"Except that we don't have Dad," I say and then it hits me. The wildfire. What if Dad was caught in that? What if he didn't get out?

I can see from Mom's face that she is thinking the exact same thing, but neither of us say anything out loud. "The barn will be the final place your father will think to meet us.

He knows we have to stop there." She goes to the bedroom and I can hear her rummaging around. I listen to Little Man grunt away while we wait and soon Mom comes out dressed in jeans and a t-shirt, a backpack in her hand.

"Here, take this," she says handing me the backpack.

"Um, I prefer my satchel," I say.

"It's not for you," she scowls, shoving the pack into my hands. I quickly realize what the pack really is.

"Oh," I say quietly as I fit it over my back and force Little Man to get situated. Mom had slit the middle so Little Man could be hidden and had even added padding to the front so that his wiggling would be hard to notice if anyone sees us. He protests for a bit, but quiets down fairly soon to my surprise.

"Load your satchel with water and food," Mom says as she does the same. She opens the weapons cabinet and pulls out a 9mm and three magazines. I strap on all my weapons and she nods when I'm finished. "Grab the shotgun and extra shells."

"I'm better with my 9," I say. "Easier to get a head shot."

"I'm not worried about the HSNs," she answers. "I'm worried about the people." She tosses me one of Dad's large brimmed hats and grabs one for herself. "It's gonna get hot."

We step from the RV into the mid-morning sun and start down the road.

2

It takes me a couple miles, but I finally realize I have never walked on flat ground. Our camp was level, but always had a slight tilt to it. This road is the first long stretch of open, flat ground I have ever set foot on.

It makes me very nervous and I constantly look over my shoulder.

"What's wrong?" Mom asks, sensing my anxiety. "You feel something."

"No," I hesitate. "It's just I feel a little exposed down here."

"Down here?" She looks confused at my statement then laughs. "Down the mountain! You can't put your back up against anything, right? It's freaking you out a little." I nod, glad I don't have to explain myself. "I understand. It's one of the many reasons we headed for the mountains when everything ended."

I can see her mind going towards darker thoughts and I quickly change the subject. "You think Dad will be at the barn?" Okay, maybe not the lightest subject, but better than where she was going.

"I hope so," she responds. "We really need that research."

"Um, and we need Dad, too," I add. She smiles weakly, but doesn't answer. "How much further is it?"

Mom pulls the map from her back pocket and partially unfolds it. She stops and looks around, checking some of the landmark notes Dad had made in the margins over the years. She points ahead and to the left. "Should be right over this hill. Only a hundred yards or so." I sigh with relief and Mom laughs. "All this flat land tiring you out?"

"It's the pavement," I answer, embarrassed. "My feet are used to dirt and mud. This road is killing me!"

We both laugh a bit, but are quiet the rest of the way until we see the barn. We get off the road and crouch down low. Mom pulls out a pair of binoculars, surveys the area and then hands them to me. "See how the back part of the barn has crumbled and looks all flattened out?"

I focus the binoculars until I see what she's describing. "Yes."

"That's where everything is stored. All we need to do is move the debris and there's a hidden trap door. All the supplies are under there."

"What about the wedge?"

"It's in pieces in the debris. Looks like junk, but we can put it together quickly and wheel it back to the RV. Your dad may not be stable, but he's not stupid."

"I don't think you should be questioning anyone's stability," I say without thinking.

She yanks the binoculars away from me and puts them back in her pack. "That may be true, but you should certainly be questioning *everyone's* stability. Including your father's. It'll keep you alive longer."

She lets the words linger there between us then gets up and moves towards the barn, keeping low and hidden in the scrub brush and grass. For the first time in my life I realize my parents can't keep me alive. I've always known that the world was dangerous and I'd have to fight to survive, but it wasn't until now that I truly understood that from here on out it's up to me to keep my butt from being food. Whether that's food for the necs or for the SATs, I don't know.

3

Mom moves us to the tree line just behind the barn and we wait forever, listening and watching.

The sun is high in the sky now and the heat is intense. Little Man starts to complain and I don't blame him. "You think we can get closer now?" Mom doesn't answer, just watches the barn. "Mom?"

"Shhhhhh," she scolds. "Just be patient."

I try, I really do, but the heat and the anxiety get the best of me and I start to fidget, grabbing up clumps of grass and tossing them to the side.

"Garret. Stop that," she growls and I realize how much she and Little Man sound alike when they make that sound. Of course, I would never, ever mention that to her, but it does make me chuckle. Mom gives me an inquiring look then finally nods. "Okay, let's see what we're in for."

I have to say I like the Mission Mom way better than Crazy Mom or Catatonic Mom. Mission Mom has it together.

We stay low and cross the twenty yards to the barn. Mom shoves me down behind the debris and swivels her head about, looking for possible attackers. Once she's satisfied she puts her finger to her lips. "Try not to make much noise. Sounds will carry and if anyone is close they'll come investigate."

We start carefully pulling away old, dried out beams and siding. After the third or fourth splinter, I pull on my gloves and Mom does the same. It takes us about thirty minutes of hard, dusty work, but we get the junk cleared off the trapdoor. That's when I see Mission Mom start to crumble.

The trapdoor is padlocked tight and the screws to the metal clasp have been drilled out so no one can take it apart.

"Crap," Mom curses and I'm pretty sure she's about to start crying. "I don't have the key. It's probably back in the RV, but knowing your father it's more than likely in his pocket. Damn him!"

"Chill, Mom," I smile and pull out the multi-tool from my satchel. I flick open the small saw blade, wedge it between the planks the lock is bolted to and start cutting. We both take turns and it's another hour before we're done, but finally the wood falls away and Mom yanks the trapdoor open.

I smell the fuel right away and Mom grimaces. "I hope the fumes haven't ruined the water or rations," she says as she steps onto the ladder that leads below. "Wait up here until I check it out."

"What?" I protest, but her look quiets me down. "You want to take the shotgun at least?"

She grabs my machete and feels the weight. "Probably not a good idea to fire a shotgun with all the fumes."

If her point is to make me feel stupid then she has succeeded. I frown and watch her descend into the darkness. She turns on her hand-crank flashlight and disappears out of sight.

All I can do is stand there and wait. I keep the shotgun firmly planted on my hip and carefully watch the area. The barn is situated in one of the few open, grassy areas in southern Oregon, having been cleared away by early settlers a couple hundred years ago. At least, that's what I'm guessing from what I've read about the area. Probably used for cattle way back when.

Every once in a while Little Man gives a squeak and I get more and more nervous as time ticks by. "Mom?" I wait, but hear nothing. "Mom? You still down there?"

Her lack of response is really starting to freak me out, but when Little Man's warnings get stronger I have to struggle to keep myself calm. I hunker down close to the debris pile and watch the tree line. There's a slight breeze and the pine trees sway back and forth, making it hard to spot any suspicious movement.

"Hush," I warn Garth and he quiets down a little, which is good since that usually means whatever he senses is moving on.

"Garret!"

It takes all my self control not to cry out loud. "What?!" I snap.

"What's your problem? Everything okay up there?" Mom asks from the bottom of the ladder.

"Yeah, it's fine. Just a little creepy, is all."

"Creepy in the middle of the day?" Mom laughs. "You sure you're okay?"

"I'm fine," I insist a little too urgently.

"Then get your butt down here. We're going to move everything to the ladder, take some fuel back to the RV and then come back for the rest. I want to get this done before sundown, so get a move on!"

I sling the shotgun over my shoulder and climb into the dark.

4

"How did all of this get down here?" I ask, stunned at the amount of supplies. "Did you and Dad bring this with you when you ran?"

"Hardly," Mom answers. "Most of it has been scavenged over the years. Anything your Dad would find useful he'd stash in one of the caches."

"How many more are there like this?"

"I don't know," she frowns. "All the caches I know about are back in the fire. I'm sure they've all burned up, even the underground ones like this. The heat alone would have ruined everything."

"Bummer."

"Yeah, bummer. Now, start lifting."

I make an exaggerated groan, but get right to work, eager to get done with it all and on the road as soon as possible. The last glance at the map showed the SAT areas to be a lot closer than I'm comfortable with. From the way Mom is hustling, I'm sure she feels the same.

It takes us a good hour before we have all salvageable supplies piled up at the bottom of the ladder. We probably would have had more supplies and gotten done faster, but Mom was right, some of the rations and water jugs smell of fuel fumes and we have to take breaks above to keep from passing out.

Mom threads a rope through the handles of three fuel

cans and hands it to me. "Climb up and start pulling. I'll push from down here."

"Sounds like I get the hard job," I complain, fatigue starting to set in.

"Yes, you do," she agrees. "But that's what seventeen year old boys are for. Manual labor."

I grumble a bit, but hustle up the ladder, set my feet on each side of the opening and start to pull. It's a lot of weight, but with Mom's help below we get the cans up onto the ground in a few minutes. Once secure, we fall to the ground panting. I reach back and pat Little Man and he just grunts, so I guess he's okay.

After a few minutes, Mom stands and tosses me the canteen. "Drink up. Time to go."

"Just a few more minutes," I plead.

"I wish we could, Garret, but we still have to walk it back to the RV and then get back here and load up."

I begin to protest once more, but Little Man's high-pitched screech stops me and I'm up on my feet in a flash. I reach over and grab the shotgun, bringing it to my shoulder and begin sweeping the area. Mom has her 9mm out and is checking behind us.

"I don't see anything," I state.

"Me neither," she responds, but Little Man doesn't let up.

"He's never wrong, Mom." She doesn't respond to this since I mention Garth directly. "There's something out there." I slowly stand up and that's when I see it. The grass by the tree line is waving back and forth, but the breeze had stopped a while ago. I nudge Mom and she turns. "In the grass," I whisper, ready to fire.

Mom reaches out and puts her hand on the barrel of the shotgun, pushing it towards the ground. "If it was runners they'd already be on us. I'm guessing it's broken. Probably quite a few." She reaches down and picks up one of the fuel cans. "Give me the shotgun." Reluctantly I hand it over and start to pull out my 9, but she shakes her head. "Grab the other two cans. We're leaving right now."

"We aren't going to kill them?" I ask, stunned.

"Why? And bring more toward the sound? No, let's just go."

"But Dad always said to kill 'em if you see 'em. The less necs in the world the better!"

"First, your father would never say necs." I begin to argue and she narrows her eyes. "Second, I'm not an idiot. You dad has never liked pointless killing. Last, killing a few broken won't do any good in the grand scheme of things. There's millions more out there. What it will do is slow us down and give time for other HSNs to get to our position. More time here also means more time for a SAT hunting party to find us. Do you want either of those things to happen?" I refuse to answer and Mom grins. "That's what I thought. Get moving."

We back away slowly from the barn and then pick up speed when we hit pavement. Little Man's warnings get less and less as we get further away and I breathe a breath of relief that all we had to deal with was the broken. Even though we didn't really deal with them. I've always thought of Mom as the weak parent, but today showed me that maybe Dad is the one that doesn't have the guts.

5

I'm so busy lost in thought that it takes me a while to notice the buzzing that is steadily getting louder. I stop and cock my head. "What is that?"

Mom must be just as lost in thought since she doesn't stop, just keeps walking.

"Mom!" I say loud enough to get her attention.

"What, Garret?" she asks, obviously annoyed and expecting another complaint from me. I raise my eyebrows and look at her expectantly and then she notices the sound.

"What is that?" I ask again. "It sounds like a lot of really angry bees."

"Get off the road now!" she says urgently. "Into the trees!"

I don't question and we both sprint deep into the shade of the trees. Mom sets the fuel can down and motions for me to do the same. She puts the shotgun to her shoulder and I pull my 9. The noise gets louder with each second and we watch the road, ready for what is coming.

"What...?" I start, but Mom shushes me.

Little Man starts to thrash about as the sound gets louder and I smack the backpack to quiet him down, but he just thrashes harder.

"Keep him quiet!" Mom warns. It's one of the few times she's directly referred to Garth which makes my blood run cold. Things must be really bad.

The sound seems to be right on us, but neither of us see

anything on the road. That's when Mom whirls about behind us and stares deeper into the trees. "It's not a road bike!" she cries, grabbing me and pulling me to my feet. "They've been circling us! Run!" She gives me a good shove and I start to object, but the noise drowns out any words I say as I see a motorcycle scream from out of a dip in the woods and shoot right at us.

A motorcycle. A dirt bike, to be precise. I've seen pictures, but of course have never heard one, so I didn't know what the sound was.

And on that dirt bike is a man. Or what could be considered a man. His head is shaved and he has a long, tangled beard that stretches down to his chest. He's shirtless, but his arms and chest are covered in pictures. Tattoos. He's wearing dark goggles and the moment he sees us his face splits into a near toothless grin.

I see his mouth start moving, like he's talking, but I don't know who could hear him over the noise his bike makes, but as he gets closer I see a thin black wire coming from his goggles and down to his mouth. He's got a two way radio and he's calling the others.

The realization we have been found by the SATs hits me and I take off through the forest as Mom lets loose with the shotgun. I hear the man cry out and the sound of the motorcycle changes. I glance back and see the bike tumble to the ground, sputter and die, the man a few feet behind it, his chest a bloody, shredded mess.

I've seen hundreds of necs get blasted and it never really bothered me a whole lot, but seeing a man splayed open is completely different. I start to gag and Mom whirls on me.

"I told you to run! Get to the RV! NOW!"

"But....?"

"Don't argue, Garret! Get the fuel cans to the RV! Get going! I'll be there soon!" As she says this she grabs the bike and pulls it upright. She mounts it like it's the most natural thing to do and points at me as she kick starts it. "GO!" Then she speeds off into the forest. Only then do I notice there's the sound of more than one engine echoing through the woods.

My crazy mother, the woman that has been a nervous wreck most of my life and would go into catatonic shock any time more than one nec would get close to the camp, that woman just hopped on a dirt bike and is now speeding *towards* danger to draw it away from me.

If we live through this all, I'll really have some serious questions for my parents.

I don't know what's the hardest part of running for your life: carrying two heavy fuel cans that are constantly banging against your legs or having an undead brother joined to your back, stuck in a backpack and getting more and more pissed off over this fact.

"Stop hitting me!" I hiss at him. "Stop!"

His little fingers dig into my shoulder and I can feel his nails scrape furrows into my skin. He rarely gets violent like this, but today is a rare day.

"Ow! Dammit, Garth!" I stop, drop the cans and unzip the pack. I grab him by the neck and squeeze. He makes little choking noises, but I know it's an act he's learned over the years. "Dad isn't here to stop me! Your faking won't work!"

I'm about to really start in on him when I hear the crack of a gunshot and the sound of a bullet whizzing past my head. I throw myself to the ground and scurry towards a thick fir tree for cover.

Another gunshot and another and bark sprays from the trunk as two bullets slam into the tree.

"Cain't hide forever, boy!" I hear a man yell. "I see where you are! Come on out and we'll have a nice talk!"

I check my 9 and peer around the tree. I can't see anyone out there and I just hope there's only one. I wait for a minute and try to build my courage. I finally take a deep breath and prepare to make a break for it. I take one more peek around the tree, but all I see is the cold steel of a pistol muzzle.

"Get up, boy," the man says, shoving the gun against my eye. "I really ain't in the mood to hike your corpse all the way back, so hows about you be a good sport and start walking?"

The man is way older than Dad, probably by a good twenty years or so, but it's hard for me to say since I've only seen pictures of other people, none up close. He's in better shape than the rider Mom killed (or I presume she killed since I doubt he'll live with his chest blown apart). He has close cropped white hair and a nasty scar running from the middle of his forehead, down across his nose, his left cheek and all the way down his neck. It could be longer, but the rest is hidden by his ratty t-shirt. He's not very tall and is actually looking up at me with a grin on his face. That's the worst part. The grin. Not because of the obvious evil intent he has in store, but because his grin shows his teeth.

Every single tooth is filed to a sharp point.

"Whatcha got there?" he asks, looking around me at the backpack. "You got some kinda pet in there? Is it cat? I haven't had cat in years and always liked 'em."

I stay silent, my one eye that doesn't have a gun stuck in it fixated on the man's teeth. I can't imagine why anyone would do that to their teeth. What purpose would it...? Oh, right...

"You dumb or somethin'?" he asks, jabbing me with the gun. "Hows about you take that pack off?"

Crap. I can't let him see Little Man. He'll kill us both.

"No," I say quietly. The man gets a puzzled look on his face.

"Um, what? Did you just say 'no' to me?"

"No. I'm not giving you the pack."

He laughs and reaches for it, but I slap his hand away. Rage crosses his face and he pulls back the gun then slams the butt across my forehead. I crumple to the ground, my head reeling and spots flash before my eyes. I shake my head to clear the spots, but it just makes things worse. Before I can push myself up he hits me again on the back of the head and it's all I can do to keep from passing out.

"You're a tough one," he snarls. "We may not gut you right away. Maybe put you in the arena and see how long you last."

I can feel him tugging at the pack, but my head hurts so

bad I can't do anything to stop him. Instead I slowly reach for my knife and hope he's too distracted to notice. When he let's out a gasp I know I'm right about the distraction.

"What the holy hell?" he cries out. "What is that thing? Is that a slick?"

I have the knife out and I'm blindly slashing before he knows it. The next sound out of his mouth is a scream of pain as the blade slices into his leg. His gun goes off as he falls to the ground and I can feel the heat of the bullet across my temple.

"You little son of a bitch! You ain't gonna have no chance to fight now!" he screams at me.

But it's too late for him. I blindly stab again and again and again. His gun goes off twice more then is silent. By the time my head clears, and my arm's too tired to move anymore, the man is dead. I struggle to my feet and sway for a moment until my eyes focus. I look down and see I've stabbed him well over thirty times. The way he fell put his torso right within reach and his chest, neck and face are mangled from all the knife wounds. I spin about and throw up, splattering my shoes with vomit.

I can't believe I did that. I keep my eyes averted, grab my 9, and stumble to the fuel cans. I lift them up and turn towards the RV, but my head hurts so much I really don't know if I'm going in the right direction or not. It's all I can do to put one foot in front of the other.

7

My head is killing me. I take off my shirt, which is an ordeal in of itself since I have to take off the backpack and wiggle the shirt around Little Man, all while he keeps screeching and smacking me right where the man had hit me. I finally get the shirt off and have it wrapped around my forehead to cover that wound and to stop the bleeding from my temple where the bullet grazed me.

The worst part is I can't stop the bleeding from where the man clubbed me in the *back* of the head. Little Man is loving it, though. He thinks it's meal time and he's happily licking the wound. Which, in a way, probably does slow the bleeding, but there is no way to know. The only thing I really know is my head is killing me.

I stumble through the forest and struggle with the fuel cans. I'd leave one and come back for it once I get the RV gassed up, but I doubt I'll be able to find my way back to the can and I decide to just suffer through. All I can hear, other than the ringing in my head, is Dad's voice saying, "Why do something twice when you can do it right the first time."

So I push on. I vomit a couple of times along the way and have to wonder if I don't have a concussion. All the symptoms fit. That means when I finally do get to rest I'll probably die in my sleep. Then Garth will finally get the necro brother he's always wanted.

I hear a twig snap and I stop. Little Man doesn't say

anything, so I don't think it's a nec, but then he's too busy at the Garret buffet to be of any help. I hear another snap and I set the cans down, pull my 9 out, and thumb back the hammer. My vision swims and I see two trees for every one that should be there, so I doubt I'll be able to hit anything if it does come at me. Well, I've got 15 rounds in the magazine and one in the chamber, so I'm bound to hit something if I start pulling the trigger.

A few minutes go by and I don't hear anything else. I have to wonder if I ever heard something to begin with or if it was just my messed up head playing tricks on me.

"Did you hear anything?" I ask Little Man, but he doesn't even bother to respond with a grunt, just keeps licking. I swat at him weakly, re-holster my pistol and pick the cans up again. They feel like they've doubled in weight since I set them down.

I can't say how long I wander through the forest, but finally I see the pavement ahead. I struggle through a drainage ditch and up the embankment to the road, never so glad to see steaming hot asphalt in my life. I turn to my left and see nothing and slowly turn to my right. There! Maybe a quarter mile down the road is the RV!

I'm saved!

I can get there, I can do this.

I will myself to take each step, putting one foot in front of the other. After a few yards I have to put one of the cans down. It's just too heavy. I'll come get it, now that I know exactly where I am. I hug the second can to my chest, letting my body take on some of the weight, not just my arm. This throws me off balance for a moment and I stumble and sway like I'm drunk. I've never been drunk, but I've read that this is what it's like.

The RV is only twenty yards away.

"Almost there, Little Man. Almost there."

Nausea washes over me and I have to stop while I heave. I have nothing left in my stomach, having not eaten since back at the barn when Mom and I took a short break, so all I spit up is saliva and bile. I've run out of water, so I mourn the lost saliva, wishing I could get it back, just to keep my mouth wet.

I shuffle along, the pain from my head almost too much to handle.

Ten yards away. So close.

Five yards away.

"We're gonna make it, Little Man," I gasp.

Two yards.

One Yard.

I'm at the door.

I'm at the door!

And the door is opening.

The door is opening?

"What? Who?" I mumble as I step back.

The last thing I see is someone reaching for me as I fall backwards.

I can hear Little Man growl and cry out.

Now...it's...all...gone...

CHAPTER FIVE

I

"**W**hat is it?"
"I don't know... It looks like a mini-slick."
"I don't like how its eyes follow us."
"Yeah, it's freaking me out."
"Should we kill it? Maybe it attacked him."
"It looks like it's hooked to him. Might kill the kid if we try."
"Kid? He's your age, K! He can't be more than eighteen!"
"I'm nineteen, dumbass."

"I'm...seventeen..." I croak, tired of the whispered conversation. As I open my eyes I can already tell from the smell I'm in the RV. And we are moving. "Who are you people?" Wait... Did I just ask that? People..?

I push myself up from the couch and Little Man gives his usual growl of protest. The girl and the boy staring at me jump and both shove their rifles in my face.

"He's not going to hurt you," I try to assure them, but my head hurts so much that my voice is weak and shaky, hardly convincing. "Can you hand me some aspirin? It's in the bathroom cupboard."

The girl and boy give each other a puzzled look, but don't move. I try to get up from the couch, but the boy shoves me back down and the girl rams the barrel of her rifle into my chest.

"Ow! What the hell?" I cry. "I just want some aspirin for my head. You know? Aspirin?" I pantomime taking a couple of pills and washing them down with water. Water! I'm so thirsty! I point to the water jug on the table. "Can I at least get a sip of water?"

They don't move. Apparently people suck.

"Let him have some water," a man's voice orders from the driver's seat. "He can't hurt us by drinking water."

"Hurt you? What are you talking about? This is my RV and you're the ones with guns!" It hits me that if we are moving then we are driving away from Mom! "Crap! My mom! We have to stop! She's back there!"

I get up fast and before the boy can stop me, I have his rifle in my hands and the barrel pressed against his forehead. The girl screams and jumps back out of reach, her own rifle aimed at my head.

"Knock it off! All of you!" the man yells and I can feel the RV slow. "Put the rifle down, kid, and I'll explain everything!"

The RV comes to a stop and the man gets out of the driver's seat and walks back to me. I don't move the rifle or take my eyes off the boy. I can see him starting to shake with fear and I realize he's a good couple of years younger than me. He has the first signs of stubble on his chin. Looks like it's going to be as bright red as the hair on his head. His blue eyes glance from me, to the man, to the rifle and back, over and over.

"Just take it easy, son," the man says.

"I'm not your son," I growl. Little Man growls with me and the man scowls.

"Okay, you're not my son, but you are someone's son. And since that thing is joined to your back, I'm guessing it's someone's son also. Want to help us out here and tell us who you are and where your parents are at?"

"No."

He stands there for a minute. "Um... No?"

"Right. No. This is my RV, my home and you've stolen it and me. You tell me who you are first." I give the rifle a little nudge and the boy whimpers. "I'm new to this whole socializing thing, so excuse me if my manners aren't up to par. Tell me who you are first then I'll decide if I want to tell you who I am."

The man shrugs. "Fine. You got trust issues. I get that.

I'm Lester Rollins. The boy you are terrifying is my nephew, Joseph. That's his sister, Karen. We're just survivors like you, trying to get by. We found the RV abandoned on the road. We had just started to scope it out when you came stumbling along."

"You're not with the SATs?" I ask.

"The sick and twisteds? No, that's not our thing." Lester gives me a hard look. "Who are you, kid? Where'd you get an outfitted RV like this?"

"My name is Garret Weir. This RV is my home. You're welcome to stay, but I'll need the girl to put the rifle down."

"Karen. Her name is Karen," Lester says.

"I don't really care until the rifle is down," I snap back. Little Man gives a couple grunts and Karen jumps. Lester immediately goes to her and takes the rifle out of her hands.

"There. Happy?"

I lower my rifle and nod. "Yeah." I fall back on the couch, but keep the rifle close. "Can you please hand me the water?"

Lester nods and Karen grabs the jug. Joseph falls to the ground in a nervous heap. He looks up at his uncle, tears in his eyes. "I think I peed myself, Uncle Les."

"That's to be expected, Jo. Don't worry; there's a creek just up the road. You can get cleaned up there."

Karen hands me the jug and I take a long drink, handing it back to her when I'm done. All three of them just stare at me. "What?"

"What do you mean, 'what'? The slick on your back! That's what," Karen says. "It's a little strange."

"Are you infected?" Joseph asks.

"Do I look infected?" I answer. They don't respond. "No, I'm not infected. And Garth doesn't have teeth, so he can't break skin and infect you."

"Garth? The thing has a name?" Karen asks. "What the hell is it?"

Lester gives her a stern look, a look my Dad has given me a thousand times, and she hushes up.

"Garth is my brother. We're conjoined twins," I respond. "I call him Little Man."

"More like Little Dead Man," Joseph laughs nervously. "How do you stand it?"

"He ain't heavy, he's my brother," I reply.

Lester laughs. "That's good, kid. Used to love that song when I was little. My mom played it over and over."

"Speaking of moms, we need to go back for mine!" I say.

"No can do, Garret," Lester frowns. "The SATs have her by now. Nothing we can do. Sorry."

2

I start to lift the rifle, but Lester is way faster. He has Karen's rifle in his hands and pointed at me before I barely flinch.

"Let's not start up again, kid," Lester says. "Hands on your lap."

"I have to go back for my mom," I glare. "This is my RV and I'm taking it back there."

"No, you aren't," Lester says. He nods to Karen and she quickly moves the rifle out of my reach. She starts to lift it to her shoulder, but Lester shakes his head. "We aren't looking to make things worse, K. Just set it up front." She does as she's asked.

"My Dad was right. It's the people I have to watch out for," I snarl. "The necs are the easy part."

"Necs?" Lester asks. "What are necs?"

"Necs. Necros," I answer. "Homo Sapien Necrosii? The HSNs?" All three look at me like I'm crazy. "I think I heard you call them slicks."

"The zombies?" Lester laughs. "What do you call them?"

"Necs."

He nods thoughtfully. "Necs... I like that. But, you're wrong, Garret. You only have to watch out for *some* people. You have to watch out for *all* the necs."

Little Man squeaks loudly and I shake my head. "Now you're wrong...Lester."

The squeaks get louder and louder and I can see the fear

build in Karen and Joseph's eyes.

"What's it doing?" Joseph asks.

"*He* is warning me that we have necros coming," I reply. "Sounds like quite a few and coming fast since I can feel them too." Once again I can tell they think I'm crazy. "Fine. Suit yourself. You'll find out soon enough."

Little Man starts to thrash. He twists about on my back, his hands smacking my shoulder.

"Make it stop," Joseph demands. "Uncle Les, make the thing stop!"

"It's not a thing!" I yell. "He's my brother and he's trying to warn us that we're about to have a whole lot of necs right on top of us!"

"Check the windows, both of you," Lester orders.

The two siblings each check out a window. Their body language tells me exactly what they see.

"They're here, aren't they?" I smirk and look at Lester. "I'm going to get up now and grab my 9. That okay?"

Lester ignores me. "What do you see?"

"Over a dozen on my side!" Karen cries.

"I've got ten over here!" Joseph whimpers. "We're dead! They're gonna get in here!"

I stand up and step towards the gun cabinet. Lester doesn't even move to stop me. "Twenty-two of them? If the last couple days have taught me anything it's that out numbered doesn't mean dead."

I pull open the cabinet, grab out a 9, pop a magazine into it and hand it to Lester. "Use this. They'll be too close for the rifle." He stares at the handgun and I grab his hand and shove it in his palm. "Trust me."

I snag my own 9, load it, and grab an extra magazine. I shove ear plugs into my ears and toss some to the others. "It's about to get very loud in here."

I push Joseph aside and slide the window open. The boy can't count, there's at least fifteen necs sprinting from the sparse pine trees right at us. I take a deep breath, ignore the pain in my head and let the breath out slowly then press the trigger.

BLAM!

Headshot. Fourteen.

BLAM!

Headshot. Thirteen.

BLAM!

Headshot. Twelve.

BLAM!

Chest shot. BLAM! Headshot. Eleven.

I glance over my shoulder and see that Lester, Joseph and Karen haven't moved. Their eyes are locked on me or Little Man.

"What the hell are you waiting for?!" I shout. This pulls Lester out of his trance and he throws the opposite window open and starts firing. Karen and Joseph struggle to get their ear plugs in as the RV is filled with the deafening barks of the 9mms.

I whittle the group down to five before they hit the RV. They pound their eroded fists against the side and Karen and Joseph jump at each impact. I have to wonder what sheltered lives they've led and why they are out here now.

Lester stops firing and I can hear necs pounding his side also.

"We're gonna have to take this outside!" I yell at Lester.

"What?!" Karen screams, her hearing obviously diminished. "You can't go outside!"

I laugh and point to the vent above. "I'm not going out the front door." I run back to the bedroom and grab a step ladder that's stashed under the bed. I have the vent open and am up on top of the RV in no time. My head hurts, but I try not to let it bother me.

The necs see me right away and most start to howl and claw at the RV's siding. Three of them have the smarts enough to rush to the ladder on the back. I take them out first. BLAM! BLAM! BLAM!

"Hold on, kid," Lester says as he tries to squeeze through the vent. "I'll help."

I give him a hand up onto the roof and we open fire, stopping only to reload. In less than a minute all the necs are toast and Lester holds out his hand.

"Great shooting, kid. I'm impressed," he says as I take his hand and give it a shake.

"Thanks," I nod. "Can I have my RV back now?"

3

Karen and Joseph huddle on the couch as Lester and I drop to the floor.

"You guys alright?" he asks them and they both nod. He looks back at me. "Garret has agreed to let us stay in the RV with him." Karen starts to protest, but her uncle quickly stops her. "We aren't thieves, K. We aren't monsters like the SATs. It's his RV and he has every right to keep it."

"Thanks," I say.

He looks hard at the two and steels himself for what he has to say next. I don't envy him.

"I've also agreed to help him find his mom," Lester says reluctantly.

"What?!"

"No!"

"Now just hold on and listen! I didn't say we were going to rescue her. I said we were going to help him find her. There's a big difference!"

"But it still means going back there?" Karen protests. "How is that different?"

"We're going to take a couple of the side roads and circle around," Lester answers. "We'll hide the RV and you two will stay here while Garret and I scope out the SATs' compound. If she's there then we'll figure out what to do then. Garret says he knows where some supplies were left back there anyway, so it's worth the trip."

"They'll kill you and eat you!" Joseph cries. "You've always said to run! Not stand and fight!"

"You aren't fighting," I say. "I am. I'm not going anywhere without my mom. If I find her there I'm going to get her out." My vision swims and I set a hand on the table to steady myself.

Karen laughs. "What are you going to do against all of them? You can barely stay standing!"

"I killed those necs, didn't I?"

"Slicks aren't people," she mutters. "It's a lot harder to kill a person."

"No. It's not," I state flatly.

Lester gives me a puzzled look, but I don't elaborate and tell them about the SAT I stabbed to death back in the forest.

"I help him find his mom then come back to the RV," Lester continues. "If he doesn't make it back in an hour then we leave. It's the deal we made."

I can tell Karen isn't happy, but she stays quiet. There really aren't a lot of options when the world has ended.

"Good! That's settled," I announce. "Do you mind driving back, Lester? I'm going to rest my head."

"Not a problem, kid," Lester grins.

Luckily, Lester seems to know the area because I have no idea where we are or where we are going. I was asleep for most of the ride.

The map! I have been so focused on Mom that I totally forgot she had the map! Which means if the SATs have her they have the map also. And that map has the locations of all the survivor groups in Oregon, including Cottage Grove.

Crap. Even if I do get Mom out alive I have to get the map too or they'll use it to wipe everyone out!

All of this swims through my head as I stumble back to the bed and collapse. As my mind starts to doze, I pray my subconscious will work out some kind of plan while I rest. Right now I couldn't plan my way out of the bathroom.

4

Being woken by your brother's heels kicking your spine is far from ideal.

"Stop it, Little Man!" I complain, absently swatting at him.

"Does that mean there's more slicks coming?"

I jump and push off the bed, looking for a weapon.

Karen holds her hands out and gives me an apologetic smile. "Sorry. I didn't mean to startle you. I was coming in to wake you up and, well..."

"He's kinda freaky, huh?" I say as I stretch. My head feels better, not perfect, but better. I give her a slight smile and for the first time really notice her.

Now, I've only read about beautiful women, so I'm not really sure what to compare her to. But if there is one feature about Karen that strikes me the most, it's her eyes. I guess they would be called almond shaped, dark brown and a little wide set. Now that I'm not dizzy I can really see them, and the rest of her features (short black hair, small nose and lots of freckles), and I find it hard to speak. Really hard to speak.

"You alright?" she asks concerned. "Is it your head?"

"No. No, I'm fine," I lie. "Just waking up is all."

She nods, but I don't think she believes me. Her cheeks flush, as I'm sure mine are too considering how much they burn, and we both stand there in awkward silence.

Little Man grunts a bit and Karen glances around my shoulder to my back.

"He really can't infect us?" she asks and I can see the shock being replaced with curiosity. There's a kindness to Karen's features that make me melt a bit. Well, melt more than I already am. I need to get myself together.

"No, I mean, not unless he bleeds on you." Her eyes go wide. "But I've never had that happen. It's fine, I mean, he's fine." I take a deep breath. "He can't hurt you."

She relaxes a bit and I find myself wanting to reach out to her. I guess this is what the books call "chemistry" or hormones. But I guess that's chemistry, too.

Karen looks at me and I swear her body shifts towards me.

"Is he awake?" Lester shouts from up front. "Tell him to get up here if he is!"

Karen frowns and her body language changes instantly. "You're not going to be happy."

"Huh? Why?" I ask. "Is there something wrong with the RV?"

She glances at the window and for the first time I notice how low the light is. I throw open the blinds and groan.

Dusk.

"You let me sleep the rest of the day?" I shout. "How could you?" I push Karen aside, a little harder than I want to, and stomp up front. "We had a deal!"

"Slow down, kid," Lester warns. "Karen tried to wake you before, but you wouldn't budge. I even came and checked your pulse to make sure you hadn't died on us. We'll camp here for the night and go scout for your mom at dawn. Most of them will be fast asleep from partying all night anyway."

I can tell he's keeping something from me and I step closer. "Partying? What does that mean?" Joseph is on the couch and he pulls his knees up close to his chest. I can see Karen fidgeting out of the corner of my eye. "What does partying mean?"

"Your mom wasn't the only one they nabbed," Lester begins. "We saw them haul a truck load of people towards their camp this morning. They're going to be feasting tonight."

I bolt towards the door, but Lester grabs me by the shoulders and slams me against the wall.

"You can't do anything right now! They'll start in on the men first and save the women!" I struggle, but he's pretty strong and I tire out quickly. "I've gotten us off the road and hidden pretty well. We'll camp here, eat something, and get some rest. We take off at first light, okay?"

I don't answer, but I stop fighting. He lets me go and holds up his hands.

"We cool?" he asks.

I look at Karen and Joseph then nod. Something about the way Karen looks at me, like she has something to say, keeps me from pressing the matter.

"Good. Joseph's a pretty good cook. How about you show him what you have to eat? We'll get some food in our bellies and then sit down and plan out how we're going to sanely and safely approach this. You good with that?"

"Yeah," I agree reluctantly.

Little Man lets out a long fart and they all jump in surprise.

Then the smell hits them and Karen rushes to open the door as Joseph scrambles for the windows.

"What the hell are you feeding that thing?" Lester complains.

"Me, mostly," I answer and shrug.

5

Joseph was able to scrabble a pretty good meal together. He was excited that I had plenty of salt in the RV. Apparently salt is hard to come by. He should have seen the barrels of salt we had back at the camp.

Thinking of the camp makes me remember Dad's warning to not trust anyone, so I keep a close eye on all three as we sit in the RV, having hidden it fairly well from the road. Keeping an eye on Karen isn't hard at all. Trying not to be the creepy staring guy is hard though. I've read enough about girls to know they don't like being stared at, but I just can't help myself. Apparently, from what I've read, that's normal too. So far, my books haven't lied to me yet. Or I'm just getting lucky.

"Stare much?" Karen asks from the couch, her lips turning up into a sneer. "It's rude, you know."

Busted. I feel my cheeks burn and I look away quickly. "Sorry," I mutter. "I just haven't been around others much."

"You mean you haven't been around boobs," Joseph laughs. Karen elbows him in the ribs and his giggles are cut short. "Ow!"

"Knock it off, you two," Lester growls. "Sound carries and these walls aren't very thick."

"Sorry," they both say, instantly quieting down. Karen gives me that weird look again and I'm starting to think it's because of Lester.

"You knock it off, too," Lester says to me. "I don't need you staring at my niece."

"Um, I'm sorry, I was just..."

"I know what you were just doing," he laughs. "I was a seventeen year old boy once, too. Just keep that in mind, Garret."

"Yes, sir," I say right away, not wanting to get on Lester's bad side if he has one.

This brings up other thoughts. Such as the fact that three people that I just met seem to be making themselves at home in my RV. I really don't know how Mom will feel about this once we find her.

If we find her...

"So, you didn't have other kids around?" Joseph asks. "No brothers or sisters?"

The second it's out of his mouth I can tell he wishes he hadn't brought up the subject.

"Nope, just me and Little Man," I answer. "And Mom and Dad."

"Your Dad, where's he at?" Lester asks, his eyes narrowing slightly. "He didn't pass on, did he?"

There's a tone in Lester's voice I don't like. I'm not sure what it is, but I realize I need to be very careful. These aren't my people. This is not my family. Trust no one. Trust no one...

"He took off before we left," I answer. "I just hope he made it out of the fire. We barely did."

"You were in the wildfire up on the mountain?" Joseph asks. "How'd you get away?"

"I drove like mad. Pretty much all I could do."

"Wow... Did any of the slicks come after you?"

"Why do you call them slicks?" I ask, changing the subject. I don't want to think about the fire and losing my home. Maybe losing Dad.

"Because they're slick, genius," Karen says sarcastically.

"You know how their skin gets? All moist and wet sometimes? That's why," Lester responds.

"The dead sweat?" I ask. "Oh, okay."

"Dead sweat? It's like learning a whole new language with you," Joseph laughs.

"Leave him alone, Jo," Lester says, turning to me. "What did you say your dad called the slicks?"

"HSNs," I respond. "And he *calls* them that...not *called*."

"My apologies, Garret. *Calls*. And HSN stands for...?"

"*Homo Sapien Necrosii*," I answer, but something gnaws at me about this...

"That's a scientific name, right? Your dad a doctor or something?" I frown and Lester gives me a huge grin. "Sorry about all the questions. Just wondering since doctors are in short supply these days."

"Are you sick?" I ask. The gnawing feeling deepens.

"Sick? No, no... Just if we find him it's good to have a doctor around." I don't respond and Lester lets the silence stand for a moment before getting up. "Well, I think I'll head up top and take the first watch. Who wants second?"

Karen and Joseph look away, fear on both their faces.

"I'll take second watch, no problem," I respond, wondering what those two are so afraid of.

"Great," Lester grins. "I'll come wake you up in four hours. Karen can take the third watch after that. That fine with you, Karen?" She has a hard time looking her uncle in the eye, but finally nods. "Great. See you in a few hours." He slaps me on the shoulder as he goes to the hatch and climbs out of sight.

"You guys okay?" I ask. "You don't seem too thrilled to be on watch."

"Should we be?" Karen grumbles. "Nothing like staying up all night waiting for the slicks to get us."

"How is that different from any other time?" I laugh, but Karen just glares and Joseph looks away. "Okay...sorry. Well, I guess I'll turn in. You guys want the back bedroom? I usually sleep in the loft bed, so it's no big deal if you want it."

"No. We'll stay up here," Karen responds. "The couch is fine."

"Okay. Well...um, goodnight."

Karen smiles slightly and I'm glad to see it. "Yeah, goodnight. You sleep tight, okay?"

I think she's mocking me, but I just smile as I go to the bedroom and slide the door closed.

6

Little Man's grumbles wake me up and I have to blink a few times before I realize I'm in Mom and Dad's bed and someone is knocking.

"I'm getting up. Hold on," I mumble.

The door slides open and I expect to see Lester, but Karen comes in. I sit up as she sits on the edge of the bed.

"Sorry about earlier," she says, but doesn't offer anything else.

"Earlier? About what?" I really have no idea what she's talking about.

"I was rude. You know, about the watch. I didn't want to say anything in front of Jo. He gets upset easily."

I can't really see her in the gloom, so I reach for the flashlight by the bed.

"No. Don't," she says and I realize she's crying.

I'm way out of my league here. What do you do when a pretty girl is crying on the edge of your bed? Books didn't prepare me for this. I pull my hand back from the flashlight as she wipes at her face.

"Sorry," she apologizes.

"No...it's fine. I mean, I'm sorry you're sad. That part's not fine, but crying is fine. Well, it isn't really, but...well...um..."

She laughs slightly. "You really don't know how to act around people, do you?"

"I didn't even know there *were* people until a couple days

ago."

She is silent for a moment. "Are you messing with me?"

"What?" I'm confused. "Messing with you? I don't understand."

"How could you not know there were people? You know about the SATs, but not others?"

"My parents kept me in the dark. They wanted me to think we were all alone. I guess so I wouldn't bug them about trying to find others. You know, because of Little Man."

"Right. I can see that," she says and scoots closer, sitting cross legged at the end of the bed. I unintentionally shift and move away, but just end up bonking my head on the wall. Karen laughs and holds up her hands. "Just getting comfortable. I'm not going to bite."

We're quiet for a while and Little Man grumbles some more.

"Does it hurt?" she asks. "Having him hooked to your spine like that?"

"No. Not at all," I answer honestly. "Unless he gets grumpy. His nails are sharp and he likes to kick."

"Why aren't *you* sick?"

"You mean infected? I'm not sure. Dad thinks since Garth and I share blood flow that I have some natural immunity. Antibodies, he calls them." I cross my legs and get comfortable. This is a subject I know a lot about. "Do you know what antibodies are?"

I see her shake her head.

"Well, antibodies are made by blood cells, but not the red ones, the white ones, and they help fight off disease like viruses and bacteria. I guess before the world died, they used to make things called vaccines from antibodies. Vaccines would make sure you couldn't get sick. Dad was hoping my blood could produce antibodies for a vaccine, but he says that my hormones are getting in the way of my blood chemistry. I guess I have to stop growing first."

"Stop growing?" She lets out a good, full laugh this time. "You're gonna keep growing? What are you, like six-two, or six-three?"

"Um, I think I'm six-feet, two-inches last time Dad measured. I'm not sure. Why, is that tall? How tall are you?"

"Five-seven," she says. "Three inches taller than my mom was."

"Where is your mom? And your dad?" I ask, not meaning to offend her, but I see her shoulders tense and she moves to leave. I quickly reach out and grab her arm. "I'm sorry. I guess I shouldn't have asked that."

Her skin is rough and I can feel small scars under my fingers before she moves my hand away.

"No...it's alright," she says quietly and I know the tears have started again. "You've been honest with me." I wait quietly. My fingers tingle a little from when I touched her and I have to slow my breathing a bit. Books do not prepare you for this.

"My mom died when I was born," she continues. "I never knew her. Dad disappeared a few months ago with Tina."

"Tina?"

"That's Joseph's mom. They were on watch and just disappeared. Uncle Lester looked for them." She starts to choke up, but pushes through. "He didn't find a trace. But, I guess that's to be expected..."

"Why?"

She looks at me and cocks her head. "What do you mean? The slicks got them."

"But wouldn't there still be some sign somewhere? Necs only eat until the bodies are cold then they move on. They don't clean up after themselves. I'd think there'd be at least scraps of clothes about." I wait for a response, but she just sits there in the dark, so I push on. "Even if your dad and Tina turned they'd be wandering around in the area. I'm just surprised your uncle didn't find anything."

"What are you saying?!" she yells, getting off the bed, her hands on her hips. "You think my uncle had something to do with it? You think he killed them or something?! Screw you, freak!"

Then she's gone. Out the bedroom and shoving the partition closed.

I have no idea what just happened. But a phrase starts running through my head, over and over, "*Methinks she doth protest too much...*"

7

I crawl up out of the hatch and see the glowing ember in front of Lester.

"Is that a cigarette?" I ask, having only read about them.

"Sure is, kid," he whispers as he stands and stretches. "Want one?"

He fishes out a pack from his jeans and offers them to me. I'm tempted, but you don't ever read anything good about cigarettes. "No. Thanks. I just haven't ever seen anyone smoking before."

"Your folks didn't smoke, huh?"

"Mom says she did when she was young, but quit before she met Dad."

"Yeah, about your mom... I've been doing some thinking." He hesitates and I can tell from his voice he doesn't want to say what he's about to say. "I don't know if it's such a great idea if you go searching for her."

"You're all welcome to leave," I say brusquely. "I'll take the RV back and hunt for her myself."

"Right... You see, kid. The SATs aren't going to be back that way. That was part of a hunting party. Their main compound is a few miles up the road, not back. If she's anywhere, she's there. We'll go back and see if those supplies are still there, but we aren't gonna search the forest." I start to protest, but he stops me. "Hold on. Just hold on. We'll get the supplies and then drive towards the SAT compound. We'll hide the RV and then scope things out and see if we can find your mom. If she's there then we'll figure it out. If she isn't there then we move on. How does that sound?"

"*We'll* move on? You mean you and Karen and Joseph? With me?"

"Yeah. It's the direction we were heading in anyway. That okay with you?"

My stomach flips and the gnaw returns. It's not okay with me at all. Plus, there's the map. I have no idea where the Cottage Grove compound is without the map. I could stay with Lester, Karen and Joseph, but then what? Would we just keep running? Plus, I just don't like this guy.

"I don't know. Let's look for my mom first," I finally answer. "We'll assess the situation at that time."

"Assess the situation at that time?" Lester laughs quietly. "You really are a scientist's son, huh?" He scoots past me to the hatch, smoking the last of his cigarette and putting it out on his boot heel. "Okay. We'll assess then." He goes to pat me on the back, but stops short. I know he doesn't want to touch Little Man. "Don't fall asleep on us now, okay? I'll make sure Karen relieves you in four hours." Then he's gone into the RV.

We never had a watch back at camp. Dad said it was a useless waste of sleep. Of course, we had a trench and two layers of razor-wired fencing between us and the necs. Out here there's only twelve feet of air between me and them. At least we can drive away if any show up.

Little Man burps and I chuckle.

"What do you think? You think we can trust them?"

He grumbles, snorts and lets out a long, slow growl.

"Really? Me neither. If things get weird I'll make sure we take the RV and go."

Grumble, grunt, grunt, snort.

"With or without Mom. I don't want to lose her, but Dad said we have to keep moving."

Growl.

"That's what he meant, though."

Growl. Grunt. Grumble, grumble, grumble. Fart.

"Oh, come on!" I reach back to smack him but one of his hands grabs mine and I stop. His fingers clench my index finger and squeeze. "I miss them too..."

He lets go of my finger and we are silent for a good long time. The night is so dark that I can barely see the trees surrounding the RV, so I just lean back and listen. There's a slight wind and the sound of the pine needles brushing against each other is so soothing I'm afraid I'll fall asleep. I shake my head a few times to clear it and sit with my knees tucked up under my chin.

The sound is slight, but I know my RV well enough that it's hard to miss. Someone has opened the door. I don't want to draw any attention, so I wait. Maybe Karen or Joseph had to go pee? But, why wouldn't they use the toilet? That's the great thing about an RV. I'm certainly not going to peak over the side and see. If it's Karen she'll think I'm some kind of pervert and that wouldn't be good. Not with how things ended earlier.

Why do I care? I just met her. I just met all of them. Dad said to trust no one, so I can't trust them. It would be better if I was on my own. Nobody to mess with my head and muddle my thoughts. No pretty girls...

The sound of footsteps walking away brings me out of my thoughts and I strain to see into the dark; to see who it could be, but with no luck. The footsteps grow faint and I figure it has to be Lester. Karen or Joseph wouldn't wander away so far. I'd be surprised if they would even go out the door.

Where is he going? No flashlight and out into the woods where necs could be anywhere. You can't see the lurkers at night. They'll pounce before you know they're there.

I keep my eyes focused on the direction I think he's gone and sure enough, after five minutes or so, I see the glow of flame way off through the woods. He's lighting a cigarette.

Grooooooooooowl.

"I feel the same way," I whisper to Little Man. "Something isn't right."

CHAPTER SIX

1

"You still awake up here?" Karen says as she climbs up through the hatch, shotgun in hand.

"Yep," I answer, but don't sound too convincing as I try to stifle a yawn.

"Well, your watch is over. Go get some sleep," she says roughly and steps aside, motioning towards the open hatch.

"I'm fine. I think I'll stay up here for a while...if you don't mind?"

She's quiet for a bit. "It's your RV. Do what you want."

I settle back down, but keep a distance between us. The early morning air has a chill and I wish I had a flannel, but now I'm committed to staying up here. Why don't I go inside and get some sleep?

"I don't know what happened earlier," I apologize. "But I'm sorry."

"It's not your fault. I'm sorry I yelled at you," Karen says quietly. "It's been hard without my dad. I miss him."

"I understand," I reply. "I miss mine too."

"But, yours is still out there. Mine is dead." Her voice toughens and I can see dealing with Karen is not an easy thing. She's up and down and all over the place.

"You don't know that," I insist, continuing before she can argue. "You said yourself that there was no trace. Sometimes no news is good news."

"You get that from a fortune cookie?" She snorts. "Great

wisdom."

"Fortune cookie? Oh, right. No, I've never had one. I read about them in some of the mystery books I have. There's always a scene where the detective has to go to Chinatown for a clue. Usually the contact makes a joke about a fortune cookie." She doesn't answer. "Have you ever had one?"

"Lots. Uncle Lester and my dad found a whole case of them a couple years ago. I didn't really like them. Tasted all grainy and weird. Joseph nearly made himself sick eating them."

"You keep any of the fortunes?"

"Why would I do that? They're just scraps of paper. Not worth anything."

"Oh," I respond. "I thought people kept the good ones."

"You read that in one of your books?"

She's making fun of me again, but I guess it's better than yelling at me.

"Yeah. I'd probably save a good one if I ever found a cookie."

"Doubt there are any left in the world. Uncle Lester said the ones we found tasted really stale and that was when I was twelve or so. I'm sure they've all rotted away now. No more fortune cookie makers, so no more fortune cookies."

"When you were twelve? You're nineteen now, right?"

"It really isn't polite to ask a woman's age. Didn't you read that in your books?"

I'm glad she can't see me because my face is burning right now. "I'm sorry. I didn't really know. Forget I asked. It was rude."

Karen bursts out laughing then covers her mouth as the sound echoes through the forest. "Crap. Sorry. I'm just joking; don't get all freaked out about it. Yes, I'm nineteen. Why? Is that too old for you?"

"Huh? What?" I have no idea what that means. "Too old for me?"

"Never mind. I forget you don't know people. Why does my age matter?"

"If you're nineteen then you were born before the world died, right?"

She's quiet for a long time. I'm about to ask again when

she speaks up. "There are so many things wrong with that question I don't know where to begin." I hear her take a deep breath. "First, the world isn't dead. The slicks are. There's quite a few people left out there. Some are good, some aren't. I've been lucky to not have to deal with the bad ones... well, too often. It's not like my dad said it was, filled with people and cars and planes and stores where you could just walk in and hand them paper and they gave you food and supplies. But, the world isn't dead."

"My parents always said it was, so I've just called it that: dead. You know, where the living are outnumbered by the necros? That's dead to me."

"Your parents... They really kept you in a bubble. When did they say the world ended?"

"You don't have to be mean," I say, my feelings hurt a bit by her tone. Dealing with other people is hard. I can see why so many parents in stories tell their kids to toughen up.

"I wasn't being mean. Sorry if it sounded like it. Just answer the question."

"They said the world died right before I was born. About seventeen years ago."

Karen laughed again, this time keeping it quiet from the start. "Seventeen years? Hah! More like twenty-seven years! I was born into this world. I never knew anything about how it was before the slicks came."

Twenty-seven years?! What is she talking about? That can't be right.

"Who told you it was twenty-seven years?" I ask. "I'm not saying you're wrong."

"Good, because I'm not!"

"I'm just saying that maybe someone lost track of the years. Maybe they were wrong."

"Wake up, Garret! Your parents told you a story, just like in your books. They told you the story they wanted you to hear. For whatever reasons they had, they kept ten years from you."

2

I just sit on the RV and wonder when my reality will stop being destroyed. First I find out there are people. Then I have to run from the only place I've called home. Now I find out I'm not only a sheltered kid that's been living in my own bubble, but I'm ten years behind everyone else.

Is anything I know real?

"Hey? You okay?" Karen asks. "I lost you there for a bit."

"Huh? What? Oh, sorry. I space off sometimes," I reply. "Just a lot to take in."

"I can imagine." She sighs and scoots a little closer to me. "The mornings are always so cold."

We're quiet for a bit, letting the early morning sounds fill the silence.

"He's kinda cute, in a way, you know" she says suddenly. "Um, I mean, um... That was kinda random, huh?"

"Who's cute?" I ask, confused. Is she talking about her Uncle? That would be weird.

"Garth," she answers, slightly embarrassed. "Little Man."

"Seriously?" I laugh, relieved. Sorta. "Cute?"

"In a sorta gross way," she answers sheepishly.

"Right...gross," I frown. "We're certainly gross."

Karen holds her hands up in protest. "No, no, I didn't mean you. You're not gross at all! Definitely not gross." I'm sure if there was enough light to see I'd see her cheeks burning. I know mine are.

"I mean," she continues. "What I mean is that it's freaky, but he's your brother and I can see that. It's cute that way."

"Kinda like you and Joseph?"

She rolls her eyes. "If he wasn't such a pest, maybe."

"Yeah, I get that. Little brothers are a pain in the butt."

"Family's in general are a pain in the butt."

"Tell me about it." We're quiet for a moment. "Listen," I start. "About your uncle...?"

The little bit Karen scooted towards me she takes away, sliding back across the RV. "What about him?"

I don't know how to ask, so I just do. "Do you trust him?"

She doesn't answer.

"I know it's a weird question. I'm sorry. Just..."

I can hear breathing quicken and I wait for the anger.

"Just he doesn't seem like a trustworthy guy?" she asks back. "Like some little voice in you keeps warning you about him?"

"Um, well, yeah." She nailed that on the head. "Sorry."

"Don't be," she sighs. "Uncle Lester has always been, well, sketchy, as my dad used to say."

"How so?" I ask, but she doesn't have time to answer as we both hear footsteps before we can continue talking. I have my 9 out and Karen has the shotgun to her shoulder in no time.

"You think it's necs?" I whisper.

"Nope, just a man out for a walk," Lester responds. "You may want to keep the chatter down. I could hear you a quarter mile off."

"Where'd you go?" I ask, my voice a little too harsh. Karen lowers the shotgun and gives me a look. "Sorry. I saw you leave earlier. Isn't really safe out there."

"It isn't safe anywhere," he responds, opening the RV door. "Since you're awake, how about coming down here and helping me out?"

"What with?"

"Cleaning a kill," he snaps, annoyed at me for all the questions. "You hungry for some fresh meat?"

"Raccoon?" Karen asks.

"Nope. They were too fast. It's a couple opossum." He closes the door and leaves me and Karen alone again.

Karen gets up and stretches. "I'm still on watch. Looks like you'll be helping gut the rats."

"They aren't rats, they're marsupials. The only marsupial in North America, actually."

She walks over and leans down close so I can see the smirk on her face. "They taste like rat. That's all that matters." She pats my cheek then yanks me to my feet. "Better get down there. I can tell you ticked him off. Keep the attitude in check and he won't hold a grudge."

"It's my RV," I insist. "He holds a grudge and he'll be walking."

The dawn has started to break and I can just make out her expression. Fear again. She forces a grin and pushes me in the chest.

"Go make nice, bubble book boy. He didn't have to risk his life and go find meat. That usually deserves a thank you, not an interrogation."

She waves me away and I really have no choice but to crawl through the hatch and face Lester.

3

O possum actually tastes pretty darn good when someone knows how to cook it. But I guess that can be said for all food. This change in my reality—edible food—I can get used to.

"That was great, Joseph," I say honestly. The others look at me like I'm crazy, which seems to be their preferred look. "No, really. If you ever have my mom's cooking you'll understand what I mean."

"Well...thanks," Joseph mutters.

Lester stretches and cracks his neck. "You want to drive or should I?" he asks me.

"I'll drive. The more practice the better," I respond, hopping into the driver's seat and starting the RV up. "Did you already put the last of the gas in the tank?"

"Sure did," Lester frowns. "It's just going to be enough to get us back to that barn you're talking about. There better be more fuel there or we'll be stuck."

"We covered things up before we left. Unless the SATs really started digging through the barn debris, they wouldn't have noticed anything."

"That's good." Lester's eyes narrow and his forehead wrinkles. I can tell he's got some internal debate going on. "How long you think it will take us to load everything up?"

"I don't know. With all of us it should only be thirty minutes or so."

He nods and squeezes my shoulder. "Then we should get going, shouldn't we?"

I slowly pull out of the woods and onto the road and we are off.

"I'm going to go catch some shut eye," Lester announces, heading back to the bedroom. "Wake me when we're almost there."

The door closes and I concentrate on the road. I'm actually relieved Lester is sleeping. Sketchy is right. I don't know what it is, but my gut keeps warning me that I'm missing something. Plus, Karen and Joseph's behavior around him is strange. I can't quite tell if they are afraid of him or if it's something else. Until I know for sure I'll keep Dad's warning at the front of my mind.

Don't trust anyone.

"Whatcha thinking about?" Joseph asks, startling me as he plops into the passenger's seat. The RV swerves a bit, but I keep it under control.

"You alright up there, 3B?" Karen asks as she wipes the plates clean and sets them in the cupboard.

"3B?" Joseph asks. "What's that about?"

"I don't know," I answer, looking over my shoulder at Karen. "What does that mean?"

"Bubble book boy," she grins. "3B."

Joseph looks from Karen to me and back to Karen. "Sounds like you two bonded last night." He gets a huge grin on his face. "I bet Uncle Lester would love to hear all about it." A dish towel flies into his face. "Hey!"

"Mind your own business, twerp," Karen growls. "We were just talking."

"Talking? Is that what it's called?"

"Oh, grow up!" Karen snarls.

"I'll try to if the slicks don't get me first," Joseph says. He starts to laugh at his joke, but falls short. "That wasn't funny, was it?"

"It's only funny if they eat you," I reply.

We're silent for a moment then all burst out laughing. I have to struggle to keep the RV straight as I get myself under control. Little Man joins in and begins to chortle grunt along. That ends the fun quickly.

Out of the corner of my eye I see Joseph struggling to keep from looking at my back. I had put the backpack on before breakfast to keep Little Man covered (and to keep his gas in), so I reach back and unzip the top.

"Take a look if you want," I offer. "He can't bite you. No teeth. Just watch his nails. Mom usually trims them for me. It's hard to reach."

Joseph looks back at Karen, waiting for approval. I look back again and see her nod. Her eyes meet mine and I smile and she tries not to return it, but I can see her lips curl slightly.

"Watch the road," she mutters.

"I thought you said he was cute?" I tease Karen.

"I never said that," she answers quickly, not looking at Joseph.

"You did so," I taunt. "Yesterday, back in the bedroom. You said he was kinda cute."

"In the bedroom? You want to have zombie babies, don't you?" Joseph laughs. "Rock-a-bye-zombie, in the treetop..."

Karen tosses a plastic cup at his head and he ducks it easily.

"Sheesh! Calm down!" Little Man grunts a bit. "Can you understand what he says?" Joseph asks, leaning over to get a better look. "Or is it all just gibberish?"

"I sorta understand what he says," I answer. "It's all just grunts and growls, so it's mostly his inflection that I understand. Also, his body language."

"Body language? He's on your back. How do you see him?"

"It's hard to misinterpret a hard kick or a quick scratch. He isn't always violent, but in the end I guess he is a nec, so violence is what he knows."

"You ever get the twin vibe?" Karen asks. She tries to sound bored, but it's obvious she's been pretending to ignore us and I know she's as interested as Joseph.

"That's really the way we do talk, to be honest," I answer, smiling again. Her lips start to curl up, but she forces them down. I focus on the road. "We're both tuned into each other's emotions. If I'm upset, even if I don't voice it, he gets upset. It goes both ways. If he gets worked up over something I have to struggle to keep calm or I end up just as flustered as him."

"Does he poop?" Joseph asks.

"Jo!" Karen scolds.

"What? Like you haven't been thinking about it."

"I haven't, thank you very much! That's just disgusting." She pauses for a bit. "But, since Jo was gross enough to bring it up..."

"Ha! See you do want to know!"

"Shut up, Jo." Her voice goes cold and Joseph quiets down. Siblings are siblings, whether alive or undead.

"No," I laugh. "He's a necro. They don't eliminate."

"Eliminate? That's what you call pooping?" Joseph looks puzzled. "What a dork."

"It's a more scientific term," I say, a little annoyed. "My dad uses it all the time. Part of growing up with a scientist."

"What about...?"

"Let him drive, Jo," Karen warns. "He needs to pay attention. One slick walks in the road and he might scream and drive us off the road."

This time I get a genuine smile.

"And, yes, I'll admit Garth is a little cute," she purses her lips. "For a slick."

"Which is cuter? Garth or Garret? Huh?" Joseph laughs, ducking his head before the second cup comes flying at him.

"Yeah, I'd like to know the answer to that question too," I join in.

"Shut up, both of you," Karen says, rolling her eyes. "Just what I need, two boys on my hands." Little Man hoots and grunts. "Great. Make that three boys. Are there no girls left in the apocalypse?"

4

"That's the barn?" Karen asks, leaning over me as she looks out the windshield. "Not much left."

"That's the point," I say, trying to keep myself focused, even though her head is right next to mine and her breath is on my cheek. "It's supposed to look like it's been picked over. The cache is underground. Let's hope it hasn't been found."

"You were supposed to wake me up when we were close," Lester grunts as he comes up front.

"Sorry," I apologize. "I didn't know we were here until I saw the barn."

Karen straightens up and moves away from me quickly. I catch a strange look Lester gives her as she steps past him to the couch.

"There's food and fuel in there?" Lester asks, shooing Joseph out of the passenger's seat. "How much?"

"Mom said there's enough fuel to get us to Washington if we needed. A lot of the food and water was spoiled by the fuel fumes, but there's enough to last a few weeks, if needed."

"Few weeks? Canned goods? Dry goods? What all's down there?"

I drive the RV off the road and straight towards the barn. "You'll see soon enough."

Little Man starts squeaking as we roll closer and I stop the

RV.

"Why'd you stop?" Lester asks. "Get closer so we don't have to carry stuff so far."

"We've got company somewhere," I say, putting the RV in park and turn off the motor. I get up and grab my 9. "Necs are out there. Last time it was brokens moving through the grass." I realize all of them understand me when I say 'brokens'. That means they know about the classifications. "We didn't notice any runners, shamblers or lurkers. Just the brokens." They don't even look my way. Interesting.

Lester nods and picks up a shotgun. He pumps a few rounds into the chamber and opens the door. "Well, let's get moving then and see what's out there." Then he's out the door.

"I didn't say there couldn't *be* runners out there now," I exclaim to Karen. "Is he crazy?"

She gives me a weak smile and grabs her rifle. "You are staying in here," she says, pointing at Joseph. "Don't even argue. Watch the tree line. You see anything then give a honk. Got it?" Joseph grumbles a bit, but nods and plops into the driver's seat. Karen is out the door almost as fast as Lester. "You coming, 3B?"

"Right behind you," I answer. I give Joseph a nod, but he only frowns at me.

The sun is pretty hot already and I know the day is going to be a sweaty one.

"You need a hat, squinty?" Karen jokes, laughing quietly as I shield my eyes.

"I think I'll make it," I say as I make sure the safety is off the 9. "You need a parasol or something? I'd hate for you to whither away in this heat."

"Parasol? What books have you been reading?"

I start to answer, but Little Man's warnings grow stronger, his heels starting to dig into me, and we get quiet.

"I don't think it's just brokens," I whisper, gun sweeping the area. "Sounds like runners. We should get back in the RV until he calms down."

"We aren't going anywhere until I see the supplies," Lester says harshly from ahead.

I'm impressed and alarmed at how good his hearing is. I'll

have to remember that.

"I don't think that's a good idea," I warn. "Little Man is pretty upset."

"I haven't stayed alive all these years by listening to slicks," he snaps back. "Keep moving."

I begin to respond, but Karen touches my arm and shakes her head. I get the warning and stay quiet.

Lester is smart enough to crouch down and we all creep up on the barn slowly, guns ready. We make it to the trap-door and I can see it's still covered up, just as we left it. It's about this time that Little Man goes into full panic mode and starts screeching like mad.

"Shush him up!" Lester orders. "You'll bring every slick in the area to us!"

"They already are," I say as the first necs break from the tree line. The RV horn sounds over and over as we start to fire.

unners. Lots of them. I know I have enough magazines in my pocket, but they are so fast I don't know if I can reload before they are on us.

"Fall back!" Lester shouts. "Run!"

The necs must have been attracted to the sounds from yesterday and from the look of their faces, they have been feeding. I pray Mom wasn't the meal.

Karen tries to turn and shoot, but I push her forward. "Just run!" I yell. "You can't get a decent shot with a deer rifle!"

She glares at me, but doesn't argue, her legs pumping madly as she sprints towards the RV. I, on the other hand, stop and face the necs, putting down seven of them before I retreat again. Even running I don't stop shooting, firing blindly at the necs.

I can hear them getting closer, gaining on me, when my 9 clicks empty. I reach into my pocket for the extra magazine, but fumble it and it falls into the grass. For a split second I debate whether to grab for it, but Little Man let's out such a high pitched screech that the thought is forced right out of my mind.

My lungs burn as I haul my butt to the RV. Karen makes it to the door, with Lester right behind her and they both turn to me. I see the terror grow on Karen's face and I know the runners are going to catch up to me. Lester yanks her inside and slams the door closed. I think I hear it lock, but that would be crazy. Why would they lock me out?

I pop the empty magazine out of the 9 and throw it at the windshield, getting Joseph's attention. I point to my 9 and pantomime a new magazine. He nods and disappears from view. I'm almost at the door and it starts to open, but is yanked shut right away. What the hell?!

I run around to the back of the RV, intending to climb the ladder to the top, but the undead growl from behind me tells me I don't have time. I keep running, hoping I can get the RV between me and the necs and realize my mistake as I round the corner. They've split and there are ten coming at me from this side, too.

Shots ring out and three drop in quick succession.

"HERE!" Karen screams.

I look up and she throws me a shotgun from the roof. I can hear Lester yelling at her, but she ignores him and puts her rifle to her shoulder and starts shooting again.

I catch the shotgun and spin around, getting it up in time to fire off two shots before the necs are on me. They lunge at me and I stumble backwards, ever mindful of Little Man as I hit the ground. I jam the shotgun in one of the nec's faces and pull the trigger. Not squeeze it like I've always been told, but pull it so hard I think I may have bruised my finger. The nec's head explodes and I close my eyes and mouth as brain and bone splatter across my face.

I can feel hands grab at me and I start swinging wildly, but my hands are slick and the shotgun slips and falls away. I kick and punch and manage to get myself to my feet. I'm surrounded by necros.

"They're too close to you!" Karen screams. "I can't get a shot!"

"I don't care! Just shoot the damn things!" I'm not sure if I am immune to their bites or not, but no one is immune to being ripped apart. "SHOOT THEM!"

"Karen! Get down here!" Lester yells and I can see him struggle with her from the corner of my eye as I face the necros.

I spin about, my arms flailing wildly as they lunge for me. Little Man screams from my back. He actually screams and it is the most human noise I have ever heard him make. More surprising is that the necs pause when they hear him. I don't waste the opportunity by hesitating and dive to the ground, grab the shotgun and start blasting. I hear Karen's rifle go off again and again also and soon I am surrounded by still corpses.

Little Man shrieks once more then goes silent, his little fists beating at my back, slower and slower until he stops. I just stand there covered in gore and try to catch my breath.

6

"**W**HAT THE HELL IS WRONG WITH YOU?!" I roar at Lester as I stand before the RV door. The only reason it's open is because Joseph threw it open before Lester could stop him. Otherwise, I think Lester would have left me outside forever. "WERE YOU *TRYING* TO GET ME KILLED?!"

"Just looking out for my own," he snarls at me.

I watch the gun in his hand and I have my shotgun to my shoulder before he can move.

"You can't look out for anything if you're dead!" I've never been so angry in my life. His eyes meet mine and I'm so close to squeezing the trigger.

"Put it down, Garret," Karen says, pulling Lester away from the door. She points to the tree line and frowns. "There are shamblers coming and probably more runners. We need to get the supplies and get back on the road."

I don't lower the shotgun. "Not with him! He doesn't go in my RV!"

Lester laughs. "Who are you kidding, kid? You won't shoot me."

"Garret? Please..." Karen pleads.

My arms start to shake and I can feel my breathing get short. Lester laughs again.

"And who says it's your RV anymore? In this world it's finders keepers, kid."

Karen is out of the RV and standing in front of me in a

blink, blocking my shot.

"Put it down, 3B. Please put it down." Her eyes start to tear up and I waiver. I can see Lester's grin widen as he knows I've already decided. I lower the shotgun and hand it to her.

"Put your gun down too," I snap at Lester. "Karen and Joseph can watch our backs while we load up."

"You ain't giving me orders, kid," Lester responds. "I've already said Joseph stays in the RV."

"Well, plans have changed, Lester. If you want to ride in my home then that's how it's going to work. I may not be worldly, but that doesn't make me stupid enough to think you won't shoot me the second all the supplies and fuel are packed. Give Karen the gun and let's get moving."

"Please, Uncle Les," Joseph says quietly. "I can stay close to the RV. I won't go far. Just let us watch the slicks while you and Garret load."

The air between Lester and me is filled with violent tension and I can see Karen shift her body closer to mine. Did she just pick sides or am I so wound up I'm reading too much into everything?

"Fine," Lester huffs, handing the gun back to Joseph. "You watch those things. Any get too close and you warn us, you hear? Don't just start firing." He looks at Joseph. "I don't need a bullet in the head, got that?" Joseph nods and Lester looks at Karen. "Got it?"

"Yes, sir," she nods.

He shoves past us all and starts towards the barn. "You coming, tough guy?"

I'm seething with rage. So much rage I'm finding it hard to breathe. Karen looks up at me and puts a hand on my chest.

"Thank you," she says quietly so Lester can't hear her. "Please keep calm. We'll talk later."

I look up at Joseph and see the tears streaming down his cheeks. He wipes at his nose and tries to smile at me.

"Okay," I relent. "You're right. We need to get out of here. But, I swear, if he..."

"I know. I'll make sure he knows it's your RV. We're just guests."

I take a deep breath and follow after Lester. I see the shamblers slowly making their way towards us and also hear the RV start up as Karen drives it as close to the barn as possible. Lester turns at the sound, but sees I'm right behind him.

"Glad you decided to help, kid," he smiles.

"Don't call me kid, Lester. My name is Garret."

His smile spreads wider, but turns colder. "Whatever you say...Garret."

We get most of the supplies loaded before more necs get close enough to be a problem. Although we've already made enough noise to bring the necros from miles around, I use my bat and machete to take care of the shamblers and the few broken creeping through the grass. I have to admit it wasn't just to keep quiet, or to save ammo, but to show Lester I can beat the crap out of things if I need to. I'm not all gunpowder and flash.

"That's the last of it!" Lester announces triumphantly. "Let's get on the road."

"Not yet," I say. "One more thing to do." I shove some of the debris away and reveal the parts to the wedge. "This goes on the front of the RV."

"What is that for?" Lester asks. "Why would you want to put that junk on?"

I roll over the first part then go back for the second. "It'll help us push through the roadways when we hit choked areas. Mom told me the roads will be crowded with abandoned cars as we go along." I dash inside the RV and grab the tool box, looking for the socket wrench.

Lester is moving the wedge to the side when I come back out. "We won't need this thing. It's a waste of time. Let's just get going."

"Well, I'm going to attach it anyway," I respond, unscrewing the nut on one of the bolts. "Better to have it and not need it than to need it and not have it."

"Your mom tell you that too?" he sneers.

"No, that would just be common sense," I snap. "If you don't want to help then fine. Go inside and leave me alone."

"Gladly, Garret," he replies, wiping his hands on his pants. "Don't be too long. We need to move out if we are going to find your mom."

I don't respond, just keep working. It's a pain in the butt trying to get the wedge secured by myself, but after about twenty minutes I have it bolted on. It looks pretty cool. I give the wedge a few good kicks to see how strong it is and end up with a couple bruised toes. I'd say it's ready to go.

"All set, Garret?" Lester asks from the driver's seat as I close the door behind me.

"I'll drive," I say, moving towards him, but Karen stops me.

"Why don't you let Uncle Lester drive?" she suggests. "You can help me organize the supplies back here."

We had to store most of the supplies in the bedroom, so she pulls me back there quickly as Lester starts up the RV and backs us on to the road.

"Keep the door open," Lester laughs. I start to say something, but Karen shushes me.

"Leave it be. Just help me with the supplies," she says. We scoot around the boxes of dried goods and gallons of water until Karen is sure we're out of sight. "You can't keep pushing him. I've known him most of my life and he has a limit. You don't want to get to that limit."

"Most of your life? He wasn't there when you were born?" I ask picking up on her wording immediately.

She looks away. "He really isn't our uncle. We've just always called him that. He was my dad's best friend before everything fell apart. It took him years, but somehow he tracked us down. I guess he and my dad had talked about possible survival sights when everything happened. They got split up right after the slicks started rising. That's the sketchy part. Daddy never went into details."

"He isn't even your real uncle?" I ask, stunned. "Why do you put up with his crap?"

"What else can I do?" she pleads. "When Dad and Tina went missing he was all we had. I can't watch Joseph on my own."

"You're not on your own now," I insist.

She looks at me for a while, studying my face then smiles. "You actually mean that don't you, 3B? You really have read too many books, you know. Trying to be a knight in shining armor..." She giggles, but stops when she sees the hurt look on my face. "I'm sorry, I shouldn't laugh. It's sweet, really, it is. But you've only known us for a couple days. You really should be thinking more about yourself. You don't know enough about the world to protect us from everything."

"I know enough," I say, patting my 9 still strapped to my hip. "I think I've shown that."

Her face grows serious and I'm afraid I've offended her somehow.

"You can't take on the world, 3B," she says quietly. "You're impressive with the slicks, but you don't know a thing about the people. I'm sorry, but I have to make sure Joseph is safe and Uncle Lester can do that." She looks back at Little Man. "Plus, you have your own burdens. You have more than yourself to keep safe."

She leans up and kisses me on the cheek and then she's gone. My face is on fire, whether from the kiss or from the anger starting to boil in my stomach, I don't know. What I do know is I am sick of Uncle Lester.

Little Man growls low in his throat, like a deep rattle and I know he feels the same way.

"We better find Mom soon," I mutter and I feel Little Man's hands slap against my back in agreement.

My insides are all torn up. I know I need to focus on finding Mom, but Karen, is just, well, she just...

For some strange reason she gets it with Garth. Maybe because she has a little brother too. Or maybe because she hasn't read as many books as I have. Am I more prejudiced because I've been exposed to so much of what the world used to be like?

Or, maybe she likes Garth because she likes you, stupid, a voice says in my head.

"Yeah, right..." I respond aloud then realize I'm talking to myself.

Trust no one. Trust no one. That's what I need to

remember. Trust no one.

That's a lot easier said than done...

CHAPTER SEVEN

"**Y**ou two stay right here, understand?" Lester orders as I wait for him outside the RV. "Keep an eye on the road and do not open this door no matter who it is. Got it?"

"Unless it's me," I say, keeping my face blank as Lester shoots me an angry look.

"If we aren't back by morning then leave," he instructs.

I start to protest, but stop, realizing no matter how much I dislike the guy, he's right. Even staying in one place that long is a gamble. It's mid-afternoon now, so morning is a long way off when you have necs and SATs roaming about.

"Gas up now, so you have a full tank," I suggest as I triple check my gear. "You don't want to do that on the run."

"Good thinking for a kid that just learned to drive," Lester grins.

"I just learned to drive, but I've been thinking all my life," I respond.

"Try not to kill each other," Karen says, giving a fake smile and a fake laugh to match. "Can you promise me that?"

Neither of us answer.

"Take care of your sister!" Lester hollers in to Joseph who is in the bedroom, refusing to see us off. Karen says it probably reminds him too much of when his parents went off and didn't come back. "Got everything?" he asks me.

"Yep," I answer and start walking.

"Other way, tough guy," Lester laughs. "Their compound is

through the woods, not down the road."

I reluctantly turn around, mad that I gave him the satisfaction of showing me up. We head away from the RV and I take a last look back over my shoulder. Karen is watching us go and she raises her hand slightly, but then lets it drop and shuts the RV door.

Little Man gives a couple of grunts. "I hear ya," I respond.

"What's he saying?" Lester asks.

"Nothing. He's just agreeing with my mood."

"What mood would that be? Love struck teenager with a chip on his shoulder?" Lester holds his hands up. "I'm just playing with ya, Garret. Don't get upset. Like I said before, I know what it's like to be a seventeen year old boy."

"I'm not a boy, Les," I grumble.

"Yes, kid, you are." He backtracks immediately. "I mean: Yes, Garret, you are. You're seventeen and don't know diddle about anything yet." I start to protest, but he just continues. "You haven't lived with people other than your parents. You didn't even know people were still alive. The only thing you know about the world is what you've read in your books and that world doesn't exist anymore. So, sorry, there is no way you can say you are a man. Which would still make you a boy."

I don't know how to argue against him, so I let it drop. I think he is actually disappointed I don't put up a fight. We're silent for a good long while as we hike through the pines and firs. Little Man grunts a few times and I laugh to myself as Lester freaks out each time, thinking he's warning us about necs. In fact, what alarms me the most is how much ground we cover without a warning.

"Where are they all?" I ask.

"Their compound is a couple more miles. We'll come at it from behind."

"No, not the SATs," I say, looking about the forest. "The necs. We haven't seen a single one since we left the RV. It's been a couple of hours and we've come pretty far. Even up at my camp I'd run into at least one a day, if not more."

"The SATs keep everything pretty well clear," he answers. "They sweep the area often to make sure there aren't any wanderers that sneak up on them."

I stop, alarmed further. "They sweep the area? Aren't they going to see us?"

"No. We're coming up on a blind spot," Lester insists, still walking. "We'll be fine for a while. Once we get real close we'll have to get a little more sneaky."

It's crap. I know everything he's telling me is crap. I may still be a boy, according to him, but I do know crap when I hear it.

He looks back at me. "You coming?"

"Yeah, I'm coming."

Little Man growls and pinches my shoulder. I don't even swat at him. He knows crap, too.

2

We crest a small ridge on our stomachs and crawl along until we have an unobstructed view of the SAT compound. It makes the camp I grew up in look like a little tiny box. It sprawls several acres with at least ten large metal buildings clustered around a single massive, metal structure. The building in the center is so large and tall that I can't see around it and have no idea what's on the other side. I can see people walking about the compound, all of them armed. Other than that there isn't any movement.

Little Man gives a tiny warning squeak, but doesn't repeat it.

"You got those binoculars?" Lester whispers. I reach into my satchel and hand him the binoculars. Lester looks over at me as I grab the extra pair I brought for myself. "Well, aren't you handy?"

"I think we've established I'm prepared."

"True enough," he agrees as he puts the binoculars to his eyes. "Okay. You know how there are four levels of security fencing?"

"Yes. All topped with razor wire. That's going to be hard to get through," I respond looking through my own pair.

"We aren't getting through that," he says. "There are mines spaced out between each row of fence. We'll blow ourselves up. We have to go in through the side gate to the right."

I move my view until I see what he's talking about. "How

are we going to get through there?" I ask, seeing that we could fit the RV through the gate, but it has four heavily armed men guarding it. Plus, behind it is a secondary gate. "They aren't just going to let us in."

"They might," Lester says.

"What do you mean?" He doesn't answer. "What do you mean?" I insist, pulling my binoculars away.

"Just hold on. Let me check a few things out."

A noise draws my attention and I see a cargo truck approach the right gate, its back tented with green canvas. Two men are in the cab with two more on the outside hanging onto each cab door. A third man is holding onto the back gate. All are just as armed as the men in the camp. The driver gives two short honks and the gate is opened for them. The truck pulls into the compound then is lost behind one of the buildings.

"What's in the truck?" I ask.

"What do you *think* is in the truck?" Lester throws back at me. "It isn't puppy dogs and ribbon bows."

"What does that mean?" I snap. "Just answer the question."

"It's people, tough guy. That's one of their procurement trucks. There's people jammed in the back there. They'll sort out the men from the women then the sick from the healthy. After that it's up to fate."

Fate. I struggle not to think of what fate my mom has been given. I don't want to have the possibilities bouncing around in my head. I have to think clearly if I'm going to find her.

"We'll keep watching for a while then fall back and eat," Lester states. "We can approach the gate at dusk. That'll be our best chance to get inside."

"What? We're just going to walk in? Why would they let us do that?"

Lester keeps the binoculars to his eyes so he doesn't have to look at me when he answers. "Because the Meets start then. We won't be the only folks going through that gate."

"The Meets?" I ask, not liking the sound of that.

Lester doesn't answer.

We sit in silence on the hillside as the afternoon dwindles away. I try to ask Lester questions about the compound, since he seems to know more about it than I thought, but he dodges the questions or flat out ignores them.

So, I sit and wait, eating some of the jerky I brought and try to conserve water, although it's roasting in the late afternoon sun.

Little Man is getting more and more agitated and he's worked into a near frenzy by the time dusk comes around and Lester and I are ready to work our way to the gate.

"He gonna be like that the whole time?" Lester complains. "He'll draw too much attention. Can you calm him down?"

"I'll try," I say, worried also. I tear a strip off a bandana from my satchel, slice my arm slightly and let the strip soak up the blood.

"What the hell?" Lester exclaims. "What are you doing?"

"Feeding him," I answer. "He doesn't need it to survive, but it'll occupy him for a while."

Lester gives me a good long look. "You've been doing that your whole life, huh?" I nod. "That's messed up, kid. In so many ways."

I let the 'kid' comment go. "You have no idea how messed up my life has been. I'm sure everyone has their own crazy stories, but none have had to deal with Little Man."

Lester shakes his head. "Well, looks like the line is starting.

We better get down there before it gets too crowded. The guards get testy once the crowd gets too big."

"We're really going to just walk in?"

"Yep. It's what everyone does. Keep your brother covered up. Won't matter too much if he moves about; he won't be the only small animal in packs. Just make sure he doesn't get too loud. It'll set the dogs off. They know a nec when they hear one."

I stop and look at Lester, stunned. "Dogs? They have dogs?"

Lester points down to the gate and I see four additional guards approaching the gathering crowd. Each has a large dog leashed tightly to their sides. I don't know enough about dogs to say what mixes they are, but each has a slightly different look. The only consistent thing is that the crowd is very aware of the dogs and even from this distance I can see the change in peoples' body language once the guards start walking them up and down the line.

"What are the dogs for?" I ask as we carefully make our way down the hill. "Can they smell necs?"

"No. They're sniffing for infection."

As soon as he says that, we come around a small group of trees and can hear the dogs barking. It's the first time I've heard actual dogs barking and I'm fascinated at how far the sound carries. Something primal in me comes to the surface at the sounds. I know what they are saying: warning, there is danger, kill that danger.

We lose sight of the gate, but the resulting gunshots paint a picture of what just happened.

"Someone was trying to hide a bite," Lester states. "You'd be surprised how many people still think they'll be okay after a slick has a taste. Stupid bastards..."

Two more shots ring out and we can hear a woman screaming, her anguish apparent. Someone is shouting for her to be quiet and the dogs are frenzied.

A final shot echoes as we come into view and I watch a woman crumple to the ground. Blood spurts from her head in a steady stream and I stop. I've never seen a person get a headshot before. It's nowhere near the same as a nec. The blood keeps spurting then slows and stops. A guard calls for someone and a man, dressed in rags with a shaved head and covered in bruises, stumbles forward with a wheelbarrow. He loads up the woman's corpse and wheels her back into the compound.

This is a mistake. This is too much. I don't know how to act around people and not only am I about to be thrust into a huge group of them, but I have to watch them get brutalized and murdered right before my eyes? Too much.

"Hey, Garret! Snap out of it! Come on," Lester says urgently. "This is not the time to get cold feet."

"But...they just shot her," I reply, still too shocked to move. "She wasn't infected, was she?"

"Doesn't matter. She was causing trouble. They don't like trouble."

"Are they going to eat her? Is that what they do with the body?"

Lester doesn't answer, just grabs my elbow and drags me towards the now almost silent crowd.

4

My fear of all the people is tempered by fascination as we get closer. I want to ask them all questions: find out where they are from, how old they are, are they family or just friends, where have they been living, why are they here. So many questions rush through my brain and I feel Little Man start to stir. He's been quiet since we came down the hill, but if I don't calm down I'll get him worked up.

"Stop looking around so much," Lester hisses. "Just keep your eyes in front. Don't draw attention to yourself."

There's a child in front of us and he keeps looking back at me. He won't look at Lester, just me. His hand is firmly gripped by the man he is with and it almost looks like twine, or rope is binding them together at the wrist.

"Hi there. I'm Garret. What's your name?" I ask innocently. Lester gives me a nudge and shakes his head.

The man with the boy looks over his shoulder at me and scowls. "Mind your own damn business, boy."

"Sorry," I respond. "I was just talking to your son, there. I didn't mean to upset you."

"You haven't upset me...yet," the man snarls and turns away.

The boy doesn't look back again.

"What a jerk," I mutter, thinking the man won't hear me. I'm wrong.

He stops and turns to me fully, pulling up his dirty, torn

flannel shirt. The grip of a pistol peeks out of his waistband. "Say it again, boy. Call me a jerk again. I dare you."

What is the guy thinking? I have a 9 on my hip, a machete strapped to my leg, a hunting knife on my belt, and my baseball bat on my back next to Little Man's pack. Does this one guy really think he scares me? It's like some stupid western novel.

"You really shouldn't put a gun there," I say, smiling. "You could shoot yourself in the crotch. Not that it would hurt much."

The man reaches for his gun and I reach for mine. It is a western! But, Lester is between us before either of us can get the weapons drawn.

"I'm sorry, sir, he's new. Doesn't quite know the 'let everyone be' rule. He's just a kid flapping his gums and didn't mean anything by it. Okay?" Lester stares hard into the man's eyes.

"Whatever," the man finally says. "Just make sure he shuts the hell up."

I begin to respond, but Lester gives me such a menacing look that my mouth snaps shut immediately.

"I'll make sure he minds his manners," Lester says. He turns to me and his face is flushed with anger. "Keep. Your. Mouth. Shut."

I nod and look away, deciding to focus on the guards. They are all very large men. I mean large. Most are taller than I am and those that aren't have more muscles than I thought possible on a person.

One in particular seems to be running everything. He's up by the gate and never moves or speaks, but all the other guards pay attention to his every shift or twitch. His eyes are scanning the crowd and he catches me looking at him. Nodding to one of the other guards he continues watching me as the guard makes his way down the line, shoving people back into the crowd and out of his way.

"You!" the guard announces. "Come here!"

Lester's head snaps my way. "What did you do?!" he hisses.

"Nothing," I shrug.

The guard comes right up to us, his rifle pointed at my belly. "You stupid or something? I said get over here!"

Lester holds up his hands. "We don't want any trouble, man. Just bringing the kid to see the Meets, is all."

"Was I talking to you?!" the guard barks. "I wasn't, was I?!"

"No, sir, sorry," Lester apologizes, lowering his head.

The guard grabs me by the collar and drags me up to the lead guard. I glance over my shoulder and see Lester watching me intently. He slowly starts to inch his way through the crowd, his eyes focused on me.

"Here you go, Travis," the guard says as he pushes me in front of his boss.

"Thanks, Milo. What's your name, kid?" Travis asks.

"Garret," I answer.

"Garret? You here with someone, Garret?"

"That guy back there," Milo says, hooking his thumb over his shoulder. "The one thinking he's being sneaky."

Travis searches the crowd and I can tell from his reaction he knows Lester. I knew this all seemed weird.

"Get you ass up here, Rollins!" Travis yells. "No use sneaking your worthless hide through the gates! We've got a watch out for you!"

A different guard grabs Lester from the crowd and shoves him towards me.

"Hey, Travis. I was just coming to see the Griffins."

"They don't want anything to do with you, Rollins. Except the fifteen pounds of flesh you owe them. You want me to take that off you and give it to 'em now?" Travis grins and I have to force myself not to flinch. His teeth are filed like the man I killed in the forest. Except Travis's are metal.

"That's what I need to see them about," Lester pleads. "I have something way more valuable than fifteen pounds of flesh."

"Oh, I'm sure you do, Rollins," Travis laughs. "Everyone has something that's better than flesh." He leans in close and, when Lester flinches, grabs him by his shirt front. "But, this world runs on flesh now. There ain't no substitute."

"Please, Travis! You have to trust me!"

"I don't have to trust sh...!"

"Where's my mother?!" I yell.

Travis, still holding Lester's shirt, looks over at me. "What was that, boy? You didn't just demand something of me, did you?"

"As a matter of fact, I did," I say moving in close. "I want to know where my mother is. Is she here?"

"There's a lotta mothers here!" Milo laughs, but shuts up instantly when Travis gives him a glare.

Lester stumbles back as Travis lets go of his shirt. The head guard looks me up and down, like he's really just seeing me for the first time. "What's your name, boy?"

"I told you already. It's Garret."

The slap comes quick and hard. My head rocks back and I put the back of my hand to my mouth. It comes away bloody and I can feel my cheek and lip swelling already.

"Your whole name, smart ass!" Travis roars.

"Garret Weir," I say cautiously.

"Weir? Weir..." Travis thinks this over for a minute. "Doesn't ring a bell. Take 'em to Butcher Bob. We're taking Rollins's fifteen pounds...and then some!"

The guards grab us and I try to struggle, but get a couple hard jabs to my kidneys for my trouble. My weapons are yanked from my body and my hands pulled behind my back. Of course, Little Man chooses that time to get active again.

He lets out a loud growl and several grunts and I can feel him thrashing hard. A couple of the guards jump back and I manage to get one arm free. I take a swing and clock the closest man to me then pull back to punch again. I never get the chance as my world explodes when Travis's fist connects with my chin. His massive uppercut nearly lifts me off my feet and my head instantly feels like it's filled with a ton of sand. Sand made of pain.

Little Man's howls silence the crowd around me and most of the guards have their rifles up to their shoulders, scanning the area for necs. Travis grabs my arm before I can fall and pulls me in close.

"That noise is coming from your pack," he grunts. "What you got in there, Garret Weir? Don't tell me you're carrying a slick!"

"None...of your...business," I whisper, barely able to get my jaw to open. Travis laughs and slugs me in the gut. All the breath is forced out of me and I feel like I'm going to puke.

"Sure about that, boy?" He tosses me to a couple of guards and they grab my arms, holding me in place. "Turn him around!" The guards flip me about and my knees get weak and I struggle to stay on my feet.

Little Man is in full on tantrum mode now and his growls and hisses are only overshadowed by the pounding of his fists and legs against my back. "Stop...Garth...please..."

I can feel the pack being pulled from my back and before I know it the crowd around us is screaming, as are the guards.

"What the holy hell is that?" Travis yells. "Is it eating him?"

The slide of rifle bolt gets my attention and I fight the weakness, trying to free myself from the guards, but even though they're freaked out by Little Man they keep their grip.

"No! Travis! Wait!" Lester shouts. "This is what I was bringing the Griffins! This is the crazy doctor's kid they've been looking for! He's the one the doctor has been talking about on the short wave to those folks in Cottage Grove! Don't shoot him!"

Travis is silent and I wait for the bullet to hit me. I wait for it all to be over.

"That's the kid? Weir... Weir!" I hear a smacking sound which I imagine is Travis slapping his own forehead. "Phew! I almost botched that up. Turn him around." I once again face Travis and this time his smile is genuine. Deadly and dangerous, but genuine. "Boy, you just made my night."

People all around are still screaming and yelling and Travis's brow furrows. "SHUT THE HELL UP!" As if a switch had been flicked the crowd goes silent, their eyes on Travis and the guards. More specifically their eyes on the rifles. "Milo, cuff Mr. Rollins here. We've got a meeting with the Griffins."

6

I'm dragged towards the gate as Lester is shoved ahead of us. He keeps looking over his shoulder at Travis, who is walking on my right side. Lester refuses to look me in the eye.

"This is worth fifteen pounds, right, Travis?" Lester asks in desperation. "This should wipe my debt clear, right?"

"Not up to me, Rollins," Travis answers. "You'll have to take it up with the Griffins."

Lester blanches and his already fear-white face becomes almost translucent.

"So, boy, what the hell is that thing?" Travis asks. "Did you get attacked or something?"

This simple question tells me a lot about Travis. Lester said the Griffins have been listening to Dad's short waves. If he's been talking about me with Cottage Grove then they would know what Garth and I are. The fact they didn't pass this info on to Travis means he's just muscle. Untrustworthy muscle. I've read enough mob and crime books to know that.

"Didn't the Griffins tell you what to look for?" I ask. I'm answered by a cuff to the side of my head and Little Man howls. The moment we walk through the second gate and are about fifteen feet into the compound Little Man's howls turn to squeaks and screeches. "You have necs coming," I warn groggily.

"Necs? What the hell are necs?" Travis asks, looking around him.

"He means the slicks, Travis," Lester answers. "Kid's never been around people. He has his own language."

"Oh, slicks, right," Travis nods. "Yeah, boy, we have plenty of slicks. You'll probably meet at least one of them."

The other guards laugh knowingly and I have to wonder what's in store for Garth and me.

We walk through what could only be called a cattle shoot. From the moment we enter the compound we are forced between two rows of fence that leads us towards the large building in the center. Armed guards are spaced out every few feet and they ignore us as we go by, keeping their eyes trained on the other people that have been let in. The guards vary in size and age (although I don't know enough about people to say what ages) and many sport nasty looking scars, eye patches, scorched scalps with stringy hair clinging to burnt skin.

"They ain't pretty, but they do their jobs," Travis says, catching me sizing them up.

As we walk along I see many of the smaller buildings for what they are and also notice all the buildings have what I guess are solar arrays bolted on top. The closest to the gates are garages with various vehicles parked or jacked up and being repaired. Each of these buildings has a large tanker truck next to it and I watch as gas is pumped into the vehicles that are in working order. Trucks, cars and motor-cycles, all highly modified and armored, sit ready for use.

After the garages are barracks of a sort. Men and women come and go from these buildings, but not all look willing. Many of the windows are open to let the air in and cool things down and the sounds coming from the windows make me blush. I've read enough to guess at what may be happening in there.

The buildings closest to the large, main building are dif-ferent. While the others are well-built, they are obviously scrapped together from many different materials. These other buildings are not scrapped together. They are very deliberate in their structure and strength. Each building, four in all, has thick steel sides with long steel girders crisscrossing every five feet. There is only one double door going into each building and that is braced with a foot thick bar and guarded by four men. One with an active flame-thrower. Whatever they keep in those they do not want escaping.

We're almost to the main building when the cattle shoot splits into three different directions. Each way has a sign suspended over it: "Have Some Fun", "Try Your Luck" and "Pay Your Debt". For the first time I really notice the people that have come here and am surprised by how many of them are missing limbs.

The line heading into the "Pay Your Debt" shoot has the most amputees. Weak men, women, and even children hobble along, their bodies missing a leg or two, an arm at the elbow or up to the shoulder. One woman is without arms or legs and is strapped to a young man's back. She cries and pleads for mercy, but no one pays her any attention.

Those entering the "Try Your Luck" shoot look dangerous. Muscled and scarred, they are hard looking people. The only emotion on their faces is pure rage. I can see muscles tremble with violence.

The majority of folks are filing into the "Have Some Fun" shoot. There is a long table set up and people drop various containers onto the table for guards to inspect. Once the guards seem satisfied with the contents they count out what look like metal chips and drop them into the people's outstretched palms. Some look like they want to argue over what they are given, but none do. They swallow their fear and anger and enter the main building.

We enter neither of these paths as a guard opens a junction just before the shoot splits off. Travis and his men take us through and we circle around the main building. The buildings on the far side are different than those in front, but I don't get a good enough look before I am shoved through a side door in the main building and forced to march up three flights of stairs.

We stop outside a thick iron door at the top landing and the six guards stationed there nod to Travis. A guard knocks on the iron door three times and we wait. Travis's eyes are focused on two bulbs that are set above the door and after a few seconds one lights green. I can see Travis relax considerably and the iron door is opened for us.

I'd hate to see what would happen if the other bulb lit up.

Inside the iron door we face a set of wooden double doors. "Hold on," Travis says quietly and steps to the double doors, knocking lightly. We wait a few minutes before the doors open and a girl, unbelievably muscled and toned, glares at us. I think she's about my age, but it's just so hard to tell. The half-shirt she wears covers her chest, but leaves the long scars that crisscross her arms and stomach for all to see.

"This him?" she asks, eyeing me up and down. "This the Carrier?"

Carrier?

Travis nods. She shrugs and motions for us to come inside as she holds the door open.

We are pushed through into a massive room lined with wood paneling and a crazy mix of furnishings. It is what I would guess a furniture store would look like with chairs and couches, beds and dressers, desks and kitchen tables filling the space so it is hard to figure out which way to walk.

Travis and the guards weave us through the maze of furnishings until we are at the far side of the room, standing before a giant red curtain.

"They're here," the girl says to the curtain.

"Make them take a seat, Veronica," a woman's voice orders from behind the curtains. "We'll be right out."

"Sit," Veronica orders.

"I've still got duties outside," Travis says.

"Sit. Now," Veronica growls. Little Man answers back with a growl to match and the girl has a twelve-inch blade in each hand in the blink of an eye. I didn't even see her move. "You brought a slick up here?!"

Travis holds out his hands, his face apologetic and scared. "It's the boy! The thing is hooked to the boy!" he cries, his body tensed and ready to be attacked. If this giant of a man is scared of this small girl then I know I should be also.

Veronica approaches me cautiously. "You move, I cut. Got it?" she asks. I nod. She peeks around my shoulder and gasps. "Holy... That's messed up."

"I know, right?" Travis says, his voice submissive. "That's what I thought."

"You? Think?" Veronica laughs then she sees Lester. In a blur she has a blade to his neck and the man starts to cry. "You shouldn't have come back, Lester. You've been black-listed. Your meat isn't worth spit around here."

"I know! I know!" Lester cries, his eyes squeezed shut. "But I brought the freak everyone is looking for! I brought him to you, to the Griffins! I could have just kept going, taken him to the Keep or maybe the Tribes, but I didn't! I brought him to you! I brought him to the Griffins!"

"And we appreciate that, Mr. Rollins," a woman says as she steps through the curtains. She is tall and beautiful. She wears a light blue blouse, which to my embarrassment does not leave much to my imagination. Her pants look like leather, but there are strange marks on them, tattoo-like marks, that I choose not to look too closely at. Her blonde hair is done in a long braid that trails down her back. And she has ice blue eyes that pierce mine. "It has been noted and that is why you are still speaking and not being fed to Big Timber right now."

"Thank you, Ms. Griffin. Thank you!" Lester blubbers. "I appreciate your mercy!"

"Mercy?" a man asks as he also comes through the curtains. He is the male version of the woman, even with a long braid down his back and the same shirt and pants. But he is a good four inches taller and has a close-cropped red beard that comes to a small point on his chin. "Sister Charlotte, did this piece of garbage that isn't worth a slick's sweat just say he appreciates our mercy?"

"Yes, Brother Charles, he did."

Lester's eye's flick madly between the two Griffins. "This kid is worth more than my fifteen pounds, right, Mr. Griffin? This should clear up my debt, yes?"

"Of course it clears up your debt, Mr. Rollins," Charles Griffin smiles. "But the deal was for two children. The boy and the girl. You didn't bring them, did you? You know how we like children."

Lester cringes and Charles continues, "Even if that was the only issue we'd let you be on your way. But there is the large matter of you running, Mr. Rollins."

"You do know the rules, right, Mr. Rollins?" Charlotte Griffin asks.

"The rules about running?" Charles asks right after her.

Lester is quiet.

"Answer them!" Veronica hisses.

"I...I-I-I know...the rules," Lester stutters and I see the front of his pants darken.

The Griffins wrinkle their noses at the same time.

"Oh, Mr. Rollins," Charles says. "Really? How embarrassing. To wet yourself in front of the ladies..."

Charlotte Griffin steps up to Lester and grabs him by the chin. "Since you did bring us such a valuable item we have already decided we won't kill you."

"But we can't just let you go, now can we?" Charles asks rhetorically. "So, as a compromise, we have decided to let you Try Your Luck."

Charlotte claps enthusiastically. "It's the only fair thing to do!"

Travis and the guards nod along, agreeing with Charlotte's exclamation.

"We are nothing if not fair, right, Mr. Rollins?" Charles asks. Lester doesn't answer. Charles glances at Veronica and she gives Lester a good, hard slap to the face. Tears well in Lester's eyes and he is soon sobbing.

Charles rolls his eyes and waves at the guards. "Take the cry baby away so he doesn't embarrass us any further."

"No! Please, Mr. Griffin! PLEASE!" Lester screams as the

guards drag him away.

"Dear sister, shall we spare him his Luck?" Charles asks, holding up his hand and halting the guards. Charlotte shakes her head no, her cold, cold eyes never leaving Lester's. "Oooh, sorry, Mr. Rollins. But the lady has spoken. I'll be kind and let you go early tonight. That way you don't suffer with worry! Good bye, Mr. Rollins, and good *Luck*."

Lester screams and shouts the entire way out of the room. I hear the iron door slam and his cries for mercy and help cease instantly.

"Ahhhh, that's much better!" Charlotte says, taking me by the elbow. "Now we can talk in private." She looks at Travis and he bows immediately as he backs out of the room. "We aren't to be disturbed, Veronica. No visitors at all."

"Yes, Mistress." Veronica nods as the Griffins escort me through the red curtains.

CHAPTER EIGHT

"You aren't going to try to harm us, are you, Garret?" Charlotte asks as she leads me into the room beyond the red curtains. "You seem like a nice boy and I would love to untie your hands so you can enjoy some food and drink, but I can't have you being violent. Can I trust you to be good?"

I study her then my surroundings. The room is as wide as the area on the other side of the curtain, but not very deep. There are two high backed, plush chairs set before a massive window. And the window is truly massive. I'm not sure what it is made of, but it is one solid pane that must stretch ten feet high and thirty feet across.

"Garret?" she asks again, patiently.

"Um...no, I won't harm you," I mutter.

"That's wonderful!" Charles says from behind as he brings in a third chair and sets it next to the others. "We abhor senseless violence! Violence with purpose... That's another matter."

Charlotte unbinds my hands and I rub my wrists to get the circulation flowing again. I expect her to move in front of me, but she remains behind and I can see out of the corner of my eye that she is studying Little Man.

"He's remarkable," Charlotte gasps. "May I touch him?"

I really don't know how to respond and Charles laughs.

"Leave him be, Charlotte! Let the boy sit and rest first!"

He takes me by the arm and leads me to my seat. My jaw drops when I near the window. It looks out on, what I guess would be called, an arena: benches for hundreds of spectators surrounding an oval dirt floor. In the floor are lines and blocks, shadows and stains. It does not look like fun games are played there.

"Impressive, isn't it?" Charlotte asks. "It took us years to perfect, but now it is nothing short of glorious!"

"Hear hear!" Charles shouts as he takes a gulp from a large goblet and quickly refills it from a glass jug. "Glorious!"

"It is based on the ancient roman gladiator arenas," Charlotte continues, taking the jug from Charles and pouring liquid into two more goblets. She hands me one and indicates for me to take a seat. "It has a few modern adaptations, though."

I sniff at the goblet and frown. "Is this wine?"

"In a way," Charles laughs. "Fruit wine. We make do with whatever we have the most of each season. I blend it myself so that it is always palatable. Drink up!"

I take a sip and my frown deepens. "It's...bitter," I say, trying not to choke.

"Gooseberry," Charlotte responds. "We added honey, but the sugar disappeared during fermentation." She takes a sip herself, her eyes watching me over the goblet. "So what do you think of our *harenas*?"

"Sand? You do know that just means sand, right?" I ask without thinking.

The brother and sister look at me for a long while before Charles bursts out laughing. "Sand! We have an educated one here, dear sister!"

"Are you, Garret? Are you educated?" Charlotte asks, but her tone isn't as jovial as Charles's.

"Um, I've read a lot," I answer, a little more humble this time.

"Read? And what have you read about Roman arenas? Please do tell."

"Well, from the size I would say this is modeled on the smaller arenas, such as found in Verona or Pompeii, not on the Coliseum in Rome." I pause, but Charlotte just nods for me to continue. "The floor looks raised and you probably have rooms underneath. There are obvious spots where perhaps walls or gates have been retracted into the floor." I stare at the dark stains in the sand. "And you use real weapons."

Charles downs his drink, stands and claps. "Bravo, young master Weir! Bravo!"

"Sit down, Charles," Charlotte scolds. "Yes, Garret. Yes to all of those observations. You really have read a lot."

"I went through a gladiator phase when I was a kid," I reply. They don't respond, just watch me and Little Man while they sip from their goblets. "Um... Are you going to eat me?"

They both look shocked at the question then burst out laughing.

"Oh, dear me," Charles says, wiping at his eyes. "Kids these days..."

"No, Garret, we aren't going to eat you," Charlotte answers. "That is not who we are. Now, don't get me wrong; we have heard all about how we are known as the SATs, and I acknowledge that during lean times some of those that reside here may not have as much restraint as would be expected of more civilized people. But us? Dear Garret, no, we are not going to eat you."

"Especially since we have no idea what's flowing through that tender meat of yours," Charles adds, pouring yet another goblet full of wine. "Being conjoined with a slick doesn't present you as the most appetizing meal." Charlotte shoots him a quick glare and he hushes up immediately as he looks away towards the arena. "Ah, I believe the evening's festivities are about to begin!"

A small man, dressed in top hat and tails, steps onto a podium set up at the side edge of the arena, just above the floor.

"Ladies and gentlemen!" the man announces. I look about and realize I'm hearing the sound from small speakers set up around the window. "Welcome to the Meets!"

The crowd, now almost filling the arena's seats to capacity, gives a lackluster cheer. The small man pouts and feigns great disappointment.

"Come now! Have more spirit! Some of you will win big tonight! Let's hear it!"

The crowd doubles its effort, but it's still pretty lame.

"Hand me the mic!" Charles demands.

"Not yet, Charles," Charlotte refuses. "Let the evening get under way first. They'll get their bloodlust up and soon be on their feet."

"Well, with what we have to go through to put the Meets together, you'd think they'd be a bit more grateful," he growls, sipping more wine. He gives me a glare over the top of his goblet. "Drink up, Garret. I insist." I take a small drink and give him a weak smile. "Good boy."

He jumps to his feet, sloshing wine from his goblet. "VERONICA!" he bellows. In an instant, the girl is at his side. I can barely track her as she moves, she's so fast. "Get me a tiny little cup! The brother must drink also!"

Veronica nods and is gone. I can hear the MC from the arena stating the evening's contests and festivities ("We've posted the Meets! You've placed your wagers! Let's get this party started!"), but my mind can't focus once I realize what Charles is up to.

"He can't drink wine," I insist. "He won't eat or drink anything regular."

Charles's grin turns malicious. "Who said anything about wine, my boy?"

I gulp and focus on the happenings below.

2

Two sets of oval, iron fencing rise out of the sand of the arena floor, creating a track, similar to horse racing tracks I've read about and just as big. At the far end of the arena two cages rise, each holding a furious nec.

"What's going on?" I ask, confused by the entire set up and also by the strange way the necros look. There's something hard about their skin, not the usual dead sweat sheen.

"Racers," Charlotte answers. "There are handlers that raise and train runners to be as fast as possible. Quite an amazing vocation really. They will search far and wide to find the best runners, capture them, and then they spend months preparing them for the arena."

"Preparing them? Like how?" I ask, as I watch two men step onto the arena floor, each approaching one of the cages.

"Their bodies are pumped full of a compound my brother created long ago," she says, giving Charles a warm smile. He nods and tips his cup to her.

"It's a polymer made from pine resin and minerals readily found in the dry lava fields around here," he continues for his sister. "Really quite simple, yet brilliant if I do say so myself."

"Please do say so," Charlotte laughs.

"Brilliant!" Charles responds, laughing with her.

"What does the resin do?" I ask.

Each man pulls a chunk of meat from a dirty, bloody bag and starts slapping the meat against their respective cage.

The necros inside go wild telling me exactly what type of meat is in the handlers' hands.

"Folks! Tonight for our first Meet we have a race! In the right cage is Speedy Gone-off-ez! In the left cage is Santa's Little Helper, the reigning champ, undefeated in the past eighteen races!" the MC announces to the crowd.

"Oooh, Santa's Little Helper! I love this guy!" Charles exclaims with pure joy. "Wait until you see him move!"

"Charles, dear, you're being rude to our guest," Charlotte admonishes her brother softly. "He asked you a question."

"Huh? Oh, yes, the resin." He takes a long sip before continuing. "The resin stabilizes their bodies. By injecting it directly into the flesh and joints, it strengthens them, making their normally spongy, slick flesh, hard and more resistant to stress. The beauty of the resin is it also allows flexibility, so their legs don't lock up and they can push those muscles as far as possible."

I stare at him, my mouth agape.

"Um, you make the necs *stronger*?" I finally ask, completely shocked that anyone would even conceive of such a thought. "What if they get loose?"

"Loose? From where? They're stored below in cages that even the strongest slick couldn't possibly breach. I'd be more scared of the people in the arena than those slicks. Not that I'd want to be the Goal."

"Goal?"

"Just watch, my boy," Charles smiles.

A third cage rises from the sand and inside is a woman. She is dressed in ragged jeans and a torn t-shirt and her eyes are wild as she looks from the crowd to the caged necs and all around the arena.

"Our first Goal is a spitfire that goes by the name..." the MC checks a note in his hand. "Scary Terry!" A section of the crowd erupts into cheers. "I see we have some fans in the stands! Good for Terry!" He looks down at the arena. "Well, enough jabber! Let's race! Handlers, are your Racers ready?" The two men pump their fists into the air. "Excellent! Scary Terry, are you ready to race?"

"I'm ready!" she shouts as she stretches her legs and twists her back, getting her muscles loose and warmed up.

"Love that enthusiasm!" the MC responds, as the handlers exit the track. "Well, I see the handlers are off the track, so without further ado...GO!"

The cage doors click open and Terry is running full out around the track, her legs pumping and feet kicking up sand. The necros are right behind her, their burst of speed stronger than anything I've ever seen.

"I didn't know runners could be so fast," I state, amazed and terrified at the same time.

"Oh, the handlers will spend weeks tracking specific runners to see if they are worthy for our Meets," Charles responds. "A few more weeks of conditioning and injections and you can see what they get: lean, mean running machines."

Terry is a quarter way around the track when three foot spikes spring up from the ground. This must be a regular part of the race since she seems to have expected it and easily leaps the spikes, her feet finding the sand again without missing a step. The necros barrel through, with Santa's Little Helper placing his right foot dead center on a spike, the metal shooting all the way through his foot. The thing gets tripped up and collapses, its entire body now pierced by spikes. It struggles to get itself free, but soon its arms are spiked also and it just lays there, writhing and howling in frustration

The crowd groans. "Oh! Tough break for Santa's Little Helper!" the MC calls out. "But I'm sure his handler will have him patched up and ready to go for next time! Looks like it's up to Speedy Gone-off-ez to chase the Goal down!"

I can see from the look on Terry's face that she has heard all of this and now has more hope she'll survive the race. Her legs pump even faster and her chest heaves from the exertion. At the halfway point, circular blades lift and fall from the track, their spinning metal kicking up sand and spraying it into the air. Terry slows her pace, trying to figure out the timing of the blades. I watch them spin up and then disappear and realize there is no pattern, it's all random. Terry learns this too late as she sets her left foot down and the outside edge of her foot, along with her ankle and calf, is sliced clean off.

"Ooooh! OUCH!" the MC barks. "That has to hurt!"

Terry stumbles to the ground, her right arm instantly separated from her torso as she falls on a second blade. All the blades settle back into the sand and Terry lays there screaming, clutching at her stump. Speedy Gone-off-ez is on her in just a few steps. I'm horrified as the crowd leaps to its feet and cheers this.

"GOOOOOOOOOOOOOOOOAAAAAAAAALLLLLL!" the MC and crowd yell in unison, while Speedy rips into Terry's throat and more blood is added to the already dark pool around her. Soon she stops struggling and is still.

"Well, that was something, wasn't it?" the MC asks the crowd. "Not to worry, folks. The cleaners and handlers will have this all taken care of in just a minute and then we'll be ready for our next race! We always aim to please here at the Meets!"

3

The races go on again and again, but none of the Goals make it; their luck not good enough tonight. As cleaners spread fresh sand in the arena, covering the thickest of the pools of blood, a realization hits me.

"What's going to happen to Lester?" I ask.

Charlotte smiles and Charles points to the arena.

"Our next Meet is a surprise addition! We have a Welcher among us that has returned to pay his debt! While he did pay in full, you all know the rule!"

"NO RUNNING!" the crowd shouts as one.

"Precisely! Now, just to make things fair I will let you, the adoring public, choose his opponent!"

This gets the crowd on their feet and they all lean forward to get a better look at the arena floor. A gate is opened on the side and I gasp as Lester is thrown out onto the sand. He is bloody and bruised with one eye so swollen it looks like someone stuffed it with purple and black cloth. His clothes have been taken away and he struggles to his feet wearing only a loincloth. I can see his mouth moving, but I can't hear what he's saying. From his body language I have to guess he's pleading.

On the far side of the arena the floor a cage is raised out of the sand then a second next to that one and a third. Inside the first cage a young girl beats at the bars, her face is contorted with rage and spit flies from her mouth. There's something about how her small body moves, how her muscles twitch, but I can't place it. The second cage holds an old man, slumped to the bottom and staring blankly out at the crowd. The last cage brings me to *my* feet: three necs slam themselves against the cage's bars. I move closer to the window and stare at the necs. Something isn't right. It takes me a moment to realize they are completely intact. No weather damage, no bite marks or fight wounds.

"The necs aren't an accident, are they?" I ask, turning to the Griffins. "You made those, didn't you?"

Charles claps and Charlotte's face beams. "You are a bright one!" Charles says. "We have other, well, priorities and just don't have the time nor resources to put as much care into their training as the freelance handlers do, but it wouldn't really be much of a sport if we put the weak slicks in there, now would it?"

The spectacle is all a little dizzying. So much blood and life lost. In the past couple days I have seen more people die than I have ever actually known. I don't have any personal connection to these people, but now that I know they exist I don't want a single one to be killed.

Not unless they have to be. I push that thought away as I turn back to the arena and wait to see which cage the crowd picks.

"Is it cage number one?" the MC asks. There is a small cheer and some applause. "Cage number two?" Almost no applause for the old man. "Or cage number three?" The crowd explodes and the MC raises his hands and they quiet down after a moment. "You know what? Since we have a Welcher to punish, how about we open all three?!"

Lester cries out and looks up at the window, but doesn't have time for pleading as the cage doors open and their occupants are freed. The small girl sprints from the cage straight at Lester, her eyes wild, her little body so fast. The old man refuses to move, he just stays in the cage, almost unaware that it is now open. Two of the freed necs run after the girl, their growls still heard above the crowd. The third nec is an obvious shambler and turns toward the old man, seeing an easy target.

"Why doesn't he get up?" I ask. "That nec is going to get

him!"

"Oh, don't worry," Charlotte replies. "The cage will kill him before the slick gets there."

When she says this I notice that the top of the cage is being retracted into the arena floor, but the bottom of the cage isn't moving.

"What? You're just going to crush him?" I exclaim. "That's insane!"

"Staying in a cage that's going to kill you is more insane, wouldn't you say?" Charles counters. "He can move at any time."

Lester's screams draw my attention away from the old man and I see the girl has chased him down, knocking him to the ground. Her hands claw at Lester's naked chest and blood and strips of flesh fly everywhere.

"Impressive, don't you think?" Charles asks. "We train them as soon as they can walk. Their fingernails are replaced with sharpened metal. We change the size as they grow."

"You...?" I can't find the words.

"Oh, that's not all," Charlotte explains. "You're father isn't the only scientist in the world. We all have our hobbies."

"My father? Wait! You know my father?" I yell, getting to my feet.

"We know of him, dear boy," Charles says, placing a hand on my arm and forcing me to sit. "It has never been our honor to meet him in person. Maybe you'll introduce us one day? He has set such the example!"

I start to answer, but Lester's shrieks pull my attention back to the arena floor.

A final scream is all Lester manages and then he's gone. The girl stands on his chest, part of him in her hands.

"Marvelous!" Charlotte claps. "She is a thing of beauty!"

The look on Charlotte's face is almost maternal and I have to wonder what the girl in the arena is to this woman.

"Yes, well, she better watch her back," Charles says

The wild girl raises her arms above her and screams, her whole body shaking with the effort. I turn away when the necs get to her.

"Well, that was disappointing," Charlotte frowns. "We'll have to work on that. Thought we had the dosage right this time."

"VERONICA! Where is that teacup?" Charles bellows.

"Sorry, sir. I couldn't find any clean ones. My apologies. I cleaned this myself."

Veronica hands Charles a tiny teacup.

"Thank you, my dear. Your extra effort will be noted. And your knife?" He holds out his hand and she places the blade in his palm. Charles looks to me as he nicks Veronica's arm and lets the blood drip into the teacup.

"Is that wise, brother?" Charlotte asks, her eyes fixed on Veronica.

"Pish posh," Charles says dismissively "Her blood is as good as any." He looks at me. "Has he had fresh blood before?"

I nod, still unable to speak after what I've just witnessed. Lester... How will I tell Karen and Joseph? Sure, he was way more than just sketchy, but... How will I tell them about any of this?

"Buck up, lad," Charles scolds me, licking the knife blade and handing it back to Veronica. She bows slightly and leaves, her eyes flicking towards me. There's a look there that I don't understand. Charles snaps his fingers. "Quit flirting and pay attention, lad! Adults are talking. You aren't really sad about Mr. Rollins, are you? He betrayed you. He betrayed us. He got what he deserved."

I cringe as the MC's voice echoes over the speakers once again.

"Well, wasn't that a great start to the evening?! How about that little one? She fought hard! The Program just gets better and better with each batch!! Outstanding! But poor old Wesley... He will be missed." The crowd bursts into laughter. "Now, back to our regularly scheduled show!"

I keep my back to the window, not wanting to see what atrocities are next.

"Turn around, Garret," Charles orders. "I can't really feed the little guy with your back facing away." I don't move, but I know Little Man can smell the blood as he starts thrashing against my back, his small grunts getting louder and louder. "Come now, my boy. Don't make this hard for yourself."

Charlotte gets up from her chair and moves towards me.

"Garret? Don't make us angry. We are having such a great time here with you tonight. Let's not spoil it." I still don't move and Charlotte gets so close to me I can feel her breath. "Please?"

I shake my head and before I know it I'm doubled over as Charlotte's fist connects with my stomach. She leans down close to my ear. "Charles is the chatty one. But I'm the real danger. Please remember that."

Charles grabs me by the arm, pulls me to my feet and spins me back towards the window. "Hard lesson learned!"

A man is led out onto the arena floor while three other men outfit him in leather armor that covers his torso and arms, leaving his legs bare. He's handed a spiked club and each of the assistants slaps him on the shoulder as they retreat. I focus on the man as soon as I hear Garth start to feed.

"Oooooh! Isn't he just adorable?!" Charlotte exclaims.

"Look at his little mouth just drink that up!" Charles chimes in.

A shiver runs through my body and I struggle to keep myself together. Why would this be any different than when I feed him my blood? Maybe because I have two psychotic siblings behind me cooing over a nec.

"You all know Jimmy Watts, right?" the MC continues.

The crowd answers with a resounding, "YES!"

"Well, Jimmy has won eight straight here! Eight straight nights of combat all to pay a debt and maybe go home with a little jingle-jingle in his pocket! All he has to do is win one more Meet and he's a free man! Are you all ready to see that happen?"

Interestingly there are boos mixed in with the cheers this time.

"Oh, I hear some of you are betting against Jimmy tonight! Well, good luck to all then!"

The MC steps down as the far wall of the arena is pulled back and ten shamblers slowly make their way onto the sand. Jimmy moves towards them, but stops when parts of the floor move and eight cages rise, their doors opening to fully reveal two broken per cage, all without legs. The creatures claw their way out of the cages and now Jimmy is facing twenty-six total necs. He backs away, giving himself more room and time to think as he assesses the different necs.

"Well, he drank that down fast enough," Charles says, a little bit of disappointment to his voice.

Little Man is energized from the fresh blood and his legs thump against my back.

"Stop it, Garth," I grumble, but he ignores me and starts thumping harder. "Stop it!" I reach back and slap him a lot harder than I mean to. He howls and I can feel his arms flail in anger and frustration.

"That's abuse!" Charles shouts. "You shouldn't do that to your own brother! What kind of monster are you?"

"Now, Charles, you know how siblings can be. We have our tiffs now and again,' Charlotte says. "Neither of us can imagine what Garret is going through."

"Still doesn't make it right," Charles grumbles.

"I agree and I am sure Garret won't be doing that again, will you, Garret?" I don't answer. "*Will you, Garret?*" The menace in her voice makes me turn around.

"No. I won't do that again."

"See, Charles? He can be reasonable."

I give a weak smile and look back at the arena, surprised that Jimmy has already killed four of the shamblers. He dances around two others and decapitates a couple broken before moving back to reengage the shamblers. The crowd cheers him on, pounding their feet against the risers and the vibrations reverberate through the building.

Jimmy ends five more necs, grabbing up one of the severed heads, showing it to the crowd. Their energy intensifies and Charles turns the speaker volume down.

"Jimmy is a favorite," he explains as he stands next to me. "He had a few close Meets, but escaped each time. We let him win last night and tonight is for the people. He's come too far to let lose. Bad for business."

"That's why he only has to face the broken and the shamblers?"

"Precisely," Charles says. "They aren't worth anything so they aren't worth losing."

4

A bell rings behind me as I watch the nec corpses dragged from the arena floor as a triumphant Jimmy is carried out on the shoulders of his assistants.

"Oh, wonderful!" Charlotte exclaims. "Dinner. I'm sure you must be famished, Garret. Am I right?"

The smell of the food that Veronica brings in makes my stomach growl and the denial I was about to voice would now be completely unbelievable. "Yes...I am hungry," I admit with reluctance.

"Oh, not to worry, my boy," Charles says, plopping a heaping mound of mashed potatoes onto a plate. "There's no friends or family in this. Gravy?"

"Gravy?" I repeat.

"Yes, Garret. Gravy. It goes on potatoes. Sometimes biscuits in the morning. Would you care for some?"

I haven't ever had gravy. Mom tried to make it a couple times, but it just ended up being scorched sludge. Kinda like all of her food. "Um, if you are having some," I answer.

"If I'm having some? Well, of course I'm having some! Who eats mashed potatoes without gravy? That's just crazy!" He hands me a plate mounded with potatoes drowned in the brown liquid. He plops two rolls on the side and gives me a fork and napkin. "Sit! Eat and enjoy!"

I take my seat and cautiously push at the food. "These look just like the mashed potatoes in the cookbooks I've read."

"You've never had mashed potatoes before?" Charlotte asks, settling into her chair. "You poor dear..."

"No, I have," I answer around a delicious mouthful. "Just not so well...um, well *mashed*. My mother isn't the best cook."

A sly look passes between the two of them, but it's gone so fast I have to wonder if it wasn't just my tired mind playing tricks.

I glance out the window to see motorcycles performing stunts. They jump through fiery hoops and over cages of necs. Many riders use no hands when doing complicated flips in the air. I've nearly licked my plate clean by the time the show is over.

"Did you enjoy the intermission entertainment as much as you did your potatoes?" Charlotte asks me.

"Yes," I nod. "They're pretty amazing."

"That's good to hear, dear. Very good to hear."

"More?" Charles asks, already loading my plate. I smile and nod.

"That entertainment comes at a high price, which is why the people come here: to see something they can't see anymore. To be wowed!" Charlotte explains. "The motorcycles require fuel and that fuel is a hard resource to come by, as I'm sure you are aware."

"Yeth," I reply, my mouth stuffed with food.

"It's something we want to talk to you about, Garret," Charles says, setting his empty plate aside. "Fuel. You see, your father spoke of it quite often over the short wave. He, of course, thought his transmissions were encrypted, but we have some very tech savvy folks working for us. It's how we found out about you."

"I thought that's why I'm here," I say. "I thought you wanted to know about me and Garth, not gasoline."

Charles's face falls and he acts hurt. It's an obvious act. "Oh my, Garret! Of course we want to know about you and Garth! But there is plenty of time for that." He glances over at Charlotte and smiles. "We are running out of fuel. Not any day soon, but the tanks will drip dry at some point. We would like to avoid that point at all costs."

"Your father knows of fueling caches all up and down the west coast," Charlotte interjects. "He and the Cottage Grove compound have spoken of them quite a bit. Unfortunately, for us, they never gave any specific details. We are hoping you might be able to help with those details."

I stop eating and look from brother to sister and back. "Me? I don't know anything about fuel caches. I really don't know much of anything except for how to keep myself and Little Man alive." I set the plate of potatoes down and stand up. "Which leads me to ask what is going to happen to me?" I ask this strangely without fear. I think the past couple days' events have numbed me to life. Tonight's events certainly have.

"That all depends on you, Garret," Charles replies. "You tell us about the fuel. You help us to understand your special situation and you will be of worth to us."

"Things that are of worth to us we value and keep," Charlotte continues.

"But I don't know where the caches are. Dad never told me."

Charles snaps his fingers and Veronica rushes in and over to him, placing a large folded piece of paper into his outstretched hand. Veronica clears the small side table of plates and Charles spreads the paper out.

The map! It's Dad's map!

"Where did you get that?!" I shout. "My mom had that map! Where is my mother?!"

5

Little Man can feel my agitation and begins screeching and thrashing. Charlotte is at my side, her hand running up and down my arm, trying to soothe me. She leans over and coos to Garth, but he just spits and foams, getting more and more worked up, just as I am.

"Sit down, Garret," Charles says calmly, but his eyes don't match his tone. "Sit down and be calm or Veronica will have to make you sit down and be calm."

"I'm not doing anything until I know where my mom is!" I yell. There is intense pain in my right hand and I'm on my knees in a second, my hand being bent back at a painful angle.

"Calm down," Veronica hisses in my ear as Charlotte walks back to her seat, wiping her hands on her pants as if she had something dirty on them. "Are you listening, freak boy? Calm down or you lose your hand. I will rip it off at the wrist. Don't push your luck."

Charles leans in close to my face, his breath smelling of wine and potatoes and something else, something more metallic, something like blood. "She will rip it off, Garret. And we will let her. Calm down and let's talk as before. Talk as friends."

"I'm not your friend," I struggle to say, the pain so intense.

"But you want to be our friend, my dear," Charlotte says. "Lester decided not to be our friend and look what happened to him."

"You won't kill me," I answer bravely. "You want to know about me and Garth."

"That's what autopsies are for, boy," Charles laughs. "Don't think for a second that you are too important to gut and hang from a pole as a lesson to all! Hell, people would pay to see that, so you are worth something dead as well as alive!"

Veronica moves my hand less than an inch and I'm forced to double over, my face to the floor. "Five seconds, kid," she growls. "Five..."

The pain radiates up my arm and into my shoulder, setting it on fire. I struggle to think, to figure out how to get out of this mess, how to get away from these crazies.

"Four..."

I can't think! I can't reason! All I can see is Dad as he shows me the map. Points out what the different circles mean. What all the markings mean.

"Three..."

The markings on the map. I can picture them. The different colors and what they mean. But...

"Two..."

There are markings on the map that Dad didn't explain. Dots...

"One..."

Dots!

"Wait! I think I know! I think I know where the caches are!" I scream.

"Let him go, Veronica," Charlotte orders. "Let's hear what he has to say."

My hand is released, but the pain remains. I struggle to get upright, every motion sending agony up and down my right arm.

Charles jabs a finger at the map. "Tell us now!"

The fear that had been gone slams back into me. Little Man howls. I look at the map and see the dots. Small orange dots spread out all over the entire map. I can see where our camp was and I follow the road down to where the barn is. Where there were supplies and fuel.

And I see an orange dot.

I start to point this out, but stop, my hand poised above

the map.

"No, Charles. I won't tell you. Not until I get to see my mom."

He blinks several times, dumbfounded. "You realize we are going to probably torture you before we kill you, right?"

I take a deep breath. "Yes. Let me see my mom and I'll tell you where the caches are."

"You want to die, Garret?" Charlotte asks so casually you would think she was asking me if I wanted to go swimming.

"No, I don't," I answer calmly. "But, I don't know where my dad is, so Mom is all that's left. Without her, what's the point? I don't know enough about the world to last long on my own. If you don't kill me, someone else will. It's only a matter of time."

Charlotte and Charles look at each other, a grin spreading on Charles's face. "We have a fatalist on our hands, dear sister!" He claps enthusiastically. "I love it!" Standing he crosses to the window and looks down at the arena. "You want to see your mother? Well, now's your chance, my boy."

He motions for me to come closer, putting his arm around my shoulders when I stand next to him.

"I had a feeling you'd ask to see her. Do you see that person down there? The one in the hood being led into the arena? That's your mother right there. Now you see her."

6

The person in the hood could be anyone. It is obviously a woman, about Mom's size, but unless I can see her face I can't know.

"I don't believe you," I respond. "She's shackled! Why would you shackle my mom? You haven't shackled any of the others."

"Well, it was either the shackles and hood or lose more of my men," Charles answers. "She's already killed half a dozen. Took eight men to bring her down and two of those men won't be walking straight for some time."

"Nice try," I laugh. "You could have at least told me a plausible story. My mom couldn't kill a half dozen *broken*, let alone one man! She's not the most stable person. Tends to freak out and freeze when things get bad. Now, please show me my mother or you don't get your fuel."

His fist is fast and I'm on my knees clutching my stomach once again.

"Don't mess with me, Garret!" he shouts in my face, grabbing my hair and yanking my head back. I can feel Little Man slapping at him, but he doesn't care, just keeps pulling until I feel like my scalp is about to come off. "That is your mother down there! You think we're idiots? Do you think I actually believe that crap about your mother being weak? She tore a man's arm off and killed another with it! That is your mother!"

He lets go of my hair and slams my head against the window, pressing my face into the glass.

"Charles," Charlotte warns. "Don't be hasty."

"Not the time, dear sister!" He pushes his knee into the small of my back, just below Little Man's kicking feet. "Hand me my pistol!"

Garth is enraged like I've never heard him before; his voice is near ear splitting, switching between howls of anguish and screeches of warnings. He's so loud I'm actually in as much pain from him as I am from having my face shoved into the window.

I hear a pistol's hammer drawn back. "Shut this thing up or I will!" Charles roars.

I struggle to shift my gaze so I can see over my shoulder. All that's in my line of vision is Charles's free hand, the one not holding my head, gripping a pistol and pointing at my back. Right about where Little Man's head is.

"SHUT IT UP!"

"I CAN'T!" I scream back. "He's trying to protect me! As long as I'm in danger he'll keep screeching!"

I watch the tension in Charles's hand and wait for him to pull the trigger.

"ARGH!" he yells, shoving away from me.

I collapse on the floor and grip my neck. Little Man's hands grasp at mine, his tiny fingers gripping around my fingers, squeezing and releasing, squeezing and releasing. "I'm okay. I'm okay," I choke out. "Calm down, Little Man."

His volume lessens, but he still protests, emitting grunts and growls punctuated by frustrated slaps and kicks.

"Ready to cooperate?" Charles asks, panting. I look over at him and have to suppress a laugh as I see his braid has come undone. He takes a seat and snaps his fingers. Veronica is behind him instantly, her fingers working to redo the braid. "I'm not giving you another chance, Garret. Now or never."

I glance out the window at the figure they call my mom.

"Take the hood off first," I say. "I want to see that it's her. Then I'll give you what you want."

Charles glares at me and I can see him fingering the trigger guard of his pistol. It's a big one, too, a chrome Smith & Wesson .44 revolver. If I get shot with that, it'll turn my head into a dandelion gone to seed. Bits flying everywhere.

"You have guts, boy," he snarls. He reaches down under the side table and grabs a black phone I hadn't noticed before. Lifting the handset he gives me a wicked smile. "This is Charles. Take off the hood. Kid wants to see his mommy." A look of puzzlement comes over his face. "They what? I don't care if the slicks are riled up. What does that have to do with the hood? Take the damn thing off so this freak will shut the hell up about it!" His face turns red, his anger building again. "Then secure the doors! Brace them however you need to! You're in charge down there; now do your job!" He slams the phone down. "Turn around and take a look."

I do as he says and watch as the MC gives a signal. One of the handlers pulls the hood off and I gasp, stunned.

I asked what else could surprise me tonight...seeing Mom's face is it.

"The crowd grows restless, Charles," Charlotte mentions. "We need to give them a show or we could have a riot soon. They've paid to see and if we don't deliver we can't blame them for getting upset."

"Get upset? To hell with the crowd! I'm upset!" Charles barks at her.

My back is to them both, my eyes fixed on Mom's face. Both lips are split and she has a nasty gash across her forehead that is oozing blood. Her left eye is swollen shut and there are various cuts and bruises up and down her bare arms. I turn and face the Griffins.

"I'll show you where the fuel is, but you have to promise to let me and my mother go right away," I say.

Charles laughs. "Not going to happen. Give me...!"

"Charles, the boy is being fair," Charlotte interrupts. She walks over to me, taking my hands in hers. "I am sure we can come to an arrangement, Garret. But first you have to tell Charles what he wants to know. Once he gets this perturbed, nothing can calm him down unless he gets what he wants. I know my brother, Garret, just as you know yours. Now is not the time to be asking for anything."

I search her eyes and realize that this may be the most truth that has come out of her mouth all evening. Looking over my shoulder at the arena, I take a deep breath.

"Fine. You get what you want," I say reluctantly. "Let me

see the map."

Charles tosses the map at me and I catch it. I flatten it out against the window, gesturing as much as possible.

"See the orange dots?" I ask, tapping the paper. I make an exaggerated show of pointing out each spot on the map. Charles gets to his feet, sidling up next to me as I point out the locations. I glance past the edge of the map and can see Mom staring up at the window, now completely aware something is happening up here. "The dots show the caches. At least that is what I think."

"You think?" Charles asks. "You aren't sure?"

"I already told you I wasn't sure. My parents didn't tell me jack about caches or plans or anything." I point to the barn's location. "But this cache had plenty of fuel. I assume the other dots have fuel also."

I place my hand on the window, pretending to lean against the glass and start to tap.

I learned Morse code when I was young. Mom, Dad and I would play a game of hiding and tapping our locations, seeing who could find each other the fastest. It also helped if we needed to communicate when we knew necs were around. Necs can't tell Morse code from a woodpecker.

"Stop fidgeting," Charles barks.

I tap to Mom that I'm okay and I'm trying to get her set free. I casually look down at the arena and she shakes her head. I insist I can get her out of here. Her eye is blinking, but I'm too far away to see what she's saying.

"I said to stop fidgeting," Charles yells, shoving me away from the window. He folds the map and tosses it to Veronica. "Send a biker to the four closest locations. I want verification that the fuel is there." He points a finger at me. "Sit your butt down. The show is about to start."

"Show?! What show?! You said you'd let my mother go!" I yell at him.

Charlotte laughs and puts her hands on my shoulders, forcing me into my seat. "That's just what you wanted to hear, Garret. There was never a deal made. We aren't Welchers after all." I feel her pat Little Man's head and he growls at her. She crosses to the window, taking Charles's arm in hers as they stare down at the arena. "This should be quite the spectacle. The crazy mom versus Big Timber. Should we warm her up with some of the lesser slicks?"

"Great idea, dear sister," Charles says, pounding on the glass. The MC looks up and Charles gives a thumbs up then puts up five fingers and brings his hand across his neck. The MC nods and starts barking orders to his assistants. "This should be quite exciting."

"You people are insane," I snarl, looking about the room for a weapon, for something to fight my way out.

"Insane? No, my boy," Charles responds without turning around. "The world is insane. We've only adapted to it. You should get inline. A little perspective goes a long way."

"Shhhh, you two," Charlotte hushes us. "They're unlocking her chains." She claps her hands together exuberantly. "This is so exciting!"

My mind is numb and I struggle to work out a plan to save Mom while I watch her stand alone in the middle of the arena. Then five cages rise from the floor and the nightmare begins.

CHAPTER NINE

I'm out of my seat and at the window in a blink. "Those are all runners! You can't put them in there with her! Stop this!"

"Sit down, Garret," Charlotte scolds. "You're embarrassing yourself."

"Embarrassing myself? You stupid cow! That's my mother down there!" I yell at her.

Her hand is fast and it stings as it smacks my cheek.

"How dare you! You rude little monster!" she screams. "I've been nothing but kind to you! If you won't sit then at least be quiet!"

I hold my cheek and Little Man grumbles in sympathy. If I make it out of here I'll be nothing but black and blue bruises.

I stay quiet and watch the nec cages open, their occupants worked into a frenzy by the smell of all the flesh in the arena. Mom just stands there, unmoving, her back to the necs and her face looking up at me. I pound on the glass and point behind her, but she doesn't move, just stands there, her good eye locked onto mine.

Is she freezing up? The woman Charles described didn't sound like my mom at all, but this woman, stuck in place, is certainly acting like the mom I know.

"Dear me, Charles, this isn't going to end well," Charlotte states. "Do we have another Meet ready in case this one is cut short? The crowd has paid to see Big Timber and this woman doesn't look like she'll make it past the warm-up."

"Not to worry, sister," Charles assures her. "I have watched this woman in action and she is remarkable."

The runners are only feet from Mom and I feel like the air has left the room. I struggle for breath and wish I could close my eyes, but I can't.

"And here we go," Charles announces as the first runner reaches for Mom.

She spins on her heels and plants a knee in the mid-section of the nec, doubling it over her leg. In one fluid motion she snaps the thing's neck, ripping its head right off. She let's the headless corpse fall and throws the head at the next closest nec, knocking the thing off balance.

A roll and a leap and she ducks under one nec, is over another that dives for her and has her fist embedded in a third, ripping its spine out through it's chest before whipping about and clubbing the fourth with the petrified spine, crushing its skull, leaving it motionless.

My jaw drops. "Did...? Did she just...?"

"It's a brand new day for you, young Garret, isn't it?" Charles laughs.

Flicking goo from her arm, Mom throws the spine to the sand and crushes it under her foot then looks up at me. I can do nothing but stare at her.

"Close your mouth, dear," Charlotte says. "Don't be a mouth breather."

I don't even question the order as I click my jaw shut. Little Man grunts and growls, his hands clawing at my shoulder.

"Ooooh! Look, Charles!" Charlotte coos. "The little one wants to see its mama!"

Charles glances at Little Man and nods. "As well it should. The mother is impressive."

Is this all happening?

"Turn around, Garret," Charlotte insists. "Let him see!"

I mechanically turn so Garth can get a better view and he quiets down then starts to hoot and spit, slapping his hands against the glass.

"Yes, yes, little one," Charlotte coos some more. "That's your mama down there! She's a fighter just like you are!"

The crowd is in a frenzy as the two remaining necs get to their feet and charge. Mom drops to the ground, letting one nec flip over her back while she sweeps the legs out from under the second nec. Her boot comes down and crushes the tripped nec's skull then she spins about and kicks out, her foot impacting with the last nec's face. She connects with such force that the nec's head separates from its torso and flies across the arena and the crowd's cheers make the window's glass vibrate and sing.

"Oh! Splendid!" Charles applauds. "Brava, Mrs. Weir! Brava!"

My mom stands in the middle of the sand, her chest heaving from the exertion. She looks at me for a moment then stares directly at Charles. Drawing her finger across her throat, she grins and points up at the window.

"How dare she," Charles growls.

The MC steps to the podium. "Well, how about that show?!" He winces at the crowd's ear-splitting response. "Don't say you didn't get your money's worth tonight! Of course, that isn't all! I know you want to see Big Timber, right?" Another deafening response. "But, how about we let this little lady get warmed up some more, eh? She dispatched five in minutes. Let's see how she does against ten!"

And the cages lift.

"Oh, Charles, Mr. MC is doing a fine job this evening," Charlotte states. "He knew you'd want to drag this out more, build the tension and anticipation for Big Timber. We should increase his rations, don't you think?" Charles doesn't answer, only glares down at Mom. "Charles? Charles, I'm speaking to you!"

He waves her off. "Not now, Charlotte. Business later..."

She rolls her eyes and focuses on Little Man instead. "May I feed him again?"

"Knock yourself out," I grunt.

"Oh! You boys are no fun at all!" she complains and snaps her fingers. Veronica is at her side in a moment, handing her a knife and strip of fabric. "At least you can be relied upon, Veronica. Thank you."

The girl nods and leaves as Charlotte cuts herself and soaks up the blood.

Little Man whips his head around at the smell and starts to spit and foam, leaning his body out as far as possible.

"Hey! Knock it off! You'll make us fall over!" I shout.

"Be nice, Garret," Charlotte scolds, which I'm beginning to believe is her favorite voice. "He's just a hungry little guy."

Little Man rips a long and harsh fart and Charlotte jumps back. "Oh, my...," she says, waving at her nose. "That isn't very civilized."

"What did you expect? You're feeding fresh blood to a dead baby," I laugh. "You think roses would sprout from his butt?"

"Quiet, please," Charles mutters, both his hands resting on the window, his face controlled rage. "The cages are rising."

I focus back on Mom and see that she is paying attention to the cages this time.

"This shouldn't take long," Charles sneers. "I'll be damned if I let her survive to fight Big Timber."

"Charles! And risk having to give all those refunds!" Charlotte exclaims.

"We don't give refunds!" he snaps back. "Anyone has a problem and they can be the one to fight Big Timber!"

Charlotte purses her lips, but doesn't say anything.

The cages are raised halfway then pause. The crowd boos.

"Come on! Come on!" Charles growls. "Get those cages moving!"

The phone behind us rings and Charlotte looks over her shoulder as she happily feeds Garth. "Are you going to answer that, brother?"

"Veronica!" Charles shouts and the girl is at the phone instantly.

Listening for a moment, she pulls the phone away and covers the mouthpiece. "Two of the cyclists have collapsed, sir. One got his leg caught in the chain mechanism. They are getting it cleaned out now and should have the cages up in a few minutes."

"People power, my butt!" Charles shouts, pointing a finger at Charlotte. "I told you we should have just used a generator."

"And waste all that fuel? Lose all that profit?" Charlotte scoffs. "Generators break down also, brother. You'll always be wrong on this point no matter how many cyclists expire." Charlotte can see my quizzical look and continues. "The entire arena is run using bicycles connected to chain drives. Saves on fuel. Sure, we lose some of the cyclists now and again, but they have a debt to pay. If they didn't want the risk they shouldn't place the bets!"

"Hear, hear!" Charles agrees.

The necs in the half raised cages grab and beat at the bars, furious they can't get at the flesh that now is circling the cages, studying them closely.

"They better get a move on!" Charles shouts at Veronica. "Call them back and tell them they have thirty seconds or heads roll and guts spill!"

"Speaking of, should we order the second course? I'm a little peckish," Charlotte asks. "Charles?"

"Whatever you want, dear sister," Charles says absent-mindedly. "It's up to you."

I can hear Charles muttering a countdown under his breath and by the time he gets to five the cages start to move once again. "Lucky..."

Mom waits directly in front of one of the cages as they lock into place, infuriating the nec inside.

"Interesting strategy," Charles states. "Usually the idea is to stay away from them. But this woman is hardly usual, is she, Garret?" He gives me a quick wink then returns his attention to the arena.

I can hear Charlotte conversing with Veronica, having finished feeding Little Man, who is now contentedly drumming his fingers along my back, and they seem deep in discussion about what to have for the second course.

"I'm not hungry," I state.

"Growing boys need their protein," Charlotte insists. "I'm having a roast sent up."

"Anyone you know?" I snipe at her.

Charles lets out a short laugh and Charlotte ignores me.

The cages unlock and the necs dash from their confines. Mom grabs the nec coming at her and tosses him aside, taking his place and shutting herself inside the cage. The crowd boos and hisses as they throw bits of trash onto the sand.

"What?! She can't do that!" Charles shouts, banging his hands against the glass. 'That's not allowed!"

"You have a rule book for these Meets, do you?" I ask, a big smirk on my face.

"Shut it, boy," he snarls back. "No more lip."

"Or you'll smack it?"

"Or I'll cut them both off and roast them for a late night snack!"

I gulp and quiet down. Charlotte tsks behind us, but doesn't intervene.

The necs surround the cage Mom has shut herself in. Their hands and arms reach through the bars at her.

"What's going on?" Charles demands. "I can't see her! What's happening?"

Most of the crowd is on its feet, jeering and cursing, calling for action and blood. Mom is completely lost from sight as the necs try to claw their way through the bars, their hunger pushing them on. One of the necs stumbles back, howling, its left arm missing at the elbow. Another falls back from the cage then another and another, all missing arms. A nec tries to shove its face through the bars, but it becomes wedged. The back of its head explodes outward as an arm bone is shoved through it.

The crowd is almost silent for a moment then swells back to its violence induced euphoria. They stomp and cheer, slapping each other on the back, calling for more.

The rest of the necs fall away from the cage, all now one-armed. Mom slams the cage door into an attacker, knocking it away. She grabs hold of the door and swings out, bringing her legs up, pile driving her boots into as many nec heads as she can. The crunch and crack of dead skulls rises above the crowd noise like gunshots and three necros fall to the sand, still forever.

"Incredible," Charles whispers.

"Maybe you shouldn't kill her?" I pose to him. "She could have value."

"Oh, she has value," Charles says and rubs his fingers together. I have no idea what this means and my face must show it because he sighs and rolls his eyes. "Cash, my boy. Currency, money, legal tender. Look at them down there! They're scrambling to place bets, change bets or add to their current wager! I get a piece of all of that, whether she wins or loses."

"*We* get a piece of that, brother," Charlotte reminds him.

"Of course, dear sister, *we* get a piece of that," he corrects. "Thirty percent of every wager. We could get more, since who is going to argue, but why be greedy, right?"

I don't answer this question, wanting to keep my lips.

Mom tosses two necros to the side, reaches into the cage and comes out with a severed arm in each hand. She swings the arms around, connecting with necs, knocking them back to give herself room to move. One of the arms tears at the elbow joint and the top half goes flying across the sand. The crowd loves this and laughter and applause fill the building.

The six necs that remain attack at once and Mom moves forward, putting herself in the center of the pack. She whips out with the long arm, clubs with the forearm, and hops from leg to leg, landing kicks with deadly accuracy.

Minutes pass and only one nec is left standing. It has no arms and the bottom half of its jaw is missing. Mom walks away from it and the crowd starts to boo, but their mood switches immediately as she spins around and throws the forearm, piercing the creature's skull. The nec wobbles for a moment then falls to the sand, the battle over.

Mom turns in a circle, her arms raised and lets the long arm fall to the ground. The crowd eats it up and the building shakes with their exuberance. She stops in mid turn and stares straight at Charles. Her mouth moves, as she shouts something up to him, but there is no way for us to hear.

I focus on her lips, trying to make out what she's saying, but can't see that far. Charles cups a hand to his ear and shakes his head, mocking her. She points at him, panto-mimes breaking him over her upraised knee then waves goodbye. The crowd oohs menacingly and many of their faces look to the window.

Charles tries to smile, but I can see he doesn't like being put on the spot. Mom continues to shout and the spectators closer to her whip their heads about to look up at Charles.

The phone rings from behind and Charlotte answers it. "What? ...No, of course not... Why would I put him on?! I just said no!" She slams the receiver down.

"Who was it, sister?" Charles asks, his eyes never leaving

Mom.

"The MC," Charlotte answers, irritated. "He wanted to know if he should have a microphone lowered into the arena for her to talk into. Many of the crowd are calling for her to speak. What a ludicrous thing to ask!"

"Do it," Charles says quietly.

"What? Are you feeling alright?"

"Do it!" he shouts. "Call him back and have a mic lowered in! If she has something to say, let her say it now! This will be the only chance she gets! I'm sending Big Timber in next!"

Charlotte doesn't respond and I glance over my shoulder. Her face is drawn and worried.

"Why are you doing this, Charles? Letting her speak?"

He looks over at me. "Do you want to hear her speak, Garret?"

"Of course," I answer. Charlotte's eyes focus on me and she glares.

"See, sister? The boy would like to hear his mother speak. Call it my compassionate side."

Charlotte lifts the phone handset and waits a moment. "Do it. Lower a mic." She slams it back down and turns to leave. "I'm going to see what is holding up the roast."

"You aren't going to stay for her great announcement?" Charles asks, shocked.

"No. I'm not."

She pushes through the curtains and is gone.

"Hmm. Wonder what's bugging her?" Charles shrugs.

We watch a microphone descend from the ceiling and I have to wonder why they would have that set up. The MC has his own microphone at the podium.

Charles looks at me and can sense my question. "It's for the dying words. The crowd loves the last breath stuff."

The mic hovers just above Mom, barely out of reach. The speakers squeal and Mom lifts her head.

"Didn't think you had the guts to listen!" she shouts and feedback squelches through the arena, causing many to cover their ears. "I can see you have my son up there. Are you alright, Garret?" I nod and she smiles weakly. "Guess I have some explaining to do, huh?" The crowd gives a hesitant laugh, knowing what she said was meant to be funny, but not getting the joke themselves. "We'll talk when this is all over. Which brings me to what I want to say. I know who you are, Griffins, and I know what you've built here. I may not end it tonight, but I am going to take my son and leave here. Clear out now. It's your only warning."

The crowd noise dwindles to silence, their eyes and heads turning towards the window.

Eerily calm, Charles steps to the phone. "Big Timber," he states flatly. "Now."

"**W**ell! Wasn't that quite the speech!" the MC laughs. "Oooooh, I'm scared now!" The audience laughs with him, but most of it sounds forced. "I just got the call from upstairs and was told the time. I know what time it is, but do you?!"

"BIG TIMBER TIME!" the crowd roars and all are on their feet once again, their enthusiasm for a fight quickly over-shadowing their unease with Mom's words.

"That's right, folks! If you will direct your attention to the far end of our illustrious arena!" The MC makes a sweeping gesture and the lights dim, while two spotlights focus on a spot at the opposite end from Mom. The sand starts to shift and a cage slowly rises. "He's ugly! He's horrible! He's the meanest slick in the history of the Universe! He's undefeated and can't be repeated! I give you BIG TIMBER!"

The cage coming up is easily twice the size of the other cages, with thick iron bars that crisscross throughout. Inside is a nec that defies what is possible. To think a human ever lived that could be so huge...

"Impressive, don't you think?" Charles asks as he stares down at the arena. "That's my baby. I found him wandering down the middle of the highway like a lost puppy. Seven good men died taking him down. Worth every life. Three of them ended up working the arena for a time before being dispatched, so it wasn't a total loss."

"This big boy, this beast, this behemoth weighs in at a whopping four hundred and fifty-four pounds of pure, flesh-eating ferocity! Modifications include a fully rosined body, saw blade implants on the outsides of both forearms, knee spikes and toe blades, you know, for that extra kick"—the crowd laughs at the little joke— "and don't forget the steel cuff surrounding his neck so he doesn't lose his head during a fight!" This gets a bigger laugh, but I can tell they've heard it all before.

"Hardly seems fair," I mutter. "How can anyone beat that?"

"They can't," Charles answers casually. "They aren't supposed to. He's the main event. One hundred and sixty-seven contenders have tried and none have even gotten him to fall over. The fastest Meet was over in two seconds. The longest lasted eight minutes." He turns and looks directly into my eyes. "You should wave goodbye to Mama. This will be the last few minutes you'll ever see her alive."

I rush the psycho and he backhands me, knocking me to the floor.

"VERONICA!" Charles shouts and she's on me in a heartbeat, trussing my arms behind my back. "Strap him to a chair and put him right next to me. I want him to watch every short second of this." She has me bound and placed next to Charles in a minute and he reaches down, grabbing me by the chin. "Close your eyes once and I'll personally slice off your lids."

I spit in his face and he punches me in return. I feel my nose break and blood starts gushing down my face and choking the back of my throat. I gag and spit, bloody foam flying everywhere. Little Man howls at the violence then hoots and reaches around, his hands pawing at my face for the blood.

Charles watches Garth wipe up the blood and lick it off his hands over and over. "That is just priceless! I wish I could show that to your mother before she dies!"

"She'll live and then she'll come for you!" I shout, although I have no reason to believe this even with what I've seen tonight. "You're about to watch your last Meet!"

"Wishful thinking, my boy. Wishful thinking."

The entire time the MC has been announcing, and even

once Big Timber was raised into the arena, Mom never stops staring up at the window. Her eyes burn with cold, homicidal fury, eerily like a nec about to feed and I have to shiver at the sight.

I ask myself once again: who is this woman?

"Your mother is pretty intense," Charles says, a hint of admiration in his voice. "I have to give her credit; she does have guts." He places a hand on my shoulder and squeezes. "Not for long though."

Little Man swipes at him and Charles pulls his hand back, clutching it to his chest. "The thing scratched me! The dirty, little beast scratched me! VERONICA!" I can see Veronica's reflection in the window and for the first time she hesitates. "Girl, get me a kit right now! I need to disinfect this scratch!"

"I...I...," she stutters.

"NOW!" Charles roars and she is gone. He looks at me. "If I feel the burn I'll kill you myself, you hear me?"

"The burn?" I ask.

"The burn of the virus, you idiot! That's how you know you'll turn!" He stares at me. "You really don't know anything, do you?! 'Feel the burn, you're gonna turn!' Every single child old enough to speak knows that!"

"I didn't get out much, remember?" I sneer. "Or is the virus already in your brain?"

His fist connects again with my nose and the pain is excruciating. "I should just kill you now!"

"You will do no such thing, Charles!" Charlotte yells. "He still has uses!"

"But look at what the mutant slick did to me!" he shouts, shoving his barely bleeding hand towards her. "You see? I could be killed! He could have killed me already!"

"Quit whining," Charlotte scolds. "You know it takes more than a scratch to infect someone." Veronica rushes in with the kit and immediately hands it to Charlotte and retreats to the shadows. "Thank you, Veronica. I apologize for my brother's over reaction."

"Over reaction?! Are you kidding?!"

She pushes a chair to the window then grabs a small stool. "Have a seat, Charles. We'll fix it up and you'll be all better, you'll see. The Meet is starting now anyway and I know you don't want to miss it."

Charles grumbles and pouts, but takes his seat while Charlotte sets herself on the stool. She opens the kit, pulling out swabs and disinfectant and starts to clean the scratch as the MC makes one last announcement.

"Ladies and gentlemen! You have seen what this woman can do! You know what Big Timber can do! For this night only, we will give you an extra sixty seconds to increase your wagers! Get that cash flowing, folks! Bet on the time, the limbs ripped off, the quarts of blood spilled! The wager menu is posted for all to see and you now only have fifty seconds! Hurry, hurry, hurry! This is a one time offer and it's going fast! Now down to only thirty-five seconds! I see you hustling! I see you bustling! Will you get those extra credits in in time? Better run! Don't walk! Don't even think of crawling! Twenty seconds left! Oh, how that clock just keeps ticking! This is it folks! Your last chance to bet on what looks to be one helluva Meet! Ten! Nine! Eight! Seven! Six! Five! Four! Three! Two!"

4

"**O**NE!" the MC shouts. "The Meet is on!"

Big Timber's cage clicks open and the giant necro shoves the door aside, making the frame quake and shudder. The door slams against the rest of the cage with such force that one of the hinges' bolts shears right off. The crowd loves this and is on their feet cheering for death and destruction.

"Oh, it looks like BT is ready to crush this little lady!" the MC yells into the mic. "And what is she doing? She's just standing there! Her back to her own demise! I don't know about you folks, but when death comes stomping, I turn around!"

I can see Mom's breathing slow and become more and more calm with each of Big Timber's earth shaking steps. She gives me a quick smile, closes her eyes and I can see her lips moving faintly, before she turns to face the giant nec.

"She better say a prayer," Charles grumbles as Charlotte finishes bandaging his scratch.

"All better, dear," Charlotte soothes. "You can watch your Meet in comfort now." She turns to look at me and frowns. "You are just a mess, Garret. And it won't do to have your brother smearing it all over your face like that. It's just not civilized!" I ignore her as she takes a damp cloth and wipes the blood away. Little Man grumbles and complains, but quiets down quickly. "There. That should be better."

Big Timber is terrifying. If I had come across him in the

woods back by home, I doubt I would have made it. I probably would have frozen in place and just let him kill me. It's like a part of a mountain came alive, died, reanimated and decide it wanted to eat you. Huge!

"Aren't you going to thank me for cleaning you up, Garret?" Charlotte asks, hurt. "It's the polite thing to do."

I don't answer. Why? She's insane. Her brother's insane. This entire arena and scene is insane. How can people live like this? Watching the misery of others, betting on that misery just so they can maybe get a little extra for themselves. It's beyond barbarism.

"Garret!" Charlotte yells. "You are being very rude!"

"I don't care," I snap. "My mother is about to fight for her life. What you consider rude or not doesn't make a damn bit of difference right now!"

I can feel Charlotte's anger, but she doesn't take the bait, instead turns to Charles and pretends like I'm no longer there. I've seen Little Man do the same thing and I have to force myself not to laugh.

"I'll be attending to other business, brother," she says to Charles. "Call me if you need me."

"Fine, sister. Do what you need to. I'd hate for you to miss the death of young Master Weir's mother, though. Are you sure you want to leave?"

I feel her eyes on me. "Yes, I am positive," she responds then stands and leaves.

"Sisters...they can be such a let down, you know?" Charles laughs. "I bet it's easier having a brother. Am I right?" The look on my face must tell him otherwise. "Right. I guess yours isn't exactly a good test subject, eh?"

"Can we just watch the Meet, please?" I reply. "If what you keep telling me is true, I don't have much time to see my mother still alive."

"Fair enough." He looks around his chair and frowns. "Veronica? My goblet, please." She has it in his hand and full in a second. "One for Garret too, please."

"No, thank you. I'm done with that stuff. I'll be watching this sober, if you don't mind."

"Suit yourself." He shrugs and nearly drains the goblet, holding it out for Veronica to fill again. "More for me."

Big Timber has his dead eyes locked on Mom and his rumbling gait picks up speed. Soon he's in an all out mad dash for her, his teeth exposed and face contorted into a rictus of ravenous rage.

Mom sets her legs, wiggling her feet into the sand. I can tell she's ready to pounce, my eyes now able to make the connection between her old "freak out" body tension and her new "kick ass" body tension. Big Timber is almost on her and the crowd is on its feet, booing and cheering. I assume they all want Big Timber to win, but I can see some of the spectators start to turn away or cover their mouths, not wanting to witness the necro rip my mom apart. How many folks are here out of pure desperation and how many are here for sport? The balance of power could turn quickly if I knew that.

"She's holding her ground," Charles laughs. "It really pisses BT off when they do that. He thinks he's being tricked if they slip away. Most don't get a second chance, though." He looks for my reaction, but I keep my face impassive. Little Man farts.

"Holy hell!" Charles waves his hand in front of his nose. "How do you live with that?" I know he doesn't expect an answer, so I don't give him one.

Big Timber's arms reach for Mom and she is under and rolling before he knows it. The giant nec spins about, swiping the air with his forearm blades, almost taking Mom's head off as she comes up from the roll. Unbelievably, she doesn't duck again, but leaps and dives over the arm, tumbling into a forward roll then kicking out with her right leg as she comes out of the roll, her foot slamming into Big Timber's left knee.

I can see the pain on Mom's face and now realize what she's up against as the monster seems unaffected by her kick. She shakes it off and springs to her feet, just out of reach. Big Timber stomps his way to her, his arms swiping again and again. Mom jumps back, matching each swipe, barely able to keep enough distance from the forearms of death.

Her feet slide out from under her and she falls hard on her butt. The crowd groans, with quite a few cheers mixed in, and I can hear an almost collective gasp as Big Timber closes in.

I have to blink a few times to make sure my eyes are working because one second it looks like the nec is going to get Mom and then she isn't there anymore and the giant is flat on his undead face. The sound is sucked from the arena for a moment then is replaced by a glass shaking roar as the crowd explodes in excitement.

"No!" Charles yells, slamming his fist down on his chair, wine sloshing from his goblet. "She can't do that!"

"She just did," I snicker, but quiet down as he turns his wine-addled eyes on me.

"This drags out much longer and I'll have to add some spice to the floor," he sneers at me. "Don't get your hopes up, my boy."

He should have figured out by now that I don't have any hopes.

5

"**R**oast is here!" Charlotte announces gleefully from behind us. "Shall I carve?"

"Please do, sister," Charles replies, smacking his lips. "I'm starving!"

"Oh, well that won't do at all," she grins. "Garret? Shall I carve for you also?"

I can't take my eyes off the arena as Mom dashes from spot to spot, just barely keeping from being beheaded or gutted.

"Garret?! I asked you a question!" Charlotte shouts. "Do not be rude or you will not be allowed to watch anymore of the Meets!'

This outburst takes me by surprise. Did she just speak to me like I was her kid? Who the hell does she think she is?

"No, I'm not hungry," I answer.

"Not hungry what?" she insists.

"Um, not hungry to eat?" I answer, completely confused.

"Always use your pleases and thank yous," Charlotte reprimands. "We've discussed politeness already this evening. I would hate to have to resort to harsher reminders, son."

There it is: 'son'. She really is starting to think she's going to replace Mom when this atrocity of a Meet is over.

"I'll carve a small plate for you anyway, dear. Growing boys, and all that..."

"Light or dark meat?" Charles asks.

"Darkish," Charlotte replies. "That Hispanic family that couldn't pay up yesterday. I think it's the daughter."

I'm doubled over and throwing up before I know what's happening. Hispanic? Daughter?

"Are you alright there, my boy?" Charles asked, alarmed. "You don't have some infection or bug we need to know about do you?"

I retch several times more, swatting Charlotte's hand away as she offers me a towel to wipe my mouth.

"Rudeness!" Charlotte insists, shoving the towel in my hand. "Last warning, young man!"

"Mmmmm, tasty! Is that ginger?" Charles asks around a mouthful of roast.

I gag, but there's nothing left in my stomach to come back up.

"Cloves, brother," Charlotte says. "It's always cloves in the roast. Ginger is for the stir fry."

"Right...cloves." He smacks his lips. "They really bring out the flavor." He leans towards me, grease and juices dripping down his chin. "They can be gamey sometimes."

I turn away quickly, pretty sure I'll throw my own stomach up inside out if I keep looking.

Veronica is at my feet cleaning up my sick. She looks up at me and then back down at my shoe, up at me and back down. I wrinkle my brow, but she doesn't meet my eye as she grabs up the soiled towels and hurries away. I glance down at my shoe and see a bit of white paper sticking out from under it. I spin about, but Veronica is already out of the room.

"Better pay attention, boy," Charles announces. "It's about to get good."

Mom dances away from Big Timber yet again and the crowd boos, their mood turning sour from the lack of real action. I watch the faces and notice how many of them look like the necros I've had to put down over the years. Their mouths twisted into grotesque sneers, many of them with sharpened teeth hungry for flesh. But, most of all, it's the dead looks in all of their eyes. These are a people that have no hope, no life left in them, and are just getting by day to day. They are as dead inside as any of the necs. I laugh to myself and think of dubbing them *Homo Sapiens Fatalis*: The Doomed Humans.

"What's so funny?" Charles asks, a bit of meat flying from between his lips and smacking against the glass. I avert my eyes as it slides down, leaving a greasy trail. "You won't be laughing in a few seconds. The ante is about to be upped."

As soon as he says this I see the sand shift about the arena and different shapes emerge. Poles, spikes, rails, fencing, saw blades; everything that I have seen in the earlier Meets now ready to trip my Mom up. I can see that the design isn't random, but meant to corral her, force her into a corner so Big Timber can rip her apart.

Mom looks about her, dodging a set of spikes that nearly impale her as they burst from the sand at her feet, and grins.

"What does she have to smile about?" Charles frowns. "She'll be dead in a matter of seconds. BT has been trained to avoid the traps. He knows his way through this maze of death like no one else."

Trained?

"Did you say trained?" I ask, unable to let my curiosity go. "He's actually trained?"

"Of course, dear," Charlotte responds. "He wouldn't be the champion he is if he was just a mindless hunk of dead flesh, now would he?"

"But you can't train a nec," I insist. "They're brain dead."

The twins look at me aghast. "Brain dead? How can you say that? Your own brother is living, well, *living dead,* proof that the slicks can think. They can't really reason, but they can think," Charlotte says.

"But, Garth is connected to me. He thinks because of our bond, because he has my blood feeding him, flowing into him!"

"And with a steady and consistent diet of fresh blood and flesh, all slicks can achieve certain levels of brain function. The gray matter changes, hard wires itself so they repeat the actions that allow them to catch and feed the best way," Charles adds. "Big Timber kills in the arena and he gets to feed. We train him with Welchers on a daily basis. Keeps his skills sharp."

And, once again, my understanding of the entire world

changes. Everything my dad taught me, that the necs were mindless killers, that they couldn't truly think, all crumbles away. I stare down at the arena and the maze of hellish obstacles and, for the first time tonight, really realize that my mom is going to die. That she isn't going to come get me, she isn't going to kill these sibling freaks, and that I am going to have to figure out how to free myself or be stuck here forever.

I hang my head in despair.

The piece of paper is still there, the corner of it stained from the vomit that Veronica hadn't quite gotten off my shoe. I grab a napkin close to me and casually wipe at the vomit, plucking the note up, hiding it in my hand.

"Still a little on you?" Charles asks, watching me. "I'll make sure and speak to Veronica about that. I don't like it when details are missed."

I grin weakly and nod. Charles watches me a little longer.

Did he see me grab the note? He turns back to the action as I cup the paper in my hand. Now, I just have to find a moment to read it.

6

Mom hops from rail to rail, ignoring the sandy floor now. She nearly loses her balance, and her legs, as Big Timber takes swipe after swipe at her, but she's able to spring away in time, leaving the nec enraged.

"Huh... No one has ever gone up before," Charles says, actually impressed. "They usually follow the maze like scared rats."

Mom has quickly figured out the "randomness" to the attacks. Leaping, dodging, ducking, spinning, turning, she avoids all the traps and has Big Timber running in circles, doubling back on himself, to get at her.

"Veronica! Phone! Now!" Charles bellows and she appears instantly, placing the receiver in his hand. He holds it up to his mouth and starts shouting. "Ditch the traps! Get the bikers out there now! I want this over with!"

"It s getting a bit boring," Charlotte agrees. "We're losing the crowd. Not enough blood. I can't believe Big Timber hasn't at least cut her."

I can as I think back on my childhood. All the times Mom had zoned out, freaked out, seemed like she wasn't there, none of those times resulted in her getting hurt. I don't remember my mom being wounded once. I've had cuts, scrapes, gouges and some terrible wounds. Even Dad had to heal up after a few close calls with some necs. He was never bitten, but he had to make hard choices getting away, leaving him with several sets of stitches.

Mom never got hurt. Not once.

The rails and spikes, all of it, falls away, back into the sand. The crowd boos, thinking there's a malfunction. Their disappointment is replaced with excitement as the doors at the edges of the arena floor open and several bikers speed across the sand towards Mom.

"Well, lookey here!" the MC announces. "No more hide and seek time! No, siree! Time to die!"

The little grin Mom has been wearing the entire Meet widens and sends Charles into a rage.

"Why does she keep smiling?" he screams. "She's going to die! Doesn't she realize that?"

"I don't think she believes it's going to happen," I say. "That's her knowing smile."

"Knowing? What could she possibly know?! She's trapped! She's the victim! She can only know what I want her to know!"

But Charles is quickly proven wrong as Mom runs at a biker, instead of away from him.

"What is she...?" Charles gapes as Mom times a jump, planting both feet into the chest of the biker, sending the armored man flying off the motorcycle and, unfortunately for him, right at the feet of Big Timber.

The crowd forgets Mom as the biker is ripped apart, his legs torn one way and his arms another, leaving a bleeding, screaming torso. The nec shoves chunks of meat into his mouth, his jaw working and chewing like mad, trying to hurry through each bite so he can stuff more in.

"NO!" Charles yells, jumping to his feet. "That is not how this works!"

"Has no one really tried any of this before?" I ask without thinking. He whirls on me and is about to strike when the phone rings. He pauses as Veronica answers it.

"They want to know if a sniper should take her out, sir," Veronica says, her hand covering the mouthpiece.

"A sniper? Why would I want a sniper...?" But he stops speaking as he looks back down at the arena and the speeding figure of my mom racing around on the fallen biker's motorcycle. "That bitch..."

"Sir? Sniper?" Veronica asks urgently.

"No," Charles answers. "We do that now and we'll have to deal with a riot. Let her have her scooter fun. For now."

"Wise choice, brother," Charlotte agrees. "But we should gather the men at the exits, just in case. Always best to be prepared for crowd control than unprepared."

"Right you are, sister," Charles responds. He nods to Veronica and she gives the order.

It was obvious Mom knew how to ride a motorcycle when I saw her mount the one in the woods when we were first attacked. But the display of skill she is showing now is amazing. Her body fluidly moves, her butt never hitting the seat, as she spins around Big Timber, using him to keep the other bikers away as none of them want to accidentally get too close and loose their heads, or arms or lives.

I see Mom scream, but can't hear her as the crowd noise is too overpowering. She arches her back and nearly loses control of the motorcycle and I can see a large gash on her back as she spins around and speeds away from Big Timber. The other bikers give chase, splitting up to try to trap her. They spin chains over their heads, ready to attack once they have her in range. Mom guns the throttle and aims straight for the far end of the arena, accelerating as she gets closer to the wall. The bikers match her speed and it looks like a race to see if they can catch her before she impacts.

"That's one way to kill yourself," Charles chuckles. "I guess ole Mom couldn't take the pressure anymore."

I grip the edges of my seat, my eyes locked on Mom. "Come on, come on, come on, come on," I whisper.

Mom is ten feet away from the wall when she stands straight up and pushes away from the motorcycle, letting the machine fly out from under her legs and smash into the wall in a ball of flame. She hits the sand and rolls to her feet, wincing slightly. The bikers giving chase whip their heads about, surprised by her move, only one of them having the presence of mind to pull back on the throttle and slow their bike. The rest hit the wall at near full speed, joining Mom's bike in a pile of fiery metal and plastic.

The crowd goes wild!

Many at the end of the collision scramble away from the heat, while others try to grab a smoking souvenir. The flames on the wall spread quickly and doors to the arena floor open from all sides, men and women rushing out with hoses and buckets, hurrying to stop the flames.

The last biker sneers at Mom and guns it, spraying up sand behind him as he races to close the distance between them. Mom sets her legs and everyone in the arena can see she is going to jump...except, apparently, for the biker. The look of surprise on his face is comical and most of the crowd erupts in laughter as he is kicked from his motorcycle and falls to the ground. Mom lets the bike sputter and fall, instead pouncing on the biker, her fist smashing into his face again and again. She rips the chain from his hand and wraps it around the man's neck, dragging him behind as she walks over to the fallen motorcycle. She's on the bike and kick starts it in seconds, before any of the firefighters are close enough to stop her.

The biker claws at his throat, the chain getting tighter and tighter as Mom races back towards our end of the arena and Big Timber. The massive nec had stopped pursuing, even retreated back, as the flames spread. Now the thing starts to run towards Mom, the lure of two warm bodies too much for it to resist.

"Now!" Charles screams. "Shoot her now! VERONICA! Call it in!"

The girl is at the phone and yelling into the receiver, but no shots are fired as Mom races across the arena towards Big Timber. When she is only a few feet away, she lets the biker go and his body tumbles to the feet of Big Timber. The nec is ripping him apart and gorging himself immediately. His distraction gives Mom enough time to turn about and come right back at him. She is off the motorcycle and once again tumbling across the sand, letting the bike speed towards Big Timber on its own.

"NO!" Charles yells, slamming his fists against the window. "NO! NO! NO!"

"Oh God, Charles..." Charlotte gasps, her hands to her mouth. "This isn't happening..."

The motorcycle hits Big Timber square in the back, crushing his legs and knocking him face first onto the sand. His right foot gets caught in the spokes of the bike's back wheel and is shredded completely before the engine sputters and dies. The crowd erupts into chaos, not sure if they should cheer or jeer, as Mom limps her way over to Big Timber.

"Where are my snipers?!" Charles screams, his face purple and red from rage. "VERONICA! WHERE ARE MY SNIPERS?!"

Veronica lets the phone dangle from her hand. "They aren't in place, sir. They usually take a break when BT is up. Now they're all down on the floor helping with the fire."

Charles moves quickly and has her by the throat. "I'll kill you for this!"

I use the time to sneak a peek at the note still clutched tightly in my hand.

I can help get you out of here, it reads. *You have to take me with you. That was one of my sisters. I can't do this anymore.*

Sister? Who was..? Oh, God. That girl. The girl in the arena.

I look up and see Charlotte eyeing me. Her eyes narrow as she sees the piece of paper in my hand. I point at the arena.

"Better pay attention!" I yell. "Looks like Big Timber is about to go one hundred sixty-seven in the wins column, with a big, whopping one in the loss column!"

Charles tosses the choking, gasping Veronica to the floor. The Griffins both rush to the window and gape at the scene below.

Mom yanks a piece of steel from the motorcycle. Big Timber struggles with himself, unsure if he should get his mangled foot free from the motorcycle or continue shoving flesh into his already overloaded mouth. I can see Mom say something to the nec and the creature lunges for her. She sidesteps and brings the metal down, piercing his skull. Grey brain and black blood ooze onto the sand and the giant collapses, still forever.

"NOOOOOOOOOOOOO!" the Griffins scream.

Mom yanks the metal from Big Timber's skull and swings it about as two guards rush her. She catches the first guard in the throat and shoulders the second guard in the chest, knocking him back, giving herself enough time to pull the metal from the first and bury it in the second's abdomen.

The crowd, having grown silent when Big Timber was killed, is now back to its bloodthirsty roar with the added violence. Mom pulls the metal free and flicks the blood from it, splattering gore across the sand. She looks up at the window and points to the Griffins then wags a finger at them.

"She killed our baby!" Charlotte screeches, her hands pulling at her hair. "She killed him like he was some common slick! Like he was an animal!"

Charles whirls on me. "If she kills ours then we kill hers! Veronica! My gun! NOW!"

Veronica fetches the pistol from the side of Charles's chair. He holds his hand out, his eyes focused on me and not her, waiting for her to place it in his open palm. Instead she places the barrel to his temple and pulls the trigger. Charles's head rocks to the side and brain and bright red blood splatter against the window.

I jump and cover my mouth. Jesus, what world do I live in?!

Charles's body sways then collapses on the ground and Charlotte begins to scream.

Spinning quickly, Veronica turns the pistol on Charlotte, but the woman dashes towards the curtain, grabbing up the roast platter and throwing it at us. We duck and she's gone, her footsteps echoing through the large room beyond.

"Should we chase her down?" I ask, ready to sprint after Charlotte.

"No, I couldn't kill her anyway," Veronica states. "They both have special pacemakers installed that monitor their heartbeats. If one dies, fine. If both die then a radio frequency is sent and the entire compound blows up in less than a minute."

"Seriously?"

"Seriously! No more time for chatting! Come on!" She grabs my arm, takes aim at the window and fires two shots, cracking the thick glass. She fires once more and the window explodes outward. "Run!"

"Wait! The map!" I dash to the side of Charles's chair and snatch up the paper, jamming it into my waistband. "Okay!"

We jump from the window, landing on the benches just feet below. The crowd has already realized the show is over and they stampede toward the exits. Screams erupt from each exit as people find the doors shut and bolted.

"Damn!" Veronica curses. "I didn't think they'd react so quickly!" She shoves spectators out of the way and heads straight for the arena floor, yanking me along.

"Where are we going?" I yell above the panicked crowd.

"Only one way out!" she shouts, pointing at the side doors on the arena floor. "Down!"

We hit the edge of the seating and Veronica jumps to the

sandy floor, tumbling, rolling then up on her feet. "Come on!"

I eye the drop and whisper a quick prayer before taking my own leap. The landing is jarring, but I don't feel much pain and am thankful I didn't break anything.

"GARRET!" Mom screams, snapping a guard's neck as she dashes towards us. She eyes Veronica and her face contorts with rage. "Let my son go, you little bitch!"

"It's okay, Mom," I yell, my hands up as I stand in front of Veronica. "She helped me escape the Griffins! She's gonna get us out of here!"

"Then you're gonna take me with you!" Veronica adds. "Right?!"

Mom's brow furrows and eyes narrow.

"Yes, we'll take you with us!" I answer, yanking Mom by the arm. "Just show us how to get out of here!"

Gunshots go off and many from the crowd start screaming. People are pushed from the edge and fall into the arena while others jump on their own. A mob makes a mad dash towards the doors we are almost at and Veronica turns and fires in the air, stopping the mob in their tracks, giving us the extra seconds to get inside.

Veronica slams and bars the doors behind us and I look around. The walls are hard clay, brick and concrete, all jammed together into a patchwork structure. The walls and ceilings are supported by huge timbers and small, yellow lights are strung up to provide some illumination. It reminds me of pictures I've seen of ore mines.

"What did you block the doors for?" I yell. "They'll all be trapped!"

"They're trapped anyway!" she shouts back. "The way out is single file! If that mob gets in here they'll overrun us and clog the passageway!"

"She's right, Garret!" Mom agrees. "It's how they brought me in. It's designed to bottleneck so if the HSNs get free they can be stopped easily."

"But...!"

"No time for debate! Move!" Veronica shouts as the wood behind us groans from the press of the mob. "They'll cave in the exit soon, once they know all the guards are out! We have minutes before we're trapped!"

"Show us the way!" Mom shouts, shoving me forward.

We weave our way past holding cells that have people calling after us, pleading for our help. I cover my ears, trying to shut out the screams and curses that echo after us. All these people that will be left to die only because they made some bad bets.

"We can't save them, Garret!" Mom yells from behind me.

"We can try!" I shout back.

"No we can't!" Veronica yells. "We don't have time!"

Mom puts her hand in the small of my back and shoves. "Keep moving!"

Little Man howls and screams, his voice rising and rising until he's in a full panic, his little fists and feet slamming and jabbing me. I'm about to scream at him to stop when we round a corner and come face to face with cage after cage of necros. No wonder he's freaking out.

"Oh...my...God," I whisper. "There's hundreds of them..."

"And all inside cages! Stop gawking and move!" Veronica calls, keeping her distance from the cages even though the cages are so small they keep the necs tightly confined with no room to move their arms and reach for us. They thrash their heads back and forth, gnashing their teeth while screeching and growling. The noise here is just as bad as the trapped people and it grates on my mind like a hot wire stabbed into a live nerve.

Mom keeps shoving me and we are past the necs in moments, forced single file into a long, dirt tunnel, but Little Man doesn't calm down at all. Instead he doubles his energy and I nearly go insane from it all.

"What's he saying?!" Mom yells.

"I don't know!" I scream back at her, but we find out soon enough as loud clicks rise above the racket of the necs.

"What was that?!" I yell.

Veronica looks back and her face is drawn and white. "Someone opened the cages!" She doesn't say anything as she pumps her legs and sprints towards the end of the tunnel.

"GO GO GO!" Mom screams. "They're coming!"

I don't look back, only focus on Veronica's back and the door beyond that seems so incredibly far away.

CHAPTER TEN

aking it to the door isn't the problem. The door being bolted and sealed is.

"You're not exactly filling me with confidence!" Mom shouts at Veronica.

"I don't get it," Veronica says, puzzled. "This is never sealed like this."

"Does it matter?" I yell, my eyes fixed on the necs rushing at us. "Is there another way out?"

Mom sees a smaller door set back into the wall. "Where does this go?"

Veronica gulps, but doesn't say anything.

Mom slaps her across the cheek. "Where does this go!?"

"The nursery," Veronica gulps. "We can't go in there."

"Like Hell we can't!" Mom kicks out and the door collapses in. She grabs me and pulls me into the room beyond.

I reach out and grab a hold of Veronica's arm. The girl is shaking with fear.

"Come on! You wanted to come with us, right?" I scream at her.

Her eyes meet mine then look past me into the room. I glance over my shoulder and nearly let go of Veronica. I shove the image aside and pull the girl into the room and slam the door.

"What the..?" Mom gasps. "I never thought it was real."

A row of hospital beds line each wall of the long room.

In each bed is a nightmare. A pregnant and squirming nightmare.

"What is this?" I say quietly, my mind struggling to take in the scene. Even Little Man goes quiet. "Are they alive?"

"Not anymore," Mom says as she grabs me and pulls me past the beds of what look like pregnant necs. Tubes and wires are stuck into them from various machines and each of the creatures hisses at us as we pass by.

"I was born here," Veronica whispers as I pull her along. "This is the Nursery."

"You said that, but what are they?" I ask.

The door behind us shakes and shudders as the necs struggle to get inside. The wood starts to splinter and crack.

"They are the Mothers," Veronica whispers again. "It's where we come from. Those of us that survive."

"Enough with the chit chat!" Mom yells. We skid to a halt before two doors. "Which one, girl?"

Veronica stares at the hospital beds and their doomed occupants.

I reach out and take her face in my hands, forcing her to look at me. "Hey, Veronica, you want to leave this place, right? That's the whole point to you killing Charles, right?"

"She killed Charles Griffin?" Mom asks, impressed.

"Shhh," I scold. "Veronica? We need to know which door to take. Do you want to die in here?"

The thought of dying in this Hell snaps her back to reality just as the necs break through the door at the far end of the Nursery. Little Man starts his screeching.

"No. No, I don't," she snarls. "I won't die here!"

A couple of well placed kicks to the door handle and Veronica has the last part of our escape route freed and we burst out into the night air.

"Follow me!" she calls out, sprinting towards one of the buildings at the back of the compound.

The night is illuminated by row upon row of floodlights posted at each corner of the compound. Alarms and sirens blare causing Little Man to protest louder, which I wasn't sure was even possible. Veronica gets about ten yards when automatic fire kicks up dirt at her feet. She comes to a screaming halt and doubles back towards us. I can see muzzle fire coming from a platform just beneath one of the light arrays and Mom and I turn and bolt towards the front of the compound and the main gate.

"The garage is this way!" I shout, bullets whizzing by my head. "We can take one of the cars!"

Veronica passes us both. I can't believe how fast she is.

"Let's hope there're keys for one that runs!" she calls over her shoulder.

Guards turn at the sound of her voice and are about to open fire when the arena doors bust and the panicked crowd streams outside like frenzied animals. People are trampled under foot as they trip and fall; children scream for their parents, but are quickly lost in the throng, their small voices overpowered; friends and family reach for each other, but the press of the mob is too great and people are shoved, pushed, crushed.

The guards turn away from us and their automatic rifles bark loudly as they fire into the onrushing crowd. Bodies collapse onto each other, but the crowd keeps moving, climbing over the fallen and pushing on.

We hit the garage and Veronica dashes to a pegboard at the back. Mom starts checking the cars that don't have hoods open or that aren't obviously missing parts.

"Garret! Down!" she screams, looking back at me.

I hit the dirt and can hear the whoosh of something swinging past my head, followed by a loud clang. Mom is sliding over a car's hood and leaping past me as I roll away from the unseen attacker. I get to my feet and see Mom bending back Milo's wrist and yanking a large wrench from his grip. I turn away as she brings the wrench down, the thick crunching sound turning my stomach.

"Check his pockets!" Veronica orders. "He'll have the gate keys on him somewhere!"

"Help me!" Mom yells and I scramble over to her. I've just witnessed so much horror and yet the sight of Milo's caved in skull nearly makes me retch. "Keep it together, Garret! You can be squeamish when we get on the road!"

I suck it up and start searching Milo's pants while Mom tugs at his jacket, searching it inside and out.

"He's got nothing on him!" Mom shouts at Veronica. "Can

we bust through?"

"Ah ha!" Veronica shouts, holding up a set of keys. She looks at the tag on the keychain then surveys the garage. For the first time I see a genuine smile spread across her face as she points to the far end of the garage. "We can bust through anything with that!"

Mom and I look to where she's pointing and behold what could only be called one helluva truck. As we run over to it, I can see the words Dodge Power Wagon stenciled and faded on the side.

"What's so special about this one?" I ask.

"V-12 engine, locked hubs for four wheel drive and enough size and force to punch through a brick wall," Veronica grins. "It's Travis's baby and the only reason it's in here is because it got a new timing belt. He'd kill us all for even looking at it."

"Sounds about right," Travis's voice growls from the front of the garage. "I'll start with you."

We all dive for cover as he opens fire. Bullets bounce around the garage, ricocheting off the other cars and metal equipment. I feel a sting at the side of my head and wince, but there's no time to investigate as Travis steps into the garage, trying to get a better line of fire on us.

Mom tosses the wrench across the garage and it clatters against the wall, distracting Travis for just a moment. It's all the time Mom needs as she clambers over the hood of the car we're hiding behind, rolls across the roof and kicks out with her right leg. Her foot connects with Travis's jaw and his head rocks back. He stumbles, the back of his hand to his face.

"I'm gonna rip you open for that," he snarls.

Mom doesn't give him a chance as she kneels low and punches him directly in the crotch. The big man sucks in breath and collapses instantly, the gun falling from his hand as he clutches between his legs. Grabbing him by the back of the head, Mom hits him hard once, twice, three times in the face and he's out cold. She searches his pockets and comes up jingling a set of keys.

"I'm guessing the gate key is on these," she says with a wolfish grin. She gives Travis a hard kick to the mouth and his teeth shatter into a hundred tiny, shiny metal bits. "Let's see you rip anything open without your chompers, punk!"

"Damn," Veronica says, impressed. "We're gonna have to compare training notes when we can."

"Oh, I already know all about you," Mom smiles. She rushes around and opens the passenger side door. "Get in, Garret! Veronica is driving!"

Veronica doesn't question, and neither do I, as we both leap into the truck. Mom is in and pulling on her seatbelt.

"You too, son. This is gonna get rough."

I adjust the middle lap belt and click it shut. Veronica secures her own and starts the truck up. It roars to life and she hits the gas, sending us rocketing from the garage and towards the double gates that lead the way out of the compound.

We hit the first gate and the metal sheers away, collapsing under the power of the truck. Bullets ping off the truck bed and Mom shoves my head down as we slam into the second gate. Instead of splitting to the side, the gate holds together, ripping from its hinges and flying up over the hood. The windshield shatters, but Mom has her legs over the dashboard and is kicking out the remaining glass in an instant. The cool night air slams into our faces as Veronica guns the engine and we speed away from the compound, the screams, gunfire and sirens getting quieter and quieter as the distance grows between us and that hellhole.

2

"We only have half a tank and you want to go where?" Veronica asks as I spread out the map on my lap.

"We parked the RV here," I say, my finger jabbing a point on the map that I hope is where Karen and Joseph still are. Not that I care too much about those two, since they obviously knew Lester was setting me up. "The RV has quite a bit of fuel. We retrieved it from one of our caches."

"The Power Wagon is diesel," Veronica states. "It won't take gasoline."

"The fuel is diesel. If it's the fuel from the barn," Mom says, looking at me. I nod as she takes the map from my hands, studying the route I pointed out. "The RV has a military grade EFV multi-fuel engine. It can run on anything from diesel to cooking oil to kerosene."

"EFV?" Veronica asks, astonished. "Isn't that Marine Corp? How'd you get one of those?"

Mom grins. "I'm a woman of mystery."

"Not sure if I like the mystery," Veronica says, watching Mom out of the corner of her eye. "If you could get one of those then you had clearance that very few had before it all went to hell."

"Who are you?" I turn and ask Mom. "What happened to the scared woman that raised me? The one that froze when a twig snapped? The one that could barely boil water let alone kill an arena full of necs?"

"We'll talk about that later," Mom answers, nodding towards Veronica. "Right now we need to get to the RV. There's more than fuel on board."

"Um, yeah, there is," I say sheepishly. "The RV is probably still occupied."

"Occupied? Garret, why would our RV be occupied?"

"Well, how do you think I got to that compound in the first place?" I snap at her. "I couldn't have found it on my own, now could I?"

She gives me a look I know well and I shrink away. Little Man grunts a few times, but he's pretty exhausted and quiets down.

"Do you need to tell me something, son?" Mom asks in a tone I do not want to refuse.

I take a deep breath and start from when I stumbled my way back to the RV and proceeded to pass out.

Her eyes go wide and her hands shoot to my head, turning it this way and that. "Concussion? You're lucky you didn't die in your sleep!"

"Let me finish," I say, swatting away her hands. I continue with how I woke up to Lester, Karen and Joseph around me and their reaction to Little Man. Mom tries to interrupt a few times, but I talk over her and she gets the idea that I'm not stopping until I'm done. When I finally do finish she has a new look in her eyes.

"You made it through all of that on your own?" she asks, bewildered.

"No, not on my own. Weren't you paying attention?"

"Sounds like you were hindered more than helped a few times," Veronica chimes in. "You deserve quite a bit of credit for making it this far. You're lucky your crush didn't get you killed."

"Crush?" I start to respond, but Mom interrupts.

"Tell me more about these kids," Mom orders, her voice serious. "You said their uncle was the surprise Meet tonight and he brought you to the compound to trade off his debt? What do you think they knew about his plans?"

I have to think hard about this. My first reaction was to believe Karen and Joseph were in on the deception, but as I told my story and went back over the events of the past couple days, my mind started to change. Now, I don't know what to believe. And there was the thing the Griffins said about how they liked kids. Was Lester really going to give Karen and Joseph over to those nutjobs? To say I'm confused is an understatement.

"Garret? Where are you?" Mom asks, waving her hand in front of my face. "What can you tell me about the kids? Did they know or not?"

"Karen isn't a kid," I answer, probably a little too fast from the look Veronica and Mom share. "I mean, she's nineteen and helps take care of Joseph, so she has a lot of responsibility."

"Uh-huh...right," Mom mocks. "I'm sure she does have a lot of...responsibility."

"I don't even know what that means." I frown.

"Do you trust her?" Mom asks.

"You're going to ask a seventeen year old boy if he trusts a nineteen year old girl?" Veronica asks. "He'd follow her to the ends of the Earth like a dog!"

"Hey!" I snap. "You look like you could be nineteen! I wouldn't follow you!"

My words are like a slap to Veronica and I can see I've hurt her.

"Okay, calm down," Mom says, patting my leg. "Let's forget the girl. What about the boy?"

"Joseph? He's scared of his own shadow! I couldn't see him really knowing anything about Lester's plan. He'd have given something away."

"You'd be surprised, kid," Veronica snorts. "Anyone is capable of anything in this world. He may not have known the details, but he probably knows his uncle well enough to know that Rollins is a slimy bastard."

"Sketchy," I correct.

"What?" Mom asks.

"Sketchy bastard. That's kinda what Karen thinks of him."

"You knew he was sketchy and you still went with him?" Mom asks, shaking her head. "I thought you had more brains than that."

I think back on all the times Karen and Joseph shared looks, or avoided answering my questions directly. I try not to admit it to myself, but now I have to really wonder if they knew he wasn't bringing me back. Back and forth, back and forth. My mind can't make itself up.

"Take a right here," I instruct and Veronica makes the turn. "Should only be a mile or so up around the bend."

"I know you haven't been around people your whole life, Garret," Mom says. "And that is why it's hard for you to figure out if these other kids can be trusted or not. You are going to have to assume that they knew and that they are just waiting for their uncle to come back."

"But..." I protest.

Mom shakes her head and looks out the windshield. "I'm sorry, Garret. I really am. I've always wanted you to be able to make some friends, especially since they sound like they adjusted to...well, you know."

"Garth, Mom. His name is Garth."

"I know what his name is!" she snaps at me. "Regardless, they can't be trusted. At least not right away. We'll tell them what happened to their uncle and see how they react. I'm a pretty good judge of character. If they knew, I'll see it on their faces. If they didn't know, well, we'll just have to go from there." She turns back to me and her face is hard. "We still have to find your father, don't forget."

Right... Dad... I *had* forgotten...

Little Man lets out a long, loud fart, but luckily we have no windshield.

Family...

No RV.

"There's no RV, Garret," Mom says as we come around the bend in the road where the RV should be.

"I can see that, Mom," I respond.

"Are you sure this is where it should be?" Veronica asks, slowing the truck down. "We don't have much fuel to go searching."

"See those two trees leaning next to each other? And that rock on the edge of the road? "I ask, pointing at both land-marks. "That's where the RV was. This is the spot."

"They could have pulled it off the road," Veronica sug-gests. "Hidden it."

"They weren't supposed to," I respond. "They were going to gas it up and then wait for us to get back. If we weren't back by morning they were going to leave."

"Leave?" Mom exclaims. "Just leave you?"

"What else could they do? You've pointed out several times they're just kids. You wouldn't want me just hanging about, would you? Exposed to any necros or SATs that may come by?"

Mom doesn't answer, but I can see she gets my point.

"We need that fuel," Veronica insists. "We won't make it to the Tribes without it."

"Leaving us in bad territory," Mom adds. "That's not good."

"What are the Tribes? And the Keep?" I ask, looking from

one woman to the other.

"Tribes are the Native Americans that banded together when everything fell apart," Mom answers. "They are brutally protective of their lands, as well they should be. Of all the population they were probably the most prepared, unfortunately, since so many were living a hand to mouth existence anyway."

"And the territory between here and there is worse?" Neither answer. "Worse than the Griffins?"

"Yes," Veronica says and she looks away. "They're our cast-offs."

"Leave it be, Garret," Mom says. "You don't need to know more. The SATs are bad, but the land without any type of order is unimaginable."

I start to open my mouth, knowing that Veronica has more information, but Mom shakes her head vigorously. I swallow my words and reach across Mom for the door handle. "Well, we should at least look to see if they left a note or if they did pull off the road."

"We don't have time for this!" Veronica snaps. "Charlotte will have bikers combing the area. We can take a few of them out, but unless you have an arsenal, they'll eventually cut us down."

"Don't have time. Don't have fuel," I repeat back at her. "Sounds more like we don't have a choice. Whether Karen and Joseph knew what Lester was up to or not, they'd still be here. We need to look." Veronica looks at Mom and she just shrugs. "Is that a yes?"

"Yes," Mom answers, opening the truck door. "Fifteen minutes then we need to hit the road. Low fuel or not, we can't just wait here."

We pile out of the Power Wagon and start to search the area, but it's near impossible in the dark.

"Is there a flashlight or something in the truck?" I ask.

"No," Veronica responds quickly. "All supplies are kept under lock and key until needed. Keeps the pilfering down."

"Which brings up our other problem," Mom says. "We have no water or food. We aren't going to last long once the sun comes up."

"More importantly, we don't have any weapons," Veronica

adds.

"You have the pistol," I point out.

"One cartridge left," she sighs. "Kinda want to keep that for myself, if you don't mind."

"One bullet won't do you much good," I start to laugh then realize what she's really saying. "Oh...right..."

A twig snaps and we all freeze. Mom picks up a hefty piece of fir lying on the ground and has it at the ready. Veronica has her pistol up and is scanning the darkness when another twig snaps.

I can hear a pitiful attempt at a 'shhhhh' and have to laugh out loud.

"Karen? Joseph?" I call out. "It's me. Garret. I have my mom with me. Come on out, guys."

"You're an idiot," Karen grumbles and I hear a hard slap.

"Ouch! Watch it!" Joseph yells.

The two siblings exit the woods only a few feet from me, both holding shotguns at the ready.

"You mind lowering those?" Veronica warns, her pistol trained on Karen. "I'd hate for an accident to happen."

"Is this your mom?" Karen asks, her eyes narrowing as she looks Veronica up and down. "She looks kinda young, isn't she? And not very modest."

"No, I'm Garret's mother," Mom says stepping forward.

Karen whips the shotgun around and points it at Mom's chest. "Where's Uncle Lester?"

"He didn't make it," I say, watching for their reactions, but it's so dark I can't really make out their features well enough.

"What happened?" Joseph asks. "Did the SATs get him while he helped you guys escape?"

"Well, *he* doesn't know anything," Mom says to Veronica.

"How about you, sweet cheeks?" Veronica asks Karen, moving to the side. I can see she's making Karen choose between covering my Mom or Veronica.

"How about me, what?" Karen snaps. "What happened to Lester?"

"Do you care?" Mom asks, taking a step closer. "He wasn't your real uncle, right?"

Karen hesitates, looking from Veronica to Mom and back. "What are they asking me, 3B?"

"3B?" Mom asks, but I wave her off.

"Lester set me up, Karen," I say. "He was trading me in to cover his debts."

"Debts? What debts?"

"He'd been gambling on the Meets," Veronica interrupts. "He was a steady loser. He ran instead of paying the fifteen pounds of flesh he owed."

"Fifteen pounds of flesh?" Joseph asks. "What does that mean? Meat? Like deer?"

"No, kid, not like deer. Like his leg or arms."

Karen lowers the shotgun. "That's where he would disappear off to... Makes sense now."

"She doesn't know anything," I say, reaching for Joseph's shotgun, taking it out of his hands.

"We still don't know for sure," Mom says, reaching for Karen's.

"No, you don't," Karen states, jumping back, the shotgun leveled at Mom once again. "But I don't know if what you say is true or not, either. So I'll just hang onto this until I'm sure."

"Don't push it, girl," Mom snarls. "You don't want to tangle with me."

"Or me," Veronica says before she takes three quick steps and has the shotgun in her hands, knocking Karen to the ground. "Jeez, Garret, I figured you'd have picked a more rugged type. She's a little weak in the knees."

"Stop!" I yell. "They don't know anything! I'll vouch for them!"

"You're being stupid, Garret! We cannot trust her!" Mom yells at me. "The boy is obviously clueless, but she's too old not to know something was going to happen!"

"If I didn't know Lester was going to hurt my parents, do you think I knew he was going to set 3B up?" Karen shouts.

"What?!" Joseph cries out. "He hurt Mom and Dad?"

Veronica lets the shotgun lower slightly. "Man and a woman? In their forties, maybe? She had short black hair? He might have had a beard? Reddish?"

Karen stares at her for a bit. "Yeah. How did you know?"

Veronica hefts the shotgun onto her shoulder and holds out her hand. Karen glares at it. "Come on, girlie. I believe you. No hard feelings."

Karen takes the hand and Veronica helps her to her feet. "Why?" Karen asks.

"Because your parents were used as Goals," Veronica answers sadly. "Rollins traded them in to cover his other debts. He lost betting on your mom. She actually made it around the track in time. That's the debt he was turning Garret in to cover."

"She's alive?" Joseph asks, excited. "My mom is alive?"

"No, kid, she's not," Veronica answers. "She attacked a guard when she found out your father didn't make it around the track. She ended up feeding Big Timber."

Joseph breaks down into tears and sobs and Karen takes him in her arms. "I don't understand anything you just said," she says. "What is going on?"

I fill Karen in on everything that happened throughout the night as we walk the mile down the road to where they stashed the RV, Mom behind us with a shotgun as Veronica and Joseph ride in the Power Wagon.

"That's awful," Karen says, stopping quickly. "I mean, I always had a feeling about Lester, but that's such a horrible way to go. Hold still."

"Hold still? Huh..? I..! OW!" I yell as Karen quickly resets my nose. She rips a part of my t-shirt off and hands it to me. "Um, thanks? I agree about Lester, by the way. No one should be subjected to that. At least Mom killed their main attraction and after everything that went down I doubt anyone will be back for anymore Meets, even if Charlotte tries to keep them going."

"Don't hold your breath there," Veronica laughs. "Charles may have been the loud one, but Charlotte was quite a bit of the brains. She'll rebuild if she has a chance. And people will always be desperate enough to go along with it."

Karen leads us off the road to a break in the trees where the RV stands waiting.

"We couldn't really hide it too well," she says. "But it made us less of a target."

"Did anyone come by?" Mom asks as she opens the door and steps inside.

"No, but we kept hearing motorcycle engines," Joseph

replies. "Kinda freaked us out. The sound just echoes around here."

"Yeah, we'd use that to our advantage," Veronica says. "Get the prey confused then close in on them." She looks at us quickly, realizing what she just said. "Sorry…"

"You do what you have to in this world," Joseph replies.

Karen and I look at him with surprise then at each other.

"Wow." Veronica grins, slapping Joseph on the back. "Pretty profound, kid."

"I have my moments," Joseph smiles.

"We better get a move on," I say." There's fuel in the bedroom. I'll grab a couple cans and we can get the truck filled."

As I step into the RV, Mom quickly tucks her hand behind her, obviously hiding something.

"What's that?" I ask, not in the mood for more secrets.

"Nothing to concern yourself about," she says and I hear a rattle as she tucks something small into her front pocket. "We have more important issues."

"Yeah, we do, but don't think I won't ask again. I'm done being left out of the loop. Once we're on the road and safely away from here, you and I are going to talk."

Mom is in my face quickly, anger flashing in her eyes. "I'm still your mother, Garret. You don't boss me around. Nothing will give you that right."

"Pretty sure my saving your butt gives me that right!" I snap.

"Don't delude yourself, Garret. I wouldn't exactly say you saved my butt."

"No, *I* saved both your butts," Veronica interrupts from the door. "How about you two put a lid on the family drama and get those fuel cans?"

"Not done," I say to Mom, pushing past her to the bedroom.

"Yes, we are!" she calls after me. "I'm closing this subject!"

"I'm not!" I shout, grabbing two cans of fuel. My hands are shaking and the cans clank against each other as I fit through the narrow bedroom door. "No more secrets! We'd be a lot more prepared if you and Dad were just honest with me!"

I hand the cans to Veronica and she gives me a weak smile, gone out the door instantly, not wanting to stick around for this.

"Your dad?" Mom laughs. "If only you knew half the crap your dad has pulled over the years!"

"So tell me!"

"No, Garret. There are certain things I'm going to leave for him to say."

"But, what if we never see him again? What if he's dead?"

"Your father isn't dead. Trust me."

"How the hell could you possibly know that? What if he didn't make it out of the forest fire?"

"Make it out...?" She looks at me and there is honest pain in her eyes. "Oh, Garret..."

"What? Tell me!"

"Your father made it out of the forest fire because he *set* the forest fire," she states.

I stare at her, stunned. "What...?"

"It was part of his protocol. He had to destroy his lab. Cover his tracks. If his research fell into the wrong hands, it would be disastrous."

"And you are just telling me this now because...?"

"Because this is the first chance I've had," she says apologetically. "I haven't always been in my right mind."

"Tell me about it!" I laugh.

The anger on her face is quickly replaced with sorrow. "I guess I deserve that."

Something itches at the back of my mind. "Wait... Wasn't Dad going to his lab to get his research? Not destroy it?"

"Have you ever seen your dad refer to any of the notes he's taken over the years?"

"Um... No," I answer after a moment's thought.

"Right. He only takes the notes for records. He has one of those brains that locks everything away inside. He has total and instant recall when he needs it. We're all lucky he's on our side."

"Is he?" I ask.

"Is he what?"

"On our side?"

Mom looks at me in surprise. "Do you really need to ask that?"

"Apparently so."

"Yes, Garret, he's on our side. And he loves you...and your brother, very much. Everything he has done has been for you...at least once you were born."

"What does that mean?"

"Sorry," Karen says from the door. "But, Miss Half-shirt has the truck fueled up and it's almost dawn. We need to leave now."

"Right," Mom says, unfolding the map and throwing it on the table. "Get Veronica and Joseph in here. We need to plan before we move. We have a long way to go before Cottage Grove and it won't be easy, even if we avoid Charlotte's people."

Karen looks at me. "You doing okay, 3B?"

I smile at her and nod. "Yes. Thanks."

She holds my gaze for a minute and is then gone.

"What's this 3B stuff?" Mom asks, obviously catching the look between us.

"Just a nickname," I mutter.

"Nicknames mean something. What is it?"

I look down and away.

"Garret? What does it mean?"

"It's nothing."

"If it's nothing then there's no reason not to tell me."

"Bubble book boy," I says hesitantly.

"Bubble book...?" Mom looks puzzled then laughs. "Ha! That's pretty fitting. Wonder I didn't think of that over the years!"

"Not much of a wonder. You haven't been known for your thinking over the years."

Mom frowns and turns to look at the map. "No...I guess I haven't," she says quietly, her back to me.

"We're here?" Mom asks, pointing at the map. I nod. "Okay. And we need to go...here." She places her finger on Cottage Grove. "We have about one hundred sixty miles between us and there. Sixty of those miles are on I-5 and will not be easy. Getting past the Tribes will be hard enough, not to mention the Scavenger freaks, but we had reports that the Keep is spreading its tentacles also. They have all of the Portland area and now most of what was Eugene. Cottage Grove is a little close for comfort."

"The Keep took Eugene weeks ago," Veronica adds. "We lost several scouts before we realized what was going on."

Mom looks at Veronica. "Anything else we should know?"

"No. Except that I-5 is hard traveling. It's clogged with vehicles. The Scavengers like it that way and usually undo any clearing that anyone does."

"Yeah, that's why we have the cow catcher on the front," I say.

"That wedge?" Veronica asks, with disdain. "Good luck."

"Don't think it will work?" Mom asks.

"For the smaller vehicles, but not for the trucks. The Scavengers place eighteen wheelers across the road. This will just run into those, won't move 'em. It's too big to maneuver around."

"Then what do you suggest?"

"The Power Wagon has enough torque to yank almost

anything off the road. I'll have to chain to them and pull. It'll slow us down, but keep the RV from crushing itself."

"You sure?" Mom asks, skeptically. "This RV has a few modifications. I think it can handle the stress."

"I'm not saying it can't help push, but if we are going at any real speed it'll just get munched. That's the whole point. The Scavengers want to slow people down. Ambush, raid and retreat. They never attack directly."

Mom rubs her face and I can see her fatigue etched in every line and wrinkle.

"You should let me drive," I say. "You can sleep until we hit I-5 then I'll let you take over."

Mom smiles. "There's a lot to do between now and then. Plus, you haven't slept either."

"I didn't end up battling in the arena, though."

"Right, but I'm trained for this, you aren't."

"Trained? How are you trained? You're a surgeon!"

"Did I look like I was just a surgeon back there? I'm a lot more than you know."

"Like what? I'd really like to find that part out because right now I have no idea who you are."

"I'm your mother and that's all you need to know."

"I just saved your butt!"

"Knock it off!" Veronica shouts. "You two aren't going through that again! We need to get on the road! We have a route! We know the dangers! Let's move some ass!"

"I have to agree with Half-shirt here," Karen says.

"Excuse me?" Veronica asks, offended.

"Don't mind her," I laugh. "She likes nicknames."

"Half-shirt?" Veronica looks down at her clothes and frowns. "I've been called worse."

"Better than what she said earlier," Joseph says with a grin.

"Shut it, brat!"

"Okay! Okay!" Mom shouts. "Enough! Veronica's right, we need to move some ass."

"I still insist on driving," I say.

"I'll tell you what," Mom replies. "I'll drive until I'm sure we are away from the SATs. Once we're clear I'll let you drive. Deal?"

"You know, I've gotten pretty good at driving," I pout.

"I'm sure you have, Garret. Deal?"

Little Man lets out a loud screech and we all freeze.

"What does that mean?" Veronica whispers.

"That means something is coming and coming fast," I answer, turning to Mom. "Deal. Let's get out of here."

Mom takes the driver's seat and starts up the RV as Little Man continues to squeak and screech. "Garret, I need you to ride shotgun...literally. Joseph, you watch the windows." She looks at Karen. "I know you can point one, but can you actually aim and fire?"

"I can," Karen answers confidently.

"Good. Then you have shotgun with Veronica in the Power Wagon. Keep yourself alert and eyes scanning. Those motorcycles can come out of nowhere."

"Keep the windows down," Veronica suggests. "You can hear the engines easier."

"Over the sound of that thing?" Karen nods towards the Power Wagon outside the windshield. "I don't think God could hear himself think over that."

"You'd be surprised," Veronica says. "Motorcycle engines have a different tuning. The pitch will rise above a V12. Trust me."

"Okay," Karen says, grabbing an extra box of shotgun shells. "I'm ready if you are."

"Any radios?" Veronica asks Mom.

"No. They don't work worth a damn. Never have really."

"We'll have to use hand signals out the windows. Do you know...?"

"I'm trained in them all. You take the lead and we'll follow. That work?"

"Works for me. See ya on the road."

Veronica nods to us and is out the door, sprinting to the truck.

Karen and I look at each other for a second.

"You going to be okay?" I ask Karen.

"No time, you two," Mom interrupts. "Get your butt moving, girl."

Karen's brow furrows, but she doesn't argue. "Take care of my brother," Karen orders and is gone in a flash.

"I will!" I shout after her, looking over at Joseph. "Don't do anything stupid and make me a liar, okay?"

"Can't make any promises," he smiles.

Little Man screeches even louder and Mom hits the gas, following right on the Power Wagon's tail.

I glance behind us as we hit the road, but can't see anything. Not coming from the woods or from anywhere.

"Why is he freaking out?" Joseph asks.

"I don't know," I answer, puzzled. "I usually have a bad feeling too if it's necs. I don't feel anything now."

I take the passenger's seat and he howls louder still.

"What do you think?" I ask Mom. She just focuses on the road, silent. "Mom?"

"Don't bother me now, Garret. I need to focus."

"But he only acts this way if there's necros around! I haven't ever seen him this upset before for just nothing!"

"He's an HSN, Garret! There's a lot you don't know about him!"

"Unless one of you guys is a slick," Joseph laughs.

"Well, we know I'm not," I laugh back. "Or you'd already be lunch."

Mom doesn't laugh, her face whiter than just a second before.

"Mom? Did you...? Are you bit?"

No answer.

"Mom?!" I ask again, panicked. "Did Big Timber bite you? I didn't see him do it, but did he?"

"No," she answers quietly.

"But...?"

"But nothing. Just watch for SATs. This isn't the time."

"It's never the time with you," I grumble.

"Now you're catching on," she replies. "We'll talk at some point. Just not now."

Little Man screeches one more time and Mom shoots him a look. He quiets down and buries his face against my shoulder.

"Wow, he hasn't done that in a while," I say.

"I haven't really looked at him in a while," Mom responds.

We both let that statement hang in the air.

"Wow," Joseph says behind us. "I thought my family was messed up..."

6

"I haven't eaten yet," Joseph says from the couch. "Can we eat?"

"Sure. Grab some jerky. It's in the cupboard," I reply, hungry myself. "Mom? You want some?"

"No, thank you," she answers quickly. "I'm not hungry."

"You have to eat," I insist. "I doubt they fed you back there. You must be starving." She doesn't answer. "I'll get you something."

I get up from the passenger's seat, but Mom grabs my arm.

"I'm not hungry, Garret. Don't bother. I won't eat."

"You really should eat, Mrs. Weir," Joseph says. "We need your energy up if you are going to be driving."

"Mrs. Weir?" Mom laughs. "I have never been called that before."

"He's right, Mom. You have to eat or you'll end up passing out."

She grimaces, but glances over at me. "Okay. I'll have some jerky."

Joseph rummages around in the cupboard and finds the tin of jerky, handing me several pieces for myself and Mom.

"I'll get some water from the jugs," he says looking about the RV. "Where are the jugs?"

"I put them in the shower stall," I answer, pointing towards the back. As I turn around I catch Mom stashing her jerky under her leg. "What the hell?"

Mom tries to look shocked and surprised, but she gives up when she sees the look on my face.

"I can't eat right now, Garret," she pleads. "You have to let this go. When we are secure in the Cottage Grove compound, I promise I'll eat."

"That's hours away if we're lucky!" I snap. "Maybe a couple of days if we have any problems on the road!"

"Which we probably will," she replies.

"You're making my case for me!"

"There is no case, son. I. Can. Not. Eat. Right. Now."

"Why?! You aren't making sense!'

"Here's some water, at least," Joseph says, placing two cups in the cup holders between us. "You have to be thirsty."

She keeps her eyes forward, on the road.

"Are you freaking kidding me?!" I yell. "Not even water? This is insane!"

Joseph gives me a worried look and retreats to the couch.

"Mom?" I calm my voice. "Mom? You can't just shut me out. You've done that my whole life. Not now, please."

This gets her attention. She looks at me, pain in her eyes. "Oh, Garret... I've never shut you out. Ever."

"Yes, you have," I insist. "All the times you'd space off. Or the looks you'd give me when I'd get back to camp from hiking or hunting. You know, as if you couldn't recognize me? How about when..."

"Enough, Garret. I know I was an awful mom."

"I'm not saying that. Not at all..."

"Then what are you saying?!" she shouts. "I don't even think you know! There are forces at work here that you cannot possibly understand!"

"Forces at work? Seriously? Is this some fantasy adventure we're in? Has the bad sorcerer put a spell on you? If you eat or drink before midnight will you turn into an ogre?" Mom's face pinches at this and my eyes go wide. "Please don't tell me you believe you have a spell on you!"

"No, of course not..."

"But it's something, right? Something out of your control?"

"Sort of. It's so complicated."

"Then just tell me! We aren't going anywhere! Tell me

what's wrong! Tell me why the mom I knew was a weak nutjob and the mom I just helped rescue is a badass killer! Tell me why, even with everything we've just been through, you refuse to eat or drink!"

She doesn't tell me any of these things. I wait, but she won't look at me, won't open her mouth to give me just a little comfort.

"Fine... Whatever..."

I cross my arms in frustration and look out the windshield at the Power Wagon. I can see Karen and Veronica having an animated discussion, friendly, I hope. Karen turns and glances back at us. She waves and I hold up my hand in response. I can tell she was expecting more and she gives me a quizzical look. I point at Mom then twirl my finger around my ear, giving the universal sign for crazy. She nods and looks away, saying something to Veronica. I can see the woman's eyes in her rearview mirror.

"You can stop mocking me," Mom grumbles. "I am still your mother and do deserve a little respect."

"I don't know what you deserve, Mom," I sigh. "You won't talk to me. You never really have. My whole life I've had to tiptoe around you because you were always off your rocker. Dad explained that things happened to you and that I needed to understand you weren't stable..."

Her eyes are on me and filled with fire. "Your father? Your father said that?!" She shakes her head, true anger raging across her features. "That bastard. That slimy bastard."

"What? Why is he slimy? He just wanted to make sure I didn't bug you or push you. What's wrong with that?"

"What's wrong...? What could possibly be wrong with driving a wedge between a mother and her son?! Oh, nothing wrong there!"

"I think you misunderstood me, Mom. He didn't try to..."

"I didn't misunderstand at all! You just don't know who your father is! You never have!"

"Sounds like you're the one trying to drive the wedge! He has always taken care of me, especially when you were off in la la land! He'd feed me when what you cooked was inedible! He trained me on how to defend myself against the necs! He taught me how to hunt, how to fish, how to survive! What have you taught me?! Huh?!" She doesn't answer, her jaw clenched tight. "Yeah... That's what I thought... I don't know why you hate him so much..."

I barely have time to brace myself against the dash as she slams on the brakes and throws the RV into park.

"Mom?! What the hell?!"

She's out of her seat and has me by the front of the shirt. "Exactly! You don't know why I have so much anger towards him! You don't know anything!"

"Then tell me!" I scream at her.

Little Man screeches and his hands slap at my shoulders.

"Because he did that to you!" she points at Garth. "Killing me in the process!"

"Did...Did you say... Did you say he killed you?" Joseph stutters, picking himself off the floor where he fell when Mom hit the brakes. "Are you...? Are you a slick?"

"Do I look like a slick?!" Mom yells. "No, you moron, I'm not a slick!"

"Hey, calm down!" We are all yelling now and Little Man is as vocal as any of us, his feet and hands flying about, punctuating his agitation. "Don't turn on Joseph! He's just a kid!"

"And so are you! But you keep insisting you're an adult! You aren't, Garret! You do not have the maturity to understand any of this!"

"I also don't have the information! How do you expect me to mature and understand adult concepts if you don't teach me about them?! Huh?! He did this to me and my brother? Tell me how! He killed you? How did he do that? Talk to me!"

Mom takes a deep breath and lets go of my shirt then falls back into her seat. "To tell you that I have to tell you who your father is..."

"I know who my father is..."

"No, I meant to say *what* your father is."

"Okay... What is he?"

She looks at me, at Joseph and back to me. "He's the man that killed the world, Garret. He caused all of this." She sweeps her hand to indicate everything outside the RV. "You're father made the virus and released it, dooming us all."

I can only stare at Mom. Did she just say that? Out of the corner of my eye I see Joseph's mouth opening and closing, opening and closing, ready to ask the million questions that I have also, but unable to voice them over the shock.

The bang at the RV door snaps me out of it and I can see that the Power Wagon has stopped and Veronica is standing in front of the RV, shotgun at the ready, sweeping the area. The RV door swings open and Karen's worried face peaks in.

"What's wrong? Why'd you stop?"

Joseph points at us. "His dad killed the world and she's dead also. Can I ride with you guys?"

"His dad..? What? She's dead? Huh? Will someone tell me what's going on?" Karen asks, perplexed. "Is this really the time for all this?"

"No, it's not," Mom says, reaching for the gear shift. "We need to move."

"Uh, wrong!" I say, grabbing the RV keys out of the ignition before she can stop me. I roll down the window and throw them into the woods. "You're gonna have to do some talking before we go anywhere!"

"Hey!"

"Are you crazy?!"

"Garret!"

They are all yelling at me now. "Karen, will you and Joseph please look for the keys?"

She blinks a few times, her mouth agape. "You mean the keys you just threw in the FREAKING WOODS?!"

"Yes, please. Those keys."

"Come on, Jo," she says, shaking her head. "We'll leave 3B and his mom to talk while we go on a pointless errand that we shouldn't have had to do if he'd just handed me the keys so they could have time to talk in private!"

I give her a weak smile, but it doesn't change her glare. The RV door slams behind them and I'm left with Mom and hopefully the truth.

"Talk," I order.

"Do you know what a dangerous game you are playing, Garret?" She snaps at me. "What if the SATs catch up with us and we don't have those keys? Did you think of that?"

"Talk."

"I will not be ordered around by a seventeen year old!"

"TALK!"

She pulls back at the force of my voice. "Fine. But we don't have time for every question, okay? I give you the big picture and we can finish this conversation on the drive. Deal?"

"Just talk. If you give me the answers I'm looking for then we might have a deal."

Mom jabs a finger at the windshield. "You have no right to put these people's lives in jeopardy! Do you think Karen is going to care about your 'answers' if the SATs catch us and murder her little brother? Do you think your 'answers' are what's on Veronica's mind when she has obviously been looking for a chance to escape the Griffins for a long while now? Do you hear yourself? Do you hear how selfish you sound?" She laughs, slapping her hand against her forehead. "Of course! I shouldn't be surprised! You sound just like him!"

I cross my arms and say nothing.

"I'll tell you what I'm going to tell you and nothing more. Take the deal or leave it. I'll go find the keys myself. If I have to tie you up and gag you to keep you from being a spoiled brat then that's what I'll do. Understand?"

I try to figure out an argument against this, but I can see Karen and Joseph, with Veronica covering them, trying frantically to find the RV keys and embarrassment washes over me. Man, am I really this much of a jerk?

"Okay. Fine. But start with me and Garth."

Mom takes a slow breath and closes her eyes, rubbing at her temples.

"Garth wasn't an accident," she starts. I want to interrupt immediately, and she can see this, so she holds up her hand, stopping my words before they get out of my mouth. "Your father has been looking for a cure to the virus ever since he released it. I'm not getting into that part right now, okay? We'll talk about you and your brother and about me, but everything else will have to wait until we're at the compound." I nod and she continues. "You and Garth weren't the first pregnancy, Garret. I miscarried three times before you two were born. Things went horribly wrong over and over."

"Did he force you to do this?"

"Like with a gun to my head? No. But he did use the guilt of service over me. I'm a surgeon, you know that. What you don't know is I was a military surgeon before everything died. I was Army Special Forces, a specific bioterrorism division. One hundred percent black ops. There is no record of me existing in the military beyond an honorable discharge after my four years of service. Your father played on that 'greater good' part of my training. That and the fact that I had the only working uterus."

"But what does this have to do with the virus?"

"He was trying to create antibodies for a vaccine. He'd had some great successes in the lab before we had to escape, but all of that research was lost before he could determine anything that would actually work. There weren't many options out in the wilds of Southern Oregon. So I agreed."

"Even though you knew it could kill your babies?"

"Desperate times, Garret. We are facing the possible extinction of the human race! My babies could die or everyone's babies could die. As a soldier, and as a surgeon, I had to think beyond myself." She fixes me with her Mom eyes. "You would do well to learn from that."

I look away, ashamed a little.

"Anyway, you and Garth made it past the first three injections without a problem. You two looked like you would be viable and healthy. Your father gave you both the last injection and we watched your vitals. It all looked great. Days went by and nothing seemed amiss. Then..."

"Then Garth died, but didn't stop moving, right?"

Mom nods, tears forming in her eyes. "I was so excited, Garret! I was going to have not one, but two boys and possibly save the world! I shouldn't have gotten my hopes up. I certainly had the experience to know better, but..."

"You couldn't help yourself."

Mom shakes her head and wipes at her cheeks. "Nope. When you started kicking like mad I knew it had gone wrong again."

"When I started kicking?"

"Even while still in the womb you had an amazing survival instinct. You knew your twin was not right. I don't know if Garth attacked you or what happened, but you were the reason for the C-section. We didn't know you were conjoined until after you were born. It was a nightmare."

"And you snapped and just checked out, right?"

Mom laughs. "Hardly. If you knew me before all of this... well, you've seen me in action lately. I didn't check out, Garret, I was infected by Garth during the birth. There's a lot of mixing of blood with a C-section. Somehow, and this is really what your father has been studying, there *were* antibodies, and those antibodies kept me from turning right away."

"Right away? You mean you could still turn?"

Mom is silent and I can see she is debating something. She slowly reaches into her pocket and pulls out what she hid from me earlier. A bottle of pills. "Your father was able to create these in his lab. They aren't perfect and the side effects are brutal, but they've kept the virus in check ever since then. They aren't a cure, just a postponement."

Wait... What is she saying?

"You're still infected?"

"I always have been. My mental issues are because of these pills."

It all starts to come together in my head. "You stopped taking the pills when we fled, right?"

"I needed to be clear to keep us safe. I have a skill set that is very valuable in a violent world like this. I couldn't get clean fast enough to get us down the mountain." Her face lights up and I see the first true, honest smile from her in a very long time. "But you took care of that. I'm very proud of you for saving us."

I blush and look away. "Thanks..."

"I know you have a ton more questions, but they will have to wait."

"One more," I say. "When Little Man was freaking out it was because of you, wasn't it? He senses the virus in you, doesn't he?"

"You know your brother better than anyone, Garret. You tell me."

Veronica flinging open the door stops my answer. "Enough family therapy! We have motorcycles heading at us through the woods! I guess six at least on our nine o'clock!"

"Keys?!" Mom asks.

"Right here!" Karen shouts, pushing past Veronica and tossing the keys to Mom. "No thanks to 3B here!"

If looks could kill...

Mom starts up the RV. "Move out now! It could already be too late!" Veronica and Karen dash from the RV and get into the Power Wagon, with Joseph rejoining us. "I hope putting your mind at ease was worth it, Garret."

It was, but I keep this to myself as she hits the gas pedal and we speed after the Power Wagon.

CHAPTER ELEVEN

mile? Maybe two?

That's how far we get when the motorcycles burst from the tree cover, three behind us and three in front.

The number is quickly turned into only two in front as Veronica runs over one of the lead bikes, crushing the vehicle and the rider. The other two dodge around her, try to fire at us, but duck as Joseph opens up on the one on his side and I start firing at the one on my side.

"Get back there and take them out!" Mom orders. "We can't let them hit the tires!"

"Up or out the back window?" I yell.

"Bedroom is full of fuel, go up! You can get a better view all around! Joseph, you need to cover both sides! Don't get comfortable, just keep moving and firing!" I leap from the seat, but Mom grabs my arm. "Be careful, please." I grin and nod.

I'm up and out of the vent in no time, struggling to keep my balance and keep hold of the shotgun at the same time. The pain hits me and I stumble, nearly falling off the edge, before I know what's going on. I look at my arm and see the gouge across my left bicep. What the...? My question is answered as a second bolt misses me by an inch and I look down to see one of the bikers taking aim with a handheld crossbow. His ability to load the bolt one handed is almost impressive enough to distract me. Almost, but not quite.

His body shudders as I pump two rounds into him. The motorcycle swerves off the road into the drainage ditch and the man's body flies over the handlebars. Nec hands spring up from the dry branches and pine needles covering the ditch and grab the body. If he wasn't dead on impact, he is now. Gotta watch out for those lurkers!

Did I just think that? Am I now the smart-ass hero like in my books? Does killing people, even SATs, mean nothing to me already? Has a world that I didn't know existed already brutalized me?

Little Man screeches, pulling me from my badly timed thoughts, and I look to my right, catching movement in the trees. Runners. Lots of them. They spill onto the road and give chase to the RV. We're going much faster than they are, but if we don't lose them they'll continue to track us. Necros don't tire out when they're on the hunt.

The second biker swerves back and forth, dodging Joseph's assault, which is a good thing since it prevents him from using the nasty looking sawed-off double barrel slung across his chest.

"Keep him hopping, Jo!" I shout, trying to take aim at the biker also, but the RV takes a hard swerve and I miss the shot. I look to the front and see there are more bikers now and Karen is struggling to keep them at bay. Veronica hits two at once and the Power Wagon gives a lurch and bump, but she keeps control, revving the engine as she speeds ahead.

Several of the bikers spot me and I flatten myself as bullets whiz by. I hear Joseph scream from below and hope he isn't hurt badly. Inching across the RV roof, I get myself to the edge and brace the shotgun against my shoulder.

The muzzle flash of my shotgun is the last thing one of the bikers below me sees. Unless he sees the pavement as he tumbles from his seat.

There I go again...

His motorcycle slams into the side of the RV and Mom compensates, but this causes me to slide dangerously close to the edge. I reach out to steady myself and the crossbow wound on my arm screams with pain. I'm able to get myself braced and steady once again, but I can tell the gouge on my bicep is worse than I thought. The cut is deep and the edges are now a dark red. It's one angry wound and I get a little woozy looking at it.

It's not like me to fall apart over a cut, no matter how bad. I've had so many accidents over the years I've grown used to the sight of my own blood. Feeding Little Man takes the squeamish right outta ya.

I push the worry out of my head and focus on the bikers. The RV is surrounded since they decided it was an easier target than the Power Wagon. Plus, Veronica's driving and Karen's good shooting was picking them off too fast. I decide to stop aiming for the bikers and just go for the bikes. Let the mob of necs still in pursuit do the killing for me.

BLAM!

One more down!

BLAM! BLAM!

There goes another!

BLAM!

OUCH! I miss the next biker and end up with a spiked chain in my right calf as one of the SATs on the side of the RV swings and embeds the chain into the RV's siding and top rail and into my leg at the same time. It's pure agony as the man leaps off his bike, his full weight being held by the chain. Luckily, some of the weight is supported by the spikes in the RV, but not enough to keep me from screaming. I twist about and hold the shotgun one handed as I fire, using my other hand to keep from getting yanked off the RV as the man scrambles hand over hand up the chain. Not the best idea to use a shotgun with one arm. The recoil knocks the gun from my hands and I stare after it as it clatters from the roof onto the pavement below.

The biker grins when he sees that I'm spiked and un-armed and pulls himself all the way to the roof. He quickly unsheathes a very large hunting knife. For some reason the sight of the knife just ticks me off. Maybe because my own knife was left behind back at the Griffins' compound. I really, really liked that knife.

"Gonna carve you up, kid!" the biker shouts, struggling to stay standing on the RV. "I'll make sure to have a taste before I kick you to the road!"

I try to get my leg free of the spiked chain, but the biker stomps down hard on my calf and I scream.

"That's right! It's gonna hurt a whole lot worse in a second!" he yells. The RV swerves and he loses his balance, falling forward onto his knees. I swing out and barely connect with his chin. The biker laughs and backhands me with a spiked glove, ripping my cheek open, making stars and sparks swim before my eyes. These freaks really like their spikes. "Too bad you only hit like a girl! We could have a little fun before I slice you open!"

The biker is about to bring his blade down right on me, and I throw up my arms to try to block him, but he stops on his own, his eyes widening.

"What the..?"

He's staring at my back and I realize Little Man's hands are flailing like mad and he's letting loose with a high-pitched wail.

"What the hell is that thing?"

"That's my brother!" I yell, kicking out with my free leg. The look of surprise on the man's face is almost worth all the pain as he tumbles back and off the RV. I hear the thump and crash as one of his buddies runs over him, loses control and ditches his motorcycle into the pavement.

I reach down and pull the chain out of my calf, spike by spike. Blood pours from the wounds and I clamp my hand down. Little Man screeches loudly even though I don't know how he can smell the blood with the wind whipping by us.

My stomach lurches and I feel woozy as I drag myself to the vent, falling through into the RV.

2

"Garret! Check Joseph now!" Mom screams.

I fight the cotton that my mind has become and pull myself up.

"I'll try," I gasp, the sharp pain in my cheek and leg, and burning pain in my arm, the only things keeping me from passing out.

Mom can tell I'm hurt from my voice and her head whips around, eyes searching my body. "What happened?! Are you okay?!"

"I'll be fine," I reply, not sure if I believe my own words. "Let me check Joseph..."

The boy is draped across the couch like a pile of clothes. Blood drenched clothes. His face is white as bone and his eyelids flutter weakly at my voice.

"Garret?" he whispers. "I got...a couple...of them..."

"Yeah, you did, Jo," I reply, probing gently for where he's shot. There is just so much blood I can't find the wound. His face tightens when my fingers touch his lower stomach and I pull up his soaked shirt as gently as possible. "Just relax, okay? I'm gonna check you out."

"Don't tell Karen I got shot," he smiles weakly. "She won't let me use my rifle anymore."

"Don't worry. It's just between us."

Slick, pink intestines bulge from the wound in his abdomen and I fight to keep from puking. His eyes study my face and he frowns.

"Does it…look as bad…as it…hurts?" he asks.

I don't respond, just look about the RV for something to press against the wound. "Sit tight, Jo. I need to get some bandages. Don't move."

"You're…funny…" he gasps, obviously not going anywhere.

The RV swerves to the left as I get to my feet and I'm slammed into the kitchen stove, the wind knocked out of me. I collapse to my knees, desperate to catch my breath. My leg is screaming, but I shove that away. Joseph is what matters now.

"Garret?! Are you okay?!"

"Fine, Mom! Just winded!"

Pulling myself up by the counter I rip open one of the drawers and pull out a dishtowel. I search a second drawer, trying to find something to help secure the towel in place, but find nothing. I'll have to apply the pressure myself and hope Mom doesn't need me for anything.

Bullets rip through the window above Joseph and I barely manage to take cover in time as I feel them fly by my head.

"Get down!" Mom shouts, yanking the wheel to the left. I hear a yell and a crash and know she has hit her target. I don't bother telling her I was already down when she shouted the warning. It would just piss her off.

"That…doesn't look…too clean," Joseph stammers, eyeing the dishtowel. "Don't…make me…sick."

"You're well past sick," I reply without thinking and quickly try to cover. "But you'll be just fine. Don't worry."

He coughs hard and cries out, blood dripping from his lips. I kneel next to him and gently press the towel to his spilling guts. He cries out again. "I'm sorry, Joseph."

"It's…okay…"

The cotton in my brain fights for control as my own wounds continually insist on attention. The burning in my arm is now a raging inferno and I glance down at it. The sight makes me gasp. "Oh… That's not good…"

I tear my sleeve completely away and reveal a bicep that has turned dark blue with bright red lines spider webbing out from the gash. There's a sharp metallic smell coming from the wound and I quickly realize the crossbow bolt had a little more to it than just metal on the tip.

"That...looks...bad," Joseph whispers, his half open eyes looking at me.

"Tell me about it." But he doesn't respond as he's racked with choking coughs, blood spraying from his mouth.

"What's going on back there?!" Mom shouts as she slams into another biker. I look up towards her and watch as she aims a pistol out her window, firing until it clicks empty. A riderless motorcycle flies by the window. "Garret?!"

I decide that subtlety is no longer an option, not with Joseph spitting up blood and my arm looking like an abstract painting. "Things aren't good back here! How's it looking up there?!"

Mom whips her head around. "What's wrong?! Tell me!"

"Joseph is hurt pretty bad! I can see his lunch working its way through his guts! I've been better too!"

"Are you bleeding?!"

I ignore her for the moment as I pull the dishtowel away to get a better position.

"Garret! Are you bleeding?!"

"Yes! I'm bleeding! I'm bleeding a lot! So is Joseph!"

"Get back from him! DO NOT LET YOUR BLOOD GET IN HIS WOUND!"

As the words echo back to me I helplessly watch three drops of blood drip from my cheek and into his gut, mixing with the never ending flow of blood there.

"Oh crap..."

"Garret?! What happened?!"

Gunshots ring out and I instinctively duck. I hear Mom return fire, but don't remember seeing her reload. If she did it was fast.

"Dammit Garret! Answer me!"

"I got some blood in his wound!"

I can hear her swearing under her breath. "Tell me what's happening!"

"What's happening?! He's bleeding! I'm bleeding! We're both bleeding! That's what's happening!"

"Don't get smart with me! What is happening to Joseph right now?!"

"Nothing! He's just lying here! What is supposed...?" My

question is answered as Joseph's eyes fly open fully, he lurches up and vomits a stream of blood across the RV. I fall back away from him, letting the blood spew by. "HOLY CRAP! HOLY CRAP! HOLY CRAP!"

The blood flow stops abruptly and he falls back on the couch, his body convulsing wildly as his jaw snaps open and closed violently.

"Mom! What do I do?" I scream, trying to hold Joseph down so he won't flop off the couch. "MOM!"

"Get away from him!"

"Get away?! Why?! Can he infect me?!"

"Infect you?! NO! You infected him! You're the Carrier, Garret! Not your brother, but you! Get back from him! The change is brutal and violent and he won't be able to control himself! He's violent and dangerous!"

"But it just happened! How can he turn this fast?!"

"GET AWAY FROM HIM NOW! You can have a science lesson later!"

The RV swerves and shakes and I tumble away from Joseph. Little Man screeches and Joseph's eyes turn my way. His body stops shaking so severely, but still shivers and shudders slightly. His lips pull back, revealing his teeth and the bloody saliva dripping off them. The growl from his throat is like something I have never heard before.

"Mom! This isn't good!" No response. I notice the RV is slowing and starting to drift towards the side of the road. "Mom?!"

I scramble away from the couch and the growling Joseph and look up front.

Mom is slumped over the steering wheel and we are heading straight for the woods.

Crap.

C hoices.

That's what life is all about: choices.

Now my choice to get control of the RV before we crash into the pine trees we are speeding towards is not a hard choice. The urgency of the impending crash makes the choice for me, but it's still hard when the flip side to that choice is leaving a freshly turned nec unattended on the couch right behind me.

That's not my favorite part of this choice.

"Mom!" I scream, grabbing the wheel and yanking it to the left, keeping us on the road. In a not so careful manner I pull Mom away, letting her fall to the floor as I grab the wheel and hit the gas pedal. The RV surges ahead and I look at the side mirror to see where the SATs are. None on my left and none on my right.

Looking forward, I see Karen crawling out the back window of the Power Wagon into the bed of the truck. She waves to me and starts pointing up just as I hear the roof vent open. Karen puts her shotgun to her shoulder and takes aim. She fires off two rounds and I hear a yell above then a thump. I can see one of the SATs tumble from the roof and smash into the road. The RV thumps and jumps as the back tires run the man over. If the fall didn't kill them then getting run over was sure to. That's one less psycho to deal with.

Karen gestures wildly at the roof and holds up three

fingers. Three?! There are three men trying to get into the RV?! Great, just great.

The howl Little Man lets out, and his fists pounding at my back, tells me Joseph is up and moving. I look down at Mom and don't see any visible wounds or blood, so that's a good thing. I'll have time to deal with her later. I look behind me and see Joseph swaying back and forth, his red eyes fixed on me. He just stands there, watching me, his mouth opening and closing, opening and closing.

Behind him a set of boots dangles from the vent.

"Jo! Behind you!" I yell then realize the absurdity of yelling at a nec to warn them. But this is Joseph. Maybe he can still be helped...

The SAT drops through the vent and the scarred, tattooed man gets to his feet, a very large pistol in his hand.

"Time to die you sons of...!"

He never finishes his sentence. As soon as his feet hit the RV floor, Joseph turns his attention from me to the man. He's on him in a blink and the man's pistol hand is knocked back and he starts firing randomly. Bullets fly by me and the windshield becomes a mess of cracks and holes. I struggle to see through the broken glass, but realize it's a lost cause. I take both feet from the floor and kick across the dashboard, clearing the shattered windshield away.

With the view cleared, Karen's eyes widen as she sees Joseph on the SAT. I glance behind me and Joseph's jaw is clamped onto the man's neck as he struggles to push the undead boy away. His struggle weakens as the blood flows out of him and Joseph feeds. I look back at Karen and she has let the shotgun fall from her shoulder. I can see Veronica inside the Power Wagon yelling at her, but have no idea what she's saying.

More gunfire and I know the other SATs are coming in. Joseph grunts then roars, tossing the dead SAT aside and focusing on the new ones that have dropped in front of him. Six more shots and Joseph roars even louder. I'm guessing they missed and are now going to pay for their bad marksmanship.

My head is pounding as I simultaneously try to focus on driving the RV, keeping enough room between the Power

Wagon in front of me, Mom on the floor, and Joseph's struggles behind me. My neck aches from all the whipping back and forth. I retch and cough as my stomach lurches and the dizzy feeling I had earlier slams back into my aching head.

"NOOOOOOO!" one of the men yells behind me and the unmistakable sound of a feeding nec makes my nausea even worse. "GET IT OFF ME!"

More gunshots and more screams. The RV comes to a major bend in the road, so I don't have time to look behind me. I see the Power Wagon's brake lights flash and I have to swerve to the left to keep from rear ending the truck. I hit the brakes and nearly slam into the steering wheel. A body tumbles forward onto Mom and I shove it away as I kick open the driver's side door and yank her up over the seat and out of the RV.

Veronica has the Power Wagon in reverse and pulls up right next to us. "What are you doing?!"

"Why'd you stop?!" I shout back. She stabs her finger forward and I see the line of trucks and cars heading for us. Each vehicle is well armored and covered in men and women, all ready for war. "oh..."

"Get back in the RV and drive!" Veronica shouts.

"Where's Joseph?!" Karen shouts over her. "What happened to my brother?!"

Little Man's screeches and then Joseph's roars behind me to answer her question.

"How...?" Her hands go to her mouth as Joseph stumbles into view, his body coated in blood, his intestines dangling from his abdomen. "No..."

"Everyone in the truck! Now!" Veronica screams. "He's a slick and gone! Leave him!"

Karen tries to scramble from the bed of the truck, but I push her back and try to heave Mom up over the side. "Help me! Karen, please!"

She hesitates, but then grabs Mom under the arms and lifts. I grab her legs and we have her in the bed of the truck and Veronica is speeding backwards as I barely make it in myself.

"We can't leave Joseph!" Karen shouts, slamming her fists against the truck cab. "Go back!"

Veronica swerves the truck directly behind the RV, right under the back bedroom windows, and stops. "Get the fuel!"

I look at her, puzzled.

"Go through the window and throw the fuel cans into the truck bed! Do it now!"

Grabbing up Karen's shotgun from the truck bed I shoot out the back window, using the butt to clear a way in. I scramble over the sill and fall onto the bed inside. Luckily the partition is closed, so I don't have to see Joseph again.

"Move your ass!" Veronica shouts from outside.

I tear down the window shades, getting them out of my way and start handing fuel cans out to Karen. She takes them mechanically, setting them roughly into the truck bed, her eyes focused past me on the bedroom door.

Joseph must hear us and he slams against the partition, making the thin wood veneer shake and buckle. Karen winces with every thump, her eyes filling with tears.

"I'm so sorry," I say to her, climbing from the RV as I hand her the last can. "I'm so sorry."

"Why?" she asks me weakly. "It wasn't your fault."

I don't answer.

"Open a can and pour the fuel into the RV!" Veronica orders. I don't question and do as she says. When the fuel is half gone she pulls away from the RV and I nearly topple over the side.

"Hey! What the hell?!"

"Keep pouring!" She continues to back up until the fuel can is empty. She pulls a lighter from her pocket and eases the Power Wagon up to the last of the fuel pooled on the pavement, tossing the lighter down, instantly setting the fuel aflame. She puts more distance between us and the RV and we watch the flame eat up the fuel, shooting towards my home.

I say a silent prayer, something about home and heart I read once, and watch as flames engulf the back of the vehicle. Red and orange cover the back then flow forward around the sides.

The SAT vehicles shimmer through the heat beyond and I see the outlines of people waving weapons of all types.

"Come on, come on," Veronica says. "Blow already!"

The SATs just reach the RV when the back end explodes, ripping the vehicle in half, launching the back part into the sky. Vehicles brake and swerve to avoid the fiery debris and the road becomes chaos. Veronica immediately takes advantage of this chaos, using the dense, black smoke as cover, whipping the truck about and back the way we came. A single, flame engulfed figure, crawls from the wreckage and stumbles into the woods, setting the underbrush and trees aflame as it goes.

Joseph...

"There's a side road back here! We'll take that until I can loop around and get us heading in the right direction!"

Neither Karen or I respond, as we watch the hell behind us grow smaller and smaller. I reach out and grip her hand. She squeezes back, nearly crunching the bones of my hand together, but I ignore the pain as we watch my home and her brother disappear forever.

We're about ten miles along the side road, more like a wide dirt trail, when Mom stirs and her eyes flutter open. Somehow Karen has managed to sob herself asleep and her head rests against my shoulder when Mom pushes herself from the truck bed.

"What happened? Where's the RV?"

"Gone," I answer. Mom tries to fight the jostling of the truck, but surrenders quickly, lying back down. "We blew it up to stop the SATs from following."

"Did you get any supplies out?"

"Nothing but fuel. We'll have to scrounge along the way for food and water. I lost the map, too." Mom shakes her head and reaches into her back pocket, producing the map. "Oh, thank God!"

Mom looks over at Karen. "Where's Joseph?"

"Crispy critter, I guess," I answer bitterly. "He ran off, setting half the woods on fire. He's cooked."

"Garret!" Mom snaps, but doesn't say anything beyond that. She braces her arms and legs against the bed to keep from sliding around. "What happened to me? Did I pass out?"

"I guess so. One second you were driving and yelling at me and the next you were slumped over the wheel."

"Yeah, that can happen."

"What can happen? Why?"

"My body is going to shut down soon and I'll turn. Fainting

is one of the first signs. I'll have seizures soon, next couple days maybe, then start vomiting blood."

"Like Joseph was doing?"

Karen mutters something in her sleep and we both wait to see if she wakes. She shifts her position, but stays asleep.

"Sort of like Joseph. That was a much more accelerated process."

"Because of my blood?"

She nods.

"And why is this? Why am I the Carrier and not Little Man?" Garth grunts when I mention him. "None of this makes sense."

Mom laughs hard, her hands on her belly. "Make sense? We live in a world where the dead rise and try to eat us! Of course nothing makes sense!"

"But you're the surgeon! Explain it to me. Why am I a Carrier, but not a nec?"

"I don't know."

"Oh, come on! You expect me to believe that?"

"You're going to have to, Garret, because I don't know! Your father doesn't even know! Whatever process happened in the womb caused this and neither of us can figure out why."

"Wait... Then you were lying earlier. Little Man didn't infect you, I did!"

Mom stays quiet.

"Why lie about that?"

"Because I didn't want to deal with all the questions. From you or from them. Do you think they'll want to help us if you're a Carrier? Walking death ready to infect them?"

"But, you're infected also. You could kill them too."

"True. Quite a pair, aren't we?" Mom looks at me closely. "Do I look as bad as you do?"

"You look pretty banged up," I answer studying the cuts and gashes, bruises and marks covering her arms, neck and face.

"That gouge on your arm isn't looking so good," she says, crawling over to me. "What did this?"

"Crossbow. One of the freaks hit me when I was on top of the RV. It hurts pretty bad."

Mom reaches past me and knocks on the back window. Veronica slides it open. "What?"

"Did your bikers use any poison on their bolts?"

"Sure they did. Something Travis put together. Pretty deadly cocktail. They only used it for hunt and kill orders. Why? You get hit?" Mom nods in my direction. "Crap. I'm surprised he isn't dead yet."

"What?!" I exclaim. "I'm going to die? From a scratch?"

"What...? Who's going to die now?" Karen asks sleepily, pushing away from me. She looks about and then bursts into tears.

Mom looks from me to Karen and back to me. She raises her eyebrows and nods towards me. I awkwardly drape my good arm around Karen and pull her to my chest. She sobs and cries, her face buried in my less than clean shirt.

"Pull over," Mom says to Veronica and she stops the truck. Mom hops out and gets into the passenger seat. She leans over to the back window. "Between Veronica's knowledge of the area and what I can make out on the map, we should be able to get to Cottage Grove and avoid as many obstacles as possible. You two just rest." She fixes me with a hard gaze. "Keep us informed on that arm. If it gets worse or you start feeling sick then tell us right away."

"Yeah, don't die back there," Veronica chimes in. "I really don't want to see what kind of slick you become." I can see the joking smile on her face in the rearview mirror, but the tone of truth still comes through in her voice. She really doesn't want to see what I'd become.

Neither do I.

Karen's sobs slow down and she pushes away from me. "Tell me what happened."

"I can't," I say quietly.

"Why not? Didn't you see it? How did he get infected? How did he turn so quickly?"

I don't answer.

She looks at me and frowns. She traces her fingers along the wounds on my face. I wince and move her hands away. "Please don't." I immediately inspect her hands, looking for any open cuts or scratches.

"What are you doing?" she asks, pulling her hands away

from me. "What are you looking for?"

"Nothing," I mutter. "Just making sure you are okay."

"Um, there's more to me than just my hands, you know."

"Yes, but..."

"But what? What aren't you saying? Tell me, 3B!" She punches my chest and I double over in a coughing fit. "Oh, God. I'm sorry. Did I do that?"

"No, it's the poison," I choke out pointing at my arm. She seems to notice it for the first time and reaches out to touch the cut. I slap her hand away. "Don't touch it! Don't touch any of me until I can get cleaned up."

"Why can't I touch you, 3B? What's wrong? Is the poison contagious or something?"

"Or something..."

She searches my eyes and I have to look away, the shame and guilt too much.

"Did you...? Did you have something to do with Joseph getting infected?" She looks around my shoulder at the surprisingly calm Little Man. "Did your brother bite him or scratch him?!"

"No...It wasn't Little Man..."

"If it wasn't him then who...?"

I can see connections being made and then her eyes grow wide as she pushes away from me, scooting to the back of the truck, instinctively putting a fuel can in front of her. "Are you...? Are you infected?"

"No, not quite," I answer, the shame stronger now. "I'm something else."

She starts to ask me more, but I can't hear her as I double over with another coughing fit. A sharp pain racks my chest and it feels like something is breaking inside me and I cover my mouth as the force of the cough increases. I pull my hands away and see blood, lots of blood.

"Garret?" Karen asks. I look up at her and see alarm, but also concern. I guess I can't stay a monster in her eyes for too long. "Garret, what's wrong?"

My head swims and temples pound. I try to respond to her, but my tongue feels too heavy and I can't get the words out. I know Karen is asking me something and I think I can hear my mom behind me, yelling from the truck's cab, but all the sounds in my head swim together creating a cacophony of painful noise.

I try to cover my ears to shut out the noise, but neither of my arms will work. The world shifts focus as I fall over on my side. Karen is in my face yelling, but I don't understand the words. I don't understand anything.

Just before the world washes away to black a small voice echoes in my head, "He ain't heavy..."

...he's your brother.

Dad?

Hey, G. Been looking for you.

For me? We've been looking for you!

I know, sorry about that. I'm okay though. Not to worry.

Not to worry?! Mom is beside herself! So am I! Where are you?

Oh, just here, there, everywhere...

That's not an answer!

You like telling me that, don't you? You somehow think I have all the answers, right? That Dad is the all knowing Oz!

No, I don't think you're a wizard or anything!

Oz wasn't really a wizard though, was he? He was a con artist that got lost. A grifter. A flim-flam man!

What does that have...? Oh, are you saying you've been conning me and Mom all this time?

Not saying that at all, G, my boy. Never said that, never will.

What are you saying?

"Garret?"

Dad? What are you saying?

"Garret? Can you hear me?"

DAD!

Right here, my boy.

Wait... You're not my Dad. You're Charles! You sicko freak! Get away from me!

Can't rightly get away from you, my boy, when I am you. It doesn't work that way.

"Garret! Hang on. Please hang on!"

Who is that?

Who is what?

That voice.

There's lots of voices in here, G.

Dad? Is that you again?

It never was, never will be. It's always you. Always about Garret.

About me? No. It's always been about Little Man. He's been the focus, hasn't he? He carries all the antibodies, right? I'm the disease, but he's the cure?

Couldn't really say. All the data burned up.

No, it didn't! Mom told me you have it all in your head!

In my head? You're mistaken, my boy! My head is splattered across the window.

Go away, Charles! I'm not talking to you! I'm talking to my Dad!

You're talking to yourself, kid. That isn't sinking in.

Lester? Great, just what I need.

Apparently it is what you need. Your fevered brain is making me talk. Trust me, I want nothing to do with you. You killed me after all.

Killed you? How did I kill you? You got yourself into that mess, not me!

But we were trying to rescue your mother. If you hadn't talked me into it I'd still be alive and we'd be driving down the road in your RV. All safe and sound. Just you, me, Karen...oh, and don't forget Joseph!

Yeah, killer, don't forget me!

I'm so confused... Why am I hearing all of your voices?

You seemed smart and cool, Garret. You could have been my big brother. But you killed me instead. Your loss...

"Garret! We're going to get you help! Just hang on!"

Help? Who can help me? I have a necro brother attached to my spine. I have a mom that's infected and probably going to turn nec any minute now. My dad is missing and he's the guy with all the answers. Who's going to help?

I never said I had the answers, G. Don't be putting words in my mouth.

You've always had the answers! I'd read books and you'd help me understand them. Concepts that don't exist anymore in this dead world, you would give me context. You'd go over it and over it until I understood. Don't say you don't have answers! You have all the answers! Where are you?

Right here, my boy.

No! Not Charles! Where's my Dad?

I'm exactly where I need to be, G. I'm exactly where you want me.

Tell me! No riddles! No codes! Tell me the truth for once!

"Calm down. Calm down. It's the fever."

What? Who is that?

That's not us, kid/my boy/G. We don't know who that is. Which means you don't know who that is.

I know I don't know who it is! I'm the one asking!

Watch your tone, son. You're all alone in here. Don't make me leave you.

What? You...? You already left!

True. But I'm never far away. I told you I'd find you. Maybe I have already.

Wait, have you been watching us? Me and Mom? Have you been following us all this time?

Couldn't really say...

"Garret? This is going to hurt. Can you hear me, Garret? You have to hold still. I'm sorry for the pain, but you can't keep moving. Someone hold him down, please!"

See! There's the voice again!

Hello?

Dad?

Lester?

Charles?

Anyone?

Joseph?

Oh, I'm still here. I'll never leave you, Garret. I'll be in your mind and on your mind forever. Murderer's guilt is what they call it.

I didn't mean to kill you! I'm sorry, I'm so sorry! Please don't hate me!

Hate? No time for hate. Just time for guilt. Guilt. Guilt.

He ain't heavy, he's your brother...

"Damn! He's bleeding out! Hand me the iron! NOW!"

Did he mention it was going to hurt, Garret?

Yes, Joseph, he mentioned it. Whoever 'he' is.

Does it hurt? Does it hurt like when you infected me and my entire body burned? Does it hurt like death?

AAAAAAAAAAAAAAAAAHHHHHHHHHH! YES! IT HURTS LIKE DEATH!

Good. Remember that. Remember this pain. Don't let it happen again. Don't kill me again.

I WON'T! I PROMISE! OH GOD! IT HURTS SO MUCH!

At least that means you're alive. Try to stay that way. Good luck, Garret. You are so going to need it!

I ain't heavy, I'm your brother...

WAIT...? WHAT?! LITTLE MAN? GARTH, IS THAT YOU?! AAAAAAAAAAAAAHHHHHHH!

6

"I need...to...throw up," I croak, struggling to open my eyes and turn my head.

"Tell me something I don't know. You've been doing it for the past forty-eight hours," I hear Karen say. "Just lean over and let it out."

I can hear the weariness in her voice and I make an extra effort to keep my eyes open once I'm done vomiting. "Forty-eight hours? How do I have anything left?"

"I've been feeding you elk broth and herb tea in-between puke sessions," she answers. "You can thank me later."

"Can I thank you now?" I ask weakly. Her hair is plastered to her forehead and the black circles under her eyes are like she painted them on. "Thank you."

She nods and grabs the bowl from the floor that I threw up in. "I'll clean this. Don't puke until I get back." She's up and out the door before I can say anything else.

Door? Where am I?

I think about sitting up to get a better look at my surroundings, but my throbbing head and protesting stomach disagree, so I stay put on my side and study what I can see.

The room is small, only enough space for the cot I'm on, the chair next to it and a small stand for a basin and pitcher. The walls are wood and the whole room smells of cedar, and a little bit of vomit and stinky me. There's a skylight in the center of the room that let's in some light, so I know I'm either on the top floor or it's a one story building.

But what building and where?

Surprisingly, Little Man is calm and quiet. I reach back to give him a pat and my arm explodes in pain.

I try not to scream, but the pain is too much.

Karen bursts through the door, panic on her face. "What?! What is it?! Is Garth okay?!"

The pain subsides as I blink at her a few times, not quite sure of what she is asking. "Did you just ask if Little Man is alright?"

"Yes! Is he? He's been struggling along with you."

I'm about to reach back again, but stop myself. "I don't know. He isn't moving and he's being really quiet."

"He's been like that the past two days. Let me check."

Karen is about to pull back the covers when Little Man lets one rip.

"Oh, God!" she cries out, covering his nose. "Yeah, he's just fine."

I laugh, but it turns into a coughing fit then I'm retching into the puke bowl again. "Ow..."

The door opens up and a young man, maybe ten years older than me (I'm getting better at figuring this out now that I've been exposed to more people), dark skinned, short black hair, peeks in. "How are the patients?"

Karen rolls her eyes. "One's awake and the other is stinking up the room. So good, I guess."

The young man steps fully into the room, his nose wrinkling. "I smell what you're saying. Hey, Garret. How are you feeling?"

"Like poo. And you?"

"I'm doing fine," he laughs extending his hand. "I'm Billy Silverthorn. I patched you up."

I shake the hand and things start to fit into place. "Silverthorn? Is that a Tribe name?" I look to Karen. "Are we with the Tribes?"

"Actually, the name is old English, but it works just as well in the Tribes. And yes, you are with the Tribes. That isn't a problem is it?"

I shake my head no, but wish I hadn't as more pain throbs across my skull. "As long as you don't try to kill us or eat us then it's fine with me. Thanks for fixing me up." I look at Karen again and see she is watching Billy closely. "What happened? How did we get here?" Karen doesn't respond. "Um, hello? Person talking here."

"What? Oh, sorry," Karen apologizes, turning her attention back to me. "It's a long story."

Billy glances from her to me while trying to hide the smirk on his face. "I'm going to let you two talk. There are other patients, you know." Darkness washes over his face, but it's gone quickly. "I'll be right back to take your vitals and redress your arm. Hang tight."

Karen stares at the door after he leaves and I clear my throat to get her attention. "Seems like a nice guy. Handsome, too."

"Yes, he is," she replies casually. "Wait, what? I mean, he's nice. Not handsome."

"You don't think he's handsome?" I tease.

"No, I didn't say that."

"Yes, you did. You just said 'not handsome'."

"Well, I didn't mean it that way. I just meant he's a nice guy." Karen's face bunches up and she studies mine. "Wait... Are you jealous?"

"Jealous? No, not at all. Why would I be jealous? That's just crazy talk."

"You are jealous! Why, because I kissed you on the cheek once? I bet you think we're going steady or something, huh?"

"Going steady?" I laugh painfully. "What is this, a Hardy Boys book?"

"Hardy Boys? I have no idea what that means."

"It was a set of mystery books from the 1920's, but later updated in the 1950's. Going steady was a term used back then a lot."

"Well, it's just something my parents would say." Her brow furrows. "Why are we arguing about this? You're jealous, just admit it!"

I'm lost. Do I admit I'm jealous to her? I don't even know if I am. But if the feeling of wanting to get up and knock Billy Silverthorn around is any indication then I probably am. Weird feeling. I don't even know the man and I want to slap him for looking at Karen. Great, just what I need, more mental and emotional confusion.

"Hello? 3B? You still with me?" Karen asks, waving her hand in my face. "You did that space out thing again."

"Oh... Sorry. I was just thinking..."

"About how jealous you are?" she says with a big grin. "It's okay. You can space out on that."

Her smile warms me up, pushing some of the pain away.

"Thanks," I smile. "Not that I'm admitting anything."

"No, of course not."

We sit quiet for a bit. "So, are you going to tell me what happened?"

Karen frowns. "Do I have to? It wasn't a fun time."

"Can I get the highlights, at least?"

She sighs. "You passed out. We thought you were dead from the poison. The SATs caught up to us again as soon as we hit the main road. There was a lot of blood and fire and smoke and screaming. I did most of the screaming. We crashed, thought we were going to die and then the Tribes stepped in and beat the SATs back. They were going to kill us themselves, something about Veronica being wanted and hunted by the Tribes, but they saw you and Garth and then totally freaked out. They got you back here, cleaned your wound and have been pretty nice ever since."

I stare at her. "Those are quite the highlights. Can we get to the details now?"

"I'd rather not, please," she says quietly. "Like I said, it wasn't a fun time."

We're silent for a bit.

"I'm sorry, Karen," I whisper. "I really am sorry."

"You have nothing to be sorry about," she answers without meeting my gaze.

"Joseph was my fault," I continue. "I didn't know I was the Carrier. I didn't-."

She stands suddenly and moves to the door. "I can't talk about this with you. Not now."

"Wait!" I yell and my head protests. I wince and she stops, concern back on her face. But she doesn't move towards me. "Wait... I just need you to know that I'm sorry."

She looks at me and so many emotions wash over her face I'm not sure if she hates me, likes me, wants to kill me, heal me, or just ignore me.

"I know you're sorry," she says finally. "But I can't talk about this with you now. Someday, but not now. Can we just be who we are right now and not dwell on what's happened? I can't go there, Garret. Not without hating you." She's on the verge of tears, but she chokes them back. "I don't want to hate you. I really don't."

I nod. "Okay. I'll let it drop. When you're ready, I'm here."

She only nods.

"So, how about we talk about why we are here. Also, where's my mom?"

Karen's demeanor changes right away and I can see she's more than relieved to switch the subject.

"Your Mom is fine. She explained everything to them and she's with some of the elders right now. They're plotting and planning something, I don't know what."

"But she's okay? She hasn't...well, she's healthy?"

"She hasn't gone slick, if that's what you're asking." She laughs weakly at the look on my face. "She told us all. She was pretty honest about your story and your father's role. She didn't exactly make him out to be the good guy."

"I'm sure she didn't. What about Veronica? Is she okay?"

Karen grimaces and her eyes narrow. "That's a tricky one. She's supposed to have a trial before the Tribal elders to-morrow. They'll decide what to do with her then."

"What?! What to do with her?! We'd all be dead without her!"

"I know that and you know that. You're mom is making a strong case for her, but..."

"But what?"

"She's done some pretty bad things for the Griffins. The Tribes aren't being very forgiving."

I can tell she's holding something back.

"What?" I ask. "What else?"

"Your mom told the tribes about what Veronica is. They aren't too happy about that."

"About what? What is she?" Then the image of the Nursery back at the SAT compound hits me. "Oh, I think I know. She's kinda like me."

"She's nothing like you!" Karen snaps.

"Whoa! Sorry. I just meant that she's engineered like me. I know she isn't really like me."

"No, she's not," Karens spits out. "And you are nothing like her."

Thankfully, there's a knock at the door and Billy is back. "My turn." He looks at us and his eyebrows raise. "Did I miss something?"

"No, Garret was just being stupid." Karen gives my hand a squeeze. A good, hard squeeze. I force myself not to wince. "I'll be back soon with some food." She looks at Billy. "Just broth?"

"He can have a little mush too. Let's see how he does with something other than liquid."

"Mush?" I groan. "Sounds yummy."

"It isn't bad, actually," Karen says as she steps to the door, fixing me with her gaze. "Be nice, 3B. I want a good report when I get back. No more being stupid."

And she's gone. Which leaves me alone with handsome Billy Silverthorn.

"**C**an you try to sit up for me?" Billy asks.

"Do I have to? It didn't go so well last time."

"I understand," Billy smiles, putting on a stethoscope. Damn, he is handsome. Jerk.

"But your reaction will tell me a lot also," he continues. "Sorry for the discomfort."

"Can't you just wave some smoking sticks over me and figure out what's wrong?"

"Um, I figured since you're the son of a surgeon you'd have a more realistic idea of how medicine works." His look becomes a little more stern. "Sit up, Garret. Please."

Guess he didn't appreciate the burning sticks joke.

"Okay, but be prepared to jump back. I'll probably spew."

"I'm used to it, trust me."

With Billy's help I slowly sit up. The dizziness and nausea are less, but I still have to take a few deep breaths to keep from puking. Little Man gives a small grunt, but I remember not to reach back this time.

"I'm guessing you and Garth have similar sleeping patterns? He was out the entire time you were."

"I wouldn't know since I'm asleep."

Billy stops and looks at me. "Is there a problem, Garret? I just met you and you're already hostile towards me. It usually takes others a day or two before they get hostile."

I try not to smile at his joke, but can't help myself. "Sorry.

Just confused and tired. Can I see my mom?"

"Soon. She's busy right now."

"That's what Karen said."

"Ah, yes, Karen. Is that the hostility? I see how you two look at each other. You been together for a while now?"

"What? Us? We? Together? No. I mean... No! We just... We aren't... I don't know."

"And you think I want to come between you?"

I don't answer.

Billy holds up his left hand in my face. "See the ring? Married. Karen's a little young for me anyway."

"She's nineteen. That's too young?"

"Not for you maybe. But I'm thirty. There's a huge difference between nineteen and thirty. Even in a crazy world like this." He taps my chest a couple of times. "Deep breath please."

I do as he asks and I'm instantly coughing, my lungs feeling like they have a huge weight on them. I hack away and am soon throwing up. Billy holds the bowl for me then hands me a towel to wipe my mouth with.

"Thanks," I say, taking small sips of water from a glass he hands me. "That sucked."

"It's better than when you were unconscious," he laughs. "I actually thought I saw a lung coming up at one point."

"Seriously?" That would be something to see.

"No, I'm kidding. It was pretty bad though. You have broken capillaries all over from the violence of the coughing though. You look like a crazy road map."

He does a few more tests and checks the dressing on my arm. "That's not looking as good as I would like. We had to cut and cauterize, it was so bad. I was able to get all of the necrotic tissue out, I think. Went through six pairs of deer intestine gloves doing it. Those aren't easy to make, you know. But your Mom said they were necessary." He looks from Little Man to me. "To say you're a bit of a medical oddity is an understatement."

"Yep, I'm a regular freak show," I frown.

"In this world? Hardly. Even with a conjoined twin, do you know how lucky you are? You're immune to the virus. I wish I could have a few weeks to check you out and study your blood."

"A few weeks? Am I going somewhere right away?" He doesn't answer. "Let me guess, I need to ask my mom."

"Exactly. Sorry."

"Why did you save us?"

"What? I didn't save you. I'm medical, not tactical."

"You know what I mean. Why'd the Tribes step in and save us? You all could have let the SATs get us. I mean, I don't know a thing about you folks, but I have learned it's an every man for themselves kind of world."

"No. I guess you don't know anything about us folks," Billy laughs. "We don't just leave people to die. There's what, one percent of the human population left? While that still may mean there's a million people living across this country, it doesn't mean we have one life to waste. You know what happens in a shallow gene pool?"

I gulp. "You want to breed us?"

"No. That's not what I mean at all." He pours some water into the basin and rinses his hands, drying them on a small towel next to the washstand. "It just means that we need as much diversity as possible to keep the species alive. While the majority of the Tribes are of Native American blood, you can hardly call us pure. We don't have that luxury any longer."

"So you saved us for some greater good? Is that what you're saying? Karen said you nearly killed us because of Veronica, but didn't because of Little Man and me."

Billy's face falls. "I'm not going to talk about her. She's different."

"How so?"

"I'm not going to say. You can ask your mother. She'll fill you in." There's a knock and Karen is back with a steaming bowl of mush. "Looks like lunch is here. Or breakfast for you, I guess. I'll be back in a couple of hours. Send Karen if you need me."

"Thanks, Doc."

"Doc? I'm not a doctor. Not officially anyway. Those are hard to come by. Unless you have one for a mom." He grins. "Call me Billy."

"Okay...Billy. Thanks."

"My pleasure, Garret. Nice talking with you. Try to get some rest." He looks at Karen. "He's full of questions, but make sure he doesn't tire out. Fifteen minutes at the most, okay?"

"Sure. Thanks, Billy," she replies as he closes the door. "Not really a bad guy, is he?"

"Eh, he's okay," I shrug and wince. "I've met worse."

Karen laughs and sits on the cot.

"We okay?" I ask, sounding more eager than I had intended.

She fights a smile. "Yes, 3B. We're okay. Just stop..."

"...being stupid. Yeah, I got it."

"Here, eat a little."

"It doesn't taste bad, right?" She's quiet. "You said it's not so bad, right?"

"I lied," she grins. "It tastes like wet paper. But it's 'nutrient dense' the cooks say. And nutrient dense is what you need."

"You realize if it tastes awful I'll just puke it back up, right?"

"You'll be fine." She raises a spoon to my mouth, but I keep my lips sealed. "3B open your mouth right now! Don't be a baby!"

I reluctantly open my mouth and she spoons in a bite. It tastes awful. "More please," I mumble around the first bite, because even with the horrible taste I realize I'd probably eat anything at this point. She gives me another bite, waits for me to finish and then another. "Oh, God, that's horrible."

"Better than nothing."

I nod and eat some more. "When's Veronica's trial?" I ask around a mouthful. "I want to be there. She saved my butt."

"She saved all of our butts. You missed the real shoot out." I can see jealousy and respect fighting for control on Karen's face. And fear. "She has abilities that are a bit disturbing. You're lucky you didn't have to witness everything."

"I'm not horribly disappointed I missed more blood," I reply, thinking back to the road fight. Thinking back to Joseph. "I'll take being unconscious for that anytime."

She frowns. "Me too."

"So... When's the trial?"

"Tomorrow morning. At dawn. Something about the spirits in the morning light."

I look at her in surprise. "Really?"

She laughs. "No." The laugh stops quickly. "They just need time to build the gallows if they decide to execute her at sundown."

"Ha, funny."

"I'm not kidding this time. That's what they said."

"Wow... Crap, that sucks."

"Yes, it does."

CHAPTER TWELVE

The room is dark when I awake, but I can see someone sitting close by. "Karen?"

"Really? Already forgot your ole mom, eh?"

"Mom? Sorry, I thought Karen would be here. She said she'd stay with me tonight."

"And that is just one more thing you need to learn about women, son. You don't ask the girl you like..."

"Mom!"

"...to stay awake all night sitting in a hard chair while you sleep. Although, I think she would have done it."

I roll my eyes, but I doubt she can see me. "Where'd she go?" I yawn and stretch, wincing slightly, my arm reminding me that it is in charge.

"I sent her to bed. Figured it was my duty to watch over you. I have more experience."

We stay silent for a while.

"How's Veronica?" I ask, not sure I want to know the answer.

"She's being treated well," Mom answers, but her voice betrays her real feelings.

"They're going to kill her, aren't they?"

"Probably. The Griffins and the Tribes have a violent history. Apparently Veronica has been a major part of that violence."

"But she helped us escape. She killed Charles! And she's

only a teenager! That should count for something."

"If she had killed me would her killing someone else count for anything? Would her age make any difference to you?"

I try to figure out an argument against that, but she's right. "No."

"Exactly."

"Can I testify?"

"What?"

"Can I testi..."

"I heard what you said; I just didn't believe you said it. You've only known this girl for a couple days. Why would you want to testify on her behalf?"

"Because she saved me. She got both of us out of that crazy place. She could have just saved herself, but she didn't. Why? Because she needs people just like the rest of us. She needed someplace to go once she did escape. She needed help."

I can feel Mom's glare. "And? What else is there?"

"And she's kinda like me. She's more than just a person. She's...different."

"Uh-huh," Mom muses. "I can see that. But, what if she saw us as a meal ticket for a while? Or she is actually working for one of the other factions. Maybe she's a spy for the Keep? There are way too many reasons for what she did."

"Everyone talks about the Keep. What is it exactly?"

"Nice try. You need to work on your segue. That's for another time, Garret. Not tonight. I just don't have it in me."

She can talk about Veronica being executed, but she can't talk about the Keep? That's not a good sign.

I yawn big and Mom laughs. "Go back to sleep, Garret. You and your brother need your strength."

She gets up and gives me a kiss on my forehead. Her lips are hot, almost like coals against my skin.

"Mom? Are *you* feeling alright?"

She doesn't answer.

"Mom? How are you feeling? Please don't hide anything from me."

"I'm fine. Don't worry."

"I'm already worrying. You feel hot. Unnaturally hot."

She sighs and I can tell she's about to leave so I reach out and grab her wrist. She gasps and tries to pull away, but I grip with all my strength. Her skin is insanely warm. I don't know how she can stand it. "How much time do you have?"

She won't answer and tries to pull away again. Little Man screeches and comes fully awake, his fists thumping against my shoulder.

"Mom, you have to answer me. Little Man doesn't lie. He knows you're close to changing."

"You don't know what he's saying, Garret."

"Bull! I know exactly what he's saying! To him you are basically a nec. How much time do you have? Answer me!"

"Don't take that tone with me!"

"I'll take whatever tone I want!" I shout. "How much time?!"

She stands there for a while, but she doesn't yell back at me. Finally she sits heavily at my feet.

"A day. Maybe...maybe not."

"A day?!" I sit upright quickly and my arm screams. "Ow! Screw it! A day?! How are we going to get to Cottage Grove? Will they even let us in?! You'll be a nec by then! You'll be the enemy!"

"They are fully aware of my situation, Garret. They'll let us in. If they want any chance at Garth's antibodies then they will play ball."

"What about the Tribes? Will they even let us go? What deals have you made with them?"

"I didn't make any deals."

She's lying.

"Mom. I'm seventeen, not stupid."

"There's an argument that seventeen and stupid are one and the same."

"Hardy har har. Seriously, please."

"I gave them certain codes to a certain place. They'll be more than happy to help us however we need."

"Codes? Oh my God, you are nothing but one mystery after another! I get an answer but end up with at least ten more questions! Are you trying to break my brain?"

"I'm just struggling to keep my own brain from breaking. I can't always be watching out for yours. You're a big boy now, Garret, time to step up and act like one."

I roll my eyes, even though she can't see me do it in the

dark. "You're such a mother sometimes."

"Get some sleep," she laughs. "And thanks for that. It's probably the best compliment you've ever given me."

I should feel good about this, but I don't. Have I always been that mean to her to count that as the best thing I've ever said to her? I'm one crappy son.

"Get some sleep," she says again. "I know you'll want to be at the trial whether they let you testify or not. Billy will have to give the okay, so the more sleep, the better your case."

"My case? I'm not the one on trial."

"No, but you're the one that will need help getting to the trial. You aren't as strong as you think you are. Get some sleep."

I yawn and chuckle. "Okay. But promise me you will try to get them to let me testify?"

"I'll see what I can do. Get some..."

"Sleep. Yeah, yeah, I know." I lay back down and pull the blanket over me. I don't even hear her leave the room before sleep takes me out.

2

"No," Billy says, shaking his head as he stands in the doorway of my room, blocking me and Karen. "You just started eating solid food."

"I wouldn't call that mush solid," I laugh. "That's stretching it a bit."

"You know what I mean," he scowls. "That was major surgery on your arm and I really don't know if there are any clots that may have formed. Moving around too much could send one to your brain or your heart, killing you instantly. You are staying put."

"Not happening," I reply. "Get out of our way, Doc. I'm going to go help Veronica."

"I already told him they won't let him testify," Karen adds, not helping in the least.

"We'll see about that," I snap.

"No. We won't," Billy responds. "Because you aren't going anywhere. Even If I did let you go, the trial is a formality. That girl has killed or captured too many of our people to let live."

"But she saved our lives! I'm not just going to let her be murdered!"

"Murder? What exactly do you know about murder, Garret? From talking with your mom it sounds like you have only been around other people for less than a week. How can you even conceive of a concept like murder? Have you wanted to murder your mom? Or your dad?"

"No," I mumble.

"Then you can't even begin to understand what is happening. Veronica is a murderer. When she is executed it will be justice, not murder. It will help a lot of suffering people put their pain to rest. Do you want others to continue to suffer? Do you think Veronica's life is worth that?"

We stare at each other for a long time. Little Man grunts a few times and kicks feebly, but quiets down when he realizes I'm not going to give him any attention.

"Are you just going to stand there all day?" I finally ask Billy.

"No, I have others that need tending. But they will have to wait until I'm sure you aren't leaving this room."

"Now who wants others to suffer?" I snort, throwing his words back at him. "I'm not backing down. Is me standing here for hours going to be good for me? Is that your prescription? Because I'm not going back to bed."

Billy glares at me then looks pleadingly at Karen. She just shrugs and I can't help but smile.

"Fine," he relents then points a finger at Karen. "You keep him from hurting himself. He gets there and sits his butt down. No testifying, no interrupting, nothing! Got it?"

"I'll do what I can," she says. "I don't want him hurt either. But he is a giant pain."

"Gee. Thanks," I respond.

"Well, you are." A darkness clouds her face and I realize what a jerk I've been. Joseph is gone. Her parents are gone. Even her backstabbing uncle is gone. Karen has nobody left. She's holding up amazingly well, but that's only because she's keeps the grief buried.

"For Karen I'll be good," I state. "She doesn't need more grief."

Billy's eyebrows raise. "You may be more mature than I thought." He steps away from the door. "Go. Be good. Try not to undo everything I worked on."

"You betcha, Doc," I grin as we step past him.

"And don't call me Doc!" he calls after us. "I'm not a doctor!"

"If it walks like a duck and talks like a duck..." I call back.

"A duck? What are you talking about?" Karen asks as we round the hall corner.

"I don't know. Something I read." I wince a little as even the slow pace sends pain jolting through my arm. Plus, my leg is still tender from those SAT spikes. Not bad, but tender. "How far do we have to walk?"

Karen laughs. "You are such a pain!"

"What? I never said I wasn't in pain. I just said it wasn't going to stop me." We each laugh a little then stay quiet as she guides me through a maze of corridors and out into the dawn light.

We aren't the only ones up for the trial. Dozens of people are making their way from the rows of wood buildings and down a long stone path that weaves its way through a thick grove of pine trees.

"I guess this is a pretty big deal," I say.

"You didn't get that from what Billy said? You aren't the quickest one are you?"

"Ha ha. No, I got it. I was just making an observation."

We keep to the side of the path since I can't move as fast as everyone else. Most just nod as they pass us. Some ignore us and a few glare. They must figure I have something to do with Veronica's past. Maybe testifying wouldn't be so smart.

"Listen," I start. "I've been pretty selfish the past couple of days. You've lost a lot more than I have."

Karen doesn't respond and I feel her body tense.

"I know there isn't anything I can do to make it better..."

"How do you know?!" she snaps, stopping in place. My feet skid on the stone path and I almost bring us both down.

"Whoa! Watch it!" I complain.

"No! You don't give me orders, 3B. You killed my brother, so you don't get to tell me what to do at all." I start to pro-test and she holds up her hand. "Shut it. You just can't let it go, like I asked, huh? I know you didn't mean for anything to happen to Joseph, but it is your fault. I'm not holding any grudge. Hell, how can I? You and your mom are all I have now! They won't let me stay here, trust me, I asked! I'm tainted goods because of Veronica! As soon as you're well enough to travel they want me gone with you."

"Wait...what? Tainted goods? Me gone? You gone? I don't understand what's going on!"

"Exactly! And that's your problem! While technically you

aren't an only child you sure do act like one! You think about yourself first! Do you realize that these people pushing past us aren't just glaring at you? They hate me also. And why? What did I do other than trust the people around me? Do you realize I'd never been threatened by a slick once until I met you?"

"You aren't actually blaming..."

"Quiet!" I shut my mouth with a snap. "What I mean is that all the bad things that have happened to me have happened because of other people. Not slicks, not this crazy world, but people! My mom dies when I'm born. My dad disappears, apparently killed by Lester. Lester, well, you know what he did. You. You bring nothing but death and destruction wherever you go. Or at least your family does. I'd be better off trying to live with the slicks! God! Why am I even helping you?!"

She let's go of my arm and stomps down the path, around a curve and is lost from my sight. I reach out and carefully lean against a tree. Now everyone keeps their eyes averted, no one meeting my gaze. I'd ask for help, but that obviously isn't going to happen.

I stumble forward slowly, going from tree to tree to keep my balance. I only get a couple tress along when Karen comes stomping back up the path. She stands right in front of me, her eyes on fire, her chest heaving with anger, and her lips pressed firmly together in a painful, angry line.

"You are a pain in my butt," she growls.

What happens next I do not expect at all. Karen grabs each side of my head and pulls it down to hers. Her lips are soft and warm and the kiss is over before I know it.

"A *giant* pain in my butt."

She takes my arm and starts helping me down the path again. I'm having a hard time focusing on walking, but I manage to get one foot in front of the other.

"Um...I...um," I stutter.

"Just keep your mouth closed, 3B. Don't ruin anything further by adding to the foot already in it."

Even if I want to respond, my opportunity is lost as we step from the path to the top of a set of stone stairs that leads down into a massive earth amphitheater. People are filling up the benches that are steeped up the sides so Karen quickly moves us to a bench and helps me to sit.

"You okay?" she asks.

"Yeah, I'm fine considering..."

She puts her finger to my lips. "Shhh. I'm going to tell your mom we're here. Stay put."

"Roger," I say, giving her a thumbs up. She smiles, but I can still see the pain behind it.

"Good. I'll be right back."

I watch her hurry down the steps to a bench where my mom is sitting and conferring with several older members of the Tribes all seated on their own bench. Karen leans over her shoulder and Mom turns quickly, looking up for me. I give a small wave and she nods then goes back to her conversation. The elders glance up at me also and most of their faces are hard and angry. This seems to be the general attitude toward me here in the Tribes. I'll be glad when we get to Cottage Grove.

3

Veronica doesn't seem to be harmed at all when they bring her out. But the shackles on her wrists and legs are short chained and she winces with each step. I'm sure they have them extra tight in case she tries to escape. I've seen her move and even with shackles she could probably do some damage and get away if she wanted to. The two guards on each side of her, both at least two-hundred fifty pounds, keep one hand firmly on each elbow. The crowd goes quiet, but their anger and venom towards her is almost as loud as if they were yelling.

I'm not sure I want to be at this trial anymore. I've only known this girl for a day. Sure, she saved my skin, but do I really want to hear everything she did when she worked for the Griffins?

A tall, thin woman, much older than Mom, gets up from the bench of elders and crosses to Veronica. The two stare at each other for a moment. Without warning the tall woman slaps Veronica across one cheek and then the other. Veronica takes it well and doesn't say a thing.

The tall woman turns to the crowd. "This abomination has been an enemy of the Tribes for too long. She has committed murder and other brutal acts of violence over the years and we have sought her head for these crimes. Today we will list each crime so there is no doubt as to what she is accused!" The woman spins about and jabs a finger in Veronica's face.

"This is not a court of law! This is a court of justice! You will not be allowed to speak and will be punished if you do speak without being asked a direct question. Do you understand?"

Veronica nods and the two once again face off. Finally the tall woman takes her seat and a small, plump man gets up, a long piece of paper in his hand.

"Veronica Descheles, you are accused of the following crimes," he announces.

My mouth drops open as he begins to read from the list. I really shouldn't be surprised considering what I know of the Griffins. What I am surprised by is the look on Veronica's face. She almost looks proud as each atrocity is read.

"My God," Karen whispers. "How can one person do all of that?"

"It's a crazy world," I answer. "People do crazy things."

Some of the crowd cry out when their loved ones' names are called. A large man has to be held back, his family dragging him up the stairs and away from the amphitheater. A little girl starts wailing and is rocked back and forth by an older woman, probably her grandmother. A young couple get up, both spitting on the ground before they leave.

Veronica takes this all in stride, the look on her face never changing.

By the time the list is read, half the crowd is gone or has been asked to leave. Several tried to rush Veronica, but were fought off.

The plump man that reads the list takes his seat once again and the elders all confer, their heads leaning in close. Minutes go by without a word from them and the crowd grows restless. Some start to mutter for them to hurry up, while others begin to chant, "Justice. Justice."

Finally the tall woman stands again and raises her hands for quiet. The grumblings of the crowd subside and she takes a deep breath.

"The reading of the crimes was not just so that the accused may know what she has done, but also so those with her know who they are with." The woman glances quickly in mine and Karen's direction then away. "In this trial we do not ask for the law to be upheld, but for justice to be meted out. That is what we will do today."

The woman looks at the rest of the elders and I can tell by their body language that they are uncomfortable. The crowd senses it also and the grumbling begins once more. The tall woman closes her eyes.

"Veronica Descheles will not be executed this evening." The crowd is on its feet and shouting instantly. It takes all of the elders to getting to their own feet, their arms raised and voices shouting for quiet. Finally they get control and the tall woman continues. "Justice will be had, though. She came here with others. One of which is a boy that is special and could help us all, not just the Tribes, but humanity as a whole."

The eyes that turn on me are filled with hate and anger. Little Man starts to squawk and Karen reaches over and pats his head. I ignore the crowd and stare at her. She touched Little Man without even thinking about it.

"What?" she asks. "Why are you looking at me like that?"

I lean over and kiss her quickly. She blushes and most of the crowd turn away, embarrassed.

"What was that for? Did you just use me as a distraction?" she asks, her cheeks burning red. "You better not have."

"That was a thank you for Little Man," I say, my cheeks burning just as hot. "No one has ever touched him before. At least no one sane."

"Oh..." she says quietly, looking away from me.

I can hear the crowd yelling and the tall woman shouting for order, but I ignore it all, reaching out taking Karen's chin in my hand, turning her back to me. Tears are streaming down her cheeks and she tries to pull away.

"What did I do?" I ask, terror gripping my chest. Did I do this wrong? She kissed me first back on the path! Am I not supposed to kiss her again? I have no idea what is going on, so many emotions flowing through me at once. "I'm sorry. I shouldn't have done that."

"No, it's not that," she sniffles, taking my hand in hers. "It's just that even with all of this insanity" –she motions to the shouting and yelling about us— "and all the pain over the past few days I just feel so guilty."

"Um, I'm lost here. Guilty for what?"

"For feeling good! For feeling safe around you! My

brother's dead, or worse, and yet I feel safe! That's crazy! That's wrong!"

She's shouting now and her grip is crushing my fingers. I ignore the pain, knowing she has to let this all out.

"What's wrong with me? I should be a sobbing mess! I should hate you with every fiber in my body! I do hate you but I also lo..." She catches herself before finishing her sentence. "It's just wrong. I'm a horrible person."

"What were you about to say?" I ask. "You said you hate me but also? Also, what?"

"Don't be a jerk, 3B," she whispers.

"Sorry. I'll leave it be," I promise. I pull my hand from hers and work the circulation back in. "For now."

We stare at each other forever. I can see angry people filing past us, stomping up the stairs to the stone path, but I ignore them and their pissed off glares. A few shout at me and I'm sure I know what they are saying, and probably should be a little afraid, but I don't care. My heart feels like it's pounding in my throat and I have to swallow over and over to make sure I'm not going to choke.

"I hate to interrupt, but we have a lot of work to do before we go," Mom says, standing on the stairs next to our bench. "We aren't exactly going to get any help, so let's get a move on."

She could have said she had gold bars falling out her butt for all Karen and I could care. We just keep looking at each other like we are all that exist.

"Um, hello?" Mom growls. "Did you two hear me?"

"We heard you, Mom," I say finally. "What's the huge hurry? Doc Billy won't let me travel anytime soon."

Mom is on me in a second and I can tell she is struggling to not throw me from my bench as she grabs my shirt. Little Man howls and Karen falls back away from the angry woman that is my mother.

"Garret! Snap out of it!" She looks over at Karen. "We talked about distractions, didn't we?" Karen nods. "Then I really don't understand what is going on here. Did you not hear a word of what Lisa Triple Bear said? Did you not hear the calls for our own deaths? Did you not hear the elders' decision?'

"Um...no?" I answer honestly.

Mom lets go of my t-shirt and stalks away, pushing her way through the few people still left in the amphitheater.

Karen and I just sit there, staring out across the amphitheater and wait for everyone to leave. Without looking at her I take her hand in mine. We sit that way even longer until something my mom said hits me.

"Wait...distraction? Talk?"

B illy stands in front of Mom, his face red with anger and frustration, while she takes inventory of supplies laid out on the table in her room.

"See!" I say. "I told you he'd be pissed."

"It doesn't matter," Mom replies. "We can't stay here. We don't have time and we aren't wanted."

"The murderer isn't wanted!" Billy snaps. "Garret is a whole other matter. While some don't believe the old legends, others do. He is welcome to stay. Life out there is no picnic for anyone, let alone a seventeen year old boy."

"Or nineteen year old girl," I add looking over at Karen who is trying to keep herself out of the way in a chair against the wall. "Where I go she goes."

"That has no bearing here," Mom snaps. "We'll talk about that later. Right now we have to get everything together and go. There isn't much time."

"Why?" Billy asks. "Why isn't there much time? All he needs is another day or so to heal that arm and he'll be fine for travel. He may not be fine for combat or running from slicks, but he can handle rough roads and some crazy driving."

Mom doesn't answer, but the coughing fit she goes into tells Billy quite a lot.

"Are you sick? What haven't you told me?"

"Nothing, Mr. Silverthorn. Just leave it."

"That's her favorite phrase. She tells everyone to leave it,"

I say. "She is sick, but there isn't anything you can do."

"Sick? How?"

"It's a long story," Mom says, giving me a disapproving look. "I don't have the time or energy to go into it. You seem to forget that I'm a surgeon, Mr. Silverthorn. I can take care of my son, thank you very much."

"Not if you're fighting for your life the entire way to Cottage Grove! How can you make sure he doesn't start bleeding while killing slicks or watching your butt for a Scavenger ambush? If you are a doctor, a *real* doctor, then you have an oath to uphold! What happened to do no harm? He's your own son, for God's sake!"

"You think I don't know all of that?!" Mom roars. "I've been dealing with this since before he was born! I've been dealing with this since before any of you people even knew what a slick was! I was on the front lines of the world ending, so I am quite aware of every single last danger there is! It still doesn't change the fact that we have to leave! Nothing changes that fact!"

"I don't want to leave," Karen says quietly.

"What?" Mom and I say at the same time.

"I don't want to leave," she says again. "Billy has said we can stay. Me and 3B, at least. He talked to the elders right after the trial. He's promised to be responsible for us in the eyes of the Tribes."

Mom turns on Billy. "You told her that? Even though you knew we were going to be leaving?"

"She's nineteen, she deserves a life that isn't all about surviving day to day and being on the run," Billy states. "The elders agree. They also don't want Garret to leave. Superstition or not, they see his arrival as more than just coincidence."

"What? More than just coincidence? It is superstition! And I don't have time for it!" Mom shouts. "Do you think I want a life of fear and madness? Do you think I want to be on the run forever? That's why we are going to Cottage Grove! To get that life! We can't get it here!" She starts coughing and I just stare at Karen.

"Right. But you're going for your life and for Garret's, not for Karen's," Billy says. "That's hardly fair."

"You really want to stay?" I ask her, slowly kneeling before her, taking her hands in mine. "I thought... I mean..."

"Yes, I want to stay," she answers. "But I want to stay with you. I want you to stay here. Let your Mom and Veronica go do the dangerous stuff and come back for us. We'll just get in the way out there." She looks past me at Mom and her eyes go cold. "We'd just be a *distraction*."

"So that's what this is about, eh?" Mom yells, instantly next to me, towering over Karen. "This is just a pissing match. The young girl versus the old woman! You better bring more than a pretty face to this fight, girlie!"

"Hold on!" I shout, struggling to my feet. "Just hold on!"

"I..!" Mom starts.

"No! Shut it!" I yell over her. "Have a seat and we are going to figure this out!" Mom glares and doesn't move.

Little Man growls low and I match it with my own growl. Mom's eyes go wide and for the first time in a long time I can see fear there. Real fear, not crazy fear. Not on the run fear, but actual from the heart fear.

"Garret, please..."

"Sit. Down."

She does and I motion for Billy to hand me a chair. He does and I sit down with myself positioned between Karen at the wall and Mom at the table.

"Let's get it all out right now," I say. "The elders let Veronica live because we need her help to get us to Cottage Grove. You convinced them that I need to get to the compound because Dad is there and he has the research that could turn the antibodies in me, or in Little Man, I'm still not sure about that part, can turn those antibodies into a cure for the necro virus. Am I right?"

"Yes, but..."

"Let me finish. Now, what I'm guessing you didn't tell them is that you have some serious need for a cure right now. Like in the next day or so. Right?"

Mom nods. Billy and Karen both start to speak, but I cut them off.

"So, no matter if Karen decides to stay, I have to go or you die, right?" Mom nods again. "So, Billy is right that you are hurrying all of this to save your own life. Not to save me. Not to save the world, but to save yourself."

Mom just stares. "It's more complicated than that, Garret."

"Oh, I'm sure it is! Now, Billy, I bet you didn't know I have read a ton of books, did you?"

"Um, no, I didn't," he answers.

"Well anyway, I have. Several of those books have various legends from around the world. One of those legends is about Thunder and Lightning. It's an old Native American legend. Do you know it?"

Billy looks embarrassed, but nods.

"Right. And the legend is actually about twins. How one is born normal and the other is born of magic. There's something about the mother being lost and the father sending the magic son away. Anyway, in the end the twins kill an ogre of some sort and the family comes back together helping the people to live in harmony. Am I right?"

"Close enough," Billy mutters.

"So all that stuff about the elders wanting me to stay because of superstition isn't true, is it?"

"Well, not completely."

"Nope. You actually want me to stay because you think I hold the key to a cure also, don't you?" Billy doesn't answer. "And if I stay then there is no reason to keep Veronica alive, is there? She wouldn't be needed to help get me to Cottage Grove which means she can be executed, right? You get your cure and your justice! Now, Karen..."

"What have I done?" she gasps. "I haven't done anything at all to you, 3B!"

"Well, that's not true. You haven't done anything bad to me, but you've got me pretty messed up inside right now. So I need to be honest with you, okay?" She nods and I see apprehension in her eyes. "I really care for you. I'd throw the L word out there, but all the books have said that just screws things up."

"You can't live by books," she whispers.

"You're 100% right!" I exclaim. "You're the only right person in this room! I can't live by books. I have to live by living! That means I have to go out there. I have to go to Cottage Grove. I have to make that journey myself. I can't let my mom die. I can't let my dad just wait there wondering if we'll ever make it alive. I *have* to go to *live*."

Tears well in Karen's eyes and I'm out of my chair in a second. Dizziness washes over me and Billy is at my arm, helping me to Karen.

"Thanks, Billy," I nod to him. I take Karen's hands back in mine. "You should stay here."

"They won't let me without you!" she cries.

"They will if I come back for you. By you staying here they know I have to come back. I have nothing out there except living. But here, right here." I tap my chest and then hers, making us both blush. "Here I have a life. Not in books, not in just survival, but a whole, complete life. Understand?"

She nods and wipes at the tears falling onto her cheeks. She's in my arms quickly and I grunt from the force. She tries to pull away, concerned, but I don't let her. "I will come back for you. It's the only way for it all to work."

I hear sniffling behind me and look over my shoulder. Mom is wiping her eyes and even Billy is having a hard time.

"Wow," Mom says. "I knew you were a lot of things, Garret, but a romantic would never have been on the list."

"It isn't romance if it's true," I respond.

"No, it's love," Billy smiles. "Are you sure you're only seventeen?"

"Last time I checked my birth certificate," I laugh. "Oh, wait, those don't exist anymore."

"Smartass," Billy chuckles. "So, I understand everything now, kinda, but I still don't think you're well enough to leave."

"He isn't, but I'll be dead soon if we don't go," Mom says, nodding towards me. "I know that's selfish of me."

"You're my mom. It'd be selfish of me to let you die."

We smile at each other for a moment and Karen squeezes my hand.

"So what now?" she asks.

"Well, now I want something to eat. Then we have to pack. Can we leave in the morning?" Mom shakes her head no. "I didn't think so. Maybe you and I can talk while the *adults* work everything else out?"

"I'd like that," Karen smiles.

A n hour. That is all the time Mom gives us to get ready.

The Power Wagon is pretty beat up and has a few extra bullet holes in it, but the motor sounds strong as Veronica revs it a couple of times. She gives a Tribal member the thumbs up. He doesn't return the sign, just walks away, washing his hands of it all. I have to admire the solid looking wedge welded onto the front. That should clear out any vehicles that get in our way.

"Here, this is food and extra bandages. Some alcohol if you need to clean your wound," Billy says, handing me a large pack. I grab it with my good arm and toss it in the cab of the truck.

"Burning daylight!" Veronica yells.

"Thank you," Mom says to Billy. "You helped save Garret's life."

"We all saved his life," Billy answers, nodding towards the elders standing to the side. They nod at us, but don't offer any words. "Get yourself well and bring him back safe. We're all counting on you for that."

Mom nods and hops into the truck bed. She rummages around for a moment and slings a hunting rifle over her shoulder, while tucking two .45s into her waistband. She thumps the top of the cab a couple of times and looks at me. "I'm ready. Say your goodbyes and let's get a move on!"

Karen has my hand in hers before I know it and pulls me

close. "Please don't die," she says quietly, trying to keep our last words as private as possible. "You need to come back."

"I will," I nod. "I promise you."

We kiss quickly and I pull away, but she grabs my shirt and yanks me back, kissing me again. Her lips are fierce and urgent and I give in to them immediately.

I have no idea how much time goes by, but soon Billy is clearing his throat and Mom is pounding on the truck again.

"I lo..." I start to say, but Karen shakes her head.

"Don't say it. Not yet. Not this way," she whispers in my ear. "Come back in one piece first."

I nod and turn away quickly, not wanting her to see the tears welling in my eyes. Mom is scowling at me from the truck bed.

Veronica has a strange look on her face as I climb into the cab. "Not even a week out in the world and you're already heartbroken. There's just no coping with teenage angst, is there," she mocks.

"Bite me," I mumble, shoving over supplies and grabbing up the waiting shotgun.

I look on the floor of the cab and see a machete in its sheath sitting there. I pick it up and check its heft. Mom taps on the back window.

"Figured you missed the big blade. Billy found one for you."

"Thanks," I say and nod to Billy. He nods back and puts an arm around Karen. She leans into him. "Take care of her, please."

"I will. We already have a cot set up in our cabin. My wife is looking forward to the company," he grins. "I'm not sure what that says about me, though."

"Ready?" Veronica asks. I nod and Mom smacks the cab again. "Good. Let's get this train wreck moving."

Karen turns her head away as we pull out and I force myself not to look in the side mirror, sure I'll start blubbering, which probably wouldn't be a good thing in front of Veronica.

"You holding up?" she asks, her eyes focused straight ahead. "Parting can be such sweet sorrow."

I glance at her. Shakespeare? I would never have guessed.

"I'll be fine," I mutter. "Let's just get to Cottage Grove."

"That's the plan," she smiles and guns the engine, shooting the truck down the dirt road and towards the main highway. "We'll connect to I-5 and hopefully avoid any problems along the way."

"You think that'll happen?"

"What? Us getting to I-5 or avoiding any problems?"

"Both, I guess."

She's thoughtful for a moment. "The Tribes said they'd make sure we aren't ambushed on their land. That puts us right onto I-5. After that we're on our own. Problems are likely. Such is the world we live in."

"Will it be SATs?"

"Could be. I don't think Travis is likely to give up a grudge. He'll want all of our heads on a spike. He wasn't with the last party that attacked, so I'm sure he's got something planned. Unless he choked on his teeth back at the Griffins' and died." She laughs loudly. "I just survived a Tribal trial, so who knows? Maybe my luck is strong and he did!"

Her laughter dies quickly which tells me she doesn't believe this any more than I do. I lean back and watch the pines and firs fly by as Veronica bounces us down the road. Every once in a while I can see an armed group of Tribal members working their way through the forest, some on horseback, but most on foot. I really hope they have more in place up ahead since Veronica is pushing the Power Wagon hard and we'll be out of Tribal protection in no time.

"Listen," Veronica says. "I heard you wanted to testify for me. I just wanted to say thanks."

"No problem," I respond.

"No, it really could have been a problem if they let you. You and your brother are the only things that kept us from all getting butchered when the Tribes first found us. All of that would have gone up in smoke if you had taken my side. I'm not saying you and your mother would have joined me on the gallows, but you certainly wouldn't have been given an armed escort off their land. They'd have dumped you on I-5 with nothing."

"You're assuming quite a bit," I reply, not sure of her assessment at all. "Ruthlessness wasn't the impression I got back there. Protectionist, yes. But ruthless? No."

She doesn't say anything, just shrugs and looks ahead.

I glance behind me at Mom and wince. She has her back to us and is hunched over in the truck bed, her arms wrapped around the hunting rifle. I can see her shoulders shaking and wonder if she's in pain. Her body heaves for a moment, is still, then heaves again.

"Hey!" I pound on the window. "Are you okay?"

Mom doesn't turn around, just waves me off. Her body heaves again and I shift my position for a better look. When I see the small pool of red black blood in the truck bed I rip open the sliding window.

"Mom! What's happening?"

She slowly turns about and I can see blood dripping down her chin and onto her shirt. "I'll be fine, Garret. We have a few hours before I go critical."

I look over at Veronica. "Can we get through everything and to Cottage Grove in a few hours?"

"Well, if I use the carpool lane, sure," she snorts then sees the look on my face. "Sorry. I don't know. It could be smooth sailing all the way or..."

She doesn't need to finish her sentence.

"Will you be okay back there?" I ask Mom.

"I'll be fine."

"I can come back there and take the rifle. You should be up here."

"You can't shoot a rifle with one bad arm," she growls. "Plus I doubt Veronica wants me shut in the cab with her right now."

"If you're going to eat my face then no, I really wouldn't!" Veronica responds. "No offense!"

"None taken," Mom grins, but is soon coughing and heaving again. "Turn around and keep you eyes open."

I watch her for a second more then turn around. If she doesn't think I can handle the rifle then what is the point of the shotgun across my lap? I glance over at Veronica and she looks back at me. I can tell she doesn't believe Mom has a few hours either. She points down to a bag I hadn't noticed by her feet.

"Billy gave me this," she says, reaching down and shaking

the bag. "Chains and shackles. Probably the same ones they used on me. It'll keep her from eating us if she gets bad before Cottage Grove."

I nod and look back out my window. I have a feeling we'll need the shackles well before Cottage Grove.

6

We hit I-5 after an hour of leaving the Tribal housing. The road seems clear for miles up ahead. I look back and see several Tribal members watching us go. I watch most of them make a hand gesture I'd seen in books that I believe to be a goodbye. Unfortunately it is one I remember being associated more with farewells to the dead than to the living. They believe us to already be ghosts, moving from the physical world to the spirit world.

We crest a hill and I lose sight of them. Mom is leaning against the back of the cab and I reach out the window and pat her shoulder. Little Man grunts and I can feel his hands reaching past my neck also. Mom turns and her eyes are nearly completely bloodshot. She looks at me and grins then sees Little Man. Her smile falters, but she brushes her fingers against my cheek then reaches past me and pats Garth.

"I wish I hadn't been so drugged out all these years," she grunts. "He really does have his own personality doesn't he?"

"I've always said so," I answer, trying not to sound smug, but the frown on Mom's face tells me I failed. "I don't mean that in a bad way. I'm just agreeing with you."

Mom nods and turns back around as she starts coughing. I can see bloody spittle flying in the wind and I wince.

"Will Dad's research help anyone that has already turned?"

She hacks and coughs a few more times before leaning back against the cab, gasping. "I don't know. He may have tried it on some test subjects, but if it did work I'd have to assume he'd have told me."

"That's quite an assumption, don't you think? The more I get to know about the 'real' Dad, the less he sounds like a team player."

She laughs/coughs. "Now you're getting it." She takes a moment to catch her breath. "But if he could reverse the necrotic process I think he would have tried it on me already."

"Unless it meant having you turn fully first. I don't think Dad would have wished that on you."

Mom clutches at her chest, more racking coughs ripping through her. She wheezes a moment and spits a large glob of bloody phlegm over the side of the truck. "You're probably right. He may be an egotistical ass, but I think he's always loved me. I know he's always loved you."

"Debris up ahead," Veronica says, pointing out the windshield.

I turn back around and see several cars sitting haphazardly across the cracked and rutted blacktop. There seems to be enough room to get around each, but it will slow us down considerably.

"It doesn't look too bad," I say hopeful.

"Yeah, that's the problem," Veronica responds.

"How do you mean?"

"Someone made sure there is access through these. Best case scenario is it was just to get by."

"And worst case scenario?"

"You're the book boy. You tell me."

I can now see how the cars are set on the road. Each one is at an angle with space enough for the truck to get past, but we'll have to zig-zag through.

"That could easily be a trap," I answer.

"I'm willing to wager that's exactly what it is." She knocks back on the window. "Stay sharp back there!"

Mom grunts something unintelligible, but she expertly raises the rifle to her shoulder and starts scanning the area. I keep my eyes peeled, watching closely as we pass each car.

Little Man is soon squawking and I whip my head about, trying to find the necs. I see movement at the side of the road and realize that all this time what I had thought were tree limbs, leaves and piles of vegetation, are actually the dried out bodies of dozens of necros. They shake and move, but none get up to pursue us. I keep my eyes on them and I'm forced to meet the dead gaze of several necs, their heads creaking about as they watch us slowly make our way past.

"What do you see?" Veronica asks.

"How do you know I see something?"

"Your body's tense and your breathing has changed. Pretty simple stuff."

"Necros. Quite a few of them in the drainage ditches."

"They coming up to get us?"

"No, they aren't."

"That seems strange, don't you think?"

"Yes, it does."

I study further and realize an important detail slipped my notice before. They're all missing their legs and hands. They've been dumped in the ditch and can't get out. They can't walk or claw their way from the ditch. I'm staring at one long line of broken.

"They've been put there," Veronica says, as if reading my thoughts.

I glance over and see she's looking out her window at the median on her side. I lean up and look her way and can see the ground is covered with broken, their jaws opening and closing with hungry longing.

"Why would anyone do this?" I ask, reaching back to calm Little Man as his squawks become more urgent.

"Why do you think? It keeps us from bolting from the truck. We're boxed in. Can't really back up either, thanks to the way the cars are placed." Surprisingly she grins at this. "I mean, I can back up in this, but most will be trapped."

"So the question is who is trying to trap us?" I ask rhetorically.

"Scavengers. Watch the cars. There could be hostiles inside waiting to pop out. They'd be at point blank range so we'd be sitting ducks."

I give up trying to calm Little Man down as the sheer volume of necs around us has him worked up well beyond my control.

"Is he going to make that noise the whole time?" Veronica

asks, annoyed.

"Yes. Get used to it." I brace the shotgun against my window frame and try to get it secured.

"We're both going to go deaf if you start firing that thing," Veronica warns.

"Huh? What?"

"Ha, funny..."

"Behind us!" Mom shouts.

I look back and see figures moving from car to car. They're too far back to make out any details, but they'll catch up to us soon at the rate we're moving.

"Hold your fire!" Veronica orders. "Save the ammo for the ones that get close!"

"Not my first rodeo!" Mom shouts back. "I know how to conserve ammo, thank you!"

"Grumpy when she's changing into a slick, isn't she?" I don't laugh or smile at this. "Sorry. That was in bad taste," Veronica apologizes.

"She changes fully and you'll be the bad taste," I mutter.

"Jeez! I was kidding! Chill out!"

The loud creaking of rusted metal stops the argument quickly and Veronica floors it. "Hang on! Show time!"

The Power Wagon does its name good by powering through the first car that's rolled across our path. Orange dust covers the windshield as the old car explodes in a mass of rust and tearing metal.

"Hell yes!" Veronica shouts as we slam through another and another car. "Three o'clock!"

I see the man coming at us with the axe before the words have left her mouth. I wedge myself against the butt of the shotgun and squeeze the trigger. My arm screams from the shock my body takes as the gun kicks back. The man collapses onto the pavement with less parts than he started with.

"Good shot! Pull that thing back in!" Veronica yells.

I yank the shotgun back into the cab just as we hit another car. This one has more stability and Veronica struggles to push past it. More people, covered head to toe in rags and animal skins, rush us and I hear Mom firing shot after shot from the truck bed.

Bodies fall and I realize none of them have firearms, only picks and axes, blades and spears. One of the spears pierces my side of the Power Wagon, ripping through the metal, its tip just missing my leg.

"Crap! Not Cool!" I shout.

"Then do something about it!" Veronica yells back, swerving to the right, shoving a parked car out of the way to avoid another one being pushed in our path. A man leaps from the moving car onto the hood of the Power Wagon. He has no teeth and his face is covered in sores and oozing pus. He grabs onto the edge of the hood with one hand and raises a metal spike with the other, ready to plunge it through the hood and into the engine. A shot rings out and the windshield is covered in a spray of blood and bone. His body tumbles to the side as Veronica turns on the windshield wipers.

"That's just wrong," I say.

"Not the most wrong thing I've ever seen," Veronica replies.

I'm sure it isn't.

I look behind and see Mom has turned around and is concentrating her fire on the attackers coming straight at us. The black blood oozes down her chin, staining her shirt further. Her eyes are now almost completely red and her lips are curling up into a very familiar and deadly sneer.

"Oh, no...," I whisper.

"She's not looking good, is she?" Veronica asks, never taking her eyes from the road.

"No...she isn't."

"Well, as long as she can keep firing at, and hitting, her targets then she's doing good!"

I want to be mad at this crazy girl that is now my ally, but she's right. As long as Mom can still fight then she's good. As soon as she stops fighting for us and starts fighting against us, well...then we have a problem.

"Jesus! These Scavengers are like freakin' roaches!" Veronica yells. "I've never seen so many at once before!"

She swerves to the left and clips two, crushing them against a car, as they try to throw what look like large rocks at us. I'm so used to having firearms at my disposal, and enemies that have them also, that it's just mind boggling to see such primitive weaponry. It makes me wonder if they are just as primitive intellectually. I haven't seen one projectile weapon. No slingshots, or bows and arrows. Nothing spring loaded even! You'd think with all of the metal and parts just lying around they'd have invented something better than hand thrown rocks.

More attackers stream over cars at us and their bodies dance as Mom pumps bullet after bullet into them. Chests bloom red with blood; heads rock back; bodies spin and bodies collapse, a kill shot just behind the first shot, ending their lives in a brutal vision of raining blood and brains.

It's soon almost more than I can take.

I hear the rifle clatter to the truck bed as Mom drops it, empty. She pulls the .45s from her waistband and opens up with those. More bodies drop, more blood is spilt and I have to force myself not to close my eyes. These are people! These aren't necros! They aren't SATs! Even if they are trying to catch us to eat us, they are doing it to survive and part of me feels for them. Most of me, however, is glad Mom is an amazing shot.

The Power Wagon thumps over bodies that have rolled in our way as Veronica shoves more cars from our path and I can see we are close to the end of the gauntlet.

"Almost clear!" Veronica shouts.

"Good, because I'm almost empty!" Mom grunts back.

A woman reaches us on my side and slams into my window. She never slowed, just kept running at the truck until she hit it. What was she thinking? How could she stop a moving vehicle that weighs tons? I crane my neck around and watch her body tumble over and over then come to a stop. Two scavengers pounce on her and start stripping off her rags. At first I think they are just taking more for themselves, as I'm sure material isn't easy to come by. But when they get down to skin and one pulls a knife I look away and squeeze my eyes closed, pushing the image of the knife coming down out of my head.

One last violent crash brings my attention forward and out the windshield. All I see is open highway in front of us. Sure there are stray cars here and there, but nothing like what we just went through.

"WOO HOO!" Veronica calls out slamming her fist into the roof of the truck over and over. "That's how it's done!"

Little Man still hasn't stopped screeching and I look to the drainage ditches, but see only a couple necs squirming about, not enough to keep him freaking out. If it isn't the necs he's warning us about then what?

My heart sinks and I look back and see Mom on her knees, facing back the way we came, the .45s held loosely in her palms. Her shoulders are shivering and the muscles in her back spasm and twitch.

"Mom?"

Her body jerks at the sound of my voice.

"Mom? Are you alright?"

Her body jerks again and her head slowly turns towards me. She's gone. My mother is gone and all that is left is a crazy-eyed, blood drooling nec.

"NOOOOOOOO!" I scream and Veronica looks back also.

"Oh crap!" she yells, slamming the brakes on.

I'm thrown forward and smash into the dash as Mom hurls against the cab, her head hitting the back window with a sickening crash, shattering the glass. The Power Wagon comes to a complete stop and Mom is flung backward into the bed. Veronica grabs the shackle bag and is out of the truck in a second. She leaps into the truck bed, kicking Mom in the face, knocking her down again. Veronica tosses the bag aside as she pulls out the chains and shackles. Mom tries to get up and again Veronica kicks her, but this time she hooks her foot under Mom's back and flips her over. She has a knee in the middle of Mom's back and grabs an arm, shackling the wrist. She grabs the other arm and does the same, threading the thick chain through a loop connecting the two.

Mom bucks and struggles, but Veronica yanks up on the chains, plants a foot on Mom's butt, spins around and shackles and chains her feet. Before I know it Veronica slaps a collar around Mom's neck, careful to keep away from her snapping jaws and attaches a chain to that also, then throws her hands up when done, shouting, "Time!"

I feel numb as I watch my own mother struggle against her bonds, the chains rattling and straining. Her eyes focus on mine and she let's out a howl.

Little Man joins her, and I press my hands against my ears, so desperate to shut it all out, to make the horror of everything go away.

CHAPTER THIRTEEN

Mom hasn't stopped thrashing about for the last 25 miles or so. Blood streams down her face from the cuts where she has continually bashed her forehead into the truck bed. Little Man matches her thrashing and I'm nearly at a point where I just want to tear him off my body and throw him out the truck window. But I can't. I probably wouldn't if I could. Probably.

"How you holding up?" Veronica asks.

I can see that the constant noise from Mom and Little Man is driving her insane too, but she's keeping it together out of respect for my loss. At least that shows she has a heart. How she stayed with the cold-blooded Griffins I don't know.

"I'm fine. Well, no, I'm not fine, but I'm not going to eat the barrel of a gun anytime soon."

"Won't eat a gun? That's a good sign. Speaking of signs, check that out," she says, pointing out the windshield. We pass an old sign that states Cottage Grove is only 27 miles away. "I'm guessing the compound is closer than that."

"I hope so," I mutter.

"You think your father will be there?"

"He better be," I growl, nearly sounding like Mom and Garth. Veronica flinches at the ferocity in my voice. "Sorry. Wait, no I'm not. Well, I'm sorry to you, but I'm not sorry for sounding mad at my Dad. He left us, regardless of his reasons, he flat out left us. We should have all stayed together."

"You really think that would have helped?" She looks at me sideways. "If the Griffins had captured him then you and your Mom would already be dead. They wouldn't have needed you. They would have just wanted him."

"They'd have needed me if Dad told them they did," I argue. "And he would have refused to help if they hurt Mom."

"You sure about that? You just said he left you. Sounds like he looks out for himself first, don't you think?"

"You don't know anything about him!" I yell.

"No, I don't. Why don't you tell me," she replies.

Oh, she's good. She's trying to get my mind off of the crazy nec family I now have by asking about my crazy scientist father. Even though I know it's just a trick to divert my attention, and probably to divert hers also, I go ahead and talk.

I tell her about growing up with a dad that drilled into me day after day all the rules and safety protocols when living in a world overrun by necs. I tell her how he calls them HSNs and that I never even heard the word slick until I ran into Karen and Joseph...and Lester. She actually seems interested in the theory that the HSNs have become a separate species, genetically altered enough to no longer be human in any way.

"The fact that they are dead kinda makes them no longer human," she laughs.

I laugh also and it feels good. I go into detail on how I would sit hidden at night inside our compound and just watch and wait to see if a nec would come by. Little Man would give a small squeak when one would get close, but hush up quickly so we wouldn't be found out. I had forgotten how much Little Man and I used to talk back and forth, me with words and he with grunts and sounds. Understanding him was never a problem for me until I got older and filled my head with books and beliefs that weren't my own. Sure, my parents argued he couldn't really talk, which I always thought was strange coming from Dad, but they were my parents so I always kinda disbelieved them.

"Wasn't it uncomfortable with him attached to you?" Veronica asks.

"Sure, but it made me stronger. I grew muscle quickly to compensate for the added weight. My back is incredibly strong now and my legs could keep up with my dad when we went hiking. I was outpacing him before I was ten."

"Impressive. What about food?"

Food. Seeing what I just saw with the scavengers, and also how the people were trading food and drink as currency back at the Griffins, I realize just how lucky I had it. Food was never a problem. I grew up with plenty to eat. It may not have been palatable when Mom was cooking, which was pretty much all the time since Dad was always on his studies, but my stomach never growled because it was empty.

I can see this strikes a chord with Veronica and I stop talking. She looks over at me, worried.

"What's wrong? Why'd you go quiet?"

"I didn't want to offend you. I guess you didn't have as much to eat as I did when the world died."

She shakes her head no. "I didn't have any parents, either, but I've been listening to you talk about that."

I hesitate, but figure she left the door open. "What happened to your parents?"

Her face becomes conflicted, and I'm pretty sure she's gonna go all crazy on me. She sighs and relaxes a bit instead.

"Guess you should know," She starts. "I didn't have parents." She pauses. "You remember the Nursery?"

"How can I forget," I exclaim. "That's not an image that washes away easily."

"Well, that was how I was born. To a dead woman that wanted to eat me if she could."

"What? How is that possible?" I gasp.

"The Griffins are scientists like your dad. But I'd put them in the 'Mad Scientist' category. You know what I'm talking about?"

"A Doctor Moreau kinda thing?" I ask, realizing as soon as I say it that she won't get the reference.

"Exactly like Doctor Moreau!" she laughs bitterly. "That's it in a nutshell! Don't look at me like that. The Griffins insisted on their killers having an education. I've read more than you know."

"Wow, I wish we had more time to talk about books. My parents were never interested..."

"Do you want to hear this or not?" she interrupts, her

voice filled with emotion.

"Oh, right, sorry. You were saying it was like Moreau."

"Except instead of combining human and animal DNA the Griffins tried to combine human and slick DNA. They failed mostly."

She turns and looks me straight in the face as silent tears fall onto her cheeks. "They failed with all the boys, but the girls? Well, we survived. We are, were, well I don't know, we're the Sisters. Human, but not quite."

"That's why you're so strong and fast, huh? The Griffins used runner DNA, didn't they?"

"Runners?"

"The fast ones. The ones that'll chase you down."

She nods. "Yeah, those. They figured out how to infect our mothers at the very last stage of pregnancy and insure they turned into runners. The infection didn't pass through the blood barrier, but it did infuse us with different abilities."

She stops talking and wipes her eyes. "Jesus, I don't know the last time I've cried."

"That girl in the arena. She was a Sister?"

"She was. Helena. We weren't close, but I made sure to keep an eye on her." She fixes me with a cold look that freezes my bones. "Charles would loan some of the Sisters out. Loan them out to high-rollers. It wasn't pretty."

I just nod my head, not quite sure I know what she means, but definitely sure I don't want to know.

"I'm freaking you out, aren't I?"

"Have you met my mother?" I laugh, trying to lighten things a bit. "Or met my brother? I don't do freaked out."

She laughs and reaches out a hand and pats my leg. I take her hand in mine and give it a reassuring squeeze. We look at each other for a second and then things get uncomfortable and I pull my hand away.

We both cough a little and clear our throats.

"How many slicks have you killed?" she asks, switching the subject to a favorite of hers.

"Wow...I don't know," I answer honestly. "I remember trying to figure that out once and Mom yelled at me for being morbid. How can anyone be morbid in a world that is dead? Isn't existence morbid in of itself?"

"It's her military training. Only the jerks keep a body count."

"Then why'd you ask? Were you hoping I was a jerk?" I grin, trying to show her I'm kidding, but she frowns anyway.

"Yeah, I was hoping I wasn't alone. I kept a body count of everyone and everything I'm sent on. One thousand and fourteen slicks at my last count."

"And people?"

"I'd rather not answer that."

"I was at the trial, Veronica. I know what you've done."

She sighs. "Six hundred and eleven. Not counting the Scavengers back there. I was too busy driving to count them."

"Really? I highly doubt that."

"Wow, thanks for the confidence."

"I just watched you hog chain my Mom. You can at least be honest."

"Okay then the total is six hundred twenty-one. I nailed ten of those bastards."

"There, was that so hard?"

"Considering I'm trying to be less of the trained dog I was forced to be with the Griffins, yes, it was hard."

"Oh...sorry."

We stay quiet for the next few miles until we both hear the engines. Truck engines. And motorcycle engines.

The SATs have found us.

2

Veronica floors the gas pedal and the Power Wagon shoots ahead. We still have to swerve around stray cars and trucks, so she can't get the speed she'd like and the string of curses coming from her mouth shows her frustration.

"Why are they still after us?" I shout.

"Because I killed Charles and we destroyed the arena! I stole Travis's truck and your Mom kicked out all of his teeth! He loved those teeth as much as he loved this truck!"

"He's really after us because of his teeth?"

"I don't know! I don't even know if he's back there at all! Shut up and let me drive!"

Looking back I can see three trucks, heavily armored and modified, with four motorcycles pacing them. A couple of flashes come from the lead truck and I realize a split second later what they are.

"Duck!" I shout as the bullets impact with the tailgate.

"Crap! They brought the sharpshooters with them!" Veronica yells. "They don't even have to catch us to stop us!"

"What?! What do you mean?!"

"Snipers! They aren't aiming for you and me they're aiming for the tires! They want to stop this truck dead and catch us alive!"

"Alive? Why?"

"Did you go stupid?! Charlotte! She can't leave the compound without it detonating and I know she didn't disarm that. It's the only thing that keeps some from killing her outright. Not everyone at the compound is working for her by choice, you know! She will want to watch us die, that's why they want us alive! She's certainly going to want me alive!"

"Can we get off I-5? Take a back road so they don't have as clear a shot?"

"You see any back roads?!"

"No, but can't we just, I don't know, go cross country?"

More bullets hit the truck and Veronica swerves about, trying to make a harder target to hit. I see her scanning the countryside, trying to figure out where we can go.

"No, cross country won't work. The motorcycles can follow us too easily. We have to ditch them completely!"

"I thought that was what we were trying to do!"

"I said to shut up and let me drive!"

Veronica slams the Power Wagon into the side of one of the derelict cars, spinning the old vehicle about. "Tell me what that did!"

I look back and see the car come to a stop, blocking even more of the road. "Almost, but not quite!"

She slams into another and another, but each time they only block a portion of the road. It slows the trucks' speed down, but the motorcycles get around them without issue and are gaining on us quickly.

"This isn't going to work, is it?" I ask, reloading Mom's .45s. "We're gonna have to make a stand!"

"Are you crazy?!" Veronica shouts. "They'll tear us apart! Charlotte didn't send the B squad after us; she sent the main team, *her* team!"

"Oh," I swallow, trying to see if I can get a bead on one of the bikers. Veronica's driving is all over the place, making it near impossible to take aim.

"Get your arm back in the truck, dumbass!" Veronica shouts, reaching over and yanking me away from the window just as we collide with a pickup truck. The side of the truck scrapes against my door and the side view mirror bends back right into the Power Wagon. Right where my arm would have been.

"Crap. Sorry. Thanks."

"Don't waste your ammo anyway," she scolds. "We'll need

it when they finally stop us. Either to shoot them or shoot ourselves. I'm not going back to being Charlotte's dog!"

"Shoot ourselves? You can shoot yourself, but I'm staying alive. Someone will come get us!"

"They'll come for you. Not for me. This was a one way trip anyway. Your Mom was supposed to shoot me as soon as you two were safely in Cottage Grove. If she didn't they'll kill Karen. That was the real trade-off."

"You...you're kidding, right?"

"Why the hell would I kid about that?! No, I'm not kidding!" She looks over at me quickly and must see the horror on my face. "It's okay. I'm cool with it. I at least get to kill some slicks and kill some SATs before I go out. Back there I would just be hanging from a rope. That's no way to die!"

"I'm not sure if I see the difference," I respond. How can she be so casual about dying? And how the hell could my Mom agree to such a thing?

"My life was over years ago," she laughs. "At least my death won't be so wasted." She focuses her intense eyes on me and I have to fight not to draw back. "Make your death count, Garret. Don't just let a slick take you down or die doing something stupid. Be a hero. The world needs every single one it can get."

I nod, but don't respond. How do you respond to that?

The motorcycles are even closer now and one of the bikers takes aim at the Power Wagon's tires. "Swerve! Now!"

Veronica doesn't question, just yanks on the wheel. I see sparks fly from where the bullet hits the pavement, right where our back right tire would have been.

"Exit! Right there!" Veronica shouts and aims straight for a clogged off ramp.

"But all the cars?!" I scream, just as we hit the first car.

The Power Wagon shudders, but slams through the car, ramming it into another, knocking that one down the embankment. I cry out as I'm thrown forward and my wound slams into the dash. I can feel some of the sutures tear.

Veronica has her foot all the way down on the gas and the Power Wagon does what it's named: it powers through everything. Until we hit the last vehicle, a school bus that has overturned at the bottom of the off-ramp.

"Come on!" she yells, grabbing the supply bag and the shotgun. She's out of the truck and sprinting past the school bus before I have the door open.

"Wait! I have to get Mom!" I scream after her, but she's gone around the bus and out of sight. "Dammit!"

I tuck the .45s into my waste band, which of course I've been taught never to do, and leap into the truck bed. My arm is in agony and I can see fresh blood seeping through the bandages and my shirt. Mom lunges at me and I dodge her attack, reaching around for the chain attached to her neck collar. She roars at me and tries to lunge again, but Little Man roars back in his tiny voice and Mom goes quiet instantly, her head cocked to the side. She grunts and growls and Little Man matches her.

While he has her attention I reach down and free her legs so she can run then jump back out of the truck bed and pull at the chain to get her to follow. A bullet hits the truck and I duck, looking up to see the bikers speeding towards me.

The first one's chest erupts and I glance behind me and see Veronica standing on top of the school bus letting loose with the shotgun. The next biker's front wheel explodes as it's hit and the man flips over the handle bars and flies through the air then slams into one of the cars, his body bouncing and rolling right to my feet.

Mom jumps from the truck bed now and is on her knees tearing at the man's throat. I pull back on the chain, desperate to get her away from the body. No son should have to watch his mother feasting on flesh.

"Come on, Garret!" Veronica shouts, firing again. The other bikers brake and duck behind cars for cover, giving us a chance. "Pull that leash and let's go!"

Little Man screeches several times and gets Mom's attention and we are sprinting away from the off-ramp and down a car clogged street, running for our lives.

3

We make it a block before the necros get wind of us and start coming out of the abandoned buildings. Mostly shamblers and broken, but I do see a few lurkers hiding their heads behind signs. No runners to speak of, but that either means they have left the area to hunt for food elsewhere or we just haven't gotten to them yet. I have my fingers crossed for the former option.

"We have to find a defensible position!" Veronica yells back at me. She's a good couple yards ahead, but I can tell she's holding back since I can't move as quickly with Mom in tow. My less than ideal health isn't helping either.

She points the shotgun towards some old restaurant and heads that way. I can hear the motorcycles behind us, but they haven't made it down the off-ramp yet. Probably hanging back until the rest of the SATs catch up. They'll try to take us by force instead of sending the bikers to pick us off.

Veronica hurries around the side of the building, cracking a couple shamblers' heads on the way, and starts working at getting a side door open. "Come on! Help me!"

"How? I have one bad arm and I'm holding my Mom with the other!" I yell at here. "Should I put the chain in my teeth?!"

She mumbles under her breath and starts looking around for something to get the door open with. "Damn! Forget this one! Let's head to the next building!"

She takes off and I am actually struggling to keep up with

her as she runs from building to building no longer holding back her pace. A loud crash of metal and glass makes me turn and I can see the SAT trucks pushing the school bus out of the way, giving them access to the main road now.

"They're coming!" I shout and Veronica turns, looking back towards the off-ramp.

I wish I could say I try to warn her, but it all happens so fast that I don't even have time to open my mouth before the nec is on her. It's a runner, a big one, and its jaws clamp down on Veronica's shoulder and it has a chunk of her flesh in its mouth by the time I can scream. She elbows the nec, knocking it away and giving her room enough to turn and blow its head right off.

I rush to her side, my eyes focused on the wound. "We can clean that! Slow the infection down!"

"Don't bother," she gasps, wincing as she pulls pieces of her shirt away from the wound. "One way trip, remember?"

The roar of motors makes us look back and we can see the trucks barreling down the street. Veronica turns to the closest door and kicks at it again and again until the lock gives way and the door cracks open. "Inside, now!"

I don't argue and rush into the gloom. It takes a couple seconds for my eyes to adjust and I have to laugh once I see where we are.

A bookstore.

"What's so funny?" Veronica asks in a harsh whisper.

"Books. I'm going to die in a book store! Ha!"

"You aren't going to die and actually this is a pretty good place to hole up in," she says checking out the racks and shelves. Many are stacked and propped against the windows and door. "Looks like someone already knew that. Books are thick and thick is good when you are trying to keep bullets from ripping you apart. Or keep slicks from getting in at you."

"Yeah, but where are those people?"

She shrugs and points to a counter by the wall. "Secure your Mom there and help me move some shelves. We need to barricade this place more."

I don't argue. Half of her shoulder is gone so my lame excuse of a wounded arm isn't going to fly. I shackle Mom to a metal bar on the counter that must have been part of the cafe part of the book store. She howls and groans and Little Man joins her, but she doesn't try to eat me at all. That's a nice thing.

As we move the shelves I start pointing out what I've read. "That one and that one. I've read that there. Hey! I didn't know this was a series!"

"Yep, there's seven of them. I've read them like three times each," Veronica joins in. "And all of those. Haven't read this one."

She tosses me an old small paperback. *Damnation Alley* by a guy named Zelazny.

"What am I supposed to do with this?" I ask.

"Put it in your pocket and save it for later," she smiles. "Gives you a reason to get out of here."

"Gives us both a reason," I insist. "We can read it together."

She gives me a weak smile, but doesn't say anything else.

We continue our game and soon have several more book-shelves propped against the doors and windows by the time the sound of the truck engines reach us.

"I'd say be quiet, but..." She hooks a finger over towards the noisy mess that is my mother. "I don't think either of us are in any shape to try to muzzle her."

"Maybe their engines are too loud and they won't hear her?"

"No, they have people on foot checking each building. They'll hear her."

"How can you be sure?"

She looks at me as if I'm stupid. "Because I used to lead these hunting parties."

"Oh...right." I guess I am stupid.

We can hear breaking glass and wood close by and I figure the SATs are checking the building next to ours.

"Get behind the counter," Veronica orders. "Weapons out, we need to check ammo." I duck behind and put the two .45s on the counter. "And extra magazines."

"Extra magazines?" I ask, my face turning red.

"Yes, the extra magazines from the bag your mom had in the bed of the truck. Those extra magazines."

"I didn't grab those. I just grabbed the guns. I...I wasn't thinking."

"No, you weren't," she snarls. She pops out magazines from each pistol and checks them. "Well, at least they're full. That's ten rounds per gun. I have six in the shotgun plus another thirty shells in the bag."

She dumps out all the shells and sets them carefully on the shelf below the counter. "Once you run out I'm going to need you to keep handing me shells until we are both empty. Considering they have three trucks that would mean there should be about six or eight SATs out there, not counting the two bikers. They won't get off their bikes though. If everything goes south they'll be instructed to race back and tell Charlotte."

"So we have maybe ten guys out there?"

"Good math, genius. Yes, about ten which gives me more than enough ammo to take them all out. You can too if you shoot straight."

"Not a problem," I respond, but the shooting pain in my arm makes me wince and Veronica frowns.

"That's not very convincing," she grumbles.

I grab up one of the .45s and pull back the slide with my bad arm. It hurts like hell, but I grit through it and give Veronica a satisfied glare.

"Okay, tough guy," she laughs. "I'm convinced."

I look at the dripping wound on her shoulder. "You want me to fix that up for you?"

"Like I said, don't bother. You know I won't bleed to death, the blood will coagulate from the virus."

Little Man screeches and squawks once, twice then doesn't stop.

"What's wrong with him?" Veronica hisses, her eyes looking from the front of the store to the back of the store. "Why is he freaking out? Is it me?"

Gunfire erupts outside and we both look to the front.

"No, sounds like some necs have found the SATs," I say, moving towards a gap in the shelves by the front window.

Veronica sidles up beside me and we peer through the gap.

"Holy crap!" Veronica exclaims. "Where'd they all come from?"

"I don't know. You'd think they would have found us

already if there were that many!"

We watch as close to fifty runners descend on the SATs. The men try to fight back but they are outnumbered five to one. Those going from building to building are ripped apart after only getting a few shots off. The ones in the backs of the trucks take some of the runners out, but they're over-powered too, torn from the truck beds. Only the men inside the trucks stand a chance.

They realize this too and hit the gas, running down the necs in front of them, mashing them into the pavement. They race down the street, turn down another, and are lost from sight.

"Guess we caught a break there," I whisper.

Mom lets out a long, high howl and all the necros in the street stop moving. Little Man squawks at her, but she doesn't stop and soon every undead eye in the street is looking at our bookstore.

"You were saying?" Veronica snaps.

4

The necros hit the front of the store like a storm. The glass shatters from the already fragile windows and undead arms and hands claw around the bookshelves.

"We can't stay here," I yell.

"Ya think, genius?!" Veronica yells back. "Doesn't matter where we go, they'll follow as long as your mom there keeps howling like a stray dog!"

"I'm not leaving her!"

"I didn't say you should!" Veronica looks at the front of the store and then towards the back. She frowns then her face changes as she looks up at the ceiling. "Okay, there were about fifty out there. The SATs took some out, but not enough." She looks at the shotgun and at the .45s. "I need to thin the herd before they get in here."

"Thin the herd? How are you going to do that?"

"I'm gonna snipe a few in front. This will clog them up and make it harder for them to get in. Help me find a ladder."

"A ladder? Where are we going to find a ladder?"

"It's a freaking book store with high bookshelves! There's a ladder here somewhere! Just shut up and help!"

I do as she says and we tear the place apart. We check every closet, every corner; every nook and cranny a ladder could possibly be, but find nothing.

"Dammit! How can a bookstore not have a ladder?" She closes her eyes for a moment and winces.

"You okay? That bite must hurt," I say, stepping towards her.

She holds her hand out and wards me off. "Not too close. You're starting to smell tasty."

I jump back and look at the .45s on the counter. A counter that has her between me and it.

Veronica laughs. "I'm just messing with you. Chill out. There's something I should probably tell you about me..."

More glass shatters and the bookshelves groan.

"What?" I ask. "What do you need to tell me?"

"Nothing," she says, waving me off. She looks up at the ceiling and the roof access mocking us. "I know where the ladder is."

"You do? Where?"

She points up. "Right where the last occupants left it. On the roof."

"On the roof...?" Then I get it. They climbed up there for safety and pulled the ladder up after them. "But wouldn't they have to come down at some point?"

"Not if they're still up there, kid."

My eyes go wide. "You mean there could be people alive up there?"

"I didn't say they were still alive. Did anything in this truck stop of a town look alive to you?"

"No. I guess not. So what does that mean?" The pounding that starts from above tells me quickly. Necs to the front, probably necs in the back already, and now we have necs up top. Great. Just great. "So no going up, huh?"

"No going up," she replies. "I'll just have to make a stand."

"You mean *we'll* have to make a stand, right?"

"No, Garret," she says, rolling her neck as she starts to bounce up and down from one foot to another. "You're going to barricade yourself in the storeroom until I tell you to come out."

"What?! You can't fight them alone! Even with the shotgun!"

"I can. I will. And you need to get moving!"

"You're crazy! You'll never survive!"

She looks at me then rushes up, grabs my face and kisses me hard on the mouth. I start to pull back, but there's a spark, a tingling, like something electric, and I grab her about the waist.

She finally breaks the kiss and pushes me away. "One way trip, remember?"

My head swims and I want to say something, but the crashing of wood and glass from the front of the store tells me I don't have time to even do that. Veronica, her face nothing but a big grin, grabs up the shotgun.

"You're a good boy, Garret Weir! Amazing really," she smiles. "Get your mom and get the hell back to the storeroom so you become an amazing man one day!"

Bookshelves start to fall and the necs come at us.

"GO!" Veronica yells and the words of goodbye I shout at her are lost as the shotgun begins to bark.

I rush over to Mom and unhook her, dragging her towards the back of the store.

I get Mom into the storeroom and shut the door, scrambling to throw whatever I can against it. I try not to think about Veronica, about the kiss, about anything except finding a solution to how I can get out of here alive.

All I have are the .45s and twenty rounds. Not good.

Pounding at the back door makes me jump and my heart sinks. I truly am surrounded.

The sounds of the shotgun stop.

"Veronica?" Nothing but nec noise. "VERONICA?!"

Mom and Little Man screech and howl as the storeroom door starts to splinter and the back door begins to buckle, having already been compromised by Veronica kicking it in. I pull the .45s out and set one on a shelf next to me, keeping it ready when the one in my hand clicks empty.

The question is will I keep one round for myself?

I can't answer this question. I'm not at that point yet and every fiber of my being screams for me to stay alive. I look around the storeroom again, hoping to see a weapon I may have missed. And I do.

In the corner is a table with paper, tape, staplers and other supplies. And on that table is what I think is called a paper cutter. It's about two feet square, the base is heavy and has a grid on it. The part that I need is the two foot long, very sharp and heavy blade that hinges on the side, ready to slice through a couple inches of stacked paper. I've read enough teen mysteries where the protagonist volunteers at the library that I know exactly what that blade can do.

The storeroom door splinters further and I can see tips of eroded fingers trying to rip through. I scramble to the paper cutter and work at the bolt that holds the blade on. Of course, it's stuck tight. I can see a tool box next to the back door, but I don't have time to grab it as the back door gives way and the necs come at me.

5

My eardrums feel like they have burst after only a couple rounds from the .45. I think I feel blood trickling down my neck, but I don't care as I place headshot after headshot. Dad would be proud.

I don't leave a bullet for myself and soon the doorway is piled high with twenty nec bodies and the others outside struggle to scramble over them. I toss the empty .45s to the floor and dash back to the paper cutter, working my fingers raw until I get the bolt loose and yank the blade from its base.

Mom is wild with rage and Little Man is screeching like never before. It's a good thing I'm semi-deaf from the gunfire or I'd certainly be from their complaining. Their noise seems to be working in my favor, though, as it confuses the necs that do scramble over the pile, making them hesitate and giving me enough time to send their heads rolling to the floor. The paper cutter blade is almost as good as my machete. Which of course, I left back in the truck with the ammo.

The necs stop trying to get at us from the back and I take a deep breath, just in time for the storeroom door to fully give way. I back myself up against the pile of nec corpses, hoping maybe I'll blend into their stink and the necros will think I've gotten away. It doesn't work as all undead eyes follow my movements. They rush me as one and I close my eyes, ready for the end.

But the end never comes. What does come is a roar that makes my teeth shake. A roar that makes all of the necs before us stop dead (or undead, I guess) in their tracks.

A roar that only a mother could make.

The resulting near silence is probably the most disturbing bit of non-sound I have ever witnessed. I slowly open my eyes and can see all of the necs have stopped only feet from me. All that stands between them and my death is Mom. And she is pissed.

Hunkered down low, she sways back and forth, hissing, growling, and spitting bloody foam at the others. They watch her and watch me, their undead brains trying to figure out what is going on. Every time one of them comes to a conclusion, and naturally that conclusion is that I am tasty flesh, she lunges forward, ripping off an arm or head or tearing their petrified guts right out of them.

I realize now is my only chance and I slowly start to dislodge the corpses behind me, glancing back to make sure I don't get grabbed from behind by a nec that hadn't heard the party is up front. I'm able to make space to get through as Mom keeps the necs back.

As I slip outside I tuck the paper blade into my belt and carefully, cautiously reach forward and grab the chain attached to Mom's collar. I slowly pull at it, leading her out the back door with me. The necs follow, but so many have found out the hard way what happens when you get too close, that even the stupidest of the things keeps a good distance. I walk us back to the road and glance over my shoulder and see the Power Wagon way back by the off-ramp.

I actually think we may make it when fresh growls and howls bring my attention back to the bookstore and I see more necs showing up. None of them have a clue as to what Mom can do and they rush towards us.

I turn and sprint towards the Power Wagon, ignoring the agony in my arm, not caring in the least if I rip every single suture. But no matter how fast I try to run, Mom holds me back, the animal that she has become wanting to fight and tear and kill, even if it is her own kind now.

God! She's now as much of a pain in my butt as Little Man!

Then it strikes me. There's one way to get her to move and follow me without hesitation. I close my eyes and bring my wrist to my teeth, tearing away the skin. As hot blood fills my mouth, and I try not to puke, I jam the wrist in Moms face and rub the blood all over her.

This gets her attention and quick. She whirls on me and any love that may still be left inside her is overpowered by the smell of my fresh flesh. I'm now sprinting full out towards the truck with Mom right on my heels. And several hundred necs on her heels.

I let the chain drop away, since Mom no longer needs any coaxing to follow me, and yank the blade from my belt. Necros are now coming from all directions and I swing out, sending heads and limbs falling to the cracked and broken pavement as I jump over corpses.

We hit the Power Wagon before I know it and I'm up over the side and into the bed in one jump. Mom is right after me and I turn and clock her, knocking her to the truck bed. I hit her two more times then toss her chain through the open back window and scramble in after it.

Little Man screams and howls as we both get wedged in the window and look out at the street and the hundreds of necs coming at us and it's all I can do from peeing everywhere. I reach back and tuck Garth's head down and finally get us through the window. As we tumble onto the bench seat the swarm of necs hits the truck, making it shudder and shake. I slam the back window closed around Mom's chain and reach for the ignition. I crank once, twice and the engine turns over.

Mom shakes off the beat down I gave her and is ripping necros apart as they try to climb into the truck. I don't understand why she fights, but I'm more than glad that she does.

I throw the Power Wagon into reverse, speeding backwards up the off-ramp until I have enough space to turn the wheel and get us around the other side of the school bus. I throw it into drive and hit the gas, crushing as many necs as I can that get in our way. We make it past the school bus and I start to head across to the on-ramp, hoping to get back on I-5, but the on-ramp is just as clogged with cars as the off-ramp so I speed under the overpass and away from the necs, and the bookstore from Hell, and head towards the farmland beyond, dodging old cars, trucks and massive potholes.

I glance in the rearview mirror and see something that makes my heart stop. The bookstore. I can see a lone figure on the roof of the bookstore. And I think I see it waving.

But that can't be, can it? I mean, the necs would have torn Veronica apart. Plus, even if she did get up on the roof it would only be a few hours before she turned from the bite. And I'm sure she had to have been bitten several more times.

But, I tell myself that it can't be Veronica. Veronica is dead and I have to push her out of my mind.

But the kiss...

I realize I still have the book in my back pocket. How it didn't fall out is going on the never ending list of mysteries in my life. I pull the book out and toss it into the glove box. Maybe I'll live to read it.

I shake my head, trying to clear it and look back in the rearview mirror. I see Mom standing in the back of the truck, her mouth open and howling back at the swarm of necs that still pursue us, although I'm putting distance between us and them quickly.

Little Man squeaks and I angle the mirror so I can get a look at him. To my surprise I see him not looking at me, but at Mom, his little dead arms reaching towards her. He squeaks again and when she doesn't respond he lets out one of his tantrum screeches and Mom's head whips around towards us.

I have to force myself to watch the road, but I keep looking in the mirror, not wanting to miss a moment of this. Little Man reaches and I lean back in the seat so he can put his little fists against the back window. Mom presses her face against the glass, smearing it with bloody pink saliva as she groans and growls. Little Man responds in kind and soon they are groaning, growling, and hooting at each other.

Dad may be the scientist, he may be the one that has spent his life studying the necs, but I may be the one that has made the most significant discovery yet.

Necs can communicate. They can talk. And somewhere in their predator brains, they can think and even feel. I've always known this about Little Man, but now maybe it's true for the rest. Doesn't mean I won't offer a well-placed head-shot if a nec comes at me, but this changes things.

I've only been out in the world for less than a full week and my perception of the truth of things has been shattered over and over again.

I really hope my brain can handle whatever gets thrown at me next. Otherwise I'll just end up a drooling, blubbering mess.

The way is slow going. I have to stop and fight Mom for the map in her back pocket, but with Little Man's distraction I'm able to get it. Since I-5 is no longer an option I try to take Highway 99 north to the compound, but that turns out to be a bad idea. Highway 99 has way too much necro activity to be safe and I have to find a back road that can take us as close to the compound as possible.

I only make it another few miles before shock and fatigue take over and I'm struggling to keep my eyes open. My body feels like dead weight, which I wonder if that is how it feels to Mom right now, and I fight for control of the Power Wagon. I see a farmhouse off the road a ways up and stop at the head of the long gravel drive.

I wait and watch to see if there is any activity inside, but see nothing and finally decide to pull up close. I get up to the house and pull the Power Wagon around back, tucking it between the house and what looks like an old garage or work shed.

Looking from the paper blade to the machete I tuck the blade into my belt again, deciding the size of the machete is a better option. I take a deep breath and open the truck door, wincing as the hinge protests, but no one tries to attack me so I slowly move towards the farmhouse's side door, machete at the ready.

The house door squeaks louder than the truck door and

both Mom and Little Man parrot the sound and I have to shush them both. Surprisingly they comply. The door opens into a kitchen area and I wait a moment for my eyes to adjust to the gloom. I sniff the air and realize I can smell food and I glance over at the stove. It's a large black cast iron stove and I can feel warmth coming from it as I place my hand near the top.

I'm not alone and I realize this almost too late as I hear Mom howl from the truck. I dash back outside in time to see a small boy put a rifle to his shoulder.

"NO!" I scream at him. "STOP!"

He looks over at me, shocked, giving me enough time to close the distance between us and slap the rifle from his hands. It goes off when it falls to the ground and I cover my head as Little Man and Mom screech in complaint. The boy is gone in a flash and I take chase, following him into the garage.

Once again my eyes have to adjust and they do in time to see a storm door close in the corner of the garage floor. I grab at it and fling it open.

The boy is at the bottom of a small ladder, huddled together with a girl even younger than he is. I hold my hands out and crouch slowly by the opening.

"It's okay," I soothe. "I'm not going to hurt you. I was just trying to find a place to sleep for the night. It's been a rough day. I promise I'm not gonna hurt you."

They tremble with fear and I have to guess the boy is maybe eight or nine and the girl is five or six. Neither have seen clean clothes or a bath in quite a long time, but that is probably to be expected way out here. They stare at me with wide, fearful eyes and I reach down.

"Come on. It's okay," I say. "I'm not going to hurt you."

"You...you...you ain't...you ain't gonna eat...you ain't gonna eat us?" the boy stammers.

"No, of course not," I laugh, but stop quickly when I realize my laughter just makes them more fearful. "I don't eat people. I'm not like the SATs."

"The...the what's?" the boy asks.

"The Sick and Twisteds. They eat people, I don't."

"You ain't with the Keep?" he asks. The girl pulls away from him a bit and starts staring at me.

"The Keep? No, I'm all by myself." Mom lets out a howl and I grimace. "Well, almost all by myself."

"Why you have a slick in your truck then?" he asks suspiciously, but his defiant tone tells me he doesn't see me as a threat. The girl points at me and the boy follows the line of her finger. He gasps and his eyes go wide. "You have one on you!"

"It's alright! They won't hurt you!" Although I'm not quite sure this is true with Mom. "They're my..." I trail off and the kids stare at me, waiting for an answer. "They're my family."

"Is that your mama?" the girl asks in the smallest voice I've ever heard. "She was bit, right?"

"Well, sorta," I answer.

"What's that on your back?" the boy asks and they move a little closer to the ladder. "Is it a baby slick? How'd you get a baby slick?"

"Well, it was a baby once. He's my brother." *He ain't heavy...* "It's a long story. You two want to come up and I can tell you about it?" I look at them sheepishly. "And if you have any food that would be great, too."

"We have some fenising," the girl blurts out.

"Hush, Sarah!" the boy scolds.

"What, Tommy? He asked if we had any food!" she snaps at him.

"Fenising?" I ask, not sure I want to know.

The boy, Tommy, struggles whether to tell me or not then sighs. "She means venison. Deer. We have some steaks left."

My mouth waters at the thought of some fresh meat and I chuckle at the irony. I guess I'm not too different from Little Man that way.

"What's his name?" Sarah asks, looking at Little Man who is now grunting and fussing.

"Come on up and I'll tell you, okay?"

They look at each other and then nod. "Okay," Tommy agrees. "But you make any moves..." He pulls a nice looking hunting knife from his belt. "I'll cut ya."

I laugh and show him my machete. "I think mine's a little bigger, but that is a nice looking knife. I used to have one like it." Sarah shies away from me when she sees the machete.

"Oh, sorry." I flip it about and lower it down handle first. "Here, you take it so you know I'm not gonna hurt you."

Sarah reaches out quickly and snatches the machete, but Tommy takes it away from her. "You're just gonna cut yourself."

"I am not!" she shouts at him.

"You are too! You always cut yourself!"

"Hey! Hey!" I say. "Knock it off. Are you two coming up or what?"

They glare at each other, but Tommy starts up the ladder with Sarah right behind.

"Don't push," he grumbles.

"I'm not," she snaps back.

I chuckle to myself as I help them up into the garage. Siblings really are siblings, no matter who they are.

7

We have to wait for the sun to go down before we can get a fire going in the stove. The smoke would be a give away if someone came looking and since I'm not sure where the SAT trucks went and Tommy and Sarah are pretty worried about the Keep, I don't argue. I even help them get blankets in place around the kitchen windows so the lantern light we cook by doesn't alert anyone.

"Where are your parents?" I ask as we finally sit down to eat some of the best smelling food I have ever come across. Not only do they have venison steaks that Sarah fetches from a cold creek running back behind their house, but we also roast up some late corn and some small purple potatoes which just fascinate me. The children look down at their plates and don't answer my question. "Are you parents close by? Will they be back?"

"No," Tommy answers flatly.

"No, they aren't close by? Or no, they won't be back?" I push.

"They're turnt," Sarah whispers. "Like your mama."

"Oh," I mutter. "I'm sorry."

Tommy slams his fork down on the table. "Why ain't you killed yours?!"

I stop mid-bite and look at him. "What? What do you mean?"

"Why ain't you killed your mama?! She's turned! She's

just gonna eat you when she can! That ain't your mama no more!" His eyes burn with anger.

I can't look at him so I focus on my plate of food, but it isn't as appetizing anymore. Mom is chained up and gagged in their storm cellar and the image of her undead stare as I closed the cellar hatch haunts me.

"I can't kill her," I mutter.

"But she's dead!" Tommy yells, but quickly quiets down as Sarah hushes him. "She ain't your mama no more."

"Yeah, you said that. I have my reasons."

"Can she be saved? Can God save her?" Sarah asks, her face full of pleading and wasted hope. "Tommy says God don't care about the slicks, but I think God cares about everything. Do you think God cares? Will He help your mama?"

I have to wonder about this. Mom, Dad especially, never really talked about God or religion. Everything I know I had to find out myself from all my books. Dad wouldn't even talk about the subject if I brought it up and Mom would just shrug or stare off in space.

"I don't know about God," I say. "I think my dad may be able to help her, though. Plus, she seems different from the other necs."

"Necs? What are necs?" Tommy asks.

"It's what I call slicks."

"So she's differ'nt like your brother?" Sarah asks, looking around me to get a better view of Little Man.

"I think so. I don't really know," I answer, patting Garth on the head. He grunts a little, but doesn't protest or try to grab me. "I hope so."

We eat quietly for a few minutes, only the sound of our forks hitting the plates filling the kitchen. Little Man grunts a few times and I realize I should probably feed him, but I'll do that when I have some alone time.

"Thanks for letting me stay here tonight," I say. "It's a huge help."

"It's fine," Tommy replies and he and Sarah exchange a look.

"What? Is there something you want to ask me?"

Tommy doesn't answer, just looks at his plate.

"Go ahead and ask. I don't mind answering any questions

you have. Not that I know a whole lot about what's going on out there, but I'll try."

"Tommy wants to know if we can come with you," Sarah blurts out.

"Sarah!" Tommy scolds. "Hush!"

A piece of venison falls from my fork as I hold it halfway to my mouth. To be honest, I didn't see this coming. Am I that self-absorbed?

"Come with me?" I look from one to the other. "I...um, I... Why would you want to do that?"

Tommy takes a deep breath. "This is the last of the venison. We have some more potatoes and late corn. That's it."

"Tommy can't shoot straight," Sarah adds.

He turns on her, but doesn't say anything, just hangs his head.

"You can't hunt then, right?" I ask. "I'm eating the last of your food? Wow, I'm sorry."

"It's okay," Tommy replies. "It would have only lasted another day or two, anyway." He looks up at me expectantly. "Can we come with you?"

"I don't know."

"See. I told you," Tommy says to Sarah and the little girl's eyes well with tears.

"Hold on," I plead. "I didn't say no. It's just it's really dangerous out there and I'm only seventeen. I don't know how to take care of kids. I can't promise you'll be any safer with me than if you try to survive here."

"We won't be alone," Sarah sniffs.

And that's the real truth of it. They are all alone here. Two small kids, no parents, now no food, and no one to tell them it will be okay. They don't have anyone to keep the bad dreams away, to sing goodnight songs to them. No stories of heroes to fight off the scary thoughts. No kisses on their knees when they fall and get scraped. They're all alone.

"Yes, of course," I nod. "You can come with me. Let's finish eating and then we'll go through what you have to see what we can bring. I don't have any food, so we need to pack all that's left." I point my fork at both of them. "That means clean your plates. This could be our last meal until we get to the compound tomorrow."

"Compound?" Tommy asks. "The hippies up by Cedar Creek?"

"You know about the compound?" *Hippies?*

"It burnt down," Sarah answers. "We tried to go there, but there ain't no one there anymore."

My stomach lurches and I fight to keep my food from coming back up. It's too precious now to waste because of some panic.

"When was that?! When did you try to go there?!"

"Two days ago," Tommy answers. "Once I knew we were almost out of food."

Two days ago...

"What happened? Tell me what you saw!"

Tommy looks away and now his eyes well with tears. Sarah just wraps her arms around herself and shakes her head.

My fist hits the table and the plates jump. "Tell me what you saw! This is important! Did it just happen? Did it look like people left? Or...?"

Tommy and Sarah grab at each other and stare at me, horrified. Little Man screeches and slaps at my neck. I take a couple deep breaths and calm myself down, but it takes all my strength.

"Please. You have to give me details. My Dad is supposed to be there. It was the last place he could be. I have to know what happened."

"No, Tommy, no, please," Sarah whimpers. "I don't want to hear it." She presses her hands to her ears and closes her eyes tight, her head shaking violently back and forth. "Nonononononononononono!"

Tommy eyes plead at me and he grabs Sarah's hands, prying them away. "It's okay. I won't say anything. I promise."

"But, I have to...!"

Tommy shakes his head. "Let's finish eating and then I'll get you tucked in. Okay, Sarah? No bad stories. Just good dreams."

She carefully opens her eyes. "No bad stories? Just good dreams?"

"Just good dreams," he insists.

Slowly she picks up her fork and finishes eating. Tommy

holds my gaze for a minute until he also starts eating again.

I look at my plate, but I'm no longer hungry. "You guys want mine?"

Sarah nods and I scrape what's left onto her plate. She wolfs it down like it's her last meal.

If I don't figure out what's happened, it could very well be all our last meals.

CHAPTER FOURTEEN

S arah falls asleep quickly, tucked into their parent's bed. Tommy and I start getting all the supplies in the house together while he tells me what he and Sarah found at the compound.

"They have these huge walls," he starts while throwing his and Sarah's clothes into a sack. I look wistfully at the clean clothes and wish I could strip down right now and scrub clean. "What are you looking at?"

"Huh? Oh, sorry. Just wish I had a clean pair of shorts," I grin.

"You can have some of daddy's clothes," Tommy offers. "He was about your size." He glances quickly at Little Man. "You'll have to cuts some holes though."

"I'm used to doing that. Thanks. It'll be great to have something clean. So, what about the walls?"

"Oh, yeah. Well they have these huge walls and before we even got close to them we could see smoke," he pauses. "We didn't get very close. Just enough to see that the gates were torn down and there were..."

I wait, but he doesn't continue. "There were what?"

"Bunch a slicks," Tommy finally answers. "All nailed to the wall." He swallows hard and struggles to speak. "It was the Keep. Daddy said that's what they do when they take a place. They crucify folks just like Jesus."

We keep packing and I let him get calmed down before I

ask, "What do you know about the Keep? My mom was going to tell me more, but she, well, you know..."

"They're bad. Really bad," he answers quickly. "Mama and Daddy kept talking about moving us 'cause the Keep was getting closer."

"Where is the Keep? Do you know exactly?"

Tommy shakes his head. "No. Daddy said they were everywhere, but I knew he was just exaggerating."

The look on Tommy's face tells me he doesn't believe his dad was exaggerating.

"Do they take prisoners? What else do you know?"

"I don't. That's about it. Like I said, we didn't get close enough to see what really happened."

"So you don't actually know if anyone was still there or not, do you?"

Tommy glares. "I'm not a chicken."

"I don't think you are. I just have to be sure, for myself."

His eyes go wide and he lets the rolled up socks he's packing slip from his fingers. "You want us to go there?"

"Yes, that's where I'm going. I have to see if my dad left a message or any clues to where he is."

"What if he's dead?" Tommy asks casually. "What then?"

"He's not dead," I insist. "I'd know if he was."

"You psychic or something?" He eyes me warily.

Funny how he and his sister accept me with a nec glued to my back, but the idea of me being "psychic" seems to bug him.

"No, I'm not psychic. It's my dad and I'd know if he's dead. Just like you'd probably know if something happened to Sarah."

He thinks about this for a moment then nods. "Yeah, okay. I think I get it. But I still don't want to go back to that compound."

I start to argue, but Little Man squawks loudly then starts in on his screeching.

"What's he doing?" Tommy asks, stepping away from me.

"Necros," I state. "Slicks. There must be some close."

A crash outside the house tells us just how close and Tommy starts to shake.

"It's okay," I say, moving to the kitchen and grabbing the

hunting rifle. I pick up my machete and slip it into my belt then slowly open the kitchen door, turning back to Tommy. "Secure this door and stay quiet. Get close to Sarah. If we have to move quickly you'll need to wake her fast."

He nods and follows me to the door as I close it. I hear the bolt slide and a thunk as he bars the door. I let my eyes adjust and crouch low, carefully making my way to the back of the house.

I peer around the corner and see several necs crowded around the garage. Little Man grunts and they turn toward me. I raise the rifle and fire, knocking one to the ground, but the three that are runners come at me fast before I can pull the bolt back and I have to swing out, using the rifle as a club.

I cave in a nec's head and jam the butt of the rifle into the gut of another before they can grab me. I'm not so lucky with the third and it hits me square in the chest, knocking me backwards and the rifle from my hands. I tumble and roll, coming up with my machete swinging. The nec's head flies and I turn to the others.

Four shamblers shuffle their way towards me and I make quick work of them, leaving only a lurker with its head hiding behind the garage and its backside sticking out. I almost feel guilty when I whack the lurker's head off. They're just too easy. If you see them.

I have to wonder why they were all gathered around the garage instead of sniffing about the house for us. Double checking I hadn't missed any necs, I go to the Power Wagon and grab a small flashlight from the glove box, then open the garage and step inside.

The storm cellar hatch is still secure and I lift it up to check on Mom, shining the light down on her. She just sits there, her legs crossed and body rocking back and forth on the dirt floor.

"Mom?" I whisper.

She doesn't respond and Little Man growls low. This gets her attention and her head whips up towards us. She tries to hiss around the gag, but it just comes out sounding like she's choking. Little Man hoots a couple times and Mom relaxes, dropping her head back down. Soon she's rocking back and forth again.

It breaks my heart, but I close the hatch and walk slowly back to the house. I knock lightly on the kitchen door and wait.

"You bit?" Tommy asks from the other side of the door.

"Nope," I answer, fatigue grinding me down. "I'm fine."

"You sure?"

"Yep, pretty sure. Open up please."

The door opens slightly and Tommy peers out. He looks me up and down, but doesn't open it any further. "You got a lot of gunk on ya."

"Yeah, that happens when you chop the heads of necs. Gunk tends to get on ya."

"Shouldn't you wash off first? I don't want that stuff touching me or Sarah."

"You'll be fine," I answer, starting to get a little more than irritated. "Just move please."

"I think you should strip off first. Mama always made Daddy strip off his bloody clothes before coming inside."

We stare at each other for a while and I realize he isn't going to budge. I set the rifle and machete down and start taking my clothes off. "You want to get those extra clothes of your Dad's for me? I'd rather not stand around naked."

He closes the door and then actually locks it behind him. I sigh and stand naked in the night air. It actually feels good, the slight breeze blowing on my skin. I look up at the night sky and watch the stars blinking in and out. Little Man hoots and I reach back and pat him. He rubs his head against my hand then chomps down on my fingers.

"Knock it off," I scold him and he grunts. "Don't do that around the kids. They'll freak out." He grunts again, hoots twice and farts.

God, I need some sleep.

2

Tommy falls asleep pretty soon after he lets me in and I spend the rest of the night searching through their house for supplies we can use. Unfortunately, there isn't a whole lot.

I do take the free time to change the dressing on my arm. It isn't pretty. The wound has gotten worse, not better. I'm pretty sure green and black aren't healthy colors.

Staring at the wound in the bathroom mirror, I have a strange feeling wash over. It feels like my life hasn't even begun to change. That who I am now is not who I'll be in the future. Sure, that's life, you grow and change. But the feeling I have is more profound. Like I'm *really* going to change. I sigh, throw on my shirt and flop onto the couch.

I manage to get a couple hours of sleep, but as soon as the dawn light hits my face I'm up and throwing gear into the back of the Power Wagon. I have Mom secured in the bed quickly and twirl the keys in my hand while I try to convince Tommy and Sarah to come with me.

"You'll be safer with me," I insist.

"No, we won't," Tommy argues. "Nothing is safe where the Keep has been."

His face is rigid and jaw set so I just nod and hop in the truck. "Hide yourselves at least, okay? Don't come out unless you know it's me. Understand?"

"We've been left before," he nods. "We know what to do."

I struggle with leaving them, but I can't really drag them kicking and screaming with me. I start up the Power Wagon and back away from the house. I wave to them as I turn around and speed down their drive. When I hit the road I can't see them in the rearview mirror and hope they'll be alright.

Tommy scratched exact directions to the compound on the map, but even with those I spend a lot of time turning around and doubling back. The dense green of the Willamette Valley is a little disorienting for me. I'm used to the browns and oranges of dry pine forests and underbrush. All this lushness makes my head spin a bit.

It takes me close to two hours, and I'm about to give up and head back, when I see wisps of smoke rising above a grove of oak trees. I pull the Power Wagon close to the grove and turn off the engine.

"You feel anything?" I ask Little Man, but he doesn't answer. Not until we get about a hundred yards closer and I hack our way through a bunch of blackberry bushes. Then he goes crazy.

"Shhhhh!" I order. "Quiet down!" He won't and I'm about to whack him when I see the compound wall. And the necs struggling and spiked to it. "Oh. Crap."

I figure if anyone is watching or listening, Little Man has already blown our cover, so I take a quick glance around and then walk right up to the wall. I don't see any gate so I must have gotten completely turned around and come from the back. I hike through the long grass and make my way to the front.

Every few feet is a necro, spikes through its hands and feet, hanging, hissing and growling on the wall. Little Man can hardly contain himself and I'm shouting at him the whole way for him to shut up and stop hitting me. We aren't exactly a crack commando team today.

With my machete in hand, ready to cut down anything that moves, I approach the demolished front gate. The smell is overpowering without the wall as a buffer and I have to cover my nose and mouth and take small, short breaths. The gate doors are made of thick wood and iron, but they look like they were easily blown from the wall. And I do mean blown. With explosives. I clomp over them and into the compound. My mind reels at the sight.

Everywhere there are body parts, and I mean everywhere. Legs, arms, heads, half torsos, full torsos, feet, fingers, hands, hair, teeth, ears. *Everywhere*. I keep the gorge down that rises in my throat and pick my way through the parts and pieces, careful not to tread on any of it.

The really weird part is, while I can tell these people were attacked by necs, none of the body parts look fed upon. None of them. That creeps me out.

I can see there were buildings lined throughout the compound, but what they were is impossible to tell since there is nothing but burnt out shells. The stench from the rotting body parts and the thickness of the smoke makes my head dizzy and it takes me a bit to focus and realize I hear someone calling my name.

"Dad?!" I shout spinning about to face the gate.

Through the haze I see someone enter the compound and I rush forward, but stop suddenly when the man before me is obviously not my dad.

He's short and old, his long white hair twisted into a dreadlocked ponytail. One eye is missing, but it must have happened a while ago since the socket is filled with old scar tissue. He's wearing a tank top and cut-off jeans. No shoes. In one hand he twirls something small and silver on a piece of leather.

"You Garret?" he asks, his voice as smoky and rough as the compound. I nod, but don't say anything. He cranes his neck for a better look at Little Man who is still squawking and complaining. "I can't believe it's true."

He stops twirling what's in his hand and brings it to his lips. He blows hard, but no sound comes out. Little Man however goes into a frenzy and starts pounding at his head and at me. The necs outside the wall howl with him.

"What are you doing?!" I yell, but I'm quickly answered as eight dogs bound into the gate and stop by the man, four lined up on each side.

"Sorry about that," he smiles. "Only way to communicate with my dogs without bringing the slicks down on me. Sure, they hear it, but it's too painful for them to track and they usually run the other direction."

"Who are you?" I yell, nipping my finger and jamming it into Garth's mouth to shut him up. He stops complaining and starts sucking at the finger right away.

"Well I'll be," the man mutters.

I smack the flat of the machete against my leg, getting his attention. "Who are you and how the hell do you know my name?"

"I'm Scootch. I know your dad."

I wait for him to continue, but he just stands there. The dogs don't twitch or move, just sit next to him stock still. They all look like they're German Shepherd mixes, but there's probably a lot more in them than just that. They're all different colors and some have blue eyes, so maybe there's some Husky too. I really need to learn more about dogs.

"You know my dad? Where is he?!"

"That I can't say," he replies, turning and walking away, back out of the compound. The dogs follow on his heels, four to a side. "He left you a message, though."

I chase after him. "What do you mean you can't say? You mean you don't know or won't tell me?"

"Don't know," he says as he stops outside the compound and points at the wall. "I have a guess or two, but he left before all this went down. I think he knew it was coming."

I'm about to ask a ton more questions when I see the message on the wall. Well, I see part of the message since it's mostly obscured by a wriggling nec.

"Morse code, right?" Scootch asks. "That's what those dots and dashes cut into the wall are, right? I don't read it myself, but I watched enough spy movies when I was your age to figure that out."

"Yeah...Morse code," I mumble as I struggle to read the entire message around the nec. It takes me a bit, but I do it and feel my world fall away.

"You ain't looking so good," Scootch says right behind me.

His voice startles me and I whirl around, my machete at his throat. "Who are you?" His dogs aren't too happy about the sudden movement and they start growling, their hackles standing up. "Call them off or I cut!"

Scootch laughs. "You kill me, they kill you. Natural order of things." He watches me closely. "Put it down, Garret. I'm here to help." He reaches slowly into his pocket and pulls something out. He bounces it in his hand a bit and brings it up so I can see it clearly.

It's a pocket knife. Something my dad used to have with him all the time.

"He said to show you this and you'd know I'm friend, not foe," he states. I start to protest, but he continues. "He said you'd argue. I'm supposed to say that the little blade is still sharp even though it's small and then ask how your thumb is."

I choke up right away and lower the machete. When I was little I took this pocket knife without asking. I had always watched Dad use the bigger blade, but not the small one. I opened up the knife, ran my thumb along the small blade, and thought nothing of it, thinking it wasn't sharp. The problem was it was even sharper than the big blade and I had sliced my thumb wide open without realizing it. The pain hit me a couple seconds later and I started screaming. Dad found me and after a couple of stitches told me, "It may be small, but it sure is sharp. Just like you."

"Sit down before you fall down," Scootch insists.

This time I don't resist and kneel on the grass, the words of Dad's Morse code message going around and around in my head.

"Don't follow. Keep Mom safe. Keep yourself and your brother safe. You three are the key to everything. Do not go North. Do not go North. Keep them safe. Keep yourself safe."

3

"I'm guessing you didn't like the message?" Scootch calls after me as I hurry back to the Power Wagon. "What did it say?"

"Not to go north," I respond as I open the truck door.

"Let me guess, you're going north?" Scootch laughs. "Yeah, he said you'd probably do whatever is the opposite of his instructions. HOLY HELL WHAT IS THAT?!"

"What?!" I yell, spinning about.

"In the truck bed! Why do you have a slick in your truck?!"

"Oh, that's just Mom. You see, I have an absent father, a dead brother attached to my back, and a recently turned mom and apparently we are the *'key to everything'*. What's so confusing about that?"

Scootch stares at me while his dogs whine at his heels. I'm guessing they want to eat Mom, but I've never had a dog, so what do I know?

"Um, kid, if your dad said to not go north, you should listen. He knows what he's talking about, trust me."

"Trust you? I don't know you!" I shout slamming the truck door. "And what would you know about my dad, anyway?"

He lifts up his tank top to show a nasty looking bandage. He peels it away and I cringe at the swollen red bite marks underneath. "He cleaned it out so fast that he beat the infection. Four days old and I still haven't turned. The man knows his stuff. I'm the proof he left so you would listen." He lets the tank drop and hooks a thumb over his shoulder. "Good thing I wasn't here or I'd be just like my friends back there, nailed to a wall, waiting to petrify."

He moves over to the truck and leans into the window. "Now, how about you shut off that engine and let's talk a bit before you go rushing off to your death."

"You're obviously not very stable. I haven't turned the engine on yet. I'll take my chances, thanks."

He grabs my arm and Mom hisses from behind me. "Wait! What?" He looks around, his eyes wide.

"Let go of my..."

"SHHHHH!"

Then I hear it. Hear them, actually. Engines. Truck engines.

"You expecting anyone else?" Scootch whispers. "Were you followed?"

"I barely found the place myself. I was turning around so much I would have noticed if someone was following me," I hiss.

Scootch raises an eyebrow. "You're an ornery little cuss, ain't ya?"

"Actually, I'm a really nice guy. At least that's what my mom says." I hook *my* thumb over *my* shoulder this time. Scootch glances back at Mom and winces. "I'm getting out of here now. I'll see ya later."

The engine sounds stop just as I'm about to turn the Power Wagon's ignition and Scootch reaches in, grabbing my hand. "Wait! They'll hear you now. You won't get far with the racket this thing makes."

He's right. I wish he wasn't, but he is. "Fine," I huff. "We'll just hang here until they pass by. Doubt they'll stay long considering the shape the compound is in."

"GARRET WEIR!" a voice booms. "WE KNOW YOU'RE HERE!"

"I don't think they're leaving soon," Scootch mutters. "Friends of yours?"

"I don't have any friends. Not here."

"GARRET WEIR! DON'T IGNORE ME, KID! I'VE GOT SOME FRIENDS OF YOURS THAT REALLY WANT TO SEE YOU!"

"More friends?" Scootch asks. "You're a popular guy for just getting into town."

"Shut up," I snarl, pushing him away from the truck as I

get out. I hop in the back of the truck and Mom lunges at me then checks herself.

Scooch gasps. "She isn't trying to kill you! What the...?"

"She's my mom. She knows me." Little Man and Mom start hooting at each other as I unhook Mom's chain and lead her from the back of the truck. "I'm going to hoof it out of here. You can come if you want, but I'm leaving now."

"What about your friends?" Scooch asks, looking back towards the compound. "They say they have your friends."

"Like I said, I don't have any friends." I jump from the truck and pull Mom along, circling back and grabbing my gear from the front seat.

"Garret!"

I stop dead. That was a small voice. A kid's voice. Tommy's voice.

"Garret, help! They got me and Sarah! Please!"

"YOU HEAR THAT, KID? YOU HAVE THIRTY SECONDS OR I FEED THE BOY TO THESE SLICKS ON THE WALL! THEN I FEED THE GIRL TO THEM! MAYBE! SHE SURE IS A PRETTY LITTLE THING!"

That voice sounds familiar also, but I'm having a hard time placing it.

"TWENTY-NINE! TWENTY-EIGHT! TWENTY-SEVEN!"

Then it hits me: Travis.

I didn't recognize the voice because the last time I heard him he had teeth. That mouth is empty now, thanks to Mom.

I turn to Scooch. "Please tell me you have some guns." I hope.

He shakes his head. "I have dogs. Don't need guns when you have dogs."

"You need guns now!" I snap. "They have guns. Lots of guns. Pretty sure dogs aren't bulletproof."

"FIFTEEN! FOURTEEN! THIRTEEN! TWELVE!"

I sigh and let go of Mom's chain as I step away from the truck and trees and back towards the compound. I'm not going to hook Mom up again. If things get bad I'll let her wander the landscape like the rest of the necs. They'll just cut her down or take her back to Charlotte and she'll end up in whatever new sick games that woman can think up.

"I HEAR YOU!" I shout. "KEEP YOUR TEETH IN YOUR

MOUTH!"

"What does that mean?" Scootch asks from behind me. Guess he's coming with.

"You'll see," I reply. I glance back and see Mom staying right inside the tree line, not following at all. She howls, and Little Man responds, then she slinks back into the shadows and I lose sight of her. I also don't see the dogs. I raise my eyebrows at Scootch.

"They're ready when we need them," he winks.

"He's right here!" a man shouts as he runs around the side of the wall, automatic rifle trained on me and Scootch. "I got him!"

"Yep, you got me," I mock, raising my hands above my head. "You're really talented!"

"Shut up and walk!" the man shouts, keeping his distance. "That way!"

"It's a circular compound, genius," I sneer. "Either way will get us back to the front."

"I said shut up!" He waves the rifle to intimidate me, but I really don't care anymore.

We get to the front of the compound and Travis laughs when he sees me. "There's our little hero! Where's that traitor Veronica?" He looks around cautiously. "WHERE YOU AT TRAITOR?!"

"She's dead," I say. "Necs got her yesterday back at the off-ramp."

"In that bookstore? Good! She deserved every single bite! You sure do leave a trail of bodies, kid." I'm about to respond, but Travis wags a finger as one of his men drag Tommy and Sarah forward. "Keep that smart mouth closed or the kids get it!"

The kids get it? Is he some pulp fiction thug?

I keep my mouth closed, not wanting anything to happen to them.

"I am supposed to thank you, by the way," he laughs. "Ms. Charlotte wants to thank you for her new toy."

"Her what?" I ask.

Travis puts a finger to his lips. "I didn't say Simon says to talk. Yeah, her toy. You know? That kid you left running through the woods like a torch with legs?"

Dear God... Joseph? He can't be talking about Joseph, can he?

"Not so smug now, are you? Didn't think the slick would live did you? Well he did, and he's quite different than the other slicks. Ms. Charlotte is having a ball putting him to the test. She just wanted you to know that."

Rage and guilt wash over me in waves.

"Yeah, that shook you up. Charlotte figured it would. She says you have too much heart," he growls. "I plan on ripping that from your chest at some point." He turns his attention to Scootch. "Who's the old man? I don't know him."

"No, you don't," Scootch replies. He steps forward with his hand extended. "Name's Scootch. Pleasure to meet you."

Travis pulls a pistol and points it at Scootch, who in turn stops in his tracks.

"I don't really care who you are, old timer. I'm here for the boy, that's all. Make trouble, you die. Move an inch more, you die. Open your mouth again, you die. Follow those rules and I might let you live. I ain't making no promises, though."

Scootch nods slowly and looks over at me.

"So, what do you want, Travis? I'm not giving you my teeth, so don't ask," I laugh.

He points the pistol at me and steps forward quickly. "If I want your teeth I'll take them!"

His hand is shaking and I can see a vein at his temple throbbing.

"Okay, okay, you can have my teeth. So what now?"

He looks around. "Where's your mommy?"

"She's dead too. Turned yesterday. Not one of the better days in my life."

Travis laughs. "You think I'm stupid?! You think I'm going to fall for that?! Veronica was good, but I don't doubt she got taken out by all those slicks. Your mom? I saw her in the arena! You're full of it!" He walks back to the kids and grabs Sarah by the arm, shoving the pistol against her cheek. "Now, where is she?!"

From back behind the compound a man's scream is cut off.

Travis waves to his other men and they run from the gate, split into two groups, and head around back, leaving only one man holding Sarah and Tommy and four others standing behind them.

"On your knees, kid!" I comply and he tosses Sarah aside, jamming the barrel of the gun against my forehead. "I don't think this is gonna go well for you!"

4

Gunfire, men screaming, and the howls of my undead mom echo to our ears. Little Man growls then screeches loudly with each of Mom's howls.

Travis keeps the pistol pressed against my head and my eyes never leave his. His face is like stone and I try to match it as we wait to hear what the final sound will be. Sweat drips into my eyes, but I don't move to wipe it away. I'm pretty sure that if I do anything other than breathe my brains will be splattered everywhere.

One last burst of automatic gunfire is heard and Mom lets out the most gut wrenching sound I think I've ever heard.

Silence.

We wait another thirty seconds and Travis smiles.

"I think your mom has truly gone bye-bye now, kid," he smirks, smacking me across the cheek with the butt of the gun.

I crumple to the grass and grab my face, wiping at the blood trickling from just under my left eye. Little Man ups his volume and Travis cocks back the hammer.

"Make that thing shut up!" he yells. "Make it shut up now or both the kids die!"

He whirls about and aims for Tommy, but lowers his gun as movement coming from the right catches his eye.

"What the..."

Mom is on him almost faster than I can track and Travis

tries to whip the gun around, but she knocks him down before he can even turn an inch. The pistol goes off once then flies out of Travis's hand as Mom tears into his throat. I close my eyes, the wet noises telling my ears everything my eyes don't want to see. That my eyes are so tired of seeing.

"Ah, Jesus!" Scootch hollers, bringing his hand up and the whistle to his mouth. "Open your eyes, boy! Not the time to be shy!"

The man holding Tommy and Sarah just stands there, his mouth agape, as he watches his boss get mutilated. The other men behind him aren't quite so shocked and they raise their rifles.

I scramble over to Travis's pistol and roll to my feet, take aim and start firing. I intentionally aim high, making sure Tommy and Sarah aren't hit. It doesn't really matter since the men instinctively duck and run further into the compound for cover. None even try to rescue Travis.

"You're gonna want to let them go," I snarl at the man holding the kids. "Right now." His hands come free and he raises them up, his eyes still glued to Mom as she now rips Travis's chest open and starts breaking ribs.

Travis's eyes find mine and I can tell he is pleading for help, but he's looking at the wrong person. It's taken me a week to learn what the world is like and now that I know I understand who I have to be in it. I'm not the carefree (for the most part) boy that picks blackberries and sits under the pine trees reading a Dickens novel or maybe a mystery by Mickey Spillane. That Garret doesn't exist anymore.

The Garret that does exist gets to his feet, crosses to Travis and puts a bullet right between the SAT's eyes. That's the Garret I am now.

Mom growls at me, her face smeared with blood and she looks like she wants to kill me for spoiling her meal. Little Man squawks at her and her head jerks in his direction. He squawks again and she slowly backs away from Travis's corpse.

"Dang," Scootch mumbles. "I've never seen a slick act that way before."

"You've never met my mom," I say. I raise the pistol towards the man behind Tommy and Sarah, who is still staring at Travis's body, and motion towards the compound. "Hey bud! How about you join your friends in the smoking ruins?"

He looks at me, looks at the pistol, looks at Travis, looks at Mom then turns and runs.

"Grab that rifle," I tell Tommy as Sarah runs to me and hugs my legs. "We need to get out of here."

Even in all the chaos and violence there is one thing I noticed: there are only two SAT trucks parked by the compound. Maybe the third truck crashed or maybe it didn't. Either way I don't want to be here if it shows up with more gun-toting crazies.

The pack of dogs come screaming around the side of the compound and stop by Scootch's side. "Can you drive?" I ask him. "You can load the dogs into the back of one of the trucks and follow me if you want."

He shakes his head. "I'm not the only one that was gone when the Keep attacked. I need to wait here for more to return."

I motion toward the inside of the compound. "What about those guys in there? They'll come to their senses soon and start shooting."

He looks down at his dogs, gives some command on his whistle and they all hunker down low and start crawling their way inside. He gives me a quick wink when the last one disappears from sight. "I think I've got it covered."

"You sure?"

"Yeah, you go ahead," he answers, his eyes watching the compound closely. "I still have to warn you away from going north."

I glance down at Sarah, still gripping my legs. "I think you may be right. I can't take them up there."

"You know where you're going?"

"Yeah, I do. I'm taking them to the Tribes and then I'll decide which direction to go. Maybe my dad will find me. He seems to be planning a few steps ahead, maybe those steps will catch up."

Snarls and screams of pain come from the compound. A rifles fires and Scootch winces, but there's no yelp of pain from any of the dogs.

"You best get going," he suggests strongly. "I'm gonna

collect the pack and wait out of sight. These guys may have friends coming."

"There's another truck about somewhere," I warn. "Keep your eyes open."

"You too."

We stand and stare at each other for an uncomfortable moment.

"We going?" Tommy asks, his arms straining at the weight of the large assault rifle.

Scootch laughs. "Get a move on. You come back this way stop by. I ain't going nowhere and we'll have the compound back in one piece soon."

I walk to him and offer my hand. He takes it gladly and shakes. "I will. I promise."

"I'll hold you to that," he smiles then moves cautiously into the compound.

I watch him drift into the smoke then lose him from sight. I've known the guy for an hour? Maybe less? And yet, I feel a pit in my stomach as I watch him go. I can see why Dad picked him to talk to me. Anybody else probably wouldn't have been able to get through to me.

"Can we go, please?" Sarah asks.

Little Man grunts, Mom growls, and Tommy slaps the rifle in his palm, nearly dropping it. How did I end up with this group?

"Yes, we can," I say, taking her hand and leading them all back around the compound and to the Power Wagon.

The truck starts right up and with Tommy's help I get us onto the road back toward their house.

"I'm glad you two are okay," I tell them.

Tommy nods and Sarah squeezes my hand, which she has barely let go of since we left the compound.

Little Man hoots and lets out a long fart and the kids start gagging as Tommy scrambles to roll down the window.

We could see the thick smoke well before we got to their driveway, so it wasn't a huge surprise to see the farmhouse crumbling to ash and embers.

"All our things," Tommy says sadly, nearly in tears. "It's all gone."

Sarah is in tears and I hold her in my arms, her head buried against my shoulder. Little Man alternates slapping at me and patting Sarah. After everything we've been through, I honestly know he understands more than anyone thinks he does.

"We'll scavenge more stuff along the way," I tell Tommy. "We'll be fine."

"But all of Mama's photos. Daddy's shot glasses."

"Shot glasses? You packed shot glasses?"

Tommy looks at me sternly. "Daddy collected them. They're very valuable."

"Right. Sorry, I didn't know."

It looks like they tried to set the garage on fire too, but didn't stick around to see if it took, leaving only one scorched wall. We salvage some tools and other supplies, loading them into the truck bed with Mom.

I can see her eyeing the kids and I have to wonder if she sees them as an extension of me or another meal. I'll have to make sure they aren't around her without me. Kinda like having a wild animal as a pet, you never know when they'll attack.

I'm back on I-5, heading south, not north, and I start to worry about the fuel level. I have Tommy navigate with the map on his lap and we soon pull off to look for a cache that's indicated.

It takes us a while to find the spot, an abandoned mine near Roseburg, but when we do it's like we stepped into Heaven. Food, bedding, fuel and more! No weapons or ammo, but we still have the assault rifle with a full magazine. I try not to think of the Scavengers we have to get through before we can get to the Tribes.

I make sure to chain Mom as far away from the kids as possible and get them tucked into a couple of the sleeping bags we find. They're a little musty...okay they're a lot musty, but they'll keep the chill from the damp mine out.

Taking the rifle, and some water and fresh bandages, I move up close to the mouth of the mine and watch the last rays of the sun settle on the hills then fade out. Bats flit by me, heading out to feed and I watch them dart above, grabbing moths and mosquitoes.

The water is flat and stale, but feels good on my throat after the day's events. My arm throbs and there is certainly a bad smell coming off it. I peel away my soiled bandage and wince. The sutures have completely come out and greenish pus oozes in large drops, with alarmingly thick, black lines spreading down my arm. I pour some of the water on it, but it only dilutes the pus. Wiping away as much as I can, and can stand to do since the slightest touch is excruciating, I tape a new bandage on and hope for the best.

If we survive the trip back to the Tribes I am sure I will catch hell from Billy. My main worry is he will want to take my arm off. I am the son of a surgeon and scientist, plus an inhabitant of a world of the dead, so I know necrotic tissue when I see it. I'll deal with that when the time comes.

Thinking of Billy instantly turns my thoughts to Karen and I try to picture her in my mind. I can see her face, her hair, how she stands, her smile. Will she still want to be around me when I show up with a nec for a mother? Will she understand when I decide I can't stay with the Tribes for long and have to get back to looking for Dad? Do *I* even understand this?

My head swims with everything I've been through. I've witnessed more death since turning seventeen than...well, I guess I haven't ever witnessed death before. Sure, I've lived with the necros my whole life, but that's a different kind of death. That death doesn't seem real since the dead are still up and walking. Except for the broken, they're just crawling along.

Death, death, death. Is it *me*? Lester would be alive if he hadn't come across me. But then he probably would have sold out Joseph and Karen at some point to cover his own butt, so I guess I saved them.

Except I didn't save Joseph. He died. He died because of me there is no doubt. My blood, my toxic blood, turned and killed him. I guess if Karen can be with me even though I killed her brother, then having Mom around won't be so bad.

The Griffins. They were sick and twisted, there's no other name for them. The torture they put people through, they deserved what they got. But what about the innocent people that lost their lives when the arena burnt down? How many mothers and fathers lost children? How many children lost parents? I caused that. All to save my own mother. Was it selfish? Probably. Would I do it over again? Yes, but I'd have more ammo.

I chuckle at this then admonish myself for such a cruel joke. I read a book once called *Catch-22*. It was about the insanity of war. Not just the brutal insanity of people actually killing each other, but the insanity that people have to force upon themselves to be in that situation in the first place. The catch-22 was that if you knew you were insane then that meant you were sane enough to know so you couldn't really be insane. And if you really were insane then you wouldn't even know it and would never tell anyone you were insane.

That's me. I'm the guy from *Catch-22*. I'm forced to be insane in this insane world, but by knowing I'm insane it makes me sane.

At least I'm not trying to get out of the Army.

Which brings up another thought: what happened to the military? Where are all the soldiers and tanks? All the law and order?

Dad told me when I was young that the country held together for a bit when the virus first started to spread, but that it got so out of control that in the end even the military couldn't keep it out and they died just like the rest. Well, Dad lied about the world dying, so did he lie about the military collapsing?

I could have gotten answers from Mom, but she's not in any shape to talk anymore. I could get Little Man to communicate with her, but a bunch of grunts and hoots, squeaks and squawks aren't going to help me. She was Special Forces. There must be more out there. More warriors willing to help.

Coyotes howl out past the hills and I shiver as the warmth of the day fades away and night truly takes hold. I look up at the stars that twinkle and flash above and smile at the thoughts of when Dad and I would leave the compound and hike to the top of a ridge at night just to watch the meteor showers that would happen a few times each year. I miss my old home. I miss my RV, my compound, my books, my woods.

Only a week has gone by...

I'm not sure when I drift off, but Sarah's screams wake me from a dream about blackberries and I'm up and sprinting back into the mine with their sweet taste still on my tongue.

"What?! What is it?!" I shout and freeze.

Mom is crouched next to Sarah and Tommy, apparently having pulled her chain loose from her neck. She jumps back when she sees me and retreats a few feet into the mine.

"She was gonna eat me!" Sarah screams.

Little Man grunts and slaps, but doesn't seem too alarmed.

"Did she hurt you?" I ask, carefully putting myself between the kids and Mom. "Did she bite you at all?"

"No, but she was gonna eat me!" Sarah insists.

"What happened?" I ask Tommy.

He shakes his head. "I don't know. Sarah started screaming and I woke up and saw your Mom curled up next to us."

"Wait...what?" Little Man hoots a couple of times and gives me a slap upside my head. "Stop!" I smack him back. "Tell me exactly what you saw, Tommy! This is important!"

"Um, she, um, she was curled up next to us, you know, sleeping," Tommy stammers.

"Sleeping? But she didn't try to hurt you or anything?"

Tommy shakes his head.

"Yes, she was going to eat us!" Sarah cries again.

"You don't think so, though, do you, Tommy?" I ask him.

He shakes his head again. "No. She was kinda like how Mama would curl up in our beds at night."

I turn and watch Mom looking from me to the kids and back. Little Man hoots and Mom responds.

"You two go back to sleep. I'll stay in here with you and make sure she doesn't do it again, okay?"

"But...!" Sarah protests.

"Don't worry, she won't get near you," I promise.

They get settled back down and it's a while before they both drift back to sleep. My mind is racing too much and I know I won't be sleeping again.

Mom squats on the ground and stares at me. I stare back and we stay that way for hours until the dawn light spills into the mine.

6

Sarah avoids looking at Mom as we load into the Power Wagon and work our way back to I-5. It's as if she is pretending Mom isn't even with us.

Tommy, however, keeps looking into the truck bed every few minutes to see what Mom is up to.

"She doing okay back there?" I ask him. He nods only. I look over at both of them. "I really don't think she will hurt you. If anything you're now on her protection list."

"Protection list? What does that mean?" Tommy asks.

"Well, mothers of all animal species have a strong protection instinct. Most will fight to the death to keep their young safe. I know she's turned, but I think my mom is different than the other necros out there. I think that protection instinct is still as strong as ever, if not stronger. She's shown that towards Little Man and me and I think she'd do the same for you."

"She'll eat us," Sarah insists.

I look at Tommy warily, but he doesn't meet my eyes. "Why do you keep saying that, Sarah?"

She doesn't answer for a moment, but when she does her voice is filled with grief and anger. "Because moms try to eat their kids when they turn!"

And I finally get it. That must have been what happened with their mother. She turned, saw them as food, and came after them. I don't want to imagine what they had to do to keep her away. I don't know if I could kill my own mother.

Sure, this was something I was taught at a very young age. Always having to be mindful of signs my parents were turning or had turned. Luckily, I have Little Man and he is my early warning system. He would have screeched bloody murder if Mom or Dad had turned and tried to come after me. Although now the evidence is overwhelming that Mom probably wouldn't have tried to eat me.

"You're right, Sarah," I tell her. "When moms, or anyone, turn they will try to eat you. But my mom is different."

"No she isn't," Sarah insists and turns her face to the passenger window, letting me know the conversation is done. Was I this difficult at that age? Yeah, I was probably worse.

"Well, until you can trust her I'll make sure she doesn't get near you, alright?"

She doesn't respond and Tommy nudges her in the side.

"Ow!"

"Don't be rude," he scolds.

She turns back to me, tears in her eyes. "That's alright. Keep her away."

"Deal," I smile, but she doesn't return it, only turns away and stares out the window.

It isn't long before we crest a hill and I see the gauntlet of abandoned cars. They look like they have been moved back in place, making a narrow, dangerous corridor. Scavenger time.

"Okay, kids, this isn't going to be easy," I say calmly. "So I need you not to panic. The last time I went through this I wasn't driving, so I need to concentrate. I want both of you down on the floor, out of sight."

They both look at me with those wide, fearful eyes, but do as I say, tucking themselves onto the floor of the truck. I swallow hard, grab the rifle and hit the gas.

I doubt a minute has gone by before they're on us. I'm able to get around, or through, about five cars when the first freaks leap out wielding their crazy clubs and axes. I mow two down that think, for some reason, a human body will stop a Power Wagon. Three more jump from the tops of cars and land in the truck bed.

Right next to Mom.

Their screams are mercifully short, but Tommy and Sarah both cry out at the sounds.

"It's okay!" I shout. "Mom took care of it!" That probably doesn't make Sarah feel any better, but Tommy nods a little.

I nearly lose control of the truck when a Scavenger leaps onto my door, his chain wrapped fist shattering my window. I slam the butt of the rifle into his face once, twice, three, four, five times before he loses his grip and falls away.

Unfortunately, getting the truck back under control proves difficult as we slam into car after car and soon the whole vehicle is spinning and stops dead, facing the wrong direction.

"Why aren't we going?!" Tommy screams.

"I'm working on that!" I scream back, seeing the dozens of Scavengers coming at us from what was behind.

I put the Power Wagon into reverse and floor the gas pedal, ramming the tailgate into the car behind us, clearing some room so I can whip the wheel round. I get us pointing in the right direction, but our path is completely blocked as dozens more Scavengers converge on the road. Even if I plow through them, most will be able to climb onto the truck and it'll only be a matter of time before they overtake us.

This all just sucks.

Picking up the assault rifle, I kick at the windshield, trying to break it loose so I have an unobstructed shot, but the Tribes did too good of a repair job and I only end up with a bruised heel.

"Crap! Cover your ears!" The kids do as I say and I pull back the slide, ready to let loose on the oncoming attackers. I'll deal with the ones behind us next. If there is a next.

My finger starts to squeeze the trigger, but before I do, Scavengers start to shudder and fall. Their bodies dance in a macabre vision of some bloody chorus line. Not that I've seen a chorus line, but I figure this would be what it looks like. If it was bloody. And set in the middle of an old highway.

The gunshots reach my ears a split second after I see their results and I whip my head about, looking for the source. From both sides of the road I can see people on horses closing in, rifles raised to their shoulders.

The Tribes! Holy crap, it's the Tribes!

I look in the rear view mirror and see the pursuers getting

closer, but the Tribes' guns aren't trained on them. Shoving the door open I hop from the truck with my rifle in hand. I run around to the back of the Power Wagon and open fire, ripping into the Scavengers that are only a couple yards away. I take most of them down before the magazine is empty. I flip the rifle about and start using it as a club on those that are still standing.

I make each and every swing count, but there are just too many of them. A club catches me across the forehead and I spin and fall, my face hitting pavement. My already broken nose turns to mush. I can't focus at all and when I feel my hair being pulled and my head yanked up I honestly think this is it.

I close me eyes, waiting for the blow or blade, but instead my head is let go and once again my nose hits the pavement. I roll to my side and kick out, but my feet hit Mom instead of a Scavenger. She rears on me and hisses, but turns back to the group of Scavengers that have us surrounded. She must have ripped her chain loose.

On shaky legs, I get to my feet and we stand next to each other waiting for the attack. When it does come, I only do about ten percent of the fighting before we are both covered in blood and gore with a stack of bodies at our feet. It's only been two days since I was last cringing at the thought of killing real people, but now, after everything I've been through, it doesn't faze me. It's not that I'm numb to it, I understand that these were people just trying to survive, but I now better understand my place in this insane world and what it means for me to survive.

Scavengers hiding in the husks of cars and trucks bolt, running from the road and scattering into the hills beyond.

I tuck back into the truck quickly. "You guys okay?" The kids both nod and it smells like one of them may have peed. I don't blame them. I may have also.

"Garret Weir?" a woman shouts, her rifle leveled at me as she approaches on horseback.

"That's me," I answer, tossing the bloody and empty rifle aside. "I can't thank you guys enough."

She sees Mom and her rifle is at her shoulder instantly. I leap in front, waving my arms. "No! Do not shoot!"

"Move! She's going to attack you!" the woman yells at me, trying to get a shot around me.

"No, she isn't!" I shout back. "She's with me! Just let me get her secured in the back again. Do not shoot!"

The rest of the rescue party join the woman (I don't recognize any of them) and they watch, dumbfounded, as I get Mom chained into the truck bed yet again.

"What?" I ask, hopping back into the Power Wagon's cab, their eyes on me. "She's my mom. You can't get between a son's love for his mom, am I right?"

7

The look on Billy Silverthorn's face the next morning is not promising.

"Garret," he starts, "I don't have good news."

"I didn't think so," I say, looking at the ever spreading black lines on my left arm. Karen grips my right hand in hers, her face stoic and brave. Her eyes are terrified though. "Let me save you the trouble, though. You can't have my arm."

Billy sighs. "I understand, Garret, but if I don't..."

I cut him off. "I know what happens. The infection spreads and I could die. But you see, I have a theory."

Billy rolls his eyes, knowing who my parents are. "I'll humor you. What's this theory?"

"From what I've read about infection, not only should there be pain, but there should be increased pain with use, right?" He narrows his eyes and nods. "Well, back on the highway, when I was fighting off the Scavengers with Mom, my arm hurt. But it started hurting less the more I used it. I think I'm different. My body is used to necrotic tissue. I've lived with it all my life."

I can see Billy struggling with his thoughts and I hold up my hand before he can respond.

"Let's just wait, okay? I'm not in any real discomfort," I lie. "If I make a turn for the worse then you can hack it off, but look at it!" I lift the arm and point to the lines. "They are going down, not up. They haven't spread to my shoulder. If they do then you can have the arm."

"If it spreads to your shoulder it could be too late," Billy insists. "Karen. Help me here."

She squeezes my hand harder. "I think we should trust 3B. He's the only one that knows what his body does. Have you ever dealt with conjoined twins where one is alive and the other isn't?"

Wow. She's just awesome. It's so nice to be with her again. Back in the bookstore, I thought... I don't know what I thought.

Billy stares at her, his mouth hanging open. "I was hoping for the opposite reaction." Karen shrugs and gives him a sly smile. "Fine!" he huffs. "I'm not going to fight you anymore. Lose your life if you want, ain't no skin off my nose."

"So...are we done?" I ask.

"Sure. Whatever," Billy grumbles. "But if anything changes I'm not asking for your permission. You have a very small window here."

"Fair enough," I grin.

"Your Mom would kill me if she..." he trails off.

"She probably still will," I smirk, awkwardly pulling my shirt on. Little Man complains, but when doesn't he?

"Is Garth doing alright?" Billy asks.

"Yep, he's as annoying as ever."

"Hey, be nice," Karen scolds me.

"Okay, you two. I have other, more cooperative folks to see. I'll see you two soon," Billy frowns as he leaves. "Try to talk some sense into him"

We both laugh as the door closes, but Karen's face doesn't hold that mirth for long.

"Are you sure about this?" she asks.

"No," I answer honestly. "But I don't want to lose my arm. And my gut says I'm right. I don't know exactly what is going to happen, but I think it's just another part of my ever changing life."

"This isn't some guilt thing over what's happened to your mom? A way for you to do penance?"

She may be right on that, but I don't dare tell her so. "No. This is what I want."

"Okay," she nods skeptically. "I'll trust you on this...for

now. First sign of trouble and I'm going to Billy. I'll even help hold you down."

"I'm counting on it," I laugh.

There's a knock on the door and a young girl peeks in. "The elders would like to see you now."

"Thanks," I reply. "I'll be right there."

"I'll check on Tommy and Sarah. I'll find you when I'm done," she says, giving me a quick kiss on my cheek.

I grab her arm before she can turn and kiss her on the lips. We stay that way for a while until she pulls away, her face flushed.

"Thank you," I tell her, my eyes focused on hers. "For being here. For helping me. I don't deserve..."

"Shut up," she jokes, smacking me in the stomach. "I'll tell you what you deserve."

And she's gone.

I make my way to the elders' meeting room. It isn't easy, as I have to avoid quite a few not so happy stares on the way. I'm not the most popular person with the Tribes.

"Mr. Weir," Lisa Triple Bear says as I shut the door behind me. "Thank you for joining us. I know you must be tired."

"Thank you for the help back on the highway," I reply, nodding to each of the elders. "It saved our butts."

"Well, about that," Lisa starts. "It is decided that that will be the last time we help you out there."

"I figured," I respond. I knew it was only a matter of time before they realized having me and Mom here was too dangerous. "You've done more than I could ask for already. I'll get Mom secured and we'll be on our way soon. You folks don't need my burden."

"You misunderstand," Lisa says. "We need your help."

I'm confused and my face must show it because all the elders start to grin.

"I'm sorry...what? How can I help?"

The door behind me opens and Billy steps in. "Sorry I'm late. Did I miss it?"

"Miss what?" I ask, looking about. "This isn't funny. What's going on?"

"Before your mother left she gave us codes we needed to open a bunker we found on our reservation," Lisa says. "That was part of the deal we made."

"The bunker was put there by your father, who knows how many years ago," Billy adds. "Before the world died."

"By my father? Here? On the reservation?" I feel like I'm going to throw up, I'm so confused. "Why would he do that?"

"The why is easy. No Federal jurisdiction," Lisa states. "The how, is still a mystery."

"He must have had help," Billy says. "But we can't find a single person that knew about it."

"People lie," I laugh. "You do know that, right?"

"Yes, Mr. Weir, we know people lie," Lisa scolds.

"Sorry." I look at them all. "I still don't see how I can help."

"Come with me," Billy says, holding the door open. "I'll show you."

I hesitate for a moment, but my curiosity gets the better of me.

We're outside and in a truck in moments and I find myself seated next to Billy as we bounce our way across an old, rutted trail to a small bluff.

"Here we are," Billy says as we walk up to the bluff.

"Yes we are," I reply. "And where are we, exactly?"

Billy steps to the bluff and reaches his hand into a small hole in the side. I hear a series of clicks and part of the bluff pushes out and slides to the side, revealing a large metal door. Billy keys in a code on a number pad in the center of the door and it starts to swing wide.

"Come on."

I follow Billy inside and lights flicker to life showing me a small version of the lab my dad had back at home.

Home... Wow...

"Anything look familiar?" Billy asks expectantly. "Do you know what any of this stuff is?"

"It's for Dad's research," I answer, running my hand along some of the instruments. "It's set up just like the one I knew." I turn and look at Billy, trying not to look hopeful. "It's exactly what's needed to help figure out the virus."

"That's what we were hoping you'd say," Billy grins. "You know how to run any of this stuff."

"Not a clue," I answer honestly.

"Think you can figure it out?"

"Seriously?" I laugh. "I'm not a scientist! I'm a seventeen year old train wreck with dead people for family."

"Yeah, but you're a Weir," he insists. "Your parents must have taught you something."

"You're wasting your breath," I laugh again as I start to walk out. I pull up short as something catches my eye. A book.

The Wizard Of Oz.

"What the..?"

I pick it up and expect to see the words I've read over and over before, but to my surprise all I see is my Dad's handwriting.

That crazy son of a...

"What did you find?" Billy asks, peering over my shoulder while he dodges Little Man's swipes.

"Instructions," I state, my mind reeling. "He left me instructions for how to recreate his experiments, I think."

Billy laughs then goes quiet. "Uh... Huh..."

"What? What's the matter?"

"That hasn't always been here. Trust me, I would have noticed." Billy runs from the lab and I follow. He shields his eyes from the sun as he scans the horizon. "How did he get past everyone?"

"Billy? What are you saying?" I ask as I grab his arm. "You can't believe my dad just left this here, can you? He's up North in the Keep, I'm sure of it."

Billy turns on me and frowns. "How do you know that?"

"He left a message on the wall back in Cottage Grove."

"He said he was at the Keep?"

"No, he said not to go North. He warned me away from there."

Billy shakes his head. 'Did it cross your mind at all that maybe he actually meant that? That maybe he thought you were mature enough to actually listen?"

"Um...no," I admit. "I figured he was playing with me."

Billy pats me on the shoulder. "Time to grow up, Garret. You can't fight your parents forever."

I slap the book against my palm and look out across the countryside.

Maybe Billy's right. Maybe Dad meant for me to listen for

a change and come back here.

He left me a book, didn't he?

I leaf through it again and this time a slip of paper falls from the pages and flutters to the floor.

"What's this?" Billy asks, reaching down and grabbing the paper. He hands it to me and I unfold it.

"G, I'm hoping you are reading this and understand what I need from you. In this book you will find precise instructions on how to create the serum I have been giving your mother for years. I have figured out a way to fine tune it a bit and anyone that needs it shouldn't have the mental and cognitive issues your mother had. This will give you and the Tribes an edge for what may be coming.

I know by now she has changed. I am truly sorry about this. I don't know what she may have been able to tell you, but I take full responsibility for everything. This entire mess is my fault.

Understand, I love you and your brother more than anything in the world. Take care of your mother, please. She may have turned, but all of my research shows she won't be like the others. I pray (yes, I said pray) that she is still with you. You three are key to the survival of us all.

Please know I am safe and with others that can help. We are working and fighting as hard as you are. You are with good people, as you will soon learn. I know I said not to trust anyone, but I was wrong. Trust the Tribes. Trust those closest to you. And, hopefully, if you aren't too mad, trust me. You have a home now. You will be safe. Rest. You deserve it.

One day we will be together again, but until that time I need you to be the man I have always known you could be. You are special, your brother is special, and while it's not fair, you both have a role to play in the future of humanity.

I love you. I miss you and I'm so sorry for everything.
Godspeed,
Dad."

"You okay?" Billy asks, placing a hand on my shoulder.

I struggle to get myself together. My throat is choked up and tears are dripping down onto the book like I'm my own personal rainstorm.

"Here, you're gonna soak that through," Billy says, taking the book from my hands. "I'm guessing that's from your dad?"

"Yeah...it is," I manage to say. I hand it to him. "Here, feel free."

Billy smiles and pushes the paper back into my hands. "No, that's for you. I'm sure you can tell me the gist."

I smile and nod, wiping the tears away. "Thanks, Billy. I'm sorry I've been a jerk."

Billy laughs and grabs me about the shoulders as we walk to the truck. "You've been a normal seventeen year old boy living under less than normal circumstances. Nothing to apologize for." He gives me a sly look and pats my chest. "Just don't let it happen again."

We both laugh as we hop in and turn the truck back towards my new home.

8

We spend the next couple of weeks inventorying the lab and making sure everything works. Dad left very detailed instructions and it didn't take long for Billy and a few others to get the hang of all the machinery. We set up solar cells to power everything, which also meant we couldn't push ourselves and work through the night, since the batteries only held an extra four hour charge.

I wouldn't have worked that hard anyway. I'm seventeen, not a workaholic like my dad. And he said to rest, which, for the first time in my life, I think I'm really able to do. I have friends now. I have people watching my back. I still have to take care of Mom and Little Man, but I'm not alone with that. The one thing about the Tribes is we all share the burden of work and living.

We all trust each other.

So, a month after coming back from Cottage Grove I find myself with Karen on the porch of the big communal lodge. It's a nice evening, but the weather has started to turn and the chill hits us quickly. Karen has been learning guitar from Billy's wife, Noel, and she sits next to me strumming out a new song.

"I know that," I say, surprised. "What is that?"

Karen looks at me sheepishly and starts to sing. I can't help but smile at her choice and join in at the very end.

"That's pretty cool," I say. "Thanks."

"Thought you'd like it," she smiles. "He Ain't Heavy, He's My Brother is not an easy song to find. But luckily Noel had a copy I could study."

"Huh," I say. "I've never heard the music to it before. Just the words. Sung badly."

She raises her eyebrows.

"Not that you sounded bad," I respond quickly. "You sounded great."

She gives me a sly smile and I see she's messing with me. We sit for a second as she practices the chords

"We should go in before it gets too cold," I suggest.

"Not before I ask you something first," Karen says, setting the guitar aside and tossing the *Damnation Alley* paperback onto my lap. "You want to tell me about this book?"

"Um, I haven't read it yet," I say quietly.

"I know, which isn't like you," she pushes. "Want to tell me why?"

I thumb the pages and try not to think of where I got the book from. Try not to think of that hellish ride. I shove the thoughts of Veronica away. Most of all, I shove the thoughts of what Travis said about Joseph away. I still haven't told her that not only is he still a nec, but he may be being held by Charlotte. I can't tell her that. She has just now started to move on, to accept that he's gone. I'd lose her in a second if I told her about Joseph. Or Veronica. Does this make me a bad person? Am I one of those well-meaning people that just screws their lives up by keeping secrets?

My parents kept secrets and look how that turned out. One's a living corpse, albeit a well cared for living corpse, and the other is missing in action somewhere out in the world. Secrets aren't good...

"Garret? Hello?" She waves her hand in front of my face. "Lost you again. Your arm feeling okay?"

"Oh, sorry. Yeah, my arm has never felt better."

Which is true. It looks strange, and honestly, doesn't always smell so great, but Billy says the tissue is no longer going necrotic. It now has the yellow color of a healed bruise. The strange part, beside it being yellow and not rotting off, is that it's much stronger than my other arm. A lot stronger.

I've kept this from everyone. Having a dead twin makes me a freak enough. Don't need everyone knowing I have a semi-dead super arm. That would be too much.

"Garret!" Karen insists. "Hello? The book?"

"I, um, right, sorry. I found it on my way to Cottage Grove. Just haven't had a chance to read it. Been so busy figuring out Dad's notes and all."

She looks at me for a moment then leans in and kisses my cheek. "Okay. You can tell me the truth when you're ready." She gets up and claps her hands together. "Apple crisp is for dessert tonight! It's gonna go fast. You want some?"

"Um, sure. Save me a piece. I'll be right in." She frowns. "I promise! I'll be in soon!"

"Okay, okay, don't get huffy." She leans down and kisses me lightly on the lips and is gone.

A couple people I've come to know wave at me as they walk by and I lift my hand to return the wave, but I'm still holding the book. They laugh, since everyone knows I read more than anyone else here at the Tribes.

The book. *Damnation Alley* by Roger Zelazny. A post-apocalyptic story set decades after a nuclear holocaust. It's about a hero that has to deliver plague medication while fighting his way across the country.

Hits a little too close to home.

And considering who handed it to me, it hits a little too close to the heart. I know where my heart should be and I'm done with being confused. And I'm done mourning. Time to move forward.

"GARRET!" two small voices yell as the screen door swings open with the force of a tiny hurricane. Two tiny hurricanes as Tommy and Sarah bolt at me and jump onto my lap.

"Ugh! You guys are heavy!" The kids laugh as I tickle them until they jump from my lap and start pulling at my arms.

"Hurry up!" they both yell. "Come on! Karen says we can feed Little Man."

"Oh, she said that did she?" I laugh as they hurry back inside.

Little Man starts to grunt and hoot, knowing food is coming. The strange thing is that everyone in the Tribes has come to accept Little Man, and Mom to a smaller extent, and we've all been storing a blood supply beyond just what's needed medically.

It's a little disgusting, if you think about it, but the kids like to feed Garth. And honestly? I think he likes it too.

"GARRET! COME ON!" Even more voices shout from the lodge. Karen got reinforcements. They've gotten used to me spacing off and know it can take some coaxing to get me inside.

"I'm coming!" I shout back, standing and tucking the book into my back pocket. I'll read it at some point, but not now.

"Ready for dessert, Little Man?" I ask, patting Garth on the head. He swipes at me a couple of times then grabs my finger, giving it a good squeeze.

"Yeah, me too."

We step inside the lodge, leaving the sound of the screen door slamming closed echoing in our wake.

One door closes, another always opens...

THE END

Jake Bible lives in Asheville, NC with his wife and two kids.

Novelist, short story writer, independent screenwriter, podcaster, and inventor of the Drabble Novel, Jake is able to switch between or mash-up genres with ease to create new and exciting storyscapes that have captivated and built an audience of thousands.

He is the author of the bestselling Z-Burbia series for Severed Press as well as the Apex Trilogy (DEAD MECH, The Americans, Metal and Ash), the Mega series, AntiBio, and the forthcoming releases by Permuted Press- the Teen horror novel Intentional Haunting and Middle Grade scifi/horror series, ScareScapes.

Find him at *jakebible.com*. Join him on Twitter and Facebook.